LIBRARY LOST

LIBRARY LOST

Laurie Graves

Hinterlands Press
Winthrop, Maine

Published by
Hinterlands Press, Winthrop, Maine
hinterlandspress.com

ISDBN: 978-0-9978453-3-4

Library of Congress Control Number: 2018912532

Chapter opener and incidental graphics: openclipart.org

Cover design by James T. Egan of Bookfly Design

r3

This book is dedicated to my mother
Rochelle June Meunier,
a mémère extrodinare,
and to all mémères everywhere.

Special thanks to Deirdre Graves, Shannon Mulkeen,
Mike Mulkeen, John Clark, Gayle Roy, and Carol Jaeger.
Their generosity, constructive criticism,
and unflagging support were invaluable.

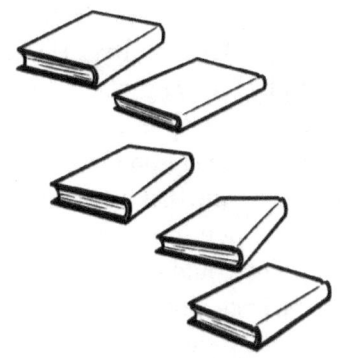

1: The Book Has Some Explaining to Do

Maya sat on the couch between her mother and her mémère. As she drank iced tea and ate the freshly popped popcorn—"No microwave for us," Mémère insisted—Maya tried not to think about Humphrey and Andy, both in Bar Harbor, about three hours from Mémère and Pépère's home in East Vassalboro. Maya just wanted to relax, to listen to Mémère's plan for the next day, which involved going shopping, and to hear her mother's brief, soft responses.

But despite her best intentions, Maya did keep thinking about Humphrey and Andy. How long had it been since she had seen Andy? No more than three hours, Maya decided. It had been in 1976, and he had been seventeen years old. But now—as Maya had just seen on TV on the evening news—Andy was at least as old as her father.

"And the president of the United States," Maya thought. "That Book sure has some explaining to do."

But Maya was too tired, and she had to admit it—shocked—to race upstairs and find out what the Book had to say for itself. "The Book should have told me," Maya thought wearily, resting her head against the back of the couch.

Then there was Humphrey, treacherous Humphrey, from the faraway planet of Ilyria. He was with Andy in Bar Harbor. "President Murphy," Maya thought, correcting herself. But why was Humphrey so close to the president of the United States? Why couldn't President Murphy see Humphrey for what he was—cruel, aggressive, and ambitious—and that he was not to be trusted? But even as Maya formed this question in her mind, she knew the answer. Andy, or President Murphy, couldn't see people the way she could. That was not his talent. Instead, it seemed, winning elections was his talent.

Mémère had stopped talking and was staring curiously at Maya. "You're quiet tonight."

"I'm tired," Maya answered truthfully. Beside Maya, her mother shifted uneasily.

"You need to get a good night's sleep so that we can have fun when we go shopping," Mémère said. "Do you want me to call my hairdresser, Dot, to find out if she has time to trim your hair tomorrow?"

Maya shook her head. On Ilyria, Feste had cut her hair, and Maya didn't want anyone else to touch it, at least not for a while.

Mémère squinted critically at Maya's hair. "It's cute, all short and curly like that, but it needs shaping."

"Not right now, Mémère," Maya said quietly but firmly, sounding more like an adult than a teenager. Maya could sense Mémère puzzling over the adult tone of voice. "Maybe in a week or two," Maya added quickly.

"All right, all right." Mémère patted Maya's leg and kissed her cheek. "I'm so glad to have you here."

After all that she had been through—going back in time, traveling to the Great Library and to Ilyria—Maya was glad to be in East Vassalboro, too, and she smiled at her grandmother, who smiled back and gave her another kiss on the cheek.

Much later that night, when the house was dark, and the only sound was the ticking of the pendulum clock in the hallway, Maya crept out of bed, went to the desk, unlocked it, and took out the Book of Everything. Maya didn't say anything until she was buried beneath the covers—hot though the night was—and even then she whispered.

"Why didn't you tell me about Andy, that he's President Murphy? Why did you have to let me see him on the evening news?"

"I'm sorry, Maya," the Book replied. "I couldn't tell you when we were on Ilyria. You might have given too much away. Andy had to discover his path on his own, not because of something you let slip. And when we got back to Earth, there wasn't time. I was going to tell you tonight."

Maya was about to remind the Book that she could keep a secret, but then Maya stopped—she knew the Book was right. On Ilyria, she and Andy had become close, and Maya might have said something, perhaps unintentionally, perhaps not. "You could have at least told me about Humphrey," Maya whispered at last.

"Humphrey?" the Book of Everything asked, and it sounded genuinely surprised.

"Humphrey. On the evening news, he was right there next to President Murphy. And Humphrey looked like he was up to no good. Same as ever."

The Book of Everything was quiet, and at first Maya was puzzled, but then she understood. "You didn't know, did you? That's what you meant when you told me that something I would see on Ilyria would help me on Earth."

"That's right. I knew something was going on, that someone with one of Cinnial's Books had come to Earth years ago, when Andy was still a senator. But I didn't know who it was."

"The Books can shield themselves and whoever has them," Maya said, remembering.

"They do. Except when they travel, there is always a little burst of energy. But as far as we know, the only time Humphrey has traveled with the Book was when he came to Earth. At the time, the feeling at the Great Library was that it was someone sent by Cinnial to help APO steal me, even though Earth is not exactly at the center of things. It really did puzzle us."

Maya thought about APO—the Association for the Preservation of Order—and of how they had been after the Book of Everything for a long, long time. "But it was Humphrey, instead, with the Book he stole from Julian."

"Ilyria and Earth have a connection," the Book replied. "Somehow, even though I didn't know about Humphrey, I had a hunch that taking you to Ilyria would be the right thing to do."

"You'll let the Great Library know?"

"I will." The Book's voice sounded amused. "I'm in constant contact with the Great Library. They have a data team, a small one, to keep track of me. And now, after your visit to the Great Library, Sydda himself will be checking in on us, from time to time."

"But what could Humphrey be doing here?"

"Who stabbed Julian?"

Maya put a hand to her face. "I did. Julian's Book brought Humphrey to Earth because of me."

"And you were also instrumental in helping Owen defeat Humphrey."

Maya sighed. "So both Julian's Book and Humphrey are out to get me. What am I going to do? You're supposed to go to Hartland with David tomorrow."

"I'll let the Great Library know what has happened. You won't be left to your own devices. I promise. And I have a plan."

"What is it?"

"I'm going to ask Sydda to let you use the Apprentice Book again, the same one you brought on Ilyria from the Great Library."

Maya was shocked. "The board will never agree to let the Book go out again."

"I think they might. The situation on this planet is more critical than it ever has been. APO has developed a device that will immobilize me. The League of Librarians has captured one of the devices, but there are probably more out there. Humphrey has Julian's Book, and they are plotting something that includes you." The Book's voice became firm. "Other planets are having similar problems, and we Books of Everything could use the help. The Apprentice Books have been shut up for way too long. They need a purpose, too. It is time for the board to relax its policy."

From the Book's tone of voice, Maya could tell that the situation with the Apprentice Books had been a long-standing argument between the Books of Everything and the board at the

Great Library. Maya decided to change the subject. "Do you think Julian's Book has let Cinnial know what's happened with Julian and Humphrey?"

"It is possible" the Book answered. "Julian's Book and Cinnial could be working together. Or, the Book could be working alone. I can't tell."

Rubbing her eyes, Maya yawned. She wanted to stay awake, but she was so very tired.

"Time for you to get some sleep. You've got a busy day ahead of you."

"I do?"

"You're going shopping with Mémère, aren't you?"

"That's right! And in the morning I have to go to the library to make a report to Jennifer, David, and Anne."

"Leave me open on your nightstand. I'll sing a song for you."

Maya set the Book on the nightstand. After that, she threw off most of her blankets and settled into bed with only the sheet covering her. Beside her, the Book began its song, but like the Toad Queen's song in the Forest of Arden, the Book's song had no words. Instead, the Book sang a song of Earth, of water rushing, of leaves rustling in the wind, of peepers in the spring, of the tides of the ocean as the moon pulled it back and forth. Soon Maya was asleep, and she slept so soundly that she didn't even remember her dreams.

The next morning at breakfast plans were made. Maya would go to the library "to go over the play with Anne Hunter and her friends," but she promised to be back by late morning. Maya felt bad about lying to her grandparents and to her mother but knew she couldn't tell them what she was really going to do.

Glancing at her mother, Maya saw that Lily was trying to gear herself up for an afternoon of shopping. Maya didn't know anyone who hated shopping as much as her mother did. Normally, Maya would have said nothing, wanting her mother to come anyway, the way a normal mother would. And there were parts of the outing that Lily actually enjoyed—lobster rolls at the Red Barn and tea at Barnes & Noble.

But now that Maya had had her eyes peeled, she could see just how much her mother wanted to stay in East Vassalboro and paint, how shopping was so boring to her that she could hardly stand it. Maya found herself saying, "Mom, you don't have to come if you don't want to."

This startled Lily. "What? Usually you want me to come along."

"I know. But you don't like shopping, and Mémère and I do. We'll have fun together, won't we, Mémère?"

"Oui, oui," Mémère answered, and Maya could tell her grandmother was surprised, too. She always reverted to French when something caught her off guard.

"Are you sure, Maya?" Lily asked.

"I'm sure. You stay home and paint. Mémère and I will go shopping." Lily frowned, fiddling with the handle of her coffee cup, and Maya said, "Come on, Mom. You know it's what you want to do."

Lily stared intently at Maya for any signs of sarcasm or moodiness. There were none, and Maya smiled at her mother as she got up from the table. "I've got to go to the library. I'll be back no later than 11:00. Then we'll be ready to go shopping. Right, Mémère?"

"Righto!" Mémère answered. Her voice was cheerful, but she, too, stared thoughtfully at Maya.

"Oh, boy," Maya thought as she left the farmhouse. "It's going to be hard to hide just how much I've changed. I knew they'd notice."

With the Book of Everything—small now—tucked in the back pocket of her jean shorts, Maya ran down the curving road, past where the stream rippled to the lake. At the four corners, Maya waited for the cars to go by, and she thought about what kind of candy she would like to buy at the Country Store that stood on one of the corners. Peanut M&M's, Maya decided, feeling the quarters jingle in her pockets as she jogged across the street.

At the small brick library, Anne Hunter, the librarian, was at her desk, and Jennifer Morgan and David Little were sitting around it, just as they had been the night before when Maya had told them she had the Book of Everything. "At least it was just last night for them. For me, it was more like two weeks," Maya thought, and it gave her a funny feeling to think of it that way. But it was true. Between her time on Ilyria and her time at the Great Library, almost two weeks had passed.

"Hello," Maya said as she approached the desk, and she noticed how tired Jennifer and David looked.

An empty chair was waiting for Maya, and "Tea?" Anne asked.

"Yes, please."

As soon as Maya had her tea, Jennifer said, "Last night, David and I brought Chet's device to the League's office in Concord. Soon APO will know we have it, but before they do, we'll have a chance to study the device. We've used Chet's phone to send messages to various people so we should be able to string them along for a day or two. As to be expected, all his contacts have code names, so we weren't able to discover who betrayed us. But we're working on that, too."

"Will APO try to get the device back?" Maya asked.

"No, I expect they will be able to deactivate it from their headquarters," Jennifer answered. "But with any luck, we'll find out how it works before they do. Even before we left, a team of librarians was looking at the device, taking it apart. Now, Maya, let's hear your story."

Maya removed the Book of Everything from her pocket and set it open on Anne's desk so that it could correct her if she made a mistake. Although the Book did make one or two corrections, mostly it remained silent as Maya told the librarians all that had happened—going back in time to 1976 to get Andy; going to a place called Caxton on the planet Ilyria, where there were no machines and cars; and meeting Feste and learning that Duke Humphrey had deposed his own brother, Owen, who was hiding in the Forest of Arden.

"The Forest of Arden?" David asked.

"And Feste?" Anne put in.

"That's right," Maya replied. "Straight out of Shakespeare, except it was all mixed up."

"Interesting," David said with a frown. "It's almost as though we're connected somehow."

"The Book said that we are," Maya said. "But it didn't say how." Maya looked expectantly at the Book of Everything, which remained silent. Rolling her eyes, Maya went on to describe how Caxton also had a Book of Everything, but that Humphrey had stolen it; how Humphrey had planned to burn down the Forest of Arden to get Owen; and how the Toad Queen, who lived in the center of the forest, had peeled her eyes and had given her three special acorns.

"What do you mean by a Toad Queen?" Jennifer asked.

"She is a giant toad with a red jewel on her head, and she lives in the middle of the forest."

"Did she literally peel your eyes?"

Swallowing, Maya remembered how much it had hurt. "Yes, with her sharp claws. First one eye and then the other."

There was a shocked silence. "Why?" David finally asked.

"So that I could see more. It would help in Caxton and on Earth."

"Did it work?" Anne asked.

Maya nodded. It had worked so well that now she had to make an effort not to see too much, not to pry into people's lives when it was unnecessary.

Next came the part that Maya dreaded telling—the theft of Earth's Book of Everything and Feste's death. Her voice was low as she related this part of the story, and Maya had to stop once or twice so that she wouldn't start crying.

Shaking her head, Anne gave Maya the tissue box she kept on her desk. "Sir John and Andy stole the Book?"

Maya took a tissue and blew her nose. "Sir John thought it would help him take Greendale and then defeat Humphrey. Andy looked up to Sir John. Then Julian—one of Cinnial's men—stole Earth's Book of Everything, but before he left, I stabbed him with his own knife."

"Just as you stabbed Chet," Jennifer said, frowning.

"Julian was going to kill Andy," Maya replied. "And then me. I didn't have a choice."

"Go on with your story," Jennifer said.

The next bit, of course, was about the Great Library, and all three librarians were very quiet as Maya described this beautiful, tranquil place that looked like a castle and was bigger on the inside than it was on the outside.

"Oh, Maya!" Anne interrupted. "None of us have even seen a picture of the Great Library, much less been there. We had no idea what it looked like."

"You're a brave girl to go that distance on little more than faith in a special acorn. You could have been killed," Jennifer said.

"I know," Maya replied, remembering how Chaos had nearly pulled her apart and how Time had saved her.

David asked, "Back to Caxton after that?"

"Yes," Maya answered, "with Elspeth, Alani, and an Apprentice Book to help me."

From there, Maya came to the end of the story: both Books were retrieved, Owen defeated Humphrey, and Julian's memory was removed by a mint that Maya had been given at the Great Library.

"Except it's not the end of the story," Maya said.

"What did you discover when you returned?" Jennifer asked.

"Andy is the president of the United States, Humphrey is here on Earth, and he's somehow involved with Andy. I mean President Murphy."

The librarians were even more quiet than they had been when Maya had described the Great Library. Maya could see how shocked they all were.

"That's a surprise twist," David finally said. "And Julian's Book and Humphrey are here because of you, Maya?"

"I think so," Maya answered.

"You're just a magnet for trouble," Jennifer said.

"I don't mean to be," Maya retorted, stung by what Jennifer had said.

Jennifer sighed. "I know. So, is the Book still going to Hartland with David?"

"Not today," Maya answered. "The Book has told Sydda about Humphrey and Julian's Book and has asked him to send an Apprentice Book to Earth to help me."

"What was his response?" Jennifer asked.

"Sydda thinks it's a good idea, but the board isn't convinced."

"What are the odds that the board will finally agree?" David asked.

Maya looked to the Book. "Better than average but not a sure thing," came the Book's answer. "They're still arguing about it." Maya related the Book's message to Anne and David, who hadn't been with the Book long enough to hear its voice. Jennifer, on the other hand, could hear the Book. "There was a time when I traveled quite a bit with the Book," Jennifer would say later.

"After this meeting, I have to go to headquarters in Concord. You'll keep me informed?" Jennifer asked.

Even though the question was rhetorical, both Anne and David answered, yes, of course they'd keep her informed.

Jennifer nodded briskly. "Good. And Maya? Be careful. Especially with knives."

Maya should have felt irritated by this advice. After all, she was not in the habit of stabbing people, and in both cases, Maya had felt that she didn't have a choice. Instead, Maya felt a shiver, as though somewhere a knife was waiting for her.

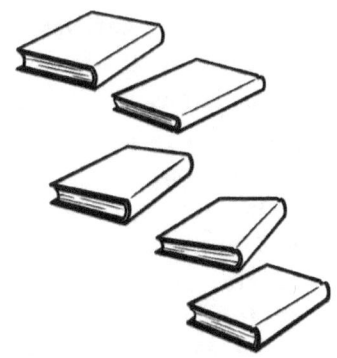

2: Suspicions

Mémère had a snappy little red car with great pickup, good gas mileage, and a standard transmission.

"I'm not ready for an automatic yet," Mémère said as she and Maya waited at the four corners in East Vassalboro for the cars to go by. "Maybe when I'm eighty-five, and my reflexes aren't as good."

"I wish we didn't get old so fast," Maya said, thinking of Sydda and some of the other people at the Great Library. Maya figured that the oldest ones must be well over 100 years old, maybe even close to 200 years old.

"You and me, too," Mémère replied. "Mon Dieu, there's a lot of traffic today."

"Crossroads of the universe," Maya said with a grin, thinking how far from the truth it was. But Mémère always said this when there was a string of cars at the four corners.

Finally, there was a break, and Mémère stomped on the gas pedal. The little red car shot across the intersection and zoomed past the Country Store. Maya laughed, wondering how many grandmothers drove like her mémère, but as they went by the library, Maya saw something that made her stop laughing.

Getting out of a car was the same white-haired man who had been at the library with Anne the day before. Maya tried to recall his name, and it wasn't until they were at the end of the Bog Road that she remembered. The man's name was Jeff Perry, and something about him made Maya uneasy.

Maya reached into her bag for her phone. Should she call Anne Hunter? And tell her what? Maya had only seen Jeff twice—briefly at the library the day before and even more briefly today. Besides, Mémère would hear whatever Maya was saying. But now that Maya had had her eyes peeled, she could tell there was something not right about Jeff Perry, and Maya had the strongest feeling that Jeff was the one who had betrayed the League of Librarians. She needed to let Anne know about Jeff without making Mémère suspicious. Texting was an option, but Maya wanted to talk directly to Anne, to be sure the librarian got the message immediately. Then Maya had an idea, and hoping there would be a direct answer, she called Anne.

As it turned out, chance was with Maya, and Anne answered her cell phone. "Hi, Maya. What's up?"

"I'm going shopping with Mémère, and we're heading to Augusta right now. But I had an idea for our play, and I wanted to tell you about it."

"Our play?" Anne's voice was puzzled, but then, "Oh, yes. Our play. What's your idea?"

"You know how we hadn't come up with a name for the bad guy who betrays everyone? Well, how about a nice, normal name like Jeff Perry?"

Anne was silent for a moment. "You're sure that's the right name?"

"Yes, that's the right name," Maya answered, wishing that she could say more. But with Mémère on one end and Jeff Perry most certainly with Anne, there wasn't much more she could say. At the same time, Maya felt as though Anne had gotten the point. "Well, goodbye. Talk to you later."

Hanging up, Anne glanced as casually as she could at Jeff Perry, who was sitting across from her in one of the rocking chairs by the window. Always intense, Jeff looked even more intense now as he watched Anne slip her phone into the pocket of her black-and-white polka-dotted skirt.

"You're putting on a play?" Jeff asked.

"Yes," Anne answered, wishing she could think as quickly as Maya. "With some of the kids in town."

"Which play?"

"We're working on one of our own. Maya, one of our young patrons, just called to suggest a few names for some of the characters. She's really good. We're lucky to have her." Smoothing her skirt over her knees, Anne decided it was time to change the subject. "What were we talking about before the call?"

"About the Book of Everything. You were going to tell me something about the League of Librarians. Have they found anything out about the Book, about where it might be?"

Anne shook her head, hoping that Jeff wouldn't notice how nervous she'd become. "No, not a thing. They're really worried. And so am I."

"Me, too." Jeff leaned forward. "Has anything like this ever happened before? Has the Book ever gone missing?"

Anne shrugged. "I don't know."

Jeff stood. "Let's hope we find the Book soon. If not..." He didn't finish the sentence.

Standing as well, Anne finished it for him. "It could be disastrous, especially if it gets into the wrong hands."

"Exactly. That's just what I was thinking. And what about Chet? We know he was after Mary and probably killed her. Has the League heard anything about him?"

Anne thought about Chet, imprisoned in one of the towers in the keep at Caxton, and she lied again. "No. He could be anywhere, Jeff. And so could the Book." Jeff was still staring intently at Anne, and she continued bravely, "It's scary not knowing where the Book is, but I have faith that Mary knew what she was doing when she decided to give it away. When the Book feels safe, it will contact us."

"I'm just surprised we haven't heard by now."

"Me, too. But maybe the Book doesn't feel safe yet."

"Maybe. You'll let me know as soon as you hear anything?"

"Of course," Anne said quickly. Too quickly?

As soon as Jeff left, Anne went to her desk and sent a text message to Jennifer Morgan and David Little. Patrons started coming in, and Anne was busy for the next hour or two as she checked books in and out. She helped a young woman—a single mother with a tiny baby—with her resume. She listened to her assistant, Beverly Penwright, read stories to the children during morning story hour. Anne even managed to smile when she gave Laura Linden a stack of books that had been ordered through interlibrary loan. Laura exclaimed, "It's just like Christmas to get all these books about life in England during the Middle Ages." But as Anne worked, she felt sick to her stomach as she thought about Jeff Perry and how, in all likelihood, he had betrayed the League.

Jeff sat in his car in the library's parking lot for a while and watched people go in and out of the small brick building. Something was definitely wrong. Yesterday afternoon, while Jeff was at work, his APO handler had informed him that the Book was in East Vassalboro, and she had asked him to check if anyone from the League had been sent. So Jeff had called Anne. Pretending to be worried about the Book, Jeff had asked about the League and whether they had changed their plans about sending anyone to Maine. Anne had told him that as far as she knew, their plans were the same, and nobody was coming to East Vassalboro. Anne's voice had sounded so trusting and so concerned that Jeff had believed her.

Later, while Jeff was still at work, he had learned that a teenager named Maya had the Book and that Chet was sure he could handle her on his own. When Jeff had called Chet, to double check, "I'll be fine," came the curt reply. Then, that night, as Jeff stayed up late, waiting and watching something on television—what, he couldn't even remember—he had received a text from Chet. The Book had been in East Vassalboro, but Chet had been wrong about Maya. She had never had the Book. Chet believed the Book was now heading south, to Florida, and that's where Chet was heading, too.

"Maya," Jeff thought. The same Maya who had come in yesterday morning while he had been with Anne? The same Maya who had just called Anne to talk about a play? The more he thought about it, the more Jeff was convinced that the Maya he had met at the library was the same Maya who had called Anne. Could she also be Chet's Maya, the one who was suspected of having the Book? After all, Maya wasn't a common name. Could there be two teenage girls named Maya in such a small town as East Vassalboro? It was possible, Jeff reflected, but certainly not a given. No, in all likelihood, they were the same Maya.

Jeff didn't believe that Anne and Maya had been talking about a play at all. After speaking to Maya, Anne's tone had changed, and the librarian had sounded stiff and guarded. Had Anne lied to him about the League? Jeff was beginning to think she had.

Jeff had been given the address of the farmhouse where Chet's Maya lived so that he could help Chet if the tracker needed backup. Jeff made up his mind to drive to the farmhouse. It would probably be a waste of time, but maybe, just maybe, he would get some kind of clue about what really had happened to Chet and the Book of Everything.

At the farmhouse, a woman, blonde and attractive, had her easel set up on the lawn, and she was painting a picture of a brick house across the street that looked just as old as the farmhouse behind her. Was this Maya's mother? Jeff decided to find out, and he knew what approach he would take. Jeff drove the car into the driveway, got out, and went over to the woman.

Frowning, she looked up. "May I help you?"

Smiling, Jeff tucked his hands into his pockets. "I hope so. I'm Jeff Perry, a friend of Anne Hunter's. I'm the Children's Librarian in Waterville."

"I'm Lily Turcotte. I'm a painter."

"I can see that. Nice picture." And it was a good picture. Even partially finished, it was full of light, and with its vivid colors, full of energy as well.

Lily considered the painting. "Thank you."

"Are you Maya's mother?"

Lily looked quickly from the painting to Jeff. "Yes, I am."

"I was wondering if Maya was here."

"No, she's not."

Jeff pursed his lips and rocked back and forth on his heels. "That's too bad. I wanted to talk to her about the play she and Anne Hunter are putting on."

"The play," Lily said, frowning again.

"Yes, the play." Jeff was starting to feel a little frustrated. Normally, he had no trouble getting information from women, who were usually attracted to his intense brown eyes and white hair. But even though Jeff had just met Lily, he could see that she was not like most women. Jeff continued, "Anne has told me how good Maya is. I thought maybe Maya could help our library with a play, too."

"Maya is a good actor," Lily said. "She takes after her father."

"I'm sorry she's not here. Maybe I can come back later?"

Lily regarded Jeff. "Maya's pretty busy."

"She's not going to give an inch," Jeff thought, and part of him admired her for this.

Jeff was just about to leave when a voice behind him asked, "Who's this?"

Jeff turned around to see a lean, older man, and there could be no doubt that he was Lily's father. Their eyes were the same shade of blue, and they both had fair complexions.

"This is Jeff Perry," Lily replied. "He's a friend of Anne Hunter's. Jeff, this is my father, Roland Turcotte."

"I'm the Children's Librarian at Waterville Public Library," Jeff added quickly. "I was hoping Maya would help us put on a play. Anne tells me Maya is good."

Roland was just as soft-spoken as Lily, but, as it turned out, not as suspicious. "Maya's good, all right. She's only been home one day, and she and Anne are already putting together some kind of play."

"Anne told me a little about that," Jeff said.

Roland laughed. "They were here late last night practicing down in the cow stall." Lily gave her father a look, and he immediately stopped talking.

Jeff tried to keep the tone of his voice casual. "Down in the cow stall? That's quite a place to practice."

"I guess it suited the action," Roland said, and Lily gave him another look.

"Very interesting," Jeff thought, but he smiled and said, "Well, I'd better be going. I hope you'll consider letting Maya help us with a play."

As Jeff walked to his car, he thought, "I need to check out that cow stall. I'll be back." Late at night, Jeff decided, when everyone was in bed, and he wouldn't be seen.

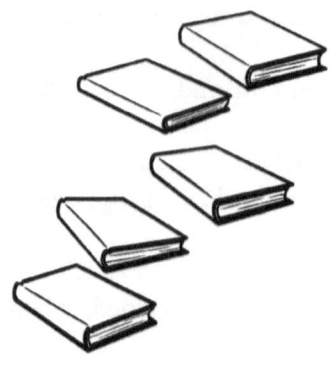

3: New Plans

In Augusta, Mémère and Maya went to their favorite stores. Mémère bought Maya shorts, tops, and some black sneakers.

"There are other colors," Mémère pointed out. "What about these bright red sneakers?"

"Mémère, I live in New York."

"But why does it always have to be black?"

Maya grinned. "It just does. If it's not black, it's not cool."

Mémère sighed, but she perked up when she found a pair of bright pink sandals that went with the top she was wearing. "And I have another top just about the same color. Plus, I can wear them with other clothes I have. What do you think?"

"Pretty snazzy, Mémère," Maya said, thinking about how Mémère's hair was always just so and how her nails were always freshly painted.

"You and Mom aren't at all alike, are you?" Maya asked as they sat in the café at Barnes & Noble. Maya had a fruity iced tea, Mémère had iced coffee, and they shared a piece of chocolate cheesecake.

Mémère laughed. "Not at all. I only have one child, a daughter, and she turns out to be quiet like her father."

"Did you ever mind?"

"Mind what?"

"That she wasn't like you."

Mémère hesitated, and Maya could see that her grandmother was deciding whether she should tell Maya the truth. Maya stared sternly at her grandmother.

"A little," Mémère finally admitted. "When Lily was young, I just wanted us to do what other mothers did with their daughters—cook together or go shopping or visit with my friends and their children. But all Lily wanted was to draw and paint. She wasn't interested in cooking, shopping, or visiting."

"She likes to go on hikes and ride her bike," Maya put in.

"Yes." Mémère laughed. "But me, not so much." Taking a sip of iced coffee, Mémère shrugged. "As Lily got older, I came to appreciate her talent, and I thought, 'Get with it, Celine. Anyone's daughter can go shopping. But not everyone's daughter can paint like my Lily does.'"

Maya could see how hard it had been for Mémère, but she could also see that now it was all right. Mémère meant what she said.

Mémère took a bite of cheesecake. "When I decided to become a nurse, it was better." She winked at Maya. "All those patients took the pressure off Lily."

Maya got a flash of Mémère as a nurse, brisk and capable yet sympathetic with her patients, and how her laughter made even the sickest ones feel a little better. "Are you sorry you retired?"

Mémère stared thoughtfully at Maya. "Why all the questions about an old woman like me?" Grinning, Maya shook her head, and Mémère said, "There's something different about you. It's only been a few months since we came to New York to see you in your play, but it almost seems as though you've aged ten years."

"Make that twenty," Maya thought. Aloud she said, "It's been quite a year."

"I know. It's hard having your father gone. I miss him, too, even though he left you and your mother for that ratty redhead."

Maya nodded, thinking with some amazement that this was really the least of her problems now. She remembered what Elspeth, from the Great Library, had said about the Books of Everything and how they put things in perspective. Somehow, with the battle between the Great Library and Cinnial, Maya's own family problems didn't seem as big anymore.

"Maya," Mémère said, and her expression was serious, "don't grow up too fast. You're only young once. You have plenty of time to be old."

"I won't," Maya replied, knowing that it was too late to follow Mémère's advice, that the Toad Queen, with her gleaming nails, had taken care of that by peeling Maya's eyes.

"But the Toad Queen warned me," Maya thought as she and Mémère finished the cheesecake. "And I could have said no."

"Should I have said no?" she wondered, as different impressions, some from Mémère and some from other people, came to Maya. She was slowly learning how to block the impressions that didn't matter, but Maya still saw more than she wanted. A man sitting next to them had just lost his job, and he was worried about money. A young woman, in love for the first time, was reliving scenes that made Maya pull back quickly. "Should I have said no?" Maya asked herself again, but she knew, deep inside, that she had made the right decision.

"Never be afraid to use your talents," her father had always told her, and seeing other people's yearnings, motivations, and fears was one of her talents. It always had been, even before she had had her eyes peeled. But despite her father's advice, Maya was a little afraid. Where would seeing take her next?

After Mémère and Maya had finished their drinks and the cheesecake, Mémère said, "I'm going to go look at the cookbooks."

"Okay. I'll stay here and read some magazines."

Mémère left, and Maya flipped through a magazine, trying to get excited about what was hot this summer and what was not. But it was no use. All Maya could think about was Humphrey and Andy—President Murphy—and whether the board would allow her to use the Apprentice Book she had taken to Caxton. Finally, Maya sighed and closed the magazine.

"Didn't see anything you liked?" a familiar voice asked.

Maya quickly looked up from the magazine. Standing in front of her was a slim, blonde woman wearing black pants and a white shirt. She smiled down at Maya, who exclaimed, "Elspeth!"

"Hello, Maya. May I sit down?"

"Oh, yes!"

Elspeth sat across from Maya, and reaching over, she squeezed Maya's hand. "It's so good to see you, Maya."

Maya returned the squeeze. "It's great to see you, too, Elspeth."

Elspeth reached into her pocket and removed a familiar small blue Book. Maya recognized it at once—it was the Apprentice Book she had used in Caxton.

Elspeth said, "I'm going to give this to you now in case your grandmother comes back while we're still talking. I can see you recognize the Book."

"I do." Maya put the Apprentice Book in her bag next to Earth's Book of Everything. "I was afraid the board wouldn't let it go out again."

"It was touch and go," Elspeth said, brushing her short, blonde hair away from her face. "There was more than one meeting, and Sydda had to use his full powers of persuasion. Even then, I don't think he would have succeeded if the Great Library's own Book of Everything hadn't been so adamant."

"The Great Library's Book of Everything?"

Elspeth nodded. "It's very, very old. It was the first Book of Everything. It stays in Sydda's office, and Sydda let the board members, one by one, consult the Book."

"And it agreed with Earth's Book?"

"It did. The Great Library's Book of Everything showed, in no uncertain terms, what would happen if Julian's Book and Humphrey prevailed. The effects would ripple outward from Earth and Caxton, and they would continue across the universe."

"I still can't believe the board let the Apprentice Book go out again."

"You have started a trend. I think that more and more Apprentice Books are going to be allowed to leave the Great Library.

I have one myself." Elspeth withdrew a small green Book from her pocket.

"Wow," Maya said, shaking her head. "You should have heard the board argue the first time. I thought they'd never stop."

"Oh, that's how boards are. Eventually they reach a decision, and sometimes it's even the right one."

"You won't be working on Books of Everything?" Maya asked.

"No, I have a new job now. I've become kind of an ambassador for the Great Library." Elspeth smiled. "Sydda was pleased with how it all turned out in Caxton. He thinks that maybe a little intervention from time to time might not be a bad thing. It also lets Cinnial know that we are keeping a tab on things in a more direct way. We are hoping this will keep him off balance. In time, others from the Great Library might be allowed to become ambassadors, too."

"Are you sorry not to be working on a Book of Everything?"

"A little, but this life is certainly more exciting."

Maya thought about the Books in her bag. "What am I supposed to do, Elspeth?"

"Andy needs to know about Humphrey. So one of the first things you have to do is warn Andy."

"But Elspeth, Andy is so old now. His hair is gray, and he hardly even looks like himself."

Elspeth laughed. "Nevertheless."

"Can't you do it? Julian's Book and Humphrey are after me, and they are both with Andy."

Elspeth was silent for a moment. "I asked Sydda if I should go tell Andy, or perhaps someone from the League of Librarians. But Sydda said, no, that it was something you needed to do because of how you see things."

"There it is again," Maya thought. "The seeing."

Elspeth leaned forward. "And to make things even more complicated, you shouldn't use the Apprentice Book for traveling unless you absolutely need to. If you do, APO will be able to track you. By coming to Earth, I've of course alerted APO that the Great Library is especially interested in this planet. However, the Book took me to New York, and I drove here so that they wouldn't know exactly where I went. And next the Book is going to take me to Florida to lead APO on a false trail. That's where they think Chet is looking for Earth's Book of Everything. At least for now."

Maya rubbed her face. "How am I going to get to Bar Harbor and see President Murphy?"

"Perhaps you could receive an invitation to the party the president is giving. You have a friend who's staying in Bar Harbor, don't you? Leah Grossman?"

"That's right! And her family has been invited to the party."

"I expect your name would be approved for the guest list, even at the last minute. And I'm guessing that your grandparents would give you a ride to Bar Harbor if you were invited to the president's party and could stay with Leah and her family."

"Do you think Andy—President Murphy—still remembers me? It's been a long time for him."

"I'm sure of it," Elspeth replied. "How could he ever forget you and all that happened to him in Caxton?"

Maya smiled somewhat ruefully. Elspeth was right. Andy wasn't likely to forget about her, the Book of Everything, Caxton, Sir John, and everything else that had taken place on that short but memorable trip to Ilyria.

Maya said, "I'll tell Leah I've always wanted to meet the president because he lived not far from where my mémère lived when she was young. Leah is one of my best friends. Also, her family likes me. I'm pretty sure I can convince them to ask if I can go to the party, too."

"Sounds like we have a good plan," Elspeth said. "At the party, you will find a way to talk to Andy and warn him about Humphrey."

"Humphrey! Won't he recognize me?"

"You were in disguise as a boy the last time you saw Humphrey. Perhaps you could change your looks even more? And wear a dress?"

Maya was about to ask more questions, when a voice behind her asked, "Maya, who's your friend?"

Maya jumped. "Mémère! This is Elspeth, a friend of Anne Hunter's. I met her at the library, and we both like plays. Elspeth, this is my grandmother, Celine Turcotte."

"I'm very pleased to meet you." Smiling, Elspeth stood and pushed the chair she had been sitting in toward the table.

"You don't have to leave on my account," Mémère said.

"Actually, I'm going on a long trip, and I need to leave shortly. It was very nice meeting you, Celine. Perhaps we'll meet again. And you, too, Maya. Give my best to Anne."

"I will," Maya said, thinking it should be sooner rather than later in case Mémère said something to Anne about Elspeth.

Elspeth left, and "Pretty woman," Mémère said.

"Yes, she is," Maya answered.

"Where is she from?" Mémère asked. "I couldn't quite place her accent."

At least Maya could answer this question truthfully. "Mémère, I really don't know."

When Mémère and Maya got back to East Vassalboro, Lily was done painting, and she asked, "Mom, do you need help with dinner? If you don't, I thought Maya and I might go for a bike ride. If you want to, that is," Lily added quickly, looking at Maya.

"Sure," Maya said, even though what she really wanted was to go to the field behind the barn where she could have a private conversation with the Apprentice Book and the Book of Everything. But Maya could see how much her mother wanted to go on a bike ride, and she decided her talk with the Books could wait until later.

"Go ahead," Mémère said. "Dinner's simple—Pépère is going to grill some chicken. I'll make a salad and maybe some kind of pasta dish. Nothing I can't handle on my own."

After Maya locked the two Books in the desk in her room, helmets were gathered, water bottles were filled, and two bikes, bought especially for riding in East Vassalboro, came out of the barn. A third bike—the one for Maya's father—stayed behind by itself, and despite all that she had on her mind, Maya felt a little sad as she thought about past bike rides they had all taken together. On those rides, Maya's father would sing snatches of songs, whistle, and bellow out commentaries as they passed scenes he liked. "What a great house!" or "Look at those horses grazing!" or, most often, "What a view!"

"For heaven's sake, Giles," Lily would say. "Do you have to be so loud?"

"Yes!" Giles would exclaim. "I do."

And despite herself, Lily would smile.

"Want to go on the loop, past Lemieux's Orchards and through North Vassalboro?" Lily asked. "The hills are easier that way, and when we're done, we can get iced tea from the Country Store and sit by the lake."

"Sure," Maya said, glad to be doing something that approached normal.

Off they went. Lily wasn't a fast rider, but she was strong, and hills never gave her much trouble. Maya was faster but not as good at hills as her mother. Somehow, though, they always accommodated each other, and it seemed to Maya that it was when they were on their bikes that they were most comfortable being together. Conversation was minimal, which suited Lily, and there was constant forward motion, which pleased Maya.

Then there was the countryside, with its deep blue sky, its woods, and lush green fields. Various smells came to Maya as she biked—the spicy scent of the evergreens punctuated by the sweet smell of the fields with their flowers, grass, and wild strawberries.

As Maya followed her mother on the country road, her troubles didn't exactly go away, but they were pushed to the back of her mind. By the time they reached Lemieux's Orchards and started going down the big hill, Maya actually felt happy as the warm summer air rushed by her face, and she listened to the whir of the tires on the road. It was when Maya was hardly thinking about President Murphy and Humphrey that it came to her how she could disguise herself so that Humphrey wouldn't recognize her. Now all Maya had to do was convince her mother, and she was so worried that Lily would say no that Maya's intuition, usually so strong, was silent on this question.

When Lily and Maya finished biking the loop and were back in East Vassalboro, they bought iced tea at the store, and Maya thought the cold drink tasted especially good. As they sat by the lake, a slight breeze came up, a cool touch on Maya's sweaty face.

"Great ride, Mom," Maya said, thinking that it would be best to start with a subject her mother would like.

"I want to go on a ride every day that it doesn't rain," Lily replied. "I love riding in the countryside."

"Me, too. Maybe sometime we can ride up to the fire tower."

"And bring a picnic," Lily added.

They sat in silence, drinking their iced tea. Maya was just about to ask her mother for permission to do something she was sure her mother wouldn't want her to do, when Lily, uncharacteristically, was the first to speak.

"Jeff Perry stopped by the house today."

Maya nearly dropped her iced tea. "He did?"

Lily was watching Maya closely. "He said he was a friend of Anne Hunter's."

"I've seen him at the library with Anne," Maya conceded.

"So he was telling the truth," Lily said quietly, and Maya could tell that her mother didn't trust him.

"Me, too," Maya thought, but aloud she asked, "What did he want?"

"For you to help with a play at the Waterville Library, where he works. Anne has been telling him how good you are."

"I hope Anne didn't give away too much," Maya thought.

Then Lily said, "Pépère told Jeff how you were all practicing in the cow stalls last night."

Maya thought, "Pépère, why did you have to tell him that?"

"So do you want to help Jeff with a play? I told him you were pretty busy."

Maya shook her head. "No, I don't. You're right. I am busy. One play is enough."

Lily smiled. "Good." She ruffled Maya's dark, curly hair.

Maya's intuition suddenly returned. "Now," a voice inside Maya said. "Ask her now."

"Mom? I want to do something for the play. It's something I've wanted to do for a long time. I want Mémère to take me to Dot's so that she can dye my hair blonde." Some of this was true. As a little girl, Maya had wanted to be blonde like her mother, and when they were in East Vassalboro in the summer, Maya would go outside and play in the sun, hoping it would bleach her hair.

"Is it blonde yet?" Maya would ask Mémère.

Mémère would look at Maya's dark curls. "No, sweetheart. I guess you'd better stay out a little longer."

Frowning, Lily looked at Maya's hair. "Blonde."

"Just for the summer. It'll grow out. And then I'll be dark again."

Lily stared steadily at Maya. "Trust me," Maya thought, meeting her mother's gaze. "Please trust me."

Lilly surprised Maya by shrugging and smiling just a little. "Let's see what Mémère says."

"Oh, why not?" Mémère said that night after dinner. "She's fifteen, not five. And Maya's right. Her hair will grow out."

"All right," Lily said. "Mom, go ahead and make an appointment for Maya."

"I'll call first thing tomorrow," Mémère said, and there was a gleam in her eyes.

Maya thought about how Mémère always liked it when a hairstyle was changed. For years, Mémère had been hoping that Lily would have her hair cut and get rid of the French twist, but as she did with so many other things, Lily remained firm about her hairstyle. Now, not only had Maya cut her hair, but she was also changing the color.

Feeling more than a little guilty, Maya looked at Mémère's happy face. "Good thing she doesn't know why I want my hair blonde."

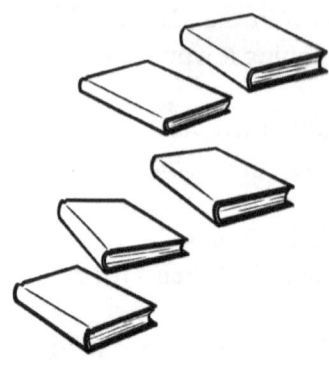

4: A Spy Is Born

T he night before Maya had her hair dyed blonde, she went into the field behind the farmhouse. It was dusk, but there was still enough light to see, and there would be for at least another hour. "I love these long days," Maya thought. In the field, no one would hear her as she talked to the two Books. The grass hadn't been cut yet for hay, and Maya was able to make a little nest for herself and the Books. When she settled down in the tall grass, not even the top of her dark head was visible.

From one back pocket in her shorts, Maya removed Earth's Book of Everything, and from her other back pocket, she removed the Apprentice one. Setting the Books in her lap, Maya carefully opened each Book. Earth's Book of Everything made that funny little whirring sound it always made when it was first opened, and the Apprentice Book made a similar sound, except the tone was a little higher.

"Well, Maya," the Book of Everything said. "You have the Apprentice Book, and the time has come for me to go with David to Hartland. I understand you've called him, and he's coming to Vassalboro tomorrow to pick me up."

"I did," Maya said. "And I'll miss you."

"It has been a pleasure to have traveled with you. There is a possibility that we will meet again. But if not, I want to wish you courage and good luck. You'll need both."

"Thanks, I guess," Maya said, thinking about the need for both courage and good luck.

The Book continued, "Trust your intuition, but don't be afraid to question it. No one's right all the time. Not even someone who can see the way you do."

"Next are you going to tell me to use the Force?"

"Now, Maya, was that necessary?" Despite the rebuke, there was a glimmer of humor in the Book's voice, and Maya thought she might have heard the faintest chuckle coming from the Apprentice Book. But the Book of Everything was serious when it spoke again. "Are you ready to help Maya?" This question was directed toward the Apprentice Book.

The Apprentice Book spoke for the first time. "I'm ready."

"Let me know if you need my help."

"I will," the Apprentice Book replied.

"I'll be keeping tabs on you."

"I know you will."

The Books reminded Maya of two brothers talking, the older one nagging the younger one, and Maya sensed that the Book of Everything was reluctant to leave.

"I've got to go north, perhaps eventually to Canada, although that still isn't clear. Hard times are likely to be coming, and the farther north I go, the better it will be," the Book of Everything said, as if reading her thoughts.

"Can you read my thoughts?" Maya asked.

"No, we Books can only see what is fixed and what is open and then guide. That's all."

"It's a lot," Maya said, with one hand on each book. "That's why APO wants to steal you."

"And sometimes it isn't enough," the Book of Everything said. "Even with all the information we have from the Great Library. But we have to keep trying, to make the effort."

Maya thought of this as she went back to the farmhouse to get ready for bed, as she washed her face and brushed her teeth, as she texted Leah and asked—begged, actually—to be invited to Bar Harbor and for Leah's father to see if Maya could go to the president's party, too.

Leah immediately texted back. "That would be great if you could come. I'll ask my father."

The Books were in the locked desk, and Maya settled into bed to read the book she had taken out from the library—*A Wrinkle in Time.* Maya smiled a little, thinking about how she couldn't have chosen a more appropriate book, but she hadn't even finished the first chapter when her phone rang. It was her father.

"Hi, Maya. How's it going?"

"Good. I'm going to have my hair dyed blonde. Mom said I could."

Her father sounded surprised. "She did?"

"It's for a play I'm going to be in. I need to change the way I look."

"Why not a wig? I like your dark hair."

"It just seemed better to dye it. A wig is so fake."

"Actors wear them all the time."

"I know. But I've always wanted to be blonde. Mémère's pretty happy."

Her father laughed. "I bet she is. Well, it's not permanent. Hair grows."

"That's what I told Mom."

Maya's father changed the subject. "Have you thought any-more about coming down for a visit?"

Maya hadn't, but she said, "Maybe in August? A week or two before school starts?"

"It'll be hot."

"That's all right."

Her father was pleased. "Good, good. Very good."

Now it was Maya's turn to change the subject. "I might be going to Bar Harbor to visit Leah and her family."

"Bar Harbor's great in the summer. You'll have fun."

"I might even be able to go to a party that President Murphy is giving. He's in Bar Harbor right now, and Leah and her family are going." Maya said, as casually as she could.

Maya's father whistled. "You're traveling in high places, kiddo."

"If you only knew," Maya thought.

"President Murphy went to NYU the same time I did. Have I ever told you that?"

Her father had, but Maya couldn't really remember what he had said. Until recently, she hadn't been that interested in President Murphy. But she was interested now. "Tell me again."

"I didn't really know him. I went to a few parties, and he was there. That's all."

"What was he like?"

"Charming but serious. There was something about him, even then. People just wanted to be around him. Even a loudmouth like me could see that."

Maya said, "If I get to go to the party, I'll be pretty nervous."

"Of course you will. It's not every day you get to meet the president of the United States."

Maya wanted to tell her father about Andy, about the Book of Everything, about Humphrey. He would know just what to say. He always did, and it was one of the reasons why Maya missed her father so much. But Maya knew she couldn't tell him about anything that had happened with the Book of Everything.

Maya swallowed. "I'll let you know if I go to the party."

"I'll be waiting to hear."

After Maya finished talking with her father, she settled back with the book. As Maya followed Meg, Charles Wallace, and Calvin, she would suddenly stop reading and think about President Murphy and Humphrey. It took her a long time to feel drowsy enough to go to sleep.

The next morning, just after breakfast was finished, Maya received a phone call from Anne. "David's here. Can you come over with the book?"

"I think so, but let me ask," Maya replied, as she turned to her mother and grandmother, who were getting ready to clear the table. "Anne wants me to go to the library before it opens so that we can work on the play. Is it all right to go?"

Lily nodded, and Mémère said, "I'll let you know if Dot has a late morning appointment, but I bet she won't have anything until afternoon. Maybe not even for a day or two."

Maya turned back to her phone. "I can come," Maya said to Anne. "I'll be right over."

Feeling sad that the Book of Everything would be going with David, Maya went upstairs and took both Books from the desk. She slipped the Apprentice Book in one of her back pockets and hesitated with the Book of Everything. Finally, she opened the Book.

"I'm really going to miss you," she said softly, so that nobody would hear her.

"I'll miss you, too," the Book said just as softly, even though only Maya could hear. Maya nodded, and her eyes stung with tears. "Time to go, Maya," the Book added gently.

"I know." Maya shut the Book and put it in her other back pocket. She rubbed her eyes, took a tissue from the box on the desk, and blew her nose. Maya sighed and then sighed again as she thought about how some of the people she loved best had left her. It had started with her father. The loneliness Maya had felt when he left had been so intense that it had made her stomach hurt, and she had hardly been able to eat. Then there was Feste, who was not just gone but dead. There were all the people from the Great Library who were so far away that, with the exception of Elspeth, Maya wasn't sure if she would ever see them again. Finally, there was the Book of Everything, which seemed more like a person than a book.

Maya was weeping now into a tissue, and she felt a hand on her shoulder.

It was Mémère. "Why are you crying, sweetheart?"

"People leave, people die," Maya said.

"I know." Mémère wrapped an arm around Maya's shoulder and let her cry.

When Maya was finished, she asked, "How can I go to the library looking like this?"

"Splash some cold water on your face. Take a little walk first. You'll be fine."

Maya followed Mémère's instructions, but she didn't walk too long because she knew David was waiting for her.

As it turned out, neither Anne nor David noticed that Maya's eyes were a little red. Even though the library wasn't officially opened, there was a man standing by the desk. Anne and David were standing, too, and they were all staring at each other. The man was slim and tall and had dirty blond hair cut so short it was just a stubble. Maya had never seen the man before, but one look told her that he was not a friend of the library.

"I've got to be going," the man said, leaning toward Anne, who pulled back a little. His voice was deep, and it rumbled with confidence. "But I wanted to remind you how important next week's town meeting is. The budget is tight. There have to be cuts."

"Of course I'll be there," Anne said, and she was not smiling. David didn't say anything. Frowning, he just stood there with his hands in his pockets.

The man left without saying goodbye, and Maya asked, "Who is that?"

Anne, usually so light and quick, sat down heavily on the chair behind her desk. "That was Greg Shepperly, the town manager." She motioned to two folding chairs by the desk, and David and Maya sat down. "He came in to tell me that he's asking the budget committee to reconsider how much money the town will give to the library. For some reason, there's a budget shortfall, and there's going to be a special town meeting about it next week."

"Your budget isn't very big as it is," David said.

"I know. But times are tough, and towns are getting squeezed by the state, which won't give the money that it promised to support the schools. Besides, Greg doesn't like this library. In fact, he'd like to see it closed. I just hope that enough library supporters come to the meeting. A lot of people go on vacation this time of year."

After all that Maya had seen and done, she shouldn't have been shocked, but she was. "Close the library?"

Anne bit her bottom lip. "Unthinkable, I know. Except Greg is thinking about it. I've heard that some on the town council are on his side, and so are some people in town."

"Why would he want to close the library?" Maya asked. It was impossible to imagine East Vassalboro without its library.

"Greg wants to close the library for a couple of reasons," Anne said. "First, he and his wife can afford to buy books whenever they want. They don't have to come to the library to get books, and they don't care that it's not that way for everyone in this town. And second, Greg thinks the library should be run by volunteers and donations. He believes the town shouldn't have to budget anything for the library. But we can't run the library that way. We'd never get enough donations to keep it open."

"But more important," David added, "without a library, people don't have as much access to ideas and other points of view, which books provide better than any other medium. Greg wants to limit and control what people know, and he's playing right into APO's hands, even though he probably doesn't realize they exist. APO's propaganda is everywhere—on TV, on the Internet, on the radio, and people like Greg are sucked in." There was a gleam in David's blue eyes. His red hair was sticking up a little, and his beard looked bushier than usual.

Despite the seriousness of the situation, Anne smiled. But then she said seriously, "David, you are so right." She turned to Maya. "You came here to give the Book of Everything to David."

Maya reluctantly took the Book, now smooth and blue, out of her pocket. "Here it is."

David took the Book. "It's quite a responsibility."

Maya asked, "Has Anne told you about Jeff Perry? I have a bad feeling about him, and I think he might be the one who betrayed the League of Librarians."

"Anne told me," David answered. "I'll be careful. But how could Jeff be on APO's side? He's a librarian, for God's sake."

Anne shook her head. "I don't know. He's always been a little vain, but I never thought of him as a traitor."

"Cinnial was a librarian, too," Maya put in softly.

"That he was." David sighed. "It's probably a good thing the Book will only be staying with me for a little while. If the Book isn't in one place for too long, it will keep APO on its toes."

"It might be going north," Maya said, remembering what the Book of Everything had told her. "Hard times are coming."

Anne and David looked grim, and Maya could tell they were thinking about the same things as she was: APO, Jeff Perry, what the hard times might be, and how they would affect Vassalboro, Hartland, Maine, the country, and even the world. Maya said a quick goodbye and left. Feeling glum, she walked up the road by her grandparents' house, all the way to the four corners at the other end of the road, past fields, houses, and woods. But the day was so fine, and the sky was so blue that by the time Maya came back home, she didn't feel quite as glum as she had when she left the library. Plus, Maya had the Apprentice Book in her pocket, and although nothing could ever replace the Book of Everything, it was comforting to know she had a Book—even an Apprentice Book—to help her.

Then, the excitement of the afternoon more than made up for the glum morning. Mémère's hairdresser had had a last-minute cancellation and was able to slide in Maya for a late afternoon appointment.

Just before Maya and Mémère left for the appointment, Leah had texted Maya. "You can come to Bar Harbor! For a visit and to the prez's party. It'll be great to see you."

"You just wait," Maya thought, grinning as she texted to Leah. "I'm going out with Mem. I'll ask Mom when I get back."

"Wow!" Mémère said at the hairdresser's, as Maya went from being a brunette to a blonde. It had been a long, stinky process. "You hardly look like yourself anymore."

Dot fluffed Maya's curls, which were now blonde. "What fun! You look great as a blonde, Maya."

Maya peered at herself in the mirror. Who was that looking back at her? The eyes and the features were the same, but the blonde hair certainly did change the way she looked. The blonde hair accentuated Maya's dark eyes and sharp, little nose, and it emphasized what her father sometimes called her "attitude." Perversely, after all the years of wanting to be blonde, Maya wasn't sure if she liked the change or not.

"It looks really good," Mémère said. "Not that I didn't like your dark hair," she added quickly.

"Don't you think she looks a little like Madonna in her younger days?" Dot asked.

Mémère frowned a little. "I hadn't thought of that, but, you know, she does."

Maya continued to stare at herself. She was pretty sure that Humphrey, who had seen her as a dark-haired boy, would not easily recognize her now. Finally Maya smiled. "It's exactly what I wanted."

On the way home, Maya said to Mémère, "I need a dress and a new pair of shoes to go with it. I know we just went shopping, but could you take me again tomorrow?"

"I don't see why not. But why do you suddenly want a dress? You hate dresses and skirts."

Maya grinned. "Because I've been invited to stay with Leah in Bar Harbor. And to go to the president's party."

"Well, I'll be darned. You had this planned all along, didn't you?" But Mémère was smiling.

Maya smiled back. "Maybe."

Lily, on the other hand, didn't smile when Maya asked her if she could go to Bar Harbor. Lily said yes—how could she refuse? —but Maya could tell her mother thought she had been devious and that Lily's trust had been misplaced when she had given permission for Maya to dye her hair blonde.

"She's right," Maya whispered that night in bed under her covers to the Apprentice Book. "I am devious."

"You have to be," the Apprentice Book said. "They can't know what's going on."

"Yeah," Maya agreed. "But still." Maya and her friends had plenty of things they wouldn't tell their parents, but what Maya was keeping from her family was so big that it seemed wrong not to tell them.

"I feel like a spy," Maya said, and this was both exciting and uncomfortable.

"In a way, that's exactly what you are," the Book said.

"And you're my companion," Maya said.

"Just like in *Dr. Who*, except I'm a book."

"Actually, you're more like Dr. Who, and I'm the companion."

Both the Apprentice Book and Maya giggled softly. Although she missed the Book of Everything, Maya was beginning to realize that the Apprentice Book felt more like a friend, that its inexperience made it less intimidating.

"Do you have a name?" Maya asked, thinking that a friend needed a name.

"No," came the answer. "We Books are not named."

Maya hesitated. "Would you like a name?"

The Apprentice Book hesitated, too. "I've never really thought about it."

"Would it be all right?"

"I guess so," the Book replied. "I don't see what it would change."

"What name would you like?"

"I don't know. There are so many names across the universe. I can't choose. Do you have one in mind?"

Maya really didn't, but then a name suddenly leaped out for her. "How about Ariel?"

"From *The Tempest?*"

"Yes, *The Tempest*. In a way, you seem like a good spirit sent to help me. Just like Ariel."

"Ariel," the Book said as though it were trying on the name for size. There was a silence for several minutes, and Maya wondered if the Book was going to reject the name.

But the Apprentice Book finally said, "I like it."

And from then on, the Book was known as Ariel.

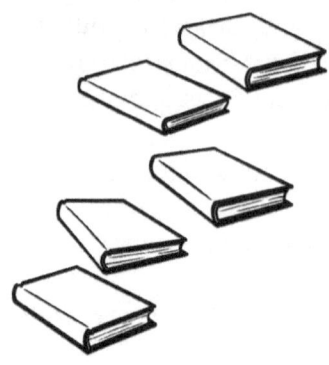

5: What Jeff Perry Found

Jeff Perry carefully made his way through the fields behind Mémère and Pépère's farmhouse. He was dressed in black, and he even wore a black cap to hide his white hair. At this time of night, Jeff did not expect anyone to see him, but he still felt the need to be careful, and Jeff shined the light from his flashlight close to the ground so that he had enough light to see but would not easily be noticed.

On the one hand, Jeff felt foolish for sneaking behind the farmhouse. "Maya is just a kid," he thought. "She's no match for someone like Chet."

On the other hand, when Jeff had met Maya at the library, he had noticed that there was something different about this girl, but he had been so focused on Mary and the missing book that he hadn't paid much attention to Maya.

Jeff stopped in the field as he thought about Anne's reaction at the library after getting the call from Maya. Anne's tone had changed after that call. What had Maya told her? Nothing good. Jeff was sure of it.

Jeff had a suspicious nature. It was one of the reasons why he had been recruited by APO and why he was so good at what he was doing. Jeff didn't trust anybody, not even his own mother. Especially his own mother, Jeff might have said, if anyone had asked him.

Jeff stood still as a warm, humid breeze blew across his face, and mosquitoes whined around his ears. If his suspicions were correct, something had happened in the cow stalls when Maya and Anne and some friends had supposedly been rehearsing a play. Jeff was hoping to find a clue that would contradict the story he had been told, a clue that would help him figure out what had really happened.

Jeff started walking again, but even with the flashlight, he stumbled into a groundhog's hole and nearly fell. Swearing under his breath, Jeff caught his balance and finally made it to the cow stalls. Opening the door, Jeff went into the room with its low ceiling and row of stalls. It was even damper inside than it was outside, and there was something about the place that gave Jeff the creeps.

Jeff groped along the wall by the door, found the light switch, and turned on the light. Everything looked just the way it should, dirty and empty. Using his flashlight because the light was so dim, Jeff examined the inside of the stalls, but nothing seemed to be out of order. It was when Jeff checked the edges of the floor by the entrance that he found the small red pen that had rolled into a crack in the floor and was barely visible. If Jeff hadn't been looking so carefully and his flashlight hadn't been so bright, he would have missed it. Prying the pen from the crack, he shined his light on it. "Green Acres Motel," Jeff read. "Portsmouth, New Hampshire."

"That's where Chet stayed on his way to Maine," Jeff thought, and he came up with a scenario. Somehow Anne had found out about Chet—despite the device that kept him shielded from the Book—and had waylaid the tracker as he was on his way to get the Book from Maya. Anne probably had help, Jeff reflected. Most likely from the League of Librarians, who had sent someone after all. There had been a fight, and in the scuffle the pen had fallen from Chet's pocket. When it was over, the librarians had taken Chet's phone and had texted the false message.

That part was clever, Jeff had to admit, putting the pen in his pocket. But what about Maya? What was her role in all of this? Surely she was too young to have figured out what to do with the Book of Everything. But then again, maybe not. And where was the Book now? "Not in Florida, I bet," Jeff muttered to himself. "It's probably still here in Maine." And Chet? Was he dead?

"Too many questions," Jeff said. "And not enough answers."

If he had been Chet, Jeff's next move would have been to creep into the house, find Maya's room, and search for the Book of Everything, just to be sure it still wasn't in East Vassalboro. And if anyone caught him sneaking around, then it would be too bad for that person.

But Jeff was not Chet. Yes, he was willing to betray his colleagues to help APO get the Book of Everything, but he was not willing to murder anyone for it. He stopped short of that. Jeff had a gun and would defend himself if someone attacked him, but to murder Maya and her family? No, and he wouldn't risk getting caught in their house where he might have to do more than defend himself.

Not knowing that Maya and her family had left for Bar Harbor. Jeff sighed as he headed from the cow stalls. He was in a quandary now. Jeff knew he should call his APO handler and tell her what he suspected. APO, with its resources, would be able to discover what had happened much quicker than he could. But what if his suspicions were wrong? APO would not be pleased. They might drop him from their payroll. Or do something much, much worse. Jeff grimaced, thinking of all the things that APO might do to him.

But what if he was right and the Book of Everything was in Maine and he could somehow get the Book on his own? Jeff had already been paid very well for his betrayal, but if he managed to get Earth's Book of Everything, then he would make even more money. So much that Jeff could leave central Maine and his little job at the library with its low salary. He could have the life he felt he deserved.

Besides, Jeff had a trump card, as his mother would have put it, and he patted his pocket, feeling the device that would shield his activities from the Book of Everything. Jeff could move freely, and the Book would never know where he was or what he was doing. The device would also disable the Book if he got close enough. Jeff reasoned that if APO had trusted him with such a valuable device, then it trusted him to be something more than a sidekick to Chet.

Jeff decided that he would give himself one day before getting in touch with his handler. Jeff thought, "And who knows what might happen in a day?"

However, the next morning, nothing came to Jeff. All day at the library, as he worked in his office and was occasionally called upon to help discipline rowdy boys on the computers, nothing came to him. When it was almost time for him to leave, still nothing had come to him.

"I'll have to call my handler," Jeff thought moodily as he began to gather his things. Someone was standing by his office door. "What do you want?" he asked curtly without looking up.

"Why, Jeff! I'm sorry to bother you."

Jeff knew that voice. It was Charlotte Nelson, the Children's Librarian from the Pittsfield Library. She always stopped by on Wednesday, hoping that Jeff would ask her to go to dinner at the Asian Cafe. Depending on Jeff's mood and his schedule, sometimes he did and sometimes he didn't. Charlotte had a thing for him, Jeff knew, and although she wasn't his type—the woman never stopped talking, and her face was plain and sharp—it amused Jeff to let her think that he might be interested in her when, in truth, Anne Hunter was more his type.

"Oh, what the hell," Jeff thought. It would be better than being alone at his apartment and thinking about the Book of Everything. Smiling, he looked up. "You're not a bother. Are you in the mood for Asian food?"

Charlotte laughed. "I sure am. And I was hoping you would be, too."

"Charlotte, this is your lucky night," Jeff thought, catching a reflection of himself in the glass on his door. He patted his hair into place. As it turned out, it was Jeff's lucky night, too.

Over wine and vegetarian dumplings, Jeff and Charlotte discussed summer reading programs, noisy kids, and book budgets that were never large enough. This discussion took them all the way to the main meal.

"Even with our expansion, there's not enough shelf space," Charlotte said, helping herself to some drunken noodles with tofu. Jeff would have preferred beef, but Charlotte was a vegetarian.

Charlotte continued, "I have to constantly cull old books to make way for the new books. I feel so bad for those old books. I always hate to get rid of them."

Jeff nodded sympathetically, even though he felt exactly the opposite. "Good riddance to those clunkers," he always said to himself as his assistants pulled the books from the shelves. Still, like most librarians, Jeff wanted more shelf space, even if he didn't have any mercy for culled books. There were always new books to add, and although his library was much bigger than Charlotte's, there was a finite amount of shelf space.

"Well, I'm luckier than David up in Hartland," Charlotte said, twirling noodles on her fork.

Jeff thought about David, who was friends with Anne. As children, Anne and David had lived next to each other, and their families were friends, too. Jeff wondered, had David been involved with what had happened to Chet?

"Oh?" Jeff asked noncommittally, stabbing his fork into a piece of tofu.

"David has such a small library, and his budget makes mine look huge." Jeff agreed, staring intently at Charlotte. She blushed, squirming just a little. "I was there just yesterday. David and I like to get together. To discuss library things," Charlotte added quickly, blinking anxiously.

Jeff understood that Charlotte was trying to tell him that she was not interested in David. "Just as well," Jeff thought. He knew David was not interested in Charlotte. Instead, it was Anne, the same as it was for Jeff. "It's nice to have other librarians to talk to," he said neutrally, actually feeling a little sorry for Charlotte.

"It sure is. Anyway, yesterday I left much sooner than I needed to, and I got to Hartland early."

"Where is this going?" Jeff thought impatiently. Charlotte always took so long telling her stories. No detail was too small to be left out. "Get to the point," Jeff always wanted to say but never did.

Jeff smiled politely. "It's good to be early."

"Yes, it is. And you know how I hate to be late. But this time I was over an hour early, and David wasn't even at the library yet. I could have called him, but I didn't want to rush him. So I just drove around for a while. Despite the poverty, Hartland is a beautiful town. There's the lake—"

"But eventually you drove back to the library?" Jeff interrupted, hoping to put an end to a description of Hartland's attractions.

"I was still early, but David's car was in the parking lot. The library's door was unlocked, so I just walked in. My goodness, David jumped." Charlotte laughed, and Jeff laughed with her. "But here's the funny thing. On his desk was the most beautiful book I have ever seen. The cover was leather, and it looked old."

For once, Jeff didn't feel like telling Charlotte to hurry up with her story. He wanted her to take her time, to get the details right.

Charlotte smiled. "When I went over to the desk, David quickly put the book in one of the desk's big drawers on the side. When I asked about the book, David told me that it belonged to a patron who thought the book might be valuable. He, the patron, had given it to David so that he could do some research on the book. You know that David is also a historian and is knowledgeable about old books?"

"Yes," Jeff answered, licking dry lips. "I do know that." Jeff also knew that David was well paid by the League of Librarians, which allowed him to work at the small library in Hartland and still be able to live decently.

"Anyway, David apologized but said he didn't have permission to show the book to anyone. I told him it was perfectly all right." Charlotte sighed. "I wonder how much that book is worth."

"If it's the Book I think it is, then it's priceless," Jeff thought, but he just shook his head in response.

"And you want to hear another funny thing?" Charlotte asked.

"I'm all ears," Jeff said.

"There was something about that book that made me want to look at it, to open the drawer if David left the room." Charlotte laughed sheepishly. "But he never left the room. He didn't even leave the desk."

"I bet he didn't," Jeff thought. Aloud, he asked, as casually as he could, "Did you notice what color the book was?"

"Oh, yes! It was the most beautiful shade of deep blue. And blue is one of my favorite colors."

Jeff smiled at Charlotte. "Mine, too."

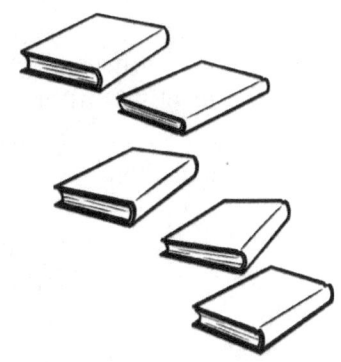

6: Library Closed

Taking a deep breath, Anne unlocked the door of the Vassalboro Public Library and stepped inside. But rather than going into her back office, as she usually did when she first came to work, Anne just stood and looked around the small library, at the wood stove—the library's logo—that kept the place cozy and warm during Maine's long, cold winters; at the blue and brown rocking chairs by the windows, where she had had so many conversations with patrons—some rich, some poor, many in between, all library lovers; at the stacks of books, a small collection, to be sure, but one that Anne had worked on diligently during her years as the library's director so that this small town could have the best library it could afford.

Blinking to stop herself from crying, Anne thought about the town meeting last night and how what she had feared would happen had actually come to pass. The town council—egged on by the town manager, Greg Shepperly—had effectively shut down the Vassalboro Public Library. Not directly, of course. Oh, no. They had been too cagey to close it outright. Instead, pleading a sudden budget deficit, the council had suggested defunding the library so the town wouldn't have to lay off a teacher. To Anne's horror, a majority at the meeting had voted with the town council, who had insisted it was time for the library to support itself. The meeting's attendance had been small. Too many of the library's supporters had gone away on vacation. "The naysayers had their way," Anne thought. "Just as Greg intended."

The library trustees had a small slush fund for emergencies, but nowhere near enough to keep the library going for six months, much less a year. And by the time the outstanding bills were paid, the slush fund would be pretty much gone. The Vassalboro Public Library would have to close.

Anne knew she should go to her office to begin the process of shutting down the library, to take care of paperwork, to make phone calls. But somehow she couldn't bring herself to go there, not just yet, and instead Anne went to the rocking chairs, sat down on the blue one, and rocked. The motion soothed her a little, but when the door opened, and Greg Shepperly came in, Anne stopped rocking. However, she stayed seated, thinking, "I won't stand for him, and I'm not going to ask him to sit down. I won't give him that. He doesn't deserve it."

Grinning and shaking his head, Greg came to the rocking chairs. He stood, staring down at her. "Well," he said, "quite a meeting last night."

"Oh, for God's sake," Anne snapped. "Don't pretend you didn't have this all planned. You've wanted to close the library ever since you took over as town manager. You and Kathy Jones, the chair of the town council, plotted and plotted. And finally you two got your way."

Still grinning, Greg sat down across from her. "You're right. I never thought the town should fund this library. And now with the deficit, the time is right."

Anne glared at Greg. "No time is ever right to defund a library. In tough times, people need a library more than ever."

"Do they?" Greg asked, and he was actually smiling. "Do they really? More than food, more than heat? Think about Fred Tully, a veteran on a fixed income. To keep the library open, we would have to raise taxes. Fred couldn't come last night, but he told me that he doesn't know what he'll do if taxes go up any more. He might have to cut out a meal. Fred doesn't have much money."

Anne bit her lip but didn't say anything. Greg had told this story last night at the town meeting, and Anne knew that Fred Tully lived on a tight budget, in a small, tidy mobile home on the edge of town. He was a regular patron of the library, a member of the town's Historical Society, and an ardent reader of historical books, fiction and nonfiction.

With a gleam in his eyes, Greg pressed his point. "You can't eat books, and they don't pay the bills."

"No, of course they don't," Anne replied, but then an image came to her of Fred's smiling face whenever he found a new history book she had added to the library's collection. "But books make life worth living, and surely that has to count for something."

Greg blinked at Anne as though she were speaking a language he didn't understand. Finally he said gently, almost genially, "Look, nobody is saying you have to close the library. Volunteers can run it. Donations can keep it going. Grants and bake sales." Greg waved his hand, a dismissive motion.

Anne stared directly at Greg. "You know better than that. We can't run the library with grants and bake sales. We need a reliable, steady income. If the town doesn't fund the library, then it will have to close."

Leaning forward, Greg stopped smiling. "I know the library has money stashed away in various accounts that you don't want to tell us about."

Swallowing, Anne shook her head. "Greg, there's no huge amount of money stashed away. There's a small fund for emergencies. That's it, and it wouldn't last for more than a few months."

"So you say." Greg's pale blue eyes were narrow. "Look, you need to stop thinking of yourself. What are we going to tell the teacher that gets laid off because of the library? And the children when their classes are too big? You should have been raising more money over the years instead of mooching from the town and the taxpayers. If you had, the library wouldn't be in this situation. It's your own fault if the library has to close. The town doesn't owe this library a penny."

Stunned by Greg's vehemence, Anne just stared at him, and he angrily shook his head. "Don't look at me with those big brown eyes. It might work on some, but not me. If you have to close the library, then close it. Get the books packed, and I'll put them out for auction. At least the town will get something from this damned library."

Standing abruptly, Greg left without saying anymore, and the empty brown rocking chair went back and forth, back and forth.

There was a tight feeling in Anne's chest, and she felt as though she could hardly breathe. "What did you expect?" she asked herself as she gripped the handles of the chair. "Did you think he was going to come around to your way of thinking?"

Even though there was a lot to do, Anne was still sitting in the blue rocking chair when Fred Tully came in a little while later. A large man with thick white hair and a gruff voice, Fred had tanned arms from spending so much time outside tending the gardens around his mobile home.

Today Fred's voice was not gruff but instead soft with sorrow. "I heard what happened at the town meeting last night. Wish I could have been there, but it was my granddaughter's seventh birthday." He shrugged apologetically. "I had to go to her party."

Not trusting herself to speak, Anne nodded and motioned to the brown rocking chair. With a sigh, Fred sat down. "Greg's been after this library for years. And now with the town's budget crisis, he finally got his way. The library's going to have to close, isn't it?"

Anne cleared her throat, and although her voice wavered, she did not cry. "Yes. And Greg was just here. We were talking about you."

"Oh?"

"Greg mentioned how you told him that it would be hard for you if taxes were raised to support the library."

Fred's face flushed. "I didn't say any such thing to him. Greg never talked to me at all about closing the library or raising taxes. I haven't seen him for a week or two."

Anne shook her head. "At last night's meeting, Greg told everyone about how you might have to skip a meal if taxes were raised."

"That man's a liar!" Fred exclaimed. "Greg had no right to say that, especially when I never said a thing about it. Yes, I'm on a tight budget. I have to be careful. But I wouldn't have to skip a meal if taxes were raised." Fred stood abruptly. "He's going to hear from me. I'm going to the town office as soon as I leave here. I'll let him know just what I think about him and his lying ways. And, Anne, I never wanted this library to close. I feel as bad about it as you do."

Fred left, and despite feeling so miserable, Anne smiled a little as she thought about the confrontation between Fred and Greg. It wouldn't change anything, Anne knew, but it gave her great comfort to think about how Fred, with his loud voice, wouldn't hesitate to blast Greg for lying.

Five minutes later, when Roland Turcotte came into the library, Anne was just getting ready to leave the blue rocking chair and go to her office. Again, Anne stayed seated, motioning toward the brown rocking chair.

Sitting down, Roland said in his gentle voice, "So sorry about what happened last night."

"I'm very glad you and Celine could come," Anne replied. "Thank you."

"We were outnumbered. Too many friends of the library had gone on vacation or had other commitments."

"I know. Fred Tully was just here and apologized for not being able to come to the meeting."

Roland smiled. "I passed him on the way to the library. Looked like Fred was on a mission."

Anne actually laughed. "He's heading to the town hall to have a discussion with Greg about lying. I guess Greg never talked to Fred about raising taxes."

Roland also laughed. "Wish I could be there for that exchange."

"Me, too."

They smiled at each other, but then the smiles went away. "There's no way to keep this library open without town support, is there?" Roland asked.

"No, the library doesn't have a big budget, but it's more than what the trustees could come up with, no matter how much fundraising they did. With our yearly book sale, along with donations, we can raise enough to buy books, but that's it."

Roland cleared his throat. "I came here to talk about the books. I suppose Greg wants you to pack them up so that he can sell them."

"That's just what he wants me to do."

"The thing is, those books don't actually belong to the town, do they?"

"No," Anne answered slowly, "I don't suppose they do. The town pays for my salary, for the building's maintenance, for heat, and electricity. But not for the books. However, Greg will find some way to get the books. You know how he is. He'll claim that the books belong to the library, and the library belongs to the town."

"But Greg won't be able to get the books if they are gone, and he doesn't know where they are."

For the first time since the town meeting, Anne felt something akin to hope. She leaned forward. "What do you mean?"

"In Sydney, right across the river from us, I have a friend with a big barn. I have a truck, and I know others who have trucks. People I can trust."

"Hide the books from Greg?" Anne asked a little breathlessly.

"Yes," Roland answered firmly. "If the books are sold, then that's it for the library. But if we hide the books, then maybe we can figure out something to save the library."

Anne marveled at how such a quiet man could have come up with such a scheme. "And it wouldn't be stealing, would it? Not technically."

"No, it wouldn't," Roland replied. "After all, the books weren't bought with town money. But we'd best move them in one fell swoop, late at night. Just in case Greg gets wind of what we're doing."

"I'll get boxes," Anne said.

"I'll get helpers with trucks," Roland said.

And a week later, the library was closed, locked, and empty. Anne's only regret was that she hadn't been there to see Greg's face when he found out the books had gone missing.

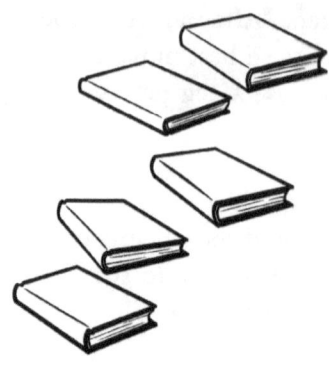

7: The President's Party

Drew Murphy, now the president of the United States and known as Andy only to old friends, stood in the great room of the huge gray-shingled house where he, his wife, and their daughter were staying in Bar Harbor on Mount Desert Island. Drew loved this part of Maine. Tucked by the ocean, Mount Desert had Acadia National Park with its old carriage roads, perfect for biking and riding horses. There were rocky shores, a sandy beach, and a ridge of small mountains with hiking trails. There were even freshwater lakes for swimming when the Atlantic Ocean felt a little too bracing.

Even though the Secret Service staff was never far away, and no vacation was ever truly a vacation where he didn't have to do some kind of work, Drew was glad to be back in Maine, which still felt like home.

The much-awaited party had begun, and those lucky enough to have been invited had started to arrive. The big room wasn't full yet, but before long, it would be, and Drew smiled as he shook hands with the various guests. There was one guest in particular that Drew was eager to meet. At the last minute, he had approved her name for the guest list, and despite the world leaders Drew had met—all of them formidable in their own way—Drew felt a little jittery as he thought about seeing her again after so many years. Drew had been waiting for this day for a long time, knowing it was likely to come this summer. It was one of the reasons why he had chosen Maine as the place for his summer vacation. Denise, his wife, and Viola, his daughter, both loved Maine, too, and they didn't need to be coaxed to take a vacation on Mount Desert Island.

It was also why Drew had invited the Grossman family to this party. Since becoming president, Drew had quietly kept track of Maya, and he knew that Maya was best friends with Leah, the youngest daughter, who came to Mt. Desert every summer with her family. This would give Maya, always resourceful, an unobtrusive way to meet him and let him know if she had seen anything important in Caxton that was relevant now.

As Drew continued to shake hands, he glanced frequently at the large entryway as groups of guests came into the room, but he didn't notice her until she was practically in front of him, waiting in line with the Grossman family. For one thing, she was wearing a dress. Drew had only seen her in jeans and trousers, but the main thing was her curly hair, dyed blonde. It was only when she looked up at him, and he recognized those dark, dark eyes that Drew knew who she was.

"Maya Hammond," she said softly, her gaze steady as she put her small hand in his large one.

"I'm pleased to meet you," Drew said, astonished by the blonde hair. "I met your father in college."

Maya nodded. "I know. He told me." In an even softer voice she said, "Humphrey is here."

There was so much noise in the room that Drew didn't hear the name, and he bent toward Maya. "Who?"

"Humphrey, Owen's brother. From Caxton."

Maya's voice was practically a whisper, but Drew heard her this time. "Where?"

She looked across the room, and Drew looked, too. By the drinks table stood Jay Sheldon, a financier and one of the richest men in the country, if not the world. He was talking to a woman named Diana Wagner, beautiful, sleek, and elegant.

"The man by the drinks table talking to the dark-haired woman?"

"Yes."

Yes. Maya had to move on, along with the Grossman family, and Drew had to smile and pretend to be interested in each guest when all he could think about was how one of the richest men he knew, a man who indicated he might give a lot of money to Drew's reelection campaign, was in fact a brutal man who had deposed his own brother, Owen, the duke of Caxton. Even more troubling were the questions Drew kept asking himself: Why was Humphrey here, and why did he want to support Drew's run for a second term as president?

On the other hand, Drew was not really surprised to learn that Humphrey had come to Earth with Julian's book. Everything was off-kilter with the country, with the world. Drew knew that APO was responsible for much of this, and he had suspected that they had somebody planted close to him. Wasn't that why he had invited Diana Wagner to come to Maine with him? Officially, she was a friend of the family. Only a few people knew Diana was really a spy. And there she was, talking to Humphrey, who was most certainly connected with APO. Diana's instincts had led her to the right person, and Maya had confirmed that Diana's suspicions were correct. Once again, Maya had been in the right place at the right time.

"I wonder what Maya will do when she grows up," Drew thought, a little bemused. "She's already a force to be reckoned with."

There was a slight lull with the incoming guests, and Denise, who was standing next to Drew, glanced at him. She leaned over and whispered, "You seem distracted."

"I am, a little."

"Well, buck up. The party has barely begun."

Denise grinned at him, and Drew grinned back, squeezing her hand.

Maya stood with a group of girls, talking to Viola. Even though the president's daughter was a few years younger than most of the girls, Viola was so confident and so self-possessed that she fit right in with them. With her dark hair and blue eyes, Viola looked very much like her father.

"She's so pretty," Maya thought.

Viola, who had been talking with Leah, turned to look at Maya. As they were regarding each other, Maya realized with a start that Viola could see things, much the same way Maya could. While it wasn't as strong with Viola as it was with Maya, it was strong enough.

Viola looked quizzically at Maya. "Have I met you before?"

"No," Maya answered.

"I feel like I know you."

"In another time, in another place..." Leah intoned, and the girls laughed, including Maya and Viola.

But then Viola was serious. "Could that really happen, do you think?"

"No," Leah said.

"Yes," Maya said in a low voice. "But I don't think it has with us."

Leah gave her a look that asked, "Where are you going with this?" It was a look Maya knew well.

Maya added quickly, "After all, there isn't a TARDIS nearby."

Everyone laughed again, and there was a general discussion about *Dr. Who* that involved a comparison of doctors and companions. There was even a lively argument between Leah and one of the other girls about who the best Doctor was, and many of the other girls joined in.

"David Tennant!"

"Are you kidding me?" Leah asked. "Matt Smith!"

"No! Jodie Whittaker. About time the doctor was a woman."

While the girls were arguing about *Dr. Who*, Maya turned to Viola and asked very quietly, "Can you see things?" It was a risky question—what if Viola didn't understand?—but Maya knew she had to ask it.

However, Maya could tell that Viola understood, and she glanced at the girls, who were still discussing *Doctor Who*. "Yes, but I don't like to talk about it."

Maya nodded. "I know. Me, too. It makes me feel different from everybody else."

Viola nodded back. "And I'm already different enough. I'm the president's daughter."

Viola and Maya had moved away from the other girls, and their heads were together. Maya felt someone looking at them, and she turned to see President Murphy from halfway across the room. He smiled slightly, but he looked serious, a little sad even.

"Do you know my father?" Viola asked.

Maya wasn't sure whether she should tell the truth or not.

"Tell me," Viola insisted.

"Yes," Maya said. "It's a long story. I can't go into it now. But I'm here for a reason."

"What reason?"

Maya glanced at Humphrey, who was still by the drinks table with Diana Wagner. Maya hesitated then made a small gesture toward Humphrey. "What do you think about this man?"

Viola wrinkled her nose. She didn't have to say anything more.

"Yeah," Maya said. "He's not good."

"Does he want to hurt my father?" Viola asked.

"Not directly. At least I don't think so. But there's more than one way of hurting someone. Have you seen him with a book? A black book?"

"A book, no. But he has a tablet, and it's always with him. Lots of times he goes off by himself to read it. He says he's checking things."

Of course. A tablet. In the twenty-first century, a grown man wouldn't carry a real book and constantly refer to it. "That would be weird," Maya thought. She knew, from experience, that the Books could change size, so it didn't surprise her that the Book could transform itself into a tablet.

Humphrey looked from Diana to the group of girls arguing about *Dr. Who*. As he studied each girl's face, Maya realized he was looking for her. Julian's Book must have warned Humphrey that she might be coming to the party.

"Would you stand in front of me?" Maya asked Viola. Even with the blonde hair, Maya didn't want to take any chances.

Viola didn't ask why. She just switched places with Maya and stood tall and straight. Even though Viola was only twelve, she was taller than Maya, and all Humphrey could see was Viola's back when he looked at them. Frowning, he turned to Diana Wagner.

"Is Mr. Sheldon looking for you?" Viola asked.

"Yeah, but I know him by a different name. Humphrey."

Viola rolled her eyes. "That's a good name for him."

"Does he have the tablet now, do you think?" Maya asked.

Viola turned to look at him. "Probably. His jacket is slung over his back. I bet it's in one of the pockets."

"I'd like to get that tablet," Maya said softly.

Across the room from Maya, a slight woman with brown hair and blue eyes was staring intently at her. Frowning, Maya stared back. It seemed to Maya that she had seen this woman before, but where?

However, before Maya could remember, something happened that had never happened before. In rapid succession, Maya saw various ways of getting the tablet. They came to her as a series of flashes. In one version, Diana Wagner tried to steal the tablet when she and Humphrey were alone. But Humphrey caught her, snapped her neck, and got away. In another, President Murphy tried to get it, but Humphrey was warned by the tablet and left before he could be confronted. Then came the last one—Viola created a distraction, and Maya slipped the tablet out of Humphrey's jacket pocket. No one was hurt; Humphrey didn't get away.

Blinking, Maya shook her head and looked for the small woman with the brown hair and blue eyes, but she didn't seem to be anywhere in the room. It didn't matter. Maya knew what should be done, and turning to Viola, she asked, "Would you help me get the tablet from Humphrey?"

With a drink in his hand and his jacket slung over his shoulder, Humphrey talked to Diana Wagner. He was drawn by her beauty and her charm, and the more Humphrey drank, the more alluring she became. However, Julian's Book had warned him about Diana.

"She's a spy," the Book had said as Humphrey was dressing for the party. "She's here to sniff things out for the president, who knows about APO and is suspicious that they have someone planted here."

"He's right to be suspicious," Humphrey had said, preening in front of the mirror. Blue shirt or red shirt? He couldn't decide.

"That may be the case," the Book had snapped. "But don't lose your head, the way you sometimes do. And don't forget that Maya is likely to be here, too. Unfortunately, she's blocked from me, so I don't know where she is. She still must have Earth's Book of Everything."

The red shirt, Humphrey decided. "I'll be cool," he said, using a term he had learned when he first came to Earth.

The Book snorted. Humphrey was many things, but he was not cool, and all too often the Book had had to extract him from tight situations resulting from Humphrey's impulsiveness and anger.

Humphrey heard the snort. "We've done all right, haven't we?"

"Not too bad," the Book replied.

Rolling his eyes, Humphrey reflected that they were doing better than "not too bad." With APO's help, they were on their way to wrecking Earth's economy, and soon, very soon, they would have Maya and Earth's Book of Everything. APO, however, didn't know about that plan. Both Humphrey and the Book had agreed that the less APO knew about Maya and the Book of Everything, the better. Humphrey and Julian's Book were perfectly willing to help APO gain money and power, but when it came to Maya, they didn't want any interference. So Humphrey had said nothing about Maya, even though he could have told APO years ago what might happen this summer.

"Just be careful," the Book had warned. "And don't drink too much."

Humphrey's shoulders twitched as he buttoned his shirt. "Don't worry. I'll be fine."

But Humphrey wasn't thinking about being careful as he talked to Diana. He was admiring her dark hair, her graceful neck, and the way she looked in her tight black dress. The Book was in his jacket pocket—he never left the Book behind. Every once in a while Humphrey scanned the room, looking for Maya, for the dark curls, for the impudent face, but he couldn't find her. He was beginning to think that the Book was wrong, that Maya wasn't going to come after all.

"Because let's face it," Humphrey thought as he pretended to listen to Diana. "The Book isn't always right." It hadn't taken Humphrey long to realize that Julian's Book did not have the same depth of information that Caxton's Book of Everything had. But Humphrey couldn't complain. Because of Julian's Book, Humphrey had seen and done things that he had never imagined when he had lived in Caxton. Sometimes Humphrey wondered if he even wanted to return to that backward place where there were no planes, guns, movies, or cars. But whenever he thought about going back to Caxton and defeating his brother, Humphrey knew that's exactly where he wanted to be.

Diana was looking expectantly at Humphrey, and he realized that she had asked him a question.

"Beg your pardon?" he asked. "It's so noisy here."

"We could go somewhere where it's more quiet," Diana suggested.

"Later, perhaps?" Humphrey said, wanting a few more drinks. "It's still early."

Just then, Viola came to the drinks table and helped herself to some ginger ale. She smiled at Diana. "You look awesome."

Diana smiled back. "You, too, honey."

Viola turned to Humphrey. "Hello, Mr. Sheldon." Her tone was cool, and her smile was brief.

Humphrey thought, "The little shit's just like her father. Always so cool." Aloud, he said, "Hello, Viola."

Nodding, Viola was about to leave, when she tripped and stumbled, and Humphrey's red shirt was wet with ginger ale.

"Damn it!" Humphrey exclaimed.

"Sorry!" Viola said, stepping back a little.

Humphrey didn't think that Viola was sorry at all, and he wanted to slap her face. He didn't, of course, but he said shortly, "That's all right. I'll go upstairs and change."

"I'll be back," he said to Diana, who was trying not to laugh, and he wanted to slap her face, too.

"I'll be here," Diana said, watching thoughtfully as Humphrey left the room.

Humphrey raced to his room on the east wing of the second floor. As soon as he changed his shirt, he grabbed his jacket and reached into one of its pockets for the Book. It wasn't there. Humphrey checked the other pocket, but all it had was the little case of tools he always carried. Humphrey began to pace in his room. The Book was gone. But how could it be gone? Had it fallen? No, he always bought jackets with deep, strong pockets. In fact, he had them custom made. The Book hadn't fallen. It had been taken.

"Viola," Humphrey said aloud, putting on his jacket. She had something to do with the Book's disappearance. Humphrey was sure of it. He left his room and quietly made his way down the hall. As he came to the stairway and the upstairs foyer, he heard voices, and one of them was Viola's. Humphrey stayed hidden in the hall.

"It will be quiet in my room," Viola said.

"All right, but we still need to be careful," another voice said.

Humphrey knew that voice, even though he had only heard it a few times. It was Maya's voice, one he would never forget. He cautiously peeked around the corner and saw two girls going down the west wing of the second floor. There was Viola, and beside her was a shorter girl in a red dress. Her curly hair was blonde, not brown. All along, Humphrey had been looking for dark hair, when he should have been looking for blonde hair. Maya was with Viola, and Humphrey was certain that they had the Book. His Book. "That girl certainly works fast," Humphrey thought, his hands clenched into fists. He would get his Book back.

Viola closed and locked the door to her room. Both girls sat on Viola's bed, and Maya took Julian's Book out of the white bag she was carrying—smaller than her messenger bag but large enough to carry two books. Maya also took out Ariel and set the two Books side by side on Viola's bed. Julian's Book was no longer a tablet.

"That's not a tablet," Viola said. "It's a book." She squinted at it. "An old one."

"That's right," Maya said, reaching for Ariel and opening it.

"Humphrey is coming," Ariel said, just as they heard a soft knock on the door.

"Girls," Humphrey said. "I know you're in there. Just give me back my Book, and I won't mention this to anyone."

"Don't give him the Book," Ariel said.

"Of course I won't," Maya replied.

"Are you talking to that blue book?" Viola asked.

"Yes, but I can't explain right now."

"Maya, I know you're with Viola. You two had no right to steal my Book." Humphrey's voice was low and urgent.

"It's not your Book," Maya said. "It's Julian's. You stole it, too."

"But it wants to be with me, not you."

"How do you know?" Maya asked, trying to gain time to think.

Maya heard Humphrey fiddling with the door. "He's picking the lock," Ariel said.

"Humphrey knows how to pick a lock?" Maya asked.

"He's been on Earth several years," the Apprentice Book said. "He's had time to learn a lot of things."

The door swung open, and Humphrey, his face ugly with anger, stood in the doorway.

Viola grabbed Maya's arm, and Maya grabbed the two Books. "Take us away from here!" Maya said to Ariel.

"No!" Humphrey cried, but then crumpled to the floor. Behind him stood Diana Wagner with a heavy glass ball used as a decoration on one of the downstairs tables. She looked into the room, blinked, and looked again. The room was empty.

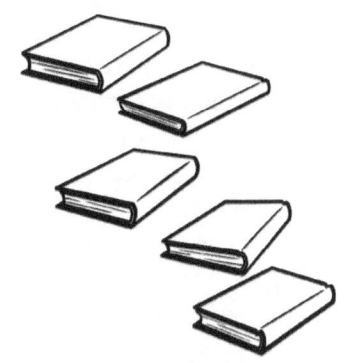

8: Rose Cottage

Maya and Viola landed with a thud on the floor not far from a big hearth. There was a low fire in it, and two men—one very large with graying hair and the other slender with red hair—were sitting in chairs in front of the hearth and toasting bread over the fire. The large man wore trousers, a waistcoat, a white shirt, and a neckcloth. The younger man was more simply dressed, with no waistcoat or neckcloth.

The big man, seeing Maya and Viola, jumped, and his piece of bread fell off the toasting fork and landed right in the fire. "Oh, very nice!" he said, whipping around to regard the blazing piece of bread, but then, just as quickly, he looked back at Maya.

"My God!" he exclaimed.

"Maya?" the red-haired boy asked. "Is that you? What happened to your hair?"

But Maya couldn't answer right away. Viola, with a pale face, was clinging to Maya's arm. "I'm going to be sick," she said.

The toasting fork fell with a clatter as the big man leaped from his chair, grabbed the metal ash bucket by the fireplace, and brought it to Viola just in time as she threw up. "That was a close one," the big man said. "I guess the Book does funny things to your stomach when you travel."

"Yes, it does, but the more you travel, the more you get used to it," Maya said, putting both Books on the round table that held the bread and butter. She would deal with Ariel later, after Viola was settled.

"I never expected to see you again," the big man said.

"And I didn't expect to see you again, Sir John." Despite Maya's irritation with Ariel and where it had taken her and the president's daughter—she could only imagine what President Murphy's reaction would be when he found out that Viola had gone to Caxton—Maya smiled at Sir John and "Simon? Is that you?"

Simon nodded. "Aye." He stood, and Maya could see he was no longer the small, skinny boy that she had met on her last visit to Caxton. He was tall now and broad shouldered and probably as old as Maya, if not older.

Beside Maya, Viola sighed, and Sir John said, "Simon, my boy, go empty this bucket."

Simon made a face but did as he was told.

Sir John turned to Viola. "Sit right here." He motioned to the chair that Simon had been sitting in, and Viola gratefully sat down. "There's something familiar about you," Sir John said, peering at Viola as he handed her what Maya hoped was a clean handkerchief. After Viola wiped her face and gave the handkerchief back to Sir John, he said, "I'll just go put this into the laundry basket. I'll get more tea, and we'll make some more toast. That will settle your stomach. Then we'll talk."

"Where are we?" Viola asked softly.

"Why, you're in Rose Cottage, my girl," Sir John answered. "Home to me, Sir John Oldcastle; my friend Harry Newton, who's not here at the moment; Simon Forster, the boy who was sitting in your chair; and the redoubtable Mrs. Hall, who takes care of the cottage. But I don't think she should see you in those clothes. I can only imagine what she would say." Sir John laughed as he left the room.

"Rose Cottage?" Viola asked. "It looks like we went back in time. And how did we get here?" She glanced at the blue Book on the table. "Did that book bring us here?"

"Yeah," said Maya, "the Book brought us here. But we're not on Earth. We're in Caxton, a city that's in a country called Albion, which is on a planet called Ilyria. Ilyria is not as advanced as Earth, and they don't have stuff like electricity, cell phones, or computers."

"How could a book take us here?" Viola asked, rubbing her face.

"The Book is connected to a place called the Great Library," Maya said, remembering what Sydda had told her. "And everything in our universe is connected. It's like a giant web, and the Great Library is in the middle of it. Everything flows through the Great Library, which collects information, then uses it to make Books like the one that brought us here. The Books are supersensitive to this giant web, and they can travel along different paths to different worlds. Also, some people are born with the same kind of supersensitivity. I was, and so were you. That's why we can see things."

Viola was quiet as she thought about what Maya had said. Sir John and Simon came back into the room. Two more chairs were pulled by the fire, and a big pot of tea was on the round table. Next to the tea were cups, plates, a loaf of bread on a board, a knife, and some butter in a dish with another knife.

"Everything that we need for tea and toast with butter," Sir John said, settling into the biggest chair, one that had been made especially for him. "Maya, Simon and I will make toast while you tell us why you are here. But first things first. Who is the girl? And why does she seem so familiar?"

"Because she looks like Andy," Simon said, as he put a piece of bread on a toasting fork.

"Of course! Those eyes!" Sir John said.

Viola frowned. "My name is Viola Murphy. How do you know my father, and why do you call him Andy? Only old friends call him that."

"In a way, we are old friends," Sir John said cautiously, and Viola looked at Maya.

"The Book can take us back in time, too," Maya said to Viola. "I met your father when he was seventeen. For me, it wasn't very long ago. For your father, it was a lot of years. Then the Book took us here, to Caxton, and we helped Duke Owen overthrow his brother, Humphrey."

"The wrongful duke," Sir John said with relish.

Viola shook her head. "My father did all those things when he was seventeen?"

"Aye," said Simon. "And I helped him escape from Greendale and get to Caxton. I showed him how to make fires, skin animals, and cook them over an open fire."

"I wonder if Mom knows about all this," Viola said, looking a little dazed.

"Probably not," Maya replied, and then shrugged, thinking of how she had caught sight of the president and his wife holding hands at the party. "But who knows? He might have told her."

Simon handed a nicely browned piece of toast to Sir John, who buttered it, put it on a plate, and passed it to Viola. "Thank you," she said, taking a bite. "That tastes good."

"Nothing like toast to settle a queasy stomach." Sir John passed Simon another piece of bread.

"Have you ever had a queasy stomach?" Simon asked, grinning a little as he put the bread on the toasting fork.

Maya and Viola also grinned, and Sir John said, "Now, Simon. There's no need to be saucy. Just make toast." But Sir John was grinning, too, and it was clear the big man was not offended by what Simon had said.

"How long has it been since Andy and I were here?" Maya asked.

"Oh, about six years," Sir John replied. "Wouldn't you say, Simon?"

"Aye," came the answer.

"You've grown," Maya said to Simon.

"Except for your hair, you're pretty much the same," Simon said. "Why is it that color?"

"So Humphrey wouldn't recognize me," Maya said. "He's on Earth, and he's with Andy, who's a grownup in my time and the president of our country. Andy was having a party, and I went to it. Humphrey was there, too. I figured if I wore a dress and dyed my hair blonde, then Humphrey might not notice me. And he didn't until the very end."

Sir John and Simon were quiet. Simon gave Sir John a piece of toast, which Sir John buttered, but rather than hand it to Maya, he took a distracted bite from one of its edges.

"What's a president?" Sir John asked.

"It's what we call our leaders," Maya answered. "The people in our country get to vote for their leaders. It's not like here."

"Of all things!" Sir John said. "How does that work?"

"Sometimes, it works out pretty well. Other times, not so much," Maya replied.

"My father's a good president," Viola put in quickly.

"I bet he is. Andy learned a lot while he was here, from our own Duke Owen." Sir John took another bite of toast. "And you say that Humphrey is on your world?"

Maya nodded. "And he has been for quite a while. He and Julian's Book have been planning something. Humphrey is pretending to help Andy, but really he's working against him. I know he is."

"I'm sure you're right about that, Maya, my girl," Sir John said. "Did you know Andy was your country's leader when you came here the first time?"

"No, I found out the night I got back, and that's when I found out about Humphrey, too."

Sir John glanced at the blue Book on the table. "I'm surprised they let you keep the Book."

"They didn't. Elspeth brought me the Apprentice Book we had when we came to Albion. Earth's Book of Everything is with someone else."

Sir John grinned. "Maya, you're always full of surprises. I like that about you, and I did right from the start."

Maya smiled at the big man's generosity. They had not always gotten along, and Sir John had done some terrible things. He had stolen her Book of Everything, and he had accidentally killed Feste, but in the end he had acted bravely and had helped take back Caxton for Duke Owen.

"And the other Book?" Sir John asked.

"That's Julian's Book," Maya answered. "I stole it from Humphrey, and Viola helped me. She can see, the way I can."

Again there was quiet. Sir John passed Simon a slice of bread, and Simon made another toast, while Viola and Maya sipped tea.

"Why did the Apprentice Book bring you here?" Simon asked.

"Good question," Maya replied, reaching for Ariel and opening it.

The Book answered slowly, "It seemed as though Rose Cottage was the best place to take you. It's the first place I thought of."

Maya shook her head and told the others what Ariel had said.

"It is an Apprentice Book," Simon said. "It's going to make a few mistakes."

"I know," Maya said, her attitude softening as she thought about Ariel.

Ariel said nothing, and later Maya would remember that silence.

"I feel much better," Viola said. "What are we going to do next?"

"Good question," Maya answered, looking out the window where she could see a profusion of red, yellow, and white roses that had given the cottage its name.

"You should tell Duke Owen about Humphrey and Julian's book," Sir John said.

Maya nodded. "But I need to get Viola back to Maine. I'm going to be in so much trouble if Andy finds out where Viola has been."

Ariel made a noise that sounded as though it was clearing its throat. "You're even in more trouble than you think. Diana Wagner saw an empty room after she hit Humphrey on the head with a glass ball. And it looks as though that's going to be fixed on Earth's time line."

"That's just great!" Maya shut Ariel with a snap and put it back on the table as she told the others what the book had said.

"Well, Maya," Sir John said. "Looks like you're going to get it no matter what you do. So you might as well be hanged for a sheep as for a lamb. Stay here for a day or two, tell Duke Owen about Humphrey, and visit with some of your friends. I know Evangeline would be keen to see you and so would Harry, Molly, Jem, and Rhys. And, besides, our Midsummer's Eve celebration is only a couple of days away. There will be a big bonfire in the courtyard with plenty to eat and drink."

"Can we, Maya?" Viola asked. "I'd love to see Caxton and the bonfire on Midsummer's Eve."

Maya bit her bottom lip. "I don't know. How are things in Caxton right now?"

"Oh, right as rain," Sir John said. "Under Duke Owen, we have order and justice. People can travel wherever they want, and there are no more confounded papers. Trees have been planted, fields have been taken care of, and the Duchy's towns get money for their schools and other functions."

"Duke Owen knows how to run things," Simon said. "When Humphrey was duke, there was no money for schools or for anything else that would help people."

"Aye," Sir John replied. "Simon's mother even gets a stipend now. His father was killed while working as a forester for the duchy. Between the stipend and what Simon sends her, his mother doesn't have to worry about not having enough to eat."

Simon's face flushed. "Sir John!"

"Oh, don't get your knickers in a twist," the big man said. "There's no shame in being poor."

"You only say that because you've never been poor," Simon replied, turning away.

Maya said quickly, "My grandparents came from poor families, and my grandmother always tells me that poor people can work hard and still be poor."

"My father grew up poor, too," Viola added softly.

Nodding, Simon looked from Maya to Viola, and his eyes were bright.

Maya thought, "Time to change the subject." She reached for Ariel and opened the Book. "What do you think? Should we stay here a couple of days?"

"Wherever you go there are dangerous possibilities," Ariel answered cautiously. "But right now it's fairly safe in Caxton. Chet is imprisoned in one of the towers, and Julian doesn't have his memory."

"Aye," Sir John said after Maya related what the Book had told her. "That Chet can't do much in the tower except watch what goes on. Whenever I go by, I see his pasty face looking down at me."

Maya had a shiver of a premonition. "He is dangerous, wherever he is. Don't forget that for a minute. And what about Julian?"

"The Apprentice Book is right. Julian can't remember a thing, and he still has that weaselly Eli to wait on him. But forgetting seems to have done Julian some good. He's mellowed over the past six years and spends a lot of his time at the University's library. We've had some good conversations. He's smart, that one is."

Shaking her head, Maya tried to reconcile her own memories of Julian, cunning and brutal, with what Sir John had told her.

"People can change," Ariel said. "It isn't easy, and mostly they don't, but it is possible, even for someone like Julian. But if you do stay, watch out for Eli. He hasn't changed."

Maya nodded, but she had one more question. "Simon, what are you doing?"

"I used to work in the stables at Caxton Castle, but now I help heal animals when they're hurt, and I help with birthing for cows, sheep, and horses. Evangeline is teaching me. Sir John is letting me stay here while I study and learn."

"The boy has a knack for it," Sir John said. "We saw it as soon as he started working in the stables. And as I have no children, I decided to be his sponsor so that he could study with Evangeline."

"That's great," said Maya, and she had a vision of Simon as an adult, becoming the first veterinarian in Caxton.

"Horses are my specialty," Simon added, smiling. "And I take care of Duke Owen's horses."

"Maya, please can we stay?" Viola asked. "Just a little while? I'd love to see the horses. I know how to ride. I've taken lessons for three years. Simon, would you show me the horses, if we stay?"

"Aye, if it's all right with Maya."

"Please?" Viola asked again.

"Okay," Maya said. "We'll stay a day or two."

Sir John clapped his hands. "There we go! I'll have Mrs. Hall fix us a special supper. And I'll rustle up some different clothes for you two. Can't have you going around Caxton like that."

"Mrs. Hall is a good cook," Simon said.

Sir John laughed. "And my boy, Simon, is a good eater. Mrs. Hall likes that."

Maya smiled. Despite the almost certain trouble she would be in when she returned to Earth, Maya was glad to be back in Caxton.

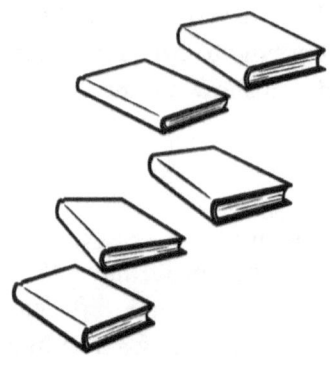

9: Beyond the Roses

As Viola walked beside Simon and Maya and looked around at the narrow streets and the half-timbered houses, she could hardly believe what had happened. She was in a place called Caxton on a planet called Ilyria, where there were no cars or electricity, and her father had been here, too. With Maya. When he was seventeen. There was something called a Great Library, where they made Books of Everything. But Maya didn't have a Book of Everything. She had an Apprentice Book named Ariel, which had mistakenly taken them to Caxton. "How lucky was that?" Viola thought, grinning. For the past few years, she hadn't been able to go anywhere by herself, and here she was, on a different planet without someone from the Secret Service watching over her.

Both Viola and Maya had on long dresses, and all the girls and women they passed in the streets were dressed the same way. Maya was carrying two reticules, one for each book.

"It's like we're in the middle of a movie," Viola thought. "But for here, it's real life."

As they turned up High Street, they passed a large, square building made with gray stones. Set back from the street, the building faced a large green, and students, all male, were bunched in small groups on the grass. Some talked, some ate, and occasionally, one student would shove another, and there would be loud guffaws.

"That's Caxton University," Simon said. "It's one of the best in Albion. Maybe even the best. Students come from all over the country to study here, partly because of the library."

"Will you go here?" Viola asked.

"Me? No. I'm studying with Evangeline. That's enough."

"Just who is Evangeline?"

"She's a healer. But she says that healing animals isn't that different from healing people."

Maya stopped suddenly. A tall, slender man with hair so blond it seemed almost white stood on the green. He was surrounded by a group of young men, and they were all talking and smiling. As Maya watched, the man with the blond hair removed a book from a satchel he was carrying, and smiling, he read a passage from it. The young men listened attentively.

"Julian looks happy," Maya said so softly it was almost a whisper.

"Aye," Simon said. "He spends a lot of time at the university. He teaches classes and leads study groups."

One young man with a sulky look stood a little apart from the group. "Who's the one off to the side?" Viola asked, not liking the young man's narrow face and sullen expression.

"Oh, that's Eli, his servant," Simon said. "Always in a bad mood."

Just then, Eli looked away from his master and the students and stared at the three of them. Frowning, he tried to puzzle out who was with Simon.

"Let's go," Maya said, walking briskly away from the university, and Simon and Viola followed her up High Street toward the castle gate.

As Julian and the students argued about free will and fate, Eli sat on a nearby bench. Eli knew all too well that his master and the students could be at this for quite a while, and he figured there was no point in standing when he could be sitting. Kicking at the grass by the bench, Eli reflected, yet again, on how much his master had changed over the past six years. As far as Eli was concerned, it was not a change for the good.

Eli clearly remembered how his master had been before he had been stabbed—in control and full of plans. Julian's restless, aggressive energy had attracted Eli right from the start, and he had positioned himself to get closer to Julian until he had become Julian's personal servant. It had all been going so well, but then Julian had been stabbed by a girl not much older than Eli.

"Maya," Eli said softly. As Julian had healed and gained strength, it became clear that he had lost something precious—his memory—and with that loss all the energy and ambition had seemed to seep out of him. Where once Julian had been plotting and scheming, he was now reading, studying, and giving lectures. Students came to their apartment at the castle, where they drank ale and had the most ridiculous discussions Eli had ever had the misfortune to hear. Right now they were on fate versus free will. Before that, there had been long debates about what made a good leader, with the general agreement that Duke Owen was one of the best.

"No, he isn't," Eli muttered. He preferred Humphrey, who had the same kind of restless, aggressive energy that Julian had had before he was stabbed.

Over the years, Eli had come to suspect that Evangeline, who had healed Julian, had been responsible for Julian's memory loss. "She gave him something that took his memory away," Eli often reflected. "I know she did." As Eli waited on the bench, his thoughts turned back to Simon and the two girls who had been walking with him. Who were they? Why did the one with the blonde hair seem so familiar?

This question nagged at Eli as he and his master returned to the castle.

We had a good discussion today," Julian said, smiling the contented smile that Eli had come to hate.

"Yes, master," Eli said with a sigh.

"Such bright young men."

"Yes, master."

"It's a pity you don't join us."

"Master, I am a servant." Eli had reminded him of this many times and knew he would have to continue doing so.

Julian frowned as if trying to remember something from his past. "A servant. Well, still, it's a pity."

"Yes, master." In truth, Eli didn't think it was a pity at all. He had no more interest in joining the discussions than he had in jumping into the River Caxton. It was one of the few times he was glad he was a servant and was therefore not allowed to join in the discussions with the students, who all came from noble families.

As Eli and Julian entered the courtyard, Eli automatically looked at the tower in the far right-hand corner, and he saw the pale face of the prisoner looking down at him. They stared at each other for a few seconds, as they always did when the prisoner was by the window, and Eli thought, not for the first time, "Here is a man like my master. Too bad he's in prison."

Later, Eli would not be able to explain why on that day, after so many years, he decided to nod at the prisoner. Was it because Eli had finally had enough of listening to his master and the students? Was it the seemingly endless discussion of fate and free will? Was it seeing the blonde-haired girl, who looked so familiar and would turn out to be Maya, as Eli would learn later? Eli really couldn't say if it was one of those things or all of those things. All Eli knew was that he was nodding at the prisoner, and it was a sympathetic nod, so brief it was detected by no one except for the prisoner. "I will help you if I can," Eli thought as he nodded, and suddenly Eli didn't feel quite as glum.

While his master was napping—no doubt tired from the exertion of discussing fate and free will—Eli went to the Barking Dog for his midday pint. His friend, Toby, who worked in the kitchen at the tavern, sat down across from Eli, and he had a huge plate of sausages, bread, and cheese. It was quiet in the tavern—the noonday rush was over, and the early evening rush hadn't begun—which made it a good time for the help to eat.

At first Toby didn't say anything. He just stabbed his food with his knife and chewed off hunks of meat, cheese, and bread. Eli knew better than to talk to Toby while he was eating. There would be no answer as Toby focused exclusively on his food. He ate slowly and methodically and with great enjoyment, savoring every bite and swallow.

Eli and Toby had been friends from childhood, living side by side in small houses on one of Caxton's backstreets. Around the same time that Eli went to work in the castle, Toby began apprenticing with the cook in the tavern. Word had spread that although Toby was young, he had a knack for roasting meat and making stews and pies. The youngest of eleven children, Toby had worked alongside his mother and sisters from the time he was small and had had to stand on a wooden crate to chop vegetables and meat. At twelve, the boy had been big enough to handle the heavy cast iron used for cooking, and not long after that, Toby had gone to the tavern to work.

About Toby, Eli's mother had once said, "He's not the sharpest, but he's loyal, and if you treats him right, he'll do most anything for you." She had given Eli a pointed look, as though she could see the day when Eli would need Toby's help. Eli had followed his mother's suggestion, knowing that she was a shrewd judge of human nature, and her assessments were seldom wrong.

"Maybe that day has come," Eli thought as Toby finished his meal. Right then, Eli didn't have any specific plans, just a vague sense that Toby might be able to help somehow. But Toby would have to be approached in a roundabout way. The large, blond-haired man was too guileless to be directly involved with any of Eli's plans.

When Toby was done eating, Eli took a drink of ale and sighed.

"What's the matter?" Toby asked, wiping his mouth on his sleeve.

"'Tis my master," Eli replied. "It pains me to see him the way he is."

"Why? He seems happy enough."

They had had this discussion before, but now it was time to take it a step further. Eli looked around the room. It was mostly empty. The only other person in the room was Lucinda Froste, the small, quick young woman who was betrothed to Toby. She was as sharp as Toby was slow, and Eli had no doubt who would be in charge when the two were married. Lucinda was on the other side of the room, and Eli felt it was safe to continue the conversation.

"Aye, I know. But he's not the man he used to be."

Nodding, Toby shrugged. "There's naught you can do for your master, so there's not much sense in worrying about it." He might have added that in truth, Eli had a good life, with an easygoing master, a warm bed, and plenty to eat. Who could ask for anything more?

It seemed that Eli could, and he continued, "Master Julian was a great man, and it's a pity he doesn't know it."

"What are you two talking about?" Lucinda stood by the table, and she sat down beside Toby.

"Eli's master," Toby replied.

"What about him?" Lucinda asked, and she gave Eli a knowing look that suggested she already knew what the problem was.

Eli decided to trust her. "My master was a great man," Eli repeated. "Before he lost his memory."

Lucinda stared at Eli for a few minutes, considering him. "Not long ago, my grandfather had a funny spell and lost his memory. But Evangeline gave him something, and his memory is coming back. Not as good as it was, but at least he knows who we are now, and he can remember some things."

Eli silently berated himself for being so slow. Of course Evangeline had something to restore a person's memory. If she took it away, Eli reasoned, then she could bring it back. Eli's deduction wasn't completely accurate—he had no way of knowing that what Evangeline had given his master didn't come from Caxton. Instead, it had come from the Great Library. Still, Eli was not completely wrong. Evangeline did indeed have potions and powders that could help restore a person's memory after a funny spell, as Lucinda had put it.

Lucinda turned from Eli to Toby. "How's that meat doing on the spit?"

Toby stood. "I'd better go check." As Toby left, he looked back as though he wanted to say something, but he just shrugged and headed for the kitchen.

Lucinda leaned forward and said very softly, "I can nab some of that potion for you. I can pretend I spilled it, and Evangeline will bring me some more."

"The duke will find out," Eli whispered back. "He has that Book, and he always knows what's going on. And I bet he especially checks on my master."

Lucinda nodded. "But tomorrow, the duke is leaving for the capital. He will be too busy to keep close tabs on your master."

"Aye, plenty of trouble in Camburgh with the old king so sick," Eli replied. "But the duke will leave Rhys in charge, and that one's pretty sharp, too."

"But Rhys won't have the Book, will he? The duke will take it with him to Camburgh. By the time the duke finds out, it will be too late. The deed will be done."

Eli grinned appreciatively at Lucinda. "You're a fast thinker."

"Aye," came the answer, and it was said in a matter-of-fact tone. "I have been since I was a little girl." She pursed her lips as she looked at Eli.

"And what do you want in return?" Eli asked, knowing her help would have a price. In Eli's experience, most help did.

"If things work out," Lucinda said, "I want a place in the castle, with Toby in the kitchen and me in charge of running things. I can't cook the way he does, but I can organize."

Eli had no doubt of this. "But what about Molly?"

"'Tis time for her to move on," Lucinda said briskly. "Molly's been there long enough. Ever since I can remember. Do we have a deal?" Her voice became even softer. "I don't want to stay in this tavern for the rest of my life. I want to be in the castle."

"Aye," Eli said. "We have a deal." Then he thought about the prisoner in the tower. "And there's one more thing..."

The prisoner—Chet Addington—had seen Eli nod at him, and Chet felt more hopeful than he had ever since Maya had brought him to Caxton. There was something about the boy's expression that made Chet think the boy was going to try to help him escape.

Chet had been stuck in this castle tower for six years. With charcoal from the fire, Chet had kept track of his long, long days as a prisoner. A lesser man—especially one like Chet, who was used to always being on the move—would have given up hope. But Chet's will to escape was still as strong as it had been when he was first imprisoned, and he would be ready, should the boy come through.

Chet had developed a routine. Every day, he exercised, and he read whatever books were brought to him—Duke Owen was as liberal with books as he was with his people—and Chet received a steady supply of books from the university's library. At first he had been surprised that he could even read them, just as he had been surprised that he could understand what the guards said, but Chet soon realized that traveling with the Book of Everything must have had something to do with this.

Chet ate the plain but hearty food that was brought to him. He observed the comings and goings in the courtyard, and there was such a good-natured bustle of people that at times Chet felt as though he were watching a television series about Europe's Renaissance that had been designed to torment him. Every month there was some kind of celebration—the changing of seasons, the longest day of the year, the first summer harvest, the last fall harvest, the shortest day of the year. When the weather was good, tables were set up in the courtyard, and they were piled with food, much of it coming from the keep's kitchen, although the villagers brought special dishes, too. When the weather was cold, there were often bonfires. And more food. And plenty to drink. And whatever the time of year, there was music. How Chet hated that music and the clumsy but spirited dancing that went with it.

There were so many celebrations that Chet wondered how the people had time to do their work, but somehow crops were planted and harvested, bread was baked, cows were milked, and flocks were tended. Nevertheless, Chet did not approve. As far as he was concerned, one or two celebrations a year were enough, and anything more was just plain indulgent. Chet thought longingly of his stern boss back on Earth. Now there was someone who knew how to run things, who knew not to waste time and energy trying to make people feel good. "Because the more you give, the more they want and take," Chet thought. "And they just don't deserve it."

"Duke Owen is too lenient with his people," Chet often muttered. And with his prisoner, too. If Chet had been in Duke Owen's place, then he wouldn't have hesitated to torture a prisoner from another world until that prisoner revealed everything he knew. But Chet was never tortured. Instead, Duke Owen would visit Chet from time to time and talk to him as casually as if Chet were a guest rather than a prisoner. "Too lenient. Too soft," Chet would repeat when the duke left. Sometimes, though, Chet had the feeling that Duke Owen had learned more than Chet had intended to reveal, but Chet resolutely pushed that thought away, saying as little as possible when the duke came to see him.

Over the years Chet had waited for some small opportunity, some opening that might help him escape, but none had come. Two guards were always sent to deliver food, books, and other supplies. Chet knew he could overcome one guard, but not two. And so he exercised and read and watched until finally today, Chet had received an acknowledgment from the boy with the blond-haired man.

"It might all come to nothing," Chet said to himself. Nevertheless, Chet was so hopeful that he wished he could have something special—a can of Diet Dr. Pepper and some Vienna Sausages or beef jerky—his on-the-road food when he was tracking the Book of Everything or an agent from the League of Librarians. If he ever got back to Earth, then Diet Dr. Pepper and Vienna Sausages would be the first thing he'd drink and eat. Chet realized, of course, that he might never get back to Earth. Chance, or something like it, would really have to be on his side for this to happen. But just escaping from the tower would be a huge accomplishment, and it was Chet's singular goal, the thing he thought about most of the time.

Chet went to his cot and lay down, with his head resting on his hands, just the way he did when he was in a motel on Earth and tracking someone. Chet's thoughts turned to the three people who had come into the courtyard just before the boy and the blond-haired man. There was the tall boy with red hair whom Chet had often seen go into the stables, and at first Chet had thought the boy was some kind of stable hand. Except the boy was more than that because when he spoke with Duke Owen in the courtyard, the duke always listened attentively and respectfully to the boy. Often a small woman came with the boy. Her long, gray hair was pulled into a careless bun, and her face was dark and wrinkled. If Chet had been superstitious, he would have called her a witch, but his mind was too practical for such labels. Instead, he thought of her as an old lady who, despite her careless appearance, also had the duke's respect.

But today, instead of the old woman, two young girls had come with the red-haired boy, and Chet could tell there was something about those girls that seemed different from the girls who usually came to the keep. However, the girl with the blonde curly hair, the one carrying two little bags with long strings, looked especially familiar. Luck was on Chet's side, and the girl in the red dress turned slightly to look at something across the courtyard. Glancing up at Chet, the girl turned away quickly, but not fast enough. Chet had time to recognize her face.

"Maya," Chet said aloud, his face still and cold.

In a rush, a memory came to Chet of where he had seen Maya with blonde, curly hair, so many years ago, and he realized with a start that she had been out of time and place.

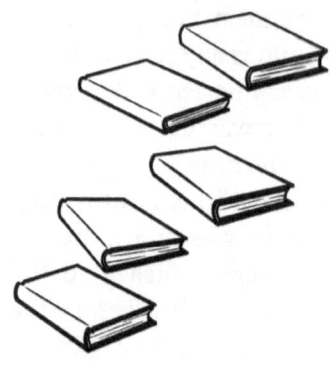

10: Julian's Book Speaks Out

Duke Owen stood quickly from his office desk as Maya entered the room. "Maya?" he said. "Your hair!"

"I know," she said. "I'll tell you all about it. But first I'd like to introduce you to someone. This is Viola Murphy, Andy's daughter."

Viola and Simon had come in behind Maya, and stepping forward, Viola smiled. "I'm pleased to meet you, Duke Owen."

"And I am pleased to meet you, too." Duke Owen sounded bemused. "Andy's daughter. Time has certainly passed since I last saw him."

Maya sighed. "In my time, he is an adult, older than you, even."

Duke Owen's mouth twitched into a grin. "Very old indeed."

Maya flushed. "I'm sorry. I didn't mean it that way."

Smiling, Duke Owen sat down and waved to chairs clustered around his desk. "No apologies necessary. I well remember when my parents seemed old. Now that I am a parent myself, suddenly it is the reverse. I do not feel all that old, but my children seem very young. As do the three of you."

"Time is relative," Maya murmured as they all sat down.

"Relative to what?" Duke Owen asked, frowning.

"Speed," said a voice. On his desk, the green Book of Everything was open, but only Duke Owen and Maya could hear it. "However, Maya was not speaking literally. I believe she meant that how old or young a person seems is relative to that person's own age. She was agreeing with you. Is that right, Maya?"

"Something like that," Maya answered.

Now it was time for Duke Owen to sigh. "There is so much I do not understand."

"I know," Maya said simply. "Me, too." She glanced at Simon and Viola. "Simon, maybe you could take Viola to the stables? I have a lot to discuss with Duke Owen."

Simon nodded. "Viola, would you like to see the horses?"

"Yes, please!" Viola answered eagerly. "Could we go for a ride?"

Simon glanced at Duke Owen. "I'm not sure about that."

"Do you know how to ride?" Duke Owen asked Viola.

"I do!"

"But not in a dress," the green Book of Everything put in.

"You have never ridden in a dress?" Duke Owen asked with a frown.

"No," Viola answered.

"In Viola and Maya's world, women often wear trousers," the green Book of Everything said.

"Perhaps Molly would have something she could wear," Simon suggested. "Viola's hair is short enough. She could pass as a boy."

Duke Owen nodded. "Molly will have something. Her son Jem is not that much taller than Viola. And give her Daffodil to ride. She is an easy-going mare, but she has spirit, too. Be back by late afternoon." Duke Owen grinned, and he almost looked boyish. "Celia doesn't know it yet, but she'll be hosting a rather large tea in the family dining room. If you come across Evangeline, be sure to invite her, too."

"Aye, I will," Simon replied. "Come on, Viola. Daff it will be for you."

With an excited bounce, Viola rose from the chair and followed Simon out of the room.

"Well, Maya, I expected to see you at some point, but I cannot say I expected to see Andy's daughter."

"It wasn't planned," Maya said. "Ariel just took Viola and me here. Your brother is on my planet, and he was trying to get us because we had Julian's Book."

"Ariel?"

"The Apprentice Book I had last time I was here." Maya flushed a little as the green Book of Everything made what sounded like a clucking sound. "The Apprentice Book said it was all right if I named it Ariel."

Taking out the little blue Book from one of the reticules, Maya put Ariel on the table and opened it.

"You let her name you?" the green Book of Everything asked.

"I saw no harm." But Ariel's voice sounded defensive. "What difference does it make if I have a name?"

The green Book of Everything replied, "It will make a great deal of difference. Naming sets you apart from the rest of us."

Duke Owen interrupted firmly, "What's done is done." He was right, but so was the green Book of Everything, as Maya would find out later. Duke Owen continued, "Tell me about Humphrey. He has been on your planet?"

Maya nodded. "For a lot of years. With his hair cut and new clothes, he looks nearly as different as I do."

"I think we need some tea to get through this," Duke Owen said.

"Yeah," Maya agreed. "I think we do."

Over tea and some of Molly's delicious knotted jumbles, Maya told Duke Owen all that had happened since she had brought Chet to Caxton—about how Andy was now President Murphy; how Humphrey was by his side; how Viola could see things the way Maya could; and how Jeff Perry most likely had a device to shield him from Books of Everything and the Great Library.

"That makes him very dangerous," the green Book of Everything put in. "He is outside our purview."

"I know," Maya said. "And one other thing. I saw Chet today. I think he recognized me."

Duke Owen frowned. "Chet is locked in that tower. He isn't going anywhere. It doesn't matter if he recognized you."

The Books were silent.

"What about your hair?" Duke Owen asked. "Why is it that color?"

"So Humphrey wouldn't recognize me at President Murphy's party."

Duke Owen shook his head. "I wish Humphrey had never gotten his hands on Julian's Book."

"Me, too," Maya said. "But he doesn't have it anymore."

"Where is the Book?"

Maya pushed the other reticule toward Duke Owen. "With me. Viola helped me steal it. Which means that Humphrey is marooned on my planet."

Putting his hand on the reticule, Duke Owen grinned. "Maya, you do not waste time, do you?"

Maya grinned back, but her answer was serious. "No, I don't. Time is too important to waste."

"So it is," Duke Owen replied. "But I was not speaking literally."

Maya smiled. "I know."

Despite the seriousness of the situation on Earth, Duke Owen and Maya, for a few comfortable minutes, just sipped tea and ate jumbles. Even though Duke Owen was much older than Maya, she could tell that he understood her just as well as she understood him.

The green Book of Everything was the first to speak. "Keep Julian's Book well hidden. Eli would very much like to find that Book for his master."

"I will." Duke Owen motioned to a chest next to the wall behind him. "It will go in this chest, which will be locked. As will my office, when I am not here. There are three office keys. One is with me, one is with my wife, and one is with my steward. Only I have the key to the chest."

"When did you marry Lady Celia?" Maya asked.

"Not long after I retook Caxton. We have two children, a girl and a boy, Rosalind and Sebastian. You will meet them later on, during tea." He looked at the reticule. "Shall we hear what Julian's Book has to say for itself?"

Maya was both fascinated and repelled. "Yes."

"Leave it shut," the green Book of Everything warned. "It will lie and try to throw you off course. In among the lies will be enough half-truths so that Julian's Book will sound reasonable."

"Best to leave that Book alone," Ariel agreed.

Duke Owen said, "I think we should hear what it has to say. We might be able to glean some information." Before the green Book of Everything and Ariel could protest any further, Duke Owen took Julian's Book out of the reticule, put it on the desk, and opened it.

Julian's Book spoke immediately, "So, here I am in Caxton. Again."

"Here you are," Duke Owen agreed.

"And Julian is not himself."

"Actually, he is his better self."

"Against his will. What are we without our memories?"

Duke Owen shrugged. "It was either that or kill him."

"And you do not like to kill unless you have to."

"That is right." Duke Owen's voice was steady.

"Such a merciful leader," Julian's Book said smoothly yet sharply. "Why not be doubly merciful and give me to Julian? With his memory gone, what can he do?"

"I am more worried about you than Julian," Duke Owen replied. "Julian has changed a lot since you left with Humphrey."

"So I've noticed. I kept tabs on him while I was on Earth. I expect he couldn't even hear me anymore now that his memory is gone."

"I'm sure he can," Maya said. "Hearing a Book has nothing to do with memory."

"Ah, Maya," Julian's Book said. "Chance certainly seems to favor you. Somehow, you are always in the right place at the right time. Ready with a knife or another Book to help you."

"The knife was Julian's," Maya pointed out.

"Indeed it was. And where is it now? Waiting for its opportunity to kill someone?"

Shuddering, Maya thought about Julian's knife with its deadly poison and how it almost seemed to have a will of its own. The knife was at the Great Library, with Sydda. He had felt it was too dangerous to stay with Maya, and she had readily agreed.

"Watch out, Miss Maya," Julian's Book mocked. "In its own way, that knife wants to come back to Julian, too."

"What do you know?" the green Book of Everything asked. "You're just a scheming Apprentice Book that is now connected to an inferior library."

It seemed to Maya that Julian's Book actually hissed. "Scheming? Oh, I am nothing compared with you Books of Everything and the Great Library. You pretend to be good because you're supposedly on the side of Time. But how many beings get crushed because of your plotting and conniving? How many lives are ruined? Maya, if I were you, I'd ditch that Apprentice Book and then never have anything to do with Sydda or the Great Library again. By the time they are done with you, you'll be wrung out, worthless. And your family? Well, I'm not even going to get into that."

"Enough!" Duke Owen said firmly, snapping shut the Book. Maya trembled a little as Duke Owen put Julian's Book in the trunk and locked it. She knew Julian's Book was lying. The Books of Everything, Sydda, and the Great Library were good—Maya could feel it deep inside. And yet, the green Book of Everything had mentioned there might be an element of truth to what Julian's Book would say. Was there? Were the Books of Everything scheming? Did people get hurt because of them?

Maya looked at Ariel, and for the first time she felt uneasy. "Can I trust Ariel?" she asked herself.

Finished with locking up Julian's Book, Duke Owen was sitting behind his desk, and he looked as though he wanted to say something to Maya but couldn't find the right words.

Finally, the green Book of Everything spoke, "Maya, going against Cinnial isn't easy. Mortmain's Library might be inferior, but his Books can still do a lot of damage. And Chaos gives him plenty of help. We Books of Everything have to plan and anticipate."

"And scheme?" Maya asked.

"I wouldn't call it that," the green Book of Everything replied quickly, and Ariel remained silent.

Duke Owen cleared his throat. "I am sorry to say this because the Books of Everything and the Great Library have done a tremendous service for Caxton and indeed for all of Ilyria. However, in my experience, the Books of Everything are not as forthcoming as they could be."

The green Book's voice had an edge. "I repeatedly warned you about Humphrey. You ignored my advice."

Duke Owen replied evenly, "That is true. I accept responsibility for that. You never lie. But sometimes, when I ask you questions, you are either evasive, or you do not tell the whole truth."

Frowning, Maya remembered how this had also been the case with Earth's Book of Everything and how frustrating it had been. Could it also be dangerous?

The green Book of Everything hesitated then sighed. "You are not always ready to hear the answers."

"And never will be?" Duke Owen asked.

The green Book of Everything didn't reply, and, again, Ariel said nothing. The tea and jumbles were gone, as was the comfortable silence between Duke Owen and Maya. Instead, there was doubt as they regarded the green Book of Everything and Ariel.

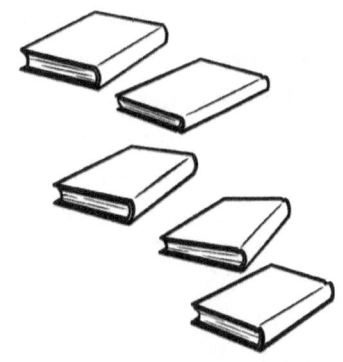

11: Bridge House

With its clear blue sky and gentle breeze, Viola didn't know how the warm summer day could be any finer. She was riding a sweet, brown mare through fields so green they almost glowed. Hedgerows bordered every field, and with the large gardens, the countryside had a patchwork look that stretched in all directions. Viola loved the broad sweep of land, punctuated by little stands of immature trees.

"No forests?" Viola asked, thinking of Maine.

"There are in other parts of the duchy," Simon replied. "But Humphrey had everything chopped down around Caxton."

"On Earth his name is Jay Sheldon," Viola said, glancing at Simon who rode easily on Percy, a large gray gelding. The powerful horse seemed to know exactly what to do, even though Simon hardly spoke to him.

"Humphrey's a rotter, whatever his name is."

Viola nodded. From the first time she had seen Jay Sheldon—or Humphrey—Viola had known he wasn't to be trusted, but she also knew that he had a lot of money and that her father was hoping for a large donation for his reelection campaign. So Viola had said nothing, the way she always did when she had a feeling about someone. Eventually, Viola would come to trust those feelings, but as a young girl, she didn't have confidence in her intuition, especially when her parents seemed to have opposite reactions.

"Well, he's on Earth now, and he doesn't have Julian's book. He can't hurt Caxton anymore." But the tone of Viola's voice was doubtful. Somehow, even though Humphrey was stranded, Viola had an image of him coming back to Caxton.

Simon snorted. "There's no knowing when that one will turn up, just like a bad penny. If there's a way, he'll find it."

"Would he kill Duke Owen?" Viola asked quietly.

"Aye, I believe he would."

For a while neither Simon nor Viola said anything. Thinking about Humphrey had brought a dark cloud to the sunny day. But then Daffodil, who was lively as well as sweet, began to trot across a large field they had just entered.

Simon was watching Viola, who really did know how to ride a horse. "Do you want to let them canter?" he asked after a short time.

"Yes!" Viola exclaimed.

Smiling, Simon's feet touched Percy's sides, and the large horse began to canter. Daffodil needed no urging, and the two horses moved smoothly and surely through the tall grass. At the edge of the field, women and children were picking berries, and they stopped to watch as Simon and Viola rode by. They waved at Simon, and he waved back. Viola waved, too. She hadn't felt this free in a long time, and she wished she could stay in Caxton, with Simon and Maya, for a month, maybe longer. Not forever. Viola knew she would miss her parents and her friends, but right now, anyway, she reveled in being able to ride alone with Simon without being trailed by someone from the Secret Service. Viola tipped her head back and laughed, and Simon, who was watching her, laughed, too. She could tell that he, like so many other people, admired her dark, gleaming hair and her blue eyes. Viola, glancing at him, liked his trim figure, his bright red hair, and, most important, his way with horses.

By the time they stopped by the River Caxton, their good mood had returned. While the horses drank, Viola looked down the river, toward the walled city, which was close to the river but far enough away so that if it flooded in the spring, the waters never reached the gates. Then she looked up the river, where she saw a bridge with a small stone house built onto it. On the other side of the river, Viola could see an apple orchard.

"Does someone live in that little house?" Viola asked, pointing toward the bridge.

"Aye," Simon answered. "Jasper, the cobbler, and his wife, Hildy. Would you like to meet them? Hildy's always ready for a cup of tea, and no one can bake over an open fire the way Hildy does."

"Not even Molly?" Viola asked.

"Molly's one of the best cooks around," Simon allowed. "But she has ovens and plenty of help. Hildy only has herself, a few pans, and an open fire."

"You're sure Jasper and Hildy won't mind?"

"Nay, not at all."

"Then, yes, please!" Again, Viola laughed but this time for the sheer joy of being able to visit someone at the last minute without any worries about security.

"You'll need a different name," Simon said, smiling as she laughed. "The way you are dressed, you look like a boy."

"Really?" Viola asked. "Do pants make such a difference here?"

"They do," Simon replied firmly. "In Caxton, if you wear a dress, then you're a lass. If you wear trousers, you're a lad."

As she shook her head, it occurred to Viola that not everything was better in Caxton than it was on Earth. "What should my name be?" she asked.

"Well, how about if we just shorten your own name to Vi. That could be for either a lass or a lad."

"Vi," Viola said, liking the sound. It was short and to the point, and it had the ring of someone who could take charge of things. "I like it." Later, it would be the name Viola would use in her professional life, when she headed a nonprofit whose mission it was to protect mustangs in the American West.

"All right, Vi," Simon said. "Let's go meet Jasper and Hildy."

Viola had been around the world with her parents and had visited many places, but she had never seen anything like Bridge House, which was tucked to one side of a bridge large enough for carts and people as well as for the cozy home. Small though it was, Bridge House was big enough to be divided into two rooms downstairs, and it even had a tiny attached shed. In one room, there was a cobbler's bench and all the tools and materials needed to make and repair shoes. Jasper was working at his bench, and he waved to Simon and Viola as they walked by the open door.

"The bread is still warm," Jasper called. He was tall and thin with wispy, gray hair, and he sat hunched over his table.

"Looking forward to it," Simon called back.

The other room was a parlor, kitchen, and dining room combined, and there was no connecting door between this room and Jasper's shop. On the wall overlooking the river, there was a row of windows, a counter, and a sink with a pump. On the wall next to the counter were shelves hung low where Hildy kept dishes and some of her cooking pans as well as various crocks, jars, and tins. In the middle of the room stood a small round oak table with four chairs. Finally, to one side sat two padded chairs each with their own little stools tucked beneath them, and when Hildy wasn't cooking, these chairs could be pulled in front of the fireplace on the wall that separated this room from the shop.

"Oh!" Viola cried, gazing around.

A petite woman turned from the sink. Her hair was white and braided into a bun that was barely visible beneath a lace cap. Her face was round and pink, and her eyes were nearly as deep a blue as Viola's. "Simon!" the woman called. "Come in, come in, and sit down. The bread is done, and as you know, the water is always hot for tea."

Looking at the fireplace, Viola saw a small cast-iron teakettle hanging over a low fire.

"Thank you," Simon said. "Hildy, this is Vi, who is visiting from far away."

Hildy's bright blue eyes took in Viola's gleaming, dark hair and smooth face, but she only said, "Welcome, Vi. Please sit down while I make the tea and cut the bread."

"Thank you, Hildy," Vi said, smiling at the old woman, who smiled back before turning to the shelves to gather the teapot and cups.

Soon, the tea was made and poured, thick slabs of warm bread were cut, and honey was drizzled on top.

"So good," Viola said with a sigh after the first chewy bite of bread and honey.

Simon didn't say anything. He just tucked into one piece of bread and then another before he even took a sip of tea. When Simon had finished two pieces of bread, he said, "I've been showing Vi the countryside. Vi's a pretty good rider."

"And how do you like our countryside?" Hildy asked.

"Beautiful!" Viola responded. "I wish I could stay here longer."

"How long will you be staying?" Hildy asked.

But Viola never had the chance to answer.

"Simon," a voice called from the open door, "I just got word that Maya is back."

Simon stood quickly. "Evangeline, good day! And yes, I know. I've seen and spoken with Maya."

Hildy stood, too. "Come in, come in. The tea is still hot, and Simon hasn't yet eaten all the bread."

Viola turned, seeing a woman who was even smaller than Hildy, but where Hildy was rosy and bright, Evangeline was as brown and firm as a nut. Viola could tell that Evangeline's dark eyes took in even more than Hildy's bright blue eyes, and Viola knew there was no need to pretend to be anything other than what she was.

Viola also stood. "I'm very pleased to meet you. Simon has told me how you're teaching him to heal animals."

Evangeline waved a hand. "Oh, sit, sit down. Yes, I could use a cup of tea. I've been traipsing about all afternoon, and I brought some salve for Jasper's hand. He's working, I suppose, even though he should give that hand a rest."

As they all sat down, Hildy nodded. "Aye, he's working. You know how Jasper is. He never stops." Hildy turned to Viola. "Jasper cut himself cleaning fish."

Evangeline shook her head. "Some people just aren't happy unless their hands are busy. That's how Jasper is. And I'm glad to see Simon hasn't eaten all the bread. I'd never turn down a slice of your bread, Hildy."

"I've had plenty," Simon said quickly, but Viola could see that he was staring longingly at the loaf and wanted a third slice.

"Pish," Hildy said. "There's plenty here. You can have as much as you like." She cut another piece for him and drizzled honey on it. Smiling, Simon took it gratefully, and Hildy patted his hand.

"She spoils you, Simon," Evangeline said, after taking a sip of tea. "But then again, you could use a little spoiling."

Embarrassed, Simon looked down at his bread, but Evangeline had turned her attention to Viola. "You came with Maya, didn't you?"

"I did," Viola replied.

"Is the boy—Andy—with her?" Evangeline asked.

Viola hesitated. "No, only me."

Again, Evangeline looked at Viola's dark hair and blue eyes. "Yes, I see." Then she said to Hildy, "Maya and Andy were here about six years ago. Maya helped Duke Owen, and she helped me, too, with Julian."

Hildy nodded. "I've heard about Maya and how without her, Humphrey might still be duke." Hildy shivered, and her rosy face was serious.

"Aye," Evangeline said thoughtfully. "Chance was on our side, that's for sure."

Viola was quiet. Before leaving Sir John's Rose Cottage, Maya had given Viola a long lecture about not saying anything about Ariel, where they came from, or anything else about their time and technology. "Say you're from away and leave it at that," Maya had advised. Viola had quickly agreed. She had read enough books that featured time travel to understand what could happen if the space-time continuum was disrupted, and it was never good.

"I'll just listen," Viola thought as she sipped her tea, and it was not hard for her to do this. Like her father, she was good at listening to people, and she spent an hour hearing and learning about various aspects of Caxton—whose horse was sick, whose baby was suffering from colic, and whose children needed shoes and were getting them because Duke Owen quietly paid Jasper to make shoes for poor families and only charge them a fraction of what he would normally charge.

Evangeline nodded. "Not good to have cold feet. Children need good, sturdy shoes with no holes."

Simon winced, and Viola understood that at one time, Simon had had holes in his shoes. But he didn't say anything, and neither did Viola.

When Simon and Viola left, Evangeline walked with Simon and Viola to where they had tethered the horses, by the river away from Bridge House and well out of earshot.

"You're Andy's daughter, aren't you?" Evangeline asked Viola.

Viola looked at Simon, and he said, "It's all right. You can tell her. She pretty much knows it all."

"Well, maybe not all," Evangeline put in. "There are still things I can't see. Nobody sees everything."

Simon smiled. "But you see quite a lot."

Evangeline shrugged and asked again, "You're Andy's daughter?" Viola nodded. "Even if I hadn't had my eyes peeled, I could tell. You're the spitting image of him."

"Eyes peeled?" Viola thought. "What could that mean?"

Evangeline asked Simon, "Where is Maya?"

"With Duke Owen at the castle. There's going to be a proper tea in Duke Owen and Duchess Celia's family dining room. Duke Owen told me to invite you if I saw you."

"I'll come," Evangeline replied. "It will be good to see Maya again. No doubt Sir John Oldcastle will be there and sing some fool song." But her small dark eyes were crinkled in a smile, and Viola could tell the old woman didn't mind the singing.

"Of course he'll be there," Simon said. "He never turns down a chance to eat Molly's food."

"Just like you," Evangeline said.

"Aye, just like me."

At first, at Duchess Celia's tea, there was no singing, just happy eating, sipping, and talking. Simon ate as though he hadn't just had three slices of bread at Bridge House, and Viola marveled at how much he could hold and still stay so slim. Viola nibbled on a piece of Molly's excellent gingerbread, but she was too full to eat much more. The family's dining room was spacious and sunny, and it had a big table, lots of chairs, padded benches along the wall by the windows, and a large sideboard loaded with treats from Molly's kitchen—bacon sandwiches, hard-cooked eggs, strawberry tarts, gingerbread, and so many other things that Viola wished she were more hungry so that she could try them all.

Because of Maya, Molly and Jem had come to the tea. A sturdy, compact man with dark curly hair was there—Viola had seen his counterpart at the White House and knew he must be one of Duke Owen's advisers. Sir John was there, of course, as was a slim man with ginger hair.

"Rhys Gruffyd and Harry Newton," Maya said, when Viola asked who they were. "Rhys works with Duke Owen, and Harry Newton lives with Sir John and Simon."

Not long after the tea had started, a young woman, the nanny, came with Rosalind and Sebastian, who were each carrying a foxhound puppy. As soon as she saw the puppies, Duchess Celia shook her head. "No."

"We thought the puppies would make the tea more fun," Rosalind said with the same calm authority Duchess Celia might have used when she was making a point with a stubborn servant.

Curly-haired Sebastian, who had just turned three, added, "Everyone loves puppies, Mama."

Rhys was standing next to Duke Owen by the sideboard, and he grinned. "Can't argue with that."

Duchess Celia looked to Duke Owen, and shrugging, he smiled. "Why not let them stay for a little while?"

Nodding, Duchess Celia smiled back, and the puppies were allowed to stay. With their long ears, black eyes, and black noses, Viola had to admit they were cute as they raced around the room, nipped Sir John and Jem on the heels, barked for treats, and yipped when Rosalind and Sebastian chased them.

"Oh, puppies and small children," Evangeline said. "What a commotion they cause!"

On a padded bench, Evangeline was sitting on one side of Maya, and Viola was on the other side. When a puppy came and pulled on the hem of her dress, Evangeline placed a hand on the puppy's head. "None of that, now," she said in a firm but affectionate voice. The puppy stopped pulling, sat down on her small haunches, and wagged her tiny tail. "There, there, off you go." The puppy gave one sharp bark, then ran off to find her litter mate.

Viola, Maya, and Evangeline all laughed, but then Maya's face grew serious.

"What is troubling you?" Evangeline asked.

"Something that Julian's Book told me," Maya replied, and on the other side of Maya, Viola was quiet as she listened to the conversation.

"And what was that?"

"How the Books of Everything plot and scheme and can hurt us and our families."

"H-m-m-m," came Evangeline's cautious reply. "Do you think Julian's Book is right?"

"I never thought about it before Julian's Book brought it up," Maya answered. "I just trusted the Books."

"And now?"

"I don't know."

Evangeline placed her hand on Maya's arm. "I have never used a Book of Everything, so I can't tell you from experience how trustworthy they are. But I know ours has given Duke Owen wise council and didn't do a thing for his snake of a brother, Humphrey."

"The Books are good. I know they are," Maya said, and Viola could see how relieved she was.

"Yes, they are," Evangeline said. "But..."

"But what?" Maya asked.

Evangeline's voice was low, and Viola could barely hear her. "It seems to me that there is a larger plot afoot that we're barely aware of."

"Like what?"

Shrugging, Evangeline shook her head. "It is just a feeling I have. Why did the Books want you to bring Chet here, of all places? You could have brought him anywhere."

Maya no longer looked relieved, and her voice was a whisper. "I don't know."

"Neither do I," Evangeline said. "Maybe you should talk to someone who does know."

"Maybe I should," Maya said slowly, her face even more serious than before.

Evangeline nudged Maya. "Ah, there he goes. Just like I thought he would. Sir John is going to sing us a song."

Sir John, having had three helpings of everything, was now standing at the back of the room. Jem, with his little flute, stood beside him.

Sir John asked Jem if he knew "Peggity, Show Me the Way."

Jem smiled. "Aye, of course I do."

Duchess Celia spoke up, "Remember, Sir John, there are children here."

Sir John inclined his head. "I will not sing the last verse."

"Very good, Sir John. See that you keep your promise."

Sir John bowed. "May I be struck with indigestion before I break my promise to you, Duchess Celia."

Everyone laughed, and Sir John also gave a mighty laugh before launching into the song about Dirk, a dim-witted man, and Peggity, his clever wife.

Soon everyone was clapping, and the puppies, exhausted, were lying stretched out beneath the table. Clapping, Viola glanced at Maya and could immediately tell from Maya's determined expression that a decision had been made—soon Maya would be going on a journey to find out more about the Books. Shivering, Viola thought about Maya's journey and how alone she would be.

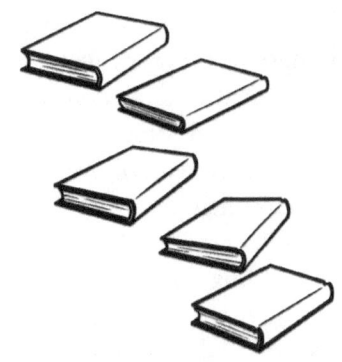

12: Back to the Great Library

Fall had come, and even though the day was sunny, and the cloudless sky was a deep blue, there was a certain chill in the air. Already the tiny birds with the whirring wings had begun their long migration to warmer lands. Sydda, in work pants and shirt, was in the garden removing the last of the cucumber plants. As he pulled the rough vines, dry yellow leaves cracked in his hand, and he thought, "That's it for the year."

And what a good one it had been for cucumbers. It gave Sydda great pleasure to think of the jars and jars of pickles that the cook and his staff had put up. The storeroom had three whole shelves of them, and Sydda hoped the pickles would last for the entire winter. There were still some edible cucumbers on the vine, and into one cart they went while into another cart went the vines with the dry, yellow leaves.

As Sydda bent to pull another vine, a sharp pain moved down his back, and he slowly straightened, waiting for the pain to go away. "I'm getting old," Sydda said aloud and without regret.

Indeed, that very morning as he had left his office to go work in the gardens, Astrid, the Great Library's assistant director, had said, "You're too old to work in the garden."

"Surely, not yet," Sydda had replied with a laugh, even though he knew she was right.

Astrid had shaken her head. "You'll see how those knees and back feel tonight."

Yes, he would. Despite his creaky back and touchy knees, Sydda continued to work in the gardens, even though his age and his status at the Great Library would have excused him from doing so. He loved being outdoors in the sun under the blue sky. He loved feeling the wind move across his face. But most of all, he loved planting seeds, watching things grow, and then harvesting vegetables.

With his hand pressed against the bottom of his back, Sydda stared at the far end of the garden, where the small forest began. Although he couldn't see it, Sydda could feel the Ancient One's presence in the center. On this island, everything looked so calm, so peaceful, and at the Great Library, everything seemed to be going just the way it should. New apprentices had come and were settling in, Books of Everything were being made, and the Great Library even had a roving ambassador—Elspeth—who was traveling from planet to planet to get a sense of how things were going across the universe.

And how were they going? "Not that well," Sydda said with a sigh, still staring at the forest.

Everywhere Elspeth had visited, things were more in flux than they ever had been, at least in Sydda's memory, which stretched back over a hundred years. Chaos, while not yet gaining the upper hand, had made real progress, and Time, increasingly, was on the defensive. Although Sydda never would have admitted it to anyone—not even to Astrid, his closest friend—he felt apprehensive. It seemed to Sydda that the Library's Book of Everything, in concert with all the other Books of Everything, was charting a dangerous course. What if the Library's Book was wrong this time? Shuddering, Sydda pictured what might happen all across the universe and to this place he had called home for so many years, a place he had come to love dearly.

When the pain in his back had eased and Sydda was about to resume his work, someone landed with a thud on the ground in front of him.

"That was smooth," said a familiar voice, and a slight figure in a red dress stood, brushing herself off with one hand.

"Sorry," came a voice from the open blue Book she was carrying.

"Maya," Sydda said, not in the least thrown by her blonde hair. "I've been expecting you."

"Sydda!" Maya exclaimed, smiling. "Well, Ariel, at least you found him."

"Ariel?" Sydda asked. "You named the Apprentice Book?"

Ariel made a sound as though it were clearing its throat in embarrassment, and Maya answered, "It just seemed so cold for the Apprentice Book not to have a name."

Sydda frowned. Somehow, the Great Library's Book of Everything had neglected to tell him this. "Interesting," Sydda said aloud.

"Will it change things?" Maya asked anxiously.

"I expect it will." Looking at Maya's red dress, Sydda asked, "You came from Caxton?"

"Yes," Maya answered with a sigh. "It's a long story. Do you have time to talk?"

"I do," Sydda replied. "What's the point of being a director if you don't have enough helpers so that you can take time to talk?" Maya smiled, just a little. "Would you like to go in for tea?" Sydda asked.

"No," Maya said. "I just came from a tea." She looked around, and at the edge of the gardens were benches. The one closest to them was empty, and although there were other workers in the garden, none were near enough to be able to overhear their conversation.

"As you like it," Sydda said.

Once on the bench, Maya launched into her story, twisting her dress in little bunches as she told Sydda all that had happened. Sydda listened without interrupting, noting Maya's small, nervous hands. In between them, Ariel sat open but did not add anything to Maya's account. Then she came to Julian's Book and the conversation with Duke Owen and the green Book of Everything. Smoothing her dress over her knees, Maya stopped talking.

"Go on," Sydda said gently. "What did Julian's Book say?"

Maya told him, and when she was done, she blinked rapidly, trying not to cry. But the tears came anyway, and Maya angrily brushed them away. Sydda was silent, and Maya said in a wavering voice, "I know. You're thinking about how much you should tell me."

Sydda sighed. "I can't deny this." Reaching over, he took her face in one of his hands, and he stared into her eyes. Maya didn't flinch, and she stared back at him.

Finally, he blinked, patted her cheek, took his hand away, and regarded the Great Library, the turrets, the towers, the white stone walls. "A castle for books," Sydda often said, but there was more. Time was very strong here, and even after all the years he had spent at the Great Library, Sydda didn't understand all of it.

"Can you at least tell me a little?" Maya asked in a low voice. "I always thought the Books were doing the right thing. But now..." She shook her head. "And I'm worried about Mom, Mémère, and Pépère. Will something happen to them because of me?"

Ariel spoke, "I think you should tell her what the Great Library's Book has planned for Maya. If you don't, I will."

"Well," said Sydda. "Well, well." He had, in fact, been thinking of doing exactly what Ariel had suggested, but the Apprentice Book's bluntness had taken him by surprise.

Ariel continued, "Maya deserves to know what might happen to her."

"I'll be going against the advice of the Library's Book," Sydda replied, but he said it absently, as though it didn't really matter.

"Nevertheless," Ariel said.

Maya sat quietly, listening intently to the exchange between Sydda and Ariel.

"All right," Sydda said, wondering if the Library's Book would be angry with him. In all his time as director, Sydda had only felt the Book's wrath once, and although it had happened long ago, Sydda still remembered it. It was not an experience he wanted to repeat, but Sydda felt that Ariel was right—Maya deserved to know about her part in the Book's plan. He wouldn't tell her everything. For the Great Library's sake, he couldn't, and Sydda sadly reflected on how much had to be held back even from those like Maya, who had become central to the plan.

Sydda cleared his throat. "When the first Book was made, the first director overoptimistically named it the Book of Everything. The Book itself was new and still unformed and therefore didn't know enough to correct the director. The director underestimated Chaos and understood the nature of Time even less than we do now. The director also didn't know that the Books have to turn their attention specifically to relevant information, much the way we do when we study something. Plus, Chaos is able to block a lot from the Books. By the time the first director realized that the Books didn't exactly know everything, many Books of Everything had been made. And then what could the director do? Change their name to the Books of Almost Everything?"

Maya smiled. "That wouldn't work."

Sydda smiled in return. "No, it wouldn't. So the name stuck. But even though the Books might not exactly know everything, they know a lot. More than any person will ever know, even somebody as old as I am. But more important, Maya, along with knowing things, they also have their own intelligence, and on their own, they work closely with Time."

"On their own?" Maya asked.

"On their own," Sydda repeated. "They do not consult us. We consult them, and working with Time, the Books try to move us in various directions. Sometimes they succeed, sometimes they don't."

"But are they good?" Maya asked.

"Yes," Sydda said. "In the long run. But in the short run, things don't always go the way they should for those involved with the Books of Everything."

"Like Chet murdering Mary Parson," Maya said. "She deliberately led Chet away from the train so I could escape with Earth's Book."

"She did indeed," Sydda replied. "And then there was Feste."

There was a stricken expression on Maya's face. "Feste? But that was an accident. Sir John and Andy stole Earth's Book of Everything and then..." Her voice trailed off, and Sydda could see that Maya understood what he meant. "That was planned all along?" she asked.

"To some degree," Sydda replied. "The Library's Book wanted to flush out whoever Cinnial had sent to Ilyria, and it figured the best way to do this was for Sir John to steal Earth's Book of Everything. The odds were high that because of Andy, Sir John would find out about Earth's Book and try to get it. As Chance would have it, you chose to have your eyes peeled, and that was the perfect opportunity."

"Was Feste's death planned?"

"No, Maya," Sydda answered gently. "Time leaves some wiggle room for Chance. Actually, Time leaves quite a lot of wiggle room. But that also lets Chaos worm its way in, and when that happens, death often comes too soon."

"What about my family? Will they be hurt? Will they be killed?"

"No," Sydda answered. "Although your Mémère will have some close calls."

Maya looked bewildered. "Mémère?"

"In all likelihood you will need her help. But in the end she'll be all right. If, of course, Chaos doesn't prevail. If Chaos does prevail, then all bets are off for everything."

With a distracted motion, Maya wiped her face, which was sweating in the cool autumn sunlight. "All right. But there's something else, isn't there?"

"Yes, Maya, and it concerns you."

"Am I going to die too soon?" Maya asked, her voice weary.

"Not as far as Time is concerned," Sydda answered firmly. "But the hope is that you will go where we librarians have never been—to Mortmain, to Cinnial's headquarters, on the planet Tufrak. As a prisoner. And Maya, this will most likely be the worst experience you have ever had or will likely ever have. Cinnial will not treat you kindly. He will try to break you."

For a while, Maya didn't say anything. Sitting on the bench, she looked at the gardens, the Great Library, and the forest. "It is so beautiful here," Maya murmured. "It feels so safe and calm."

"It's because Time is in control here," Sydda said. "Quite different from where Chaos has the upper hand. So much ugliness and disorder. So much destruction and suffering. And some people are always drawn to Chaos. It's easier to destroy than to create."

Finally Maya nodded. "And you're telling me all this because you want it to be my choice to go to Mortmain."

"Yes," Sydda said.

"Made from free will," Ariel added. "Not pushed unknowingly by the Books of Everything."

"Why me?" Maya asked, but her tone was curious, not bitter.

"Blame Chance," Sydda said wryly. "She chose you out of many."

"Is Chance alive?" Maya asked.

"In a way," Sydda said. "She takes form wherever she appears. You have probably seen her but were not aware of it."

"And when will I have to make this choice?"

"Soon," Sydda answered. "In Caxton in the next day or two."

"Chet is part of this, too. He saw me today. He's in Caxton for a reason, isn't he?"

Sighing, Sydda nodded. "It's going to be a mess. An awful mess. But if you allow yourself to be captured, then you just might be able to discover what it takes to defeat Cinnial. You're so small. He'll sense your potential, but he'll underestimate you. And you'll figure something out. You always do. And one more thing. Don't be afraid to use your Book for traveling. Everything is in such flux right now that it really doesn't make a difference if your travel is noticed."

Maya swallowed, then swallowed again. "I'm scared," she whispered.

"You have every reason to be," Sydda replied gently.

"But you can do it," Ariel said. "I know you can."

"Will you be with me?" Maya asked the Apprentice Book.

"Yes, but I don't know for how long."

"What will happen to you?" Maya asked.

"When they find me, they'll get what information they can and then in all likelihood destroy me." Ariel's voice was calm, and it was clear to Sydda that the Apprentice Book had already accepted the possibility of its own destruction. Sydda could also see that Maya knew this and had decided what she was going to do.

After asking a few more questions, Maya left with Ariel. Sydda walked slowly back to his office in the Great Library. The Library's Book was open, the way it always was, on a large wooden stand by Sydda's desk. Although Sydda was a slight man, he sat down heavily in his chair.

"You told her," the Library's Book said in its high, clear voice.

"I did," Sydda answered, waiting for harsh words from the Book.

But the Book's voice was surprisingly mild. "I expected you would."

"You did? Had you planned this all along?"

"No. Come on, Sydda. After all the time we have spent together, you should know by now that I can't make you do anything."

Sydda sighed. "I do know this. But I was wondering if by telling me not to let Maya know what is likely to happen, then this would encourage me to do the opposite."

"Now, now. You are not that contrary. But you have certainly become suspicious."

The Book's voice was wry, and Sydda smiled. "With reason, you must admit."

"Yes, with some reason," the Book said. "I thought it would be better for Maya if she didn't know. It would spare her some worry. But you and Ariel decided otherwise, and who knows? Maybe you're right. Choosing out of free will might just be the nudge we need to set things in the right direction."

"And I won't be around to help, will I?" Sydda asked.

"No," the Book answered, and its voice was sad. "This will be your last autumn."

Sydda nodded. "That's what I thought."

There was silence for a while as neither the Book nor the old man said anything. No words were needed. Sydda and the Book had been together for a long time, and they knew each other very well. Sydda had brought joy, openness, and new ideas to the Great Library, which was not something every director, no matter how good, had done.

"You've been an excellent director," the Book finally said. "I will miss you."

"I've done my best, and no matter how it ends for me, I wouldn't have chosen another life. Not for anything." Sydda smiled, and the look on his face was radiant. Then he said briskly, "Well, well. There's much to do, and I had better get started, first with Astrid, then with the board, then with everyone else. We've been planning for this day for a while. Time to get things going."

Sydda left the office and the Great Library's Book of Everything. Sydda would have been surprised to learn that the Book was actually brooding about the course that had been chosen. Over the years, Cinnial had become powerful, and with Chaos on his side, the outcome was far from certain. A crisp, salty breeze blew in from an open window, moving some of the papers on Sydda's desk and ruffling the pages of the ancient Book of Everything.

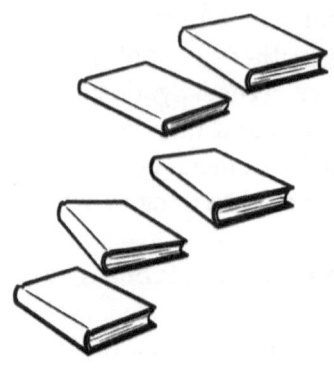

13: Before the Bonfire

Even though Duke Owen had left for Camburgh—to confer with the old king—the Midsummer Festival went on as planned. Tables had been set up in the courtyard, wood had been stacked for a bonfire, and Molly and her staff had been cooking feverishly in preparation for the feast hosted by Duke Owen and Duchess Celia.

"After all," Sir John said to Viola that morning over breakfast in Rose Cottage's small, bright dining room. "Midsummer's Eve comes but once a year."

"What will it be like?" Viola asked, looking from Sir John to Harry to Simon.

"Plenty of food," Sir John said. "Molly outdoes herself for the Midsummer Festival."

"Lots of ale," Harry said with a laugh, and Sir John laughed, too.

"And dancing," Simon put in shyly, staring at Viola.

"Dancing," Viola said, smiling. "I won't know any of your dances, but it will be fun to watch."

"Pish posh," Sir John said. "'Tisn't very complicated. Mostly it's just whirling around the bonfire."

Listening, Maya pushed her eggs around her plate, but she remained silent. She knew she should take Viola back to Earth, but the girl was so excited about the Midsummer Festival that Maya hated to spoil her fun. Maya thought, "But what if tonight is the night I'm taken to Cinnial? What will happen to Viola?"

"You're awfully quiet, Miss Maya," Sir John said. "What has your Book told you?"

The laughter stopped as Sir John, Viola, Simon, and Harry regarded Maya. Smiling sadly, she shook her head.

"Can't tell us, eh?" Sir John asked shrewdly, and with a start, Maya realized she was doing the same thing that the Books of Everything did, deciding which information to share and which to keep secret.

As they all stared at her, Maya thought, "It's for their own good." But was it really? Was it right to keep such a big secret? Shouldn't they be warned, too? Again, Maya shook her head.

Viola set her teacup down with a determined clatter. "I don't want to go back. Not yet. I'm not ready."

Smiling just a little, Maya looked at Viola. They were sharing a bedroom at Rose Cottage, and they had gotten to know each other, talking late into the night, long after everyone else was asleep. In both words and looks, Viola reminded Maya so much of Andy. However, unlike Andy, Viola could see and sense things. As she regarded Viola, Maya got an idea of what it must have been like for her own mother and father, living with a child who always seemed to know what was going on, and for the first time, Maya felt a twinge of sympathy as she realized it could not have been easy for her parents.

Maya decided to tell Viola, Sir John, Harry, and Simon some of what she knew. "Last night after tea, I went to the Great Library."

"Did you, by God?" Sir John asked. "We never knew you left Rose Cottage."

"From your point of view, I was gone less than a minute," Maya replied.

"And what did you learn?" Harry asked, casually scraping strawberry jam onto a piece of toast.

"Something big is likely to happen either tonight or in the next day or two," Maya blurted out, unable to keep it in any longer. "I'm going to be captured and taken to Cinnial in Mortmain." She turned to Viola. "It's not safe for you here. That's why I need to take you back to Maine. Probably this morning. And the rest of you?" Here Maya shrugged. "I don't know what will happen to you."

There was no clattering of teacups, no spreading jam on toast. Even Sir John was absolutely quiet, and Maya shifted uneasily in her seat as everyone looked at her.

Harry was the first to break the silence. "Do you have a choice in this?"

"I do," Maya said. "I could go back to Maine, give Ariel to the League of Librarians, and never have anything to do with you or the Great Library again. Cinnial would leave me alone because, without the Books of Everything, I'd just be..." Maya didn't finish the sentence.

"Normal," Viola said wistfully. "You'd just be normal."

Sir John's fist came down on the table, and everyone jumped. He bellowed, "Normal? Are you out of your mind? How could you ever be normal, after doing all the things you did? Coming here. Having your eyes peeled. Going to the Great Library." Sir John wiped his red face and said more gently, "Miss Maya, you'd never be normal. At best, you'd just be miserable, wondering what was happening at the Great Library and what you could have done to stop things going from bad to worse. At worst, on your planet, the enemies of the Books of Everything would be out to get you because you know too much. Maya, my girl, you're in too deep to be normal."

Maya knew Sir John was right. Hadn't the Toad Queen told her as much before peeling her eyes? "Once it is done, it is done. You can never go back to the way you were before, and you will be different from most of your kind."

Maya nodded slowly. "I can run away, or I can be captured, but I'll never be normal."

"So, what next?" Simon asked.

"I don't want to go back," Viola said. "Not yet."

"You'll be stranded here if I'm captured," Maya said.

"There's Caxton's Book of Everything," Simon pointed out.

"It's with Duke Owen," Maya replied.

"Oh, he'd come back lickety-split if you were taken from here," Sir John said. "Don't you doubt it for a minute."

Maya was about to argue with Sir John when a flash came to her, of Simon and Viola escaping from Caxton in a wagon, and there were four people in the back, two children—Sebastian and Rosalind—and two adults—Evangeline and Mémère Celine. Evangeline was lying flat and was almost hidden, and Mémère, wearing bright pink, was bent over her. There was something important Simon and Viola would do together. Maya didn't get a clear sense of what this was, but she knew without a doubt that Viola was part of the plan, too.

Maya looked at Simon. "Promise me you'll watch her. Promise me you'll take her away if things get rough. Tonight, make sure a wagon and horses are ready. Just in case. And watch out for Rosalind and Sebastian. Evangeline, too." Then Maya added reluctantly, "And my grandmother."

"Your grandmother?" Simon asked, frowning.

Maya nodded. "Yes. She might be coming here to help Evangeline."

"Aye," Simon said, turning to Viola. "I promise."

Viola blushed a little and nodded without saying anything.

Later that afternoon, Maya stood in the bedchamber she was sharing with Viola, who was in the garden with Simon. Their heads were together, and they were laughing as they looked down at something on the ground—a frog, perhaps—and Maya smiled as she watched them from the window.

"They are becoming very close," said Ariel, who lay open on the bed.

"I know." Turning from the window, she went to the bed and sat next to Ariel. "But Viola's only twelve. She has to go back to her parents when this is all over."

"She will. But Viola might return one day, when she is older."

"You always meant to bring us here, didn't you?"

"Yes, it's part of the plan, for you and for Viola."

"Oh, Ariel." Maya felt her eyes sting with tears at the thought of what she had to face and of what Viola might have to face, too. "Do the Books always use kids like this?"

"Not always," Ariel answered. "But more than we should." Here Ariel actually sighed. "Children and teenagers are often overlooked. The right ones can do a lot before the adults catch on."

"Ariel, promise me that you'll let Elspeth know what's happening and tell her to come get Viola when things are settled. Whenever that is."

"I've already done that," Ariel said. "And Elspeth will take your Mémère back, too."

Maya's breath caught as she thought about Mémère in Caxton, but then her attention turned back to Ariel. "And what am I going to do about you? Just carry you in a reticule and let Cinnial get you?"

"Yes, if you hide me or give me to someone else, then Cinnial will know this was planned from the start, and in all likelihood he'll just kill you. We have to make it look like a surprise, or none of this will work. Remember, you have to try not to be captured. But don't try so hard that you'll escape."

"All right," Maya replied, wondering how in the world she was going to manage this. "And Ariel? I sure hope this plan, whatever it is, works."

"Me, too," Ariel said sadly.

"Tonight," Eli said, as Lucinda handed him a vial with a potion to make Master Julian remember. They were in the tavern, in midafternoon, when it was quiet and nearly empty. Toby was in the kitchen, chopping meat for pies. Eli continued, "Everyone will be so busy eating and drinking and dancing that they won't know what's going on until it's too late."

"I'll take care of those guards, don't you worry," Lucinda replied. "I'll give them ale with something to make them sleep. I have a cousin who works in the keep's kitchen, and I'll tell her

I've come to help them get ready. It's Midsummer Festival. They won't be suspicious. Then I'll bring the prisoner to Master Julian's apartment, where you'll both be waiting."

Eli grinned in appreciation. He enjoyed working with Lucinda, who was just as sharp as he was. Eli was beginning to think she was wasted on his friend Toby, and as he took the vial, he even briefly considered how he might win Lucinda over. Eli gave his head a slight shake, knowing they would never get on as a married couple. Sooner or later, with their temperaments, they would clash over matters both big and small.

Lucinda's bright eyes took in his considering look. "I'm best with Toby. You know that."

"Aye," Eli said.

Lucinda's lips quirked into a small, rueful smile. "We'd be at each other's throats in no time."

"Still, just think what we could do if we put our heads together. And both of us from poor families. We'd show them, we would."

"Aye," Lucinda answered softly, and she even touched his hand. Then she stood up, saying briskly, "I'd better go in the kitchen and see if Toby needs help with anything."

"Yes," Eli said softly. "You'd best go to Toby."

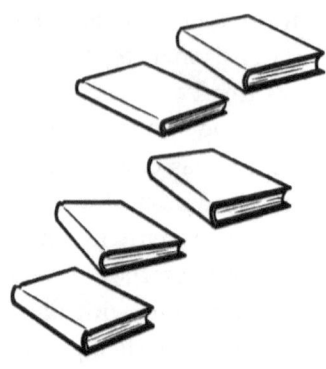

14: The Fire Burns

Finally, finally it was night. The tables were piled with food and drink, and from the town and from all over the countryside, people had come to celebrate. The courtyard was full of people drinking, eating, and laughing. The bonfire had been lit, and the musicians were playing. Julian smiled as he watched people, including Simon and Viola, flash around the fire. Hands were held tightly as Midsummer was welcomed yet again.

"It was so much fun," Viola would say later. "At least at first."

Outside the whirling ring of dancers, the younger children had made their own wobbly ring that broke down at times as somebody fell but continued just as soon as footing was regained. Rosalind and Sebastian were in that ring, laughing and urging everyone to go faster, faster.

Julian planned to dance well into the night. He might have lost his memory, but he had not lost his looks, and women of all ages were more than willing to dance with him. Alyce, a brunette with a pert face, was already smiling at him. She was the older sister of one of his students, and Julian decided he would ask her for the first dance. Just as he was about to make his way over to her, Eli was at his side with a mug of ale, pressing it into Julian's hand.

"I thought you might want something to drink before the dancing starts," Eli said. "You know how you are. Once the dancing gets going, you hardly stop."

Julian laughed genially. "True, true."

Eli grimaced, but it passed so quickly Julian didn't notice it. "Drink up, master."

Julian took a big drink and handed the mug back to Eli.

"Drink it all," Eli urged. "You'll need to keep up your strength."

Julian laughed. "So I will." He finished the ale and moved toward Alyce, who was still smiling at him. But suddenly, Julian felt dizzy, and he stumbled. If Eli hadn't been there to catch him, Julian would have fallen.

"Are you all right, Master Julian?" Eli asked.

Julian pressed a hand against his forehead. "I don't know. I feel so funny. I think I need to sit down for a while."

Alyce ran to see what was the matter, but Eli waved her away. "My master's feeling a little dizzy. I'll take him to his apartment to rest."

"Is there anything I can do to help?" Alyce asked, frowning at Julian, who looked at her and smiled weakly.

Eli said, "Nay, nay. I'll tend to him. I'm sure he'll be all right. Master Julian's been through much worse."

In his apartment, Julian collapsed in his padded chair by the fireplace. Groaning, he bent over and rested his head in his hands. "Eli, I feel so awful. My head, my head." Grimacing, Julian closed his eyes and fell into a sort of swoon, where he was both conscious and not conscious. Julian knew where he was, and he knew that Eli was standing beside him, watching anxiously. But images, hidden for the past six years, started coming to him. Some of them were pleasant—as a child, playing with his sister and his friends; going to the seaside with his large, extended family, all just as fair as he was; learning to drive and roaring down the highway in his first car. And best of all, being chosen to go to the Great Library. There had been hundreds and hundreds of applicants from his planet, but he was the one the committee had chosen. Although Julian was momentarily taken aback by the grimace of jealousy on his sister's face when he told her the news, it didn't suppress the joy he felt over being chosen to go to the Great Library.

As he remembered his sister's face, Julian thought for the first time, "I should have paid more attention to the way my sister felt. What is in her is also in me."

Then other memories gripped Julian, and he was at the Great Library, as an apprentice among many apprentices. Sydda had personally given them a tour of the Great Library. As he and the others followed the spry director, Julian was again seized by a fierce joy because he had been chosen to come to this place with so many books, both paper and virtual. As he followed Sydda, Julian thought, "If I work hard, someday I'll make Books of Everything."

Beside him, a tall young man with brown hair, a square jaw, and intense blue eyes seemed to be as taken with the Great Library as Julian was.

"All these books," he murmured to Julian. "All this information. All this knowledge."

Julian, his face still open and bright, nodded at the young man, who was about his own age.

"My name is Cinnial," the man said.

"I'm Julian."

Grinning, they looked at each other, and Julian sensed that a strong friendship would develop between the two of them. That the friendship would later become something more binding, more suffocating, more destructive, Julian couldn't foresee. At that moment, Julian was filled with awe and love for the Great Library, and he could tell that Cinnial felt the same way. Even the Library's Book of Everything hadn't foreseen what would happen, how jealousy and resentment would pave the way for Chaos to worm its way into the Great Library and insinuate itself into Cinnial and Julian. Chaos wasn't able to stay at the Great Library for long before being bounced out, but it was long enough.

The following memories came in a rush: The rejection—neither Julian nor Cinnial would be chosen to make Books of Everything; the resentment and anger; the defection; the plotting and planning; and across the universe, all the killings and the blood. Then he recalled how Maya had stabbed him and how the old woman, Evangeline, had given him a mint to supposedly ease his pain. Julian now realized the mint had taken away his memory.

Grimacing, Julian was filled with a remorse he had never before allowed himself to feel. Because alongside the recovered memories came the images of the life he had lived for the past six years in Caxton, a life of teaching and students that he might have had at the Great Library if he hadn't decided to follow Cinnial, the closest friend he had ever had.

"I was happy," Julian whispered as he thought of his time in Caxton. His head cleared, and with a mournful expression, Julian looked up at Eli. "I was happy," he repeated. "There was something in the ale, wasn't there? Why did you make me remember?"

With his mouth open, Eli stared at his master but was saved from having to respond by a soft but sharp rap on the door. "Eli, are you there? It's me, Lucinda. I've got the prisoner. Let us in before anyone sees us."

Eli opened the door, and Lucinda, followed by Chet, walked into Julian's apartment.

"That was lucky," Chet said as Lucinda quickly closed the door behind them.

"Aye," said Lucinda. "I was sure someone would notice you, even though it's dark, and some people have drunk so much that they wouldn't notice if their own dead mother was dancing around the fire."

Julian rubbed his bleary eyes. "It was more than luck. I can guarantee it."

"Is he himself?" Lucinda asked quietly, glancing at Eli.

But Julian heard her. "My memories are back. And I wish to God they weren't." Julian's face was pale and pinched as he regarded first Eli then Lucinda and finally Chet. "You're the prisoner from the tower, aren't you?"

"Yes, my name is Chet Addington." He held out his hand, and Julian shook it firmly but without enthusiasm.

"And I'm Julian Jortensen." He turned to Eli. "Now that your plot to help me regain my memory has succeeded, I suppose you're going to tell me what's next on your agenda."

Eli cleared his throat and looked at Lucinda, who shrugged.

"There is no plan, is there?" Julian asked, and his shoulders drooped.

"I can't stay here," Chet said. "In a few hours, when the guard changes, they'll notice I'm missing and will start searching. And there's something else. A girl named Maya is here." His face flushed. "She's from my land, and it's because of her that I was in that tower for six years."

Julian actually laughed. "Maya is here? That girl certainly gets around."

"She sure does," Chet said, his voice low. "Maya has a Book of Everything, or she wouldn't be in Caxton. When Maya recently came to the castle, she was carrying two stupid looking little bags with long strings. One bag, I bet, had her own Book of Everything. She would never leave it behind, no matter where she was staying. And the other bag must have had something important, too, or she wouldn't have brought it here. I was watching the courtyard when Maya left, and I noticed she only had one bag. I think she left the other one with Duke Owen."

"What could have been in that bag?" Lucinda asked.

"Another Book?" Eli ventured.

"I know what it is," Julian said wearily. "It's my own Book. The one that Humphrey took from me just before I lost my memory. For the past two nights I've been dreaming about a book, and it was calling to me. And now that my memory is back, I can feel that it's here."

"I bet Maya stole it from Humphrey," Chet said. "He's been in my land for quite a few years."

"See what I mean about Maya?" Julian said.

"But, master," Eli protested, "she stabbed you with your own knife."

"That she did," Julian responded absently. "But she did it in self-defense. And no matter how you look at it, Maya has a knack for being in the right place at the right time."

"I'd like to knacker her," Chet said, and the look on his face indicated that he wasn't kidding.

Like an old man, Julian rose slowly from his chair. "I'm afraid you're not going to get that chance. Because if we find my Book, then Maya will be going with me to Mortmain, to Cinnial, who will most certainly want to, ah, question her." Julian shook his head, and there was a sad expression on his face.

"Cinnial," Chet said quietly, almost with reverence. "You're with Cinnial?"

"I am and have been for a very long time."

"Where do you think Duke Owen kept the book?" Eli asked quickly.

Julian shrugged. "In his office? In his own apartments?"

"Duke Owen's office is on the other side of the great hall," Eli said. "We wouldn't even have to go outside to get there."

"Then let's start with Duke Owen's office," Chet said, giving Julian a searching look.

Lucinda said, "I'd better go back to the tavern. Not that there will be much business on Midsummer's Eve. But Toby will miss me. I'm supposed to help him make pies for tomorrow's meals. We go through a lot of pies at the tavern."

Chet gave a slight nod. "Thank you. I won't forget how you helped me escape."

Looking from Eli to Julian to Chet, Lucinda curtly nodded back. "We'll see how this all goes. Good luck." Then she left.

"A resourceful girl," Chet said to Eli.

"Aye," Eli answered. "But she's betrothed to my best friend."

Chet just snorted. "Let's go to Duke Owen's office."

Eli led the way, with Chet following close behind and Julian lagging.

"Lucky the dancing has started, and the meal is over. Molly and her helpers will be in the courtyard with everyone else," Eli said.

Chet patted the knife and belt he had stolen from one of the guards. "I'll take care of anyone who comes too close."

Eli shifted uneasily. "Let's hope it doesn't come to that. We don't want to attract any attention. At least not yet."

Chet didn't say anything, and soon they were by the door to Duke Owen's office.

"Got anything to pick a lock?" Chet asked, and Eli removed a small wire from his pocket.

They were undisturbed as Eli picked the lock and opened the door. Chet grabbed one of the lamps from the great hall, and they all slipped into the room. The lamp, burning low, cast a small circle of light around Duke Owen's uncluttered office.

"Where would it be?" Chet muttered.

Julian pointed to a chest against the back wall. "It's in there. Locked, of course."

Eli crouched by the chest and slid the wire into the lock, which didn't give as easily as the one on the door. Several minutes went by as Eli probed, but finally there was a snap, and Eli was able to pull open the lock. Chet held the lamp high as they looked into the chest. In the dim light they saw papers, bags of money, and several books. As Chet and Eli reached for the bags of money, Julian stared down at his Book, off to one side in a corner, as though it didn't want to associate with the other books.

"Master?" Eli asked, after grabbing two bags of gold.

"Yes." Julian sighed, reluctantly reaching down for his Book and opening it.

"Took you long enough," the Book observed sharply. "You have changed." Then the Book's voice rang out in a warning, "Watch out for Duchess Celia. She is by the door."

"What are you doing here?" Duchess Celia asked indignantly, standing on the threshold.

Before Eli, Julian, or the Book could say anything, Chet was across the room. His knife was in one hand, and with the other he grabbed Duchess Celia, stabbing her. She cried out, fell to the floor, and then was still.

"What have you done?" both Julian and the Book asked together.

"I took matters into my own hands," Chet said to Julian. "Something you seem incapable of doing."

"He has a point," Julian's Book said. "But to kill Duchess Celia. That will most certainly raise a ruckus. Still, we might be able to use her death to our advantage."

"We've got to get out of here before Duke Owen finds out and uses his Book to come back," Julian said, suddenly shaken from his torpor by the sight of so much blood on the floor.

"Not yet," Julian's Book replied. "Didn't you hear what I said about using Duchess Celia's death to our advantage? Besides, there's still a lot we have to do, and according to my source, Duke Owen won't know what's happened for a couple hours. When he comes back, he won't be thinking clearly."

"Nemesis?" Julian asked.

"Correct," the Book said. "Chaos allowed us to use her this evening. She is in Camburgh, at the king's dinner, and right now she is singing in her, ah, inimitable voice. While Nemesis is entertaining the guests, none of them, including Duke Owen, will be thinking about anything else."

"Who is Nemesis?" Eli asked.

"It's a long story," Julian said. "But she works with Chaos. She takes the shape of a blonde woman, very pretty. And her voice is mesmerizing."

"I saw her in the courtyard tonight," Chet said suddenly. "She was flirting with that fat knight. Everyone was watching her."

"It's probably why nobody saw you come here. Nemesis is like that. Everyone was too busy looking at her to notice you." Julian shook his head. "Duke Owen will be focusing on Nemesis, just like everyone else in the room. By the time he comes to his senses, it will be too late."

"Right," Chet said, putting his knife back in the sheath. "Let's make plans about what we're going to do next."

And that's just what they did.

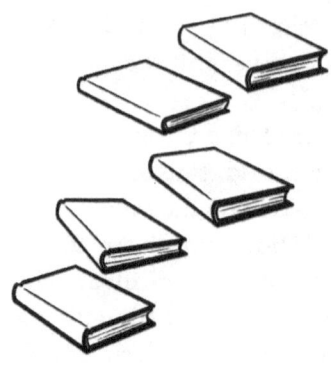

15: Humphrey Returns

Humphrey woke slowly with the worst headache he had ever had. His vision was blurry, and blinking, he tried to make out where he was and what had happened. At first, Humphrey was completely disoriented, and his pounding head was all he could think about. But gradually his vision cleared, and Humphrey saw that he was in a bedroom—the one he had been given at the house where the president and his family were staying. Then it all came back to him—the party, Viola spilling her drink, the stolen book, seeing Viola with a girl who turned out to be Maya, following them to Viola's room. And then blackness.

Humphrey struggled to sit up but felt so dizzy that he gave up.

"Better take it slow," a voice said. President Drew Murphy was sitting in a chair not far from the bed, and beside him sat Diana, looking lovely and grim.

"Where are the girls?" Diana asked in a low, urgent voice. "If you don't tell me, I'll break all your fingers one by one."

Humphrey thought, "The girls? They could be anywhere. Who knows where the Book took them?" Aloud, he answered simply and honestly, "I don't know."

Drew looked from Humphrey to Diana, and Humphrey realized that the president knew who he was. "Maya must have told him," Humphrey thought. "I'd like to get my hands on that damned girl."

"Diana," Drew asked, "could you leave us? I want to talk to Jay in private."

"Are you sure?" she asked.

"I'm sure. I'll be fine. We searched him. He doesn't have any weapons, and we found the ones hidden in the room."

"All right." Diana's tone indicated that she didn't want to leave, but the order was coming from the president of the United States. So Diana left.

"Well, Humphrey," Drew said sternly. "What brings you to Earth? Of all the places in the universe, why here? And where are the girls? Tell me all that happened, and tell me the truth."

Humphrey wished that his head didn't hurt so much, that he wasn't lying on a bed while being questioned by a man with such keen intelligence.

Humphrey decided he would start with the truth. "Viola and Maya stole my Book, and I followed them to Viola's room to get it back. I wasn't going to hurt them. I just wanted them to give me what was mine."

"Right. But you didn't get the Book did you?"

Humphrey grimaced. "No, Maya had her own Book, and it took them away when I, ah, went into the room."

"And why do you suppose the Book took them away?" Drew asked.

"How should I know?" Humphrey replied. "They're kids. Sometimes kids do strange things."

"But one of those kids is Maya, and she's not like other kids, is she?"

"No, she isn't," Humphrey admitted slowly, and there was a grudging admiration in his voice.

"She stole your book for a reason."

"Maya had no right to take it," Humphrey retorted. "And she used your daughter as an accomplice."

Drew actually grinned. "Yes, I'm sure she did. Maya is very resourceful."

"She'd better watch out," Humphrey snapped. "She's up against a force far more powerful than she is."

Drew wasn't grinning anymore. "What do you mean by that? And how does this affect my daughter?"

Another voice said, "He means that Maya's up against Cinnial and, of course, Chaos."

Both Humphrey and Drew jumped. Standing on the other side of the bed was a tall, slender man with hair so blond it was almost white. In his hand was a small, black Book, and it was open.

"Julian!" Humphrey exclaimed. "And the Book."

Blinking at the man who had once tried to kill him, Drew glanced at the door behind him.

Julian wearily shook his head. "We can be gone before you even start calling for help."

Drew nodded curtly. "Do you know where my daughter and Maya are? And what are you going to do?"

"Your daughter and Maya are in Caxton," Julian answered after listening to his Book. "I'm going to bring Humphrey back to Caxton, and then I'm going to take Maya to Cinnial. Your daughter will be left behind in Caxton. Although she can see, it's not as strong with her as it is with Maya, and we have no need of her."

"Viola can see?" Drew asked. "Of course she can! From the time Viola could talk, she always seemed to know what was going on, sometimes even before we did. Why didn't I notice it?"

Julian smiled grimly. "Hindsight's uncanny, isn't it? So much makes sense, now that you think of it."

"You won't hurt my daughter?" Drew asked.

"I have no interest in your daughter," Julian replied and then repeated patiently, "I'm going to bring Humphrey back to Caxton and then Maya to Cinnial. If you want your daughter back, then you'll have to use Earth's Book to get her." Julian put his hand on Humphrey's arm and said to the Book, "Take us back to Caxton."

Humphrey's stomach lurched as he traveled with Julian and the Book to Caxton, back to the castle that he had won and then lost to his older brother. They landed in Duke Owen's office, and waiting for them were Eli and Chet. The first thing Humphrey noticed was how dim the light was. One lone lamp flickered in the darkness, and Humphrey knew that among other things, he was going to miss electricity, which could make a room as bright as day, even at midnight. Unused to traveling directly with the Book, Humphrey stumbled, grabbing the desk to keep from falling.

"Sit down," Julian said, motioning to the chair behind the desk.

Swallowing, Humphrey sat down quickly. As he did, he noticed a body on the floor, and Humphrey realized he could smell blood. "Who is that?"

The men glanced at each other. "Duchess Celia," Julian finally said. "Chet killed her."

"Why?" Humphrey asked, remembering how he had once loved her. But she had never loved him. For Celia, it had always been Owen, and Humphrey yet again wondered bitterly why everything always came to his older brother. Love, respect, loyalty, wealth, even looks—Owen always seemed to get it all, even when he was hiding in the Forest of Arden.

"She caught us breaking into Duke Owen's office to look for Julian's Book," Chet answered shortly. "I had to take care of her so she wouldn't tell anyone about it."

Humphrey was beginning to get his bearings. "I suppose you did." Through APO, Humphrey had learned about Chet's many exploits and had even met the tracker a few times. While Humphrey was truly sorry that Duchess Celia was dead, he was glad to have Chet on his side.

"But why are you in Caxton?" Humphrey asked.

"Maya brought me here, and your brother kept me in that damned tower of his for six years."

Humphrey thought, "Julian's Book had never mentioned a thing about this." Shaking his head, Humphrey asked, "Why didn't you come back to Earth with Julian?"

"I figured I'd be more useful here. I want to help you capture Maya and her Book," Chet answered, and if the light hadn't been so dim, Humphrey would have seen a gleam in Chet's eyes. "Julian will bring me back to Earth later."

"So, what's the plan?" Humphrey asked Julian.

To Humphrey's surprise, Chet answered the question, and it was then that Humphrey realized there was something not quite right about Julian. The tracker said, "You are going to wait here until Duke Owen comes rushing back from Camburgh to find his wife dead on the floor. Then, you are going to take care of him as you see fit. I suggest killing Duke Owen and getting him out of the way. Duke Owen has already made one comeback. You don't want him to make another."

"Yes, he has," Humphrey said stiffly. "And that damned Maya helped him. I'd like to take care of her, too."

"Maya certainly has a lot of enemies," Julian said.

Chet snorted. "She's worked hard to make us her enemies. Like you said, she's got a knack."

No one could argue with this, not even Julian, who had changed so much, and for a while the office was quiet. From outside came the sound of music and people laughing.

"Midsummer Celebration?" Humphrey asked.

Eli spoke for the first time. "Aye, and everyone's either drunk or with someone they ought not be with."

His lips pursed, Chet shook his head, but Humphrey actually smiled, remembering past Midsummer Festivals when he, too, had been drinking and had kissed another man's wife.

"How much time before my brother finds out about Duchess Celia?" Humphrey asked.

"About an hour," said Julian's book, which was open on the desk. "Nemesis is just getting started."

"Who?" Humphrey asked, and Julian explained who Nemesis was.

"Then I guess there's time enough for a drink," Humphrey said.

The Book's reply was saucy. "Isn't there always time for a drink with you?"

"Always," Humphrey answered.

Humphrey sent Eli out to fetch a pitcher of ale and some mugs. Chet and Humphrey had moved Duchess Celia to the back of the room, and one of the tapestries from the wall had been taken down to cover her still body.

"I need a knife," Humphrey said.

"There's one at the bottom of the chest," Julian's Book said. "Snotty thing. It's got a dark green stone on the handle, and this made it think it was better than the rest of us in the chest. I set that little hick of a knife straight."

"The knife belonged to my father," Humphrey said, hesitating slightly before searching the chest. Did he really want to kill his brother with that knife?

The Book must have sensed Humphrey's dilemma. "What difference does it make? Dead is dead, no matter the knife."

"True enough." Humphrey found the knife along with its sheath and belt. "Do all objects have thoughts and feelings?"

This time Julian answered, and his voice was mournful, "Yes, if you can see deep enough. We all come from the same place, and it doesn't matter whether we're flesh and blood or wood or steel or jewels. That essence is there, in all of us, alive or not. We are all connected."

Humphrey thought, "That one sure is a New Age woo-woo." He had seen plenty of them on Earth, and one of his girlfriends had had an impressive collection of crystals. That relationship hadn't lasted long. Then came an uneasy thought. "I hope Julian doesn't muck things up."

The blond man had changed so much that he hardly seemed like the same person.

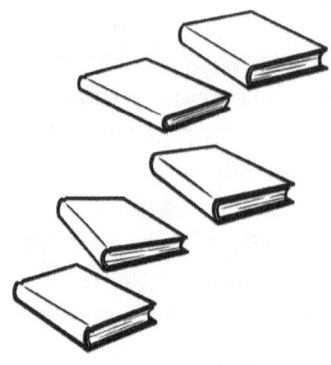

16. Eli Takes Action

Eli felt like lashing out at someone, anyone, as he left Duke Owen's office. If a cat had crossed his path, he would have kicked it. And a dog? The same thing. Fortunately, none of the castle's dogs and cats crossed his path as he stormed across the great hall to the courtyard to fetch drinks from the casks next to the long table with the pitchers and mugs.

As Eli had plotted and schemed, he had always been certain that bringing back his master's memory would restore Julian to the man he had been before Evangeline had taken those memories away. "The old hag," Eli thought, scowling. "I'd kick her a good one, if I saw her. What right did she have to do that? She's ruined him, that's what she's done."

Eli felt his face flush, and there was a hard knot in his chest that made him feel as though he couldn't breathe. Had his master been grateful when his memories returned? No. Instead, Julian had reproached Eli and had even said he had been happy when he couldn't remember who he was. Happy! Not having anything better to kick, Eli lashed out at the great hall's door frame, and he was rewarded with a throbbing toe that felt as though it was on the verge of being broken. But Eli didn't care. All he could think about was Master Julian. It was beyond Eli's comprehension how his master could have been happy with his new life, doddering back and forth to the university, teaching students, having them over for pastries and tea and sometimes something a little stronger. Late into the night they would talk and argue, with his master intervening from time to time when the arguments got a little too heated. His master, with his hot temper, cooling things down? If Eli hadn't seen it for himself, then he never would have believed it. And, oh, what his master and the students discussed. As far as Eli was concerned, there weren't two words of sense spoken together between his master and those students.

Out into the courtyard Eli rushed, and there by the table with the mugs and pitchers, stood none other than one of the prime sources of his troubles—Evangeline, who was filling her mug from a cask. When Evangeline turned, there was a relaxed, slightly silly expression on her face, and Eli realized that the old woman was drunk, which meant her guard would be down. Although he had been ordered to get drinks, Eli patted the knife that he wore by his side and decided that there was going to be a change in plans. Lord Humphrey could wait for his drink.

Eli's first impulse was to stride over to Evangeline and slit her throat. While Eli might have been angry, his instinct for self-preservation, always strong, intervened as he pictured what would happen to him if he killed one of the duke's favorites right out in the open where there would be many witnesses. No, he would lure Evangeline away from the crowds and into the shadows, where no one would see him kill her.

Taking a deep breath to calm himself down, Eli walked over to Evangeline and tried to give her a friendly nod. But his teeth were gritted, and there was no smile in his eyes.

"If it isn't the grumpy Eli," Evangeline said. "Enjoying the festival?"

"Nay," Eli replied, thinking fast. "I've just come from the Barking Dog. My friend Toby has cut himself bad and needs your help. Will you come?"

"Of course I'll come." Evangeline set her mug down on the table. She patted a large leather pouch that she wore belted by her side. "Lucky I'm always ready with supplies. You never know what's going to happen on Midsummer's Eve."

"Hurry!" Eli urged, moving away from the table. "He's lost a lot of blood."

"I'm coming." Evangeline followed Eli away from the table, across the courtyard. "Damned fool," she grumbled. "Doesn't that Toby know how to handle a knife?"

"Aye," Eli said, leading her through the castle's open gate into the dark, empty town. "Toby's good. But everybody makes mistakes."

Evangeline should have heard a warning in this, but all she did was grunt in acknowledgment.

Eli took her down a side street that led to the Barking Dog, and he was so intent on getting his revenge that he didn't realize he was being followed. When in the dark street, Eli turned suddenly and yelled, "This is for my master," somebody heard Evangeline as she cried out in pain and surprise when the knife went into her shoulder.

"Stop!" called a gruff voice.

A coward at heart, Eli did not wait to see who had followed him. Instead of making sure the job was finished, he sheathed his knife and ran, disappearing into the darkness of Caxton, to the Barking Dog and to Lucinda.

It was Maya who had followed Eli and Evangeline. She had drunk no ale and had eaten very little. Her senses were as sharp as ever, and the only time her attention had been distracted was when a blonde woman, coldly beautiful, had been flirting with Sir John by the food table. Maya had had a bad feeling about this woman as she tucked one hand into Sir John's arm and patted his cheek with the other hand. Maya turned for a moment to watch Sebastian and Rosalind spin around with their friends, and when she glanced back at Sir John, the woman was gone.

Not long after, Maya saw Evangeline leave with Eli, and she realized the healer was in danger. For a moment Maya had debated whether she should stay and watch or follow Eli and Evangeline. Maya had followed Ariel's instructions by not standing too close to the entrance of Julian's apartment, therefore making it too obvious she was spying, and Maya was reluctant to go.

But her fear for Evangeline was so great that Maya knew she couldn't just leave Evangeline, who was tipsy, to Eli's devices. Remembering the image she had had of Evangeline in the wagon, Maya was sure Eli was going to hurt the old woman. So, reluctantly, she followed the pair from the courtyard.

When Evangeline had cried out, Maya's suspicions were confirmed, and she hurried to the fallen figure on the street as Eli ran away. Maya knelt beside Evangeline.

"Maya," Evangeline said softly, "I've been such a fool."

"No one can see everything." Maya put her hand on the woman's cheek.

Evangeline sighed. "Well, we all have to go sometime. I would have liked to stay a little longer, but when your time is up, it's up."

"No," Maya replied firmly. "I know someone who can help you."

Pulling Ariel from the reticule she had cinched around her waist, Maya said, "Take us to my room in Rose Cottage."

In less than a second, Maya and Evangeline were by Maya's bed. Fortunately, Evangeline was so small and light that Maya was able to lift the healer, grimacing and groaning, onto the bed.

Evangeline's face was pale. "Now what?" she asked weakly.

"I'm going to get someone who can help you."

"Who?"

"My mémère."

"Your what?"

"My grandmother. But first I need to light a lamp so that we can see when we come back."

And as soon as the lamp was lit, Maya and Ariel were gone.

The Apprentice Book brought Maya directly to Mémère's bedroom, but they landed quietly to one side, and at first

Mémère didn't notice them. She had on a bright pink top and the new pink sandals she had bought when she had gone shopping with Maya. Smiling, Maya remembered how Mémère had been sure the two would match. But Mémère didn't look happy, and shaking her head, she muttered, "That stupid town manager."

Turning to leave the room, Mémère jumped when she saw Maya. "Mon Dieu, you scared me!" Then she squinted at Maya. "What are you doing in that dress? And is that blood?" She shook her finger at Maya. "Don't tell me it's for that play of yours. Something funny is going on, isn't it?"

Maya's voice caught. "Oh, Mémère, so much is going on that I don't have time to tell you all that's happening. But somebody is hurt and bleeding and needs your help. Will you come with me? And bring your first aid kit?"

"Oui, oui," Mémère replied. "But where are we going? And why are you here? You're supposed to be in Bar Harbor."

"After you've taken care of Evangeline, I'll tell you more. But hurry!"

Mémère was about to argue, but Maya spoke with such urgency and authority that she just shrugged. "I guess I won't be going to book group tonight."

Mémère rushed out of the room and returned quickly with a larger than usual first aid kit. "After all," Mémère would say later. "I was a nurse."

"Ready?" Maya placed her hand on Mémère's arm.

"I'm ready. But where are we going?" Mémère asked again.

"To another planet and another time. Hold on, Mémère. You're probably going to feel sick to your stomach."

Then they were standing beside the bed with Evangeline. Clutching her stomach, Mémère stumbled, but Maya had a firm grip on her grandmother's arm, and she didn't fall.

Maya said, "It will pass in a few moments."

Nodding, Mémère swallowed and swallowed again. Then she looked down at Evangeline.

The old woman smiled weakly. "That's quite a granddaughter you have."

"That's for sure," Mémère said briskly. "Maya, we need more light. And help me get this dress off so I can see the wound."

When another lamp had been lit and the dress had been removed, Mémère peered critically down at Evangeline's wound. "It could be worse. You were lucky."

Smiling a little despite the pain, Evangeline glanced at Maya. "Yes, lucky. Or something like that."

Mémère said, "I'm going to clean the wound and stitch you up. I have something that will help with the pain. Maya, could you get me a cup of water?"

There was a cup next to the pitcher on the washstand, and Maya poured water into the cup, setting it on the small stand beside the bed. Opening her kit, Mémère found a bottle of extra-strength Tylenol, twisted the cap, and took out two pills. Evangeline raised her eyebrows but didn't protest as Mémère helped her take the pills and the water.

As Evangeline settled back into the bed, Maya said, "There's more water in the pitcher, and the washcloth and towel hanging on the side are pretty clean. Mémère, I am so sorry, but I have got to go. Something big is about to happen, and I have to be there."

But Mémère, who was usually so soft and easygoing with Maya, replied sternly, "Maya Celine Hammond, you aren't going anywhere until you tell me where we are and what's going on."

Evangeline put in, "You can't just leave her like this without any explanation at all."

"All right, all right!" Maya exclaimed. In a rush that sounded incoherent even to herself, Maya launched into a whirlwind description of the Books of Everything, Chet, APO, the League of Librarians, Andy, Duke Owen, Humphrey, Caxton, Sydda, the Great Library, Cinnial, and Julian. Frowning, Mémère didn't say a word as Maya spoke.

Blinking rapidly, Maya concluded, "Viola, President Murphy's daughter, is here, too. I'm going to send her and Simon, a boy who lives in this house, to take you out of Caxton and bring you and Evangeline someplace where you'll all be safe. And remember Elspeth, the woman you met at Barnes & Noble?

Sometime soon, she's going to get you and Viola and bring you back to Earth. But right now, I've really got to go." Reaching over, she gave her grandmother a fierce hug. "Thank you, Mémère. I never should have gotten you involved in all this." Maya sniffed. "But I did, and even though it was the right thing to do, I'm sorry."

Evangeline asked, "Did you understand any of that?"

"A little, but not much," Mémère admitted. "But I knew something was going on, that there was something different about that girl." She gave Maya a long, hard stare and then looked down at Evangeline. "Well, now I'm going to stitch that wound."

Evangeline replied, "When you're done, I'll fill in some of the gaps in Maya's story, even though I don't know as much as she does. Take care that those stitches are small. I don't want a big scar." She stared at Mémère's hands. "And those are some pink fingernails that you have. Is that common where you come from?"

Mémère said, "Oh, be quiet. I know what I'm doing." But Mémère's lips twitched into a smile as she washed Evangeline's shoulder and prepared to stitch the wound.

Even Maya smiled just a little, and then she and Ariel were gone.

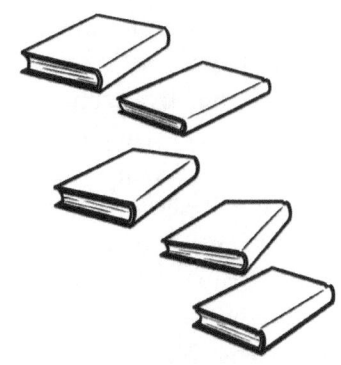

17: The Fall of Duke Owen

A riel took Maya back to the courtyard, where the bonfire was still blazing, and a ring of dancers was still spinning around it. But all Maya could think about was Mémère. Had she done the right thing bringing her here?

Viola and Simon were off to one side, resting from their wild dancing, and Rosalind and Sebastian were not far away, sitting on the ground. Sebastian had his thumb in his mouth, and Rosalind looked around for either their nanny or their mother, Maya guessed.

After tucking Ariel into the reticule and cinching it around her waist, something made Maya glance at the keep and at the window of Duke Owen's office, where she saw the soft glow of lamplight. She looked up at the tower where Chet was imprisoned, but there was no light, no face by the window. Closing her eyes, Maya could sense that Humphrey was back and that Chet was with him in Duke Owen's office. It was time for Simon and Viola to leave with Sebastian and Rosalind right now, while they could.

She rushed over to Simon and Viola. "Is the wagon ready?"

"Aye," Simon replied, taking in the blood on Maya's dress. "What's happened? Are you hurt?"

"No, but Evangeline is. Eli stabbed her." Simon looked as though he was ready to bolt from the courtyard, but Maya put a hand on his arm. "Don't worry. She's going to be all right. I went to my planet and got my grandmother, who is a healer and has special medicine. She's stitching Evangeline's wound, and they're at Rose Cottage. But there's something worse. Look at the window of Duke Owen's office. Humphrey is back, and Chet is with him."

All three of them stared at the window, and Viola, who had been silent, said, "Maya's right. Something bad is about to happen. Let's get the kids and go. Rosalind and Sebastian know you, Simon. Go talk to them."

Nodding, Simon went to the children and crouched beside them. "Your mother and your nanny are both busy tonight, and they want you to come with me. I'm going to take you to a special place where your father used to stay. It's a treat your mother had planned but wanted to keep as a surprise."

Rosalind looked doubtful, but Sebastian, nearly asleep, just nodded, his thumb still in his mouth. "Come on, children," Simon said gently. "You'll get to ride in a wagon with me and Viola."

Rosalind looked at Viola, who nodded encouragingly. "All right." The child got up and took Simon's hand. "Come on, Sebastian."

A wobbly, sleepy Sebastian stood and took Simon's other hand.

Maya said to Simon, "Go get my grandmother and Evangeline at Rose Cottage and ride as far away from here as you can." Then she turned to Viola. "Elspeth, a friend from the Great Library, knows what is happening and that you and Mémère are here. She will take you back to Earth. I don't know when, but you won't be stranded on Ilyria." Maya faltered and ended with a tremble. "Be safe!"

Viola nodded and then hugged Maya. "Be safe, too!"

Letting go of the children, Simon put a hand on Maya's shoulder. "Aye, take care. But no doubt you are heading directly into trouble. That's what you do."

Maya smiled ruefully. "I guess it is. And, Simon? Listen to Viola. Remember, she can see, too."

Simon gave Viola an appraising look, but all he said was, "All right, children. Let's go." He gathered curly-haired Sebastian in his arms, and Viola took Rosalind's hand. Maya watched them go across the courtyard, to the stables. Her heart was beating hard and fast, and her mouth was dry. "Be safe, be safe," she whispered as they disappeared into the stables.

Taking a deep breath, Maya turned toward the keep, and at first slowly, then resolutely, made her way from the courtyard to the empty great hall. The night was still young, and there was plenty of food and drink outside. Molly and Sir John were spinning around the bonfire, and so were her helpers. As Maya entered the great hall, the music and the laughter became dimmer, and Maya focused on the office door, which was not entirely shut. Quietly, quietly, she crept to the door, stopped, and listened. Peering into the room, Maya could see the desk as well as Chet, Julian, Humphrey, and Julian's Book. Immediately, Maya knew what had happened. Julian had found his book and had brought Humphrey back from Earth.

Crouching, Maya waited for someone to discover her, but at first nobody did. They—Julian's Book included—were too intent on their own conversation.

"How long now?" Humphrey asked.

"Soon," Julian's Book answered. "Nemesis has finished singing, and everyone is leaving the great hall in Camburgh Castle. No doubt Duke Owen is leaving, too, even though I can't see him."

"Where is that damned boy with the ale?" Humphrey asked.

"He had his own business to attend to," the Book replied. "But he was not entirely successful."

"What do you mean by that?" Julian asked.

"Eli had it in for Evangeline because of what she did to you, and he lured her into a back alley. Then he stabbed her, but he didn't kill her."

Julian shook his head. "Stupid boy."

Chet was pacing back and forth in front of the desk. "Never mind about the old woman. At least she's out of the way. Humphrey, we need to think about what you are going to do after you've dealt with Duke Owen."

Outside the office, Maya thought, "Duke Owen! Stay away. Please stay away." But she knew he was coming just as surely as she knew something terrible had happened to Duchess Celia, whose still, lifeless presence Maya could sense.

"Yes," Humphrey agreed. "I'll need men on my side if I'm going to retake the castle."

"There's Lieutenant Reed. He's not so far away, up in Pictland, to the north, where he has been since Duke Owen banished him," Julian's Book replied.

"I could go get him," Humphrey said. "And bring him back. Then he could find men who are still loyal to me."

"Hurry, then," Julian's Book urged. "Duke Owen will be coming back soon."

There was silence in the office, and Maya fidgeted by the door. She had no idea what she should do. Go warn Duke Owen? That's what Maya wanted to do, but she also knew that she was supposed to let herself be captured. As Maya deliberated, going back and forth between various options, the decision was made for her as the door opened suddenly, and Chet stood in the doorway.

"There you are!" Chet said. "Always where you shouldn't be." Grabbing her arm, he pulled her into the office and slammed shut the door.

"No!" Maya cried, and her terror was genuine as Chet loomed over her, his free hand twitching by his knife.

Julian spoke sharply, "Remember, she's not for you. She's for Cinnial."

Chet swallowed, and his hand moved away from the knife. But Chet did allow himself to rip the reticule from Maya's waist, and again Maya's terror was genuine as she cried out, "No! That's mine."

Chet leered at her. "Not anymore, it isn't." And he slapped the reticule on the desk.

Julian said wearily, "Sit down, Maya. You should have stayed with your friends in the courtyard. But you didn't. At any rate, it will soon be over."

Maya stared curiously at Julian, and she could tell that his memory was back. "But he really has changed," Maya thought. What would that mean? Before Maya had time to think about this, Humphrey was back with Lieutenant Reed, who had to sit down for a few minutes to recover from traveling with Julian's Book.

Swaying slightly, Humphrey placed the Book on the desk, and the Book said, "Maya, I see you've joined us."

"Not because I wanted to," Maya answered truthfully.

The Book laughed. "I'm sure of that. No, you joined us because you're a busybody who can't seem to stay out of trouble."

What could Maya say? Simon had made a similar but kinder comment, and she hadn't been able to disagree with him.

The Book continued, "But never mind that. We'll get to you and your little Book later. Julian, tell Chet to make sure that Maya doesn't escape. Maya is a slippery one, she is."

Julian quietly related the Book's message.

"I know that better than anyone," Chet replied, pushing Maya to a chair, forcing her to sit down, and clamping a hand on her shoulder, which he squeezed in a tight grip. Maya winced but didn't cry out.

The Book asked, "Julian, has Lieutenant Reed's stomach settled enough for him to go find men who will follow Humphrey?"

"Aye," Lieutenant Reed answered Julian's repeated question. "Just barely."

"Then tell him to get going," the Book said. "Duke Owen will be here soon."

Lieutenant Reed left, and Maya wondered frantically how she could warn Duke Owen that he was coming back straight into a trap. Looking at the reticule with Ariel, Maya squirmed, but Chet's hand squeezed even harder. Maya bit her lip. She realized she wasn't going anywhere until they were done with Duke Owen. And suddenly, Duke Owen was in the room with them. His curly hair was disheveled, and there was a grim, stricken expression on his face as he looked frantically around. He took in Chet, Julian, Humphrey, Maya, and then the body on the floor under the tapestry.

"So it's true!" he said raggedly, and for a second, his shoulders drooped.

"Of course it's true," Julian's Book replied. "Do you think your own Book would lie to you?"

"No!" Duke Owen's voice was bitter. "It never lies. It just doesn't tell the whole truth."

The green Book was open. "Duke Owen, I..."

"Never mind. I'm done with you." Throwing his Book to the floor, Duke Owen reached for his knife.

Roughly lifting her from the chair, Chet pushed Maya toward Julian. "Guard her, so that I can help Humphrey."

Nodding, Julian took Maya's arm, but his grip was much weaker than Chet's. Maya knew she could easily break away from him and bolt out the door while Humphrey and Chet confronted Duke Owen. It's what Maya desperately wanted to do— to get as far away from this room as she could and maybe even catch up with Simon's wagon. "Run, run!" a part of her urged. "Go while you can." But a deeper part of her said, "No, stay right where you are." So choking a little in fear, Maya stayed.

Duke Owen faced Humphrey and Chet. "Cowards," he spat out. "To kill a woman like that."

Humphrey shook his head. "Not that it matters much, but I didn't kill her."

"I killed her," Chet said calmly.

"Why?" Duke Owen asked. "What had she ever done to you?"

"She was in the way," Chet stated, and his voice sounded as neutral as though he were discussing the weather instead of explaining why he had killed someone. "And besides, she was married to you, who kept me a prisoner in that tower."

Duke Owen glared at Chet. "You'll pay for this."

"I don't think so," Chet said. "You're outnumbered, and not to brag, but I've killed a lot of people."

"Maybe we don't have to kill him," Humphrey said slowly. "Maybe we could just make him my prisoner."

Staring at Humphrey, Maya understood that he didn't necessarily want to kill Duke Owen. Instead, he wanted to prove he was a better leader than his brother. She saw that this was what he had wanted all along, and if the situation hadn't been so grim, Maya might have even felt a little sorry for Humphrey.

For a brief instant, Chet looked contemptuously at Humphrey before turning and springing toward Duke Owen.

"Watch out!" Maya cried.

But Duke Owen was ready, slashing Chet's arm. Staggering briefly, the tracker snarled and regained his footing. Maya watched in horror as Duke Owen and Chet fought, and it took longer to end than she would have imagined. Duke Owen fought with fury and energy. But Chet was right that he hadn't been bragging. Chet handled his knife coolly, with efficiency, waiting for that small opening he knew would come. Striking quickly, Chet drove his knife deep into Duke Owen's stomach. Gasping, Duke Owen dropped his knife.

"Wait!" Humphrey called out.

But Chet didn't wait, stabbing Duke Owen again. Maya cried out as Duke Owen fell to the floor. As the duke died, the room was silent. Julian let go of Maya's shoulder, and she covered her face with her hands as a series of images came to her and then went: Duke Owen at the lodge in the forest of Arden; his triumphant return to Caxton; the recent tea with Duchess Celia, Duke Owen, the puppies, Sebastian, and Rosalind.

Julian's hand came back down on Maya's shoulder, but it felt more like a pat than a grip.

Breaking the silence, Maya began to sob. Duke Owen was dead, and so was Duchess Celia. For Caxton, the past six years had been good ones, but that time was over.

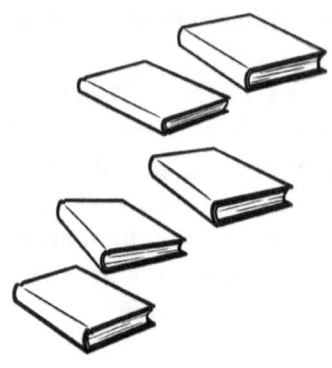

18: Duke Humphrey

Julian's Book said, "Now we can return to Cinnial."
"Will he want me?" Julian asked.

"Of course he'll want you," the Book answered sharply. "You'll have two of the Great Library's Books for him. True, one is an Apprentice Book, but it doesn't matter. Between the two, he'll be able to find his way back to the Great Library. It will take a while, but eventually Cinnial will get the information he needs to find the route that Time has hidden."

"To the Great Library?" Maya asked, her face pale.

"To the Great Library," Julian answered sadly.

"I need to talk to you alone," the Book said firmly. "Now."

Looking like a naughty student who had been called to the principal's office, Julian turned to Chet and Humphrey. "I have to go back to my apartment."

"Go ahead," Humphrey said, and then paused. "We can manage without you."

Chet snickered just a little, but he didn't say anything.

The Book said to Julian, "Take Maya, her Book, and the Green Book."

Julian obediently gathered the Books and took a trembling Maya by the arm.

Humphrey cleared his throat. "Will you be coming back?"

"No," the Book answered.

"Can you handle Maya?" Humphrey asked.

"We can handle Maya," the Book replied. "Don't you worry."

"Well, then." Humphrey was reluctant to see the Book go, even though he knew that it didn't belong to him and that the book was where it wanted to be, with Julian. Despite all the time they had spent together on Earth, Humphrey had always been aware that the Book desperately wanted to be back with the man who had created it and had given it life, that their bond was so strong it couldn't ever be broken.

The Book said crisply, "Caxton is yours again. You won't have me, but I expect that when this is over, Cinnial will reward you with one of his books, if he can spare one. And that will be a big help, especially without a Book of Everything to interfere." Julian's Book paused. "Humphrey, we've done all right together."

Humphrey nodded curtly, but he was pleased. He had been with the Book long enough to know that praise did not come readily or easily and that this was the closest thing to a compliment Humphrey was likely to get.

But Julian's Book couldn't resist having the last word. "Remember all the things you learned from APO. You don't want to make the same mistakes you made last time you were in charge."

Humphrey flushed a little but nodded. "I'll remember."

"You won't forget to come back and get me?" Chet asked Julian.

"I won't forget," Julian replied.

"Come along," said the Book to Julian. "We still have a lot to do."

Julian, the Books, and Maya left. The room was quiet, and Humphrey felt disoriented. Somehow, even though he had been waiting for years for this moment, everything had happened so fast, and it gave Humphrey an odd feeling to think of his brother and the duchess dead on the floor not far from where he sat. On Earth, when he had imagined this scenario, Owen and Celia had always been his prisoners, and they had been very much alive.

"He fought well," Chet said in an offhanded voice, probing at the slash on his arm. "Most would have gone down quicker than that."

"Owen was always a good fighter," Humphrey replied. "Better, really, than I am. But he was never as eager to fight as I was."

"He seemed pretty eager today."

"You had just killed his wife."

Chet nodded. "Who else needs taking care of?"

"Quite a few," Humphrey replied and then collecting himself, he added firmly, "But they are going to be imprisoned first and then have a trial. The people of Caxton need to think that things are at least going a little fairly."

Chet snorted. "Why?"

"Because last time, except for some who were close to me, most of the duchy was against me. That's how come Owen won so easily."

"You don't need to be soft."

Humphrey said quietly, "I won't be. Sir John, Harry, Rhys, Molly, her son Jem. They'll all pay. But last time we cracked down too hard and too fast. We need to move slower, with the vise being tight, but not too tight." Humphrey really had not needed the Book's warning. Through APO, books, and especially movies, Humphrey had learned a lot on Earth. He was neither as smart nor as compassionate as Owen, but he wasn't a fool, either. Humphrey had come to the conclusion that by following Julian's harsh advice, he had gained the fear and hatred of the people in the duchy rather than their loyalty. This was a subject Julian's Book had never broached. However, during his years on Earth, Humphrey had thought about it a lot, how Julian's anger had kindled Humphrey's own anger and how the blaze had gotten out of control. But Humphrey had decided not to mention this bit of insight to Julian's Book. Humphrey had discovered that when it came to Julian, the Book was more than a little touchy.

"Duke Owen gave his people too much," Chet stated. "More than they deserved. He's turned them into moochers."

"No doubt," Humphrey replied. "But they need to have a little, to give them hope and to string them along. Are you with me while you're here?"

Chet met Humphrey's level stare. "Of course I'm with you."

Humphrey nodded curtly. "Good. No more acting on your own. I'm in charge now, and despite what you might think, I'm not like my brother. Kill someone again without my orders, and you'll wish you were back in that tower. Understood?"

"Yes," Chet said, bowing stiffly. "As long as I'm here, I'll follow you."

Humphrey nodded again. "See that you do."

Before long, Lieutenant Reed came back with fifteen men who had submitted to Duke Owen but who were more than willing to bend the knee to Humphrey. As Humphrey considered them, he saw that they were all drunk. Shrugging, Humphrey reflected that he'd be drunk, too, if he had been at the Midsummer Festival. "Still," Humphrey thought, "there's nothing like a coup to sober up a man." And he knew he could count on them.

"All right," Duke Humphrey said crisply to the men. "Here's what's going to happen. But first of all, I'm going to need different clothes."

Thirty minutes later, a bench had been pulled outside and pushed beneath the windows of the great hall. Some of the men loyal to Humphrey came out and dispersed themselves among the crowd. Humphrey and Chet, flanked by the rest of the men, came outside and stood by the bench. At first, nobody noticed them. The musicians played as people danced, drank, and ate.

Climbing onto the bench, Humphrey just stood there for a while. In front of him his men were arrayed with their swords and knives, and Chet, almost smiling, was right in the middle. Not surprisingly, the first to notice Humphrey were the people closest to the bench, and they became silent as they stared at him. Their silence and their attention slowly spread until the musicians stopped playing, and the dancers stopped whirling.

"By God!" a voice bellowed. It was Sir John, who was standing next to Harry, Molly, Jem, and Rhys. But Humphrey had anticipated this, and some of his men were in a circle around the little group. Harry, Rhys, Molly, and Jem glanced around them, and it was clear they had assessed the situation. Sir John, on the other hand, had eyes for no one other than Humphrey.

"What are you doing back here!" The big man's voice blasted through the courtyard. "And where is Duke Owen?"

Humphrey had a loud voice, too, and he knew that now was the time to use it. While Humphrey might not have been as thoughtful and as well read as Owen, he did have one advantage over his older brother—he was a quick thinker. And although Owen had indeed been better looking, Humphrey's aggressive energy gave him a certain kind of charisma that drew men—and women—to him.

"Owen, my brother, is dead," Humphrey proclaimed in ringing tones. Everyone gasped, and if Molly, Jem, Harry, and Rhys hadn't held Sir John back, he would have charged toward the bench.

"Did you kill him?" Sir John roared, straining against the hands that held him.

"No, I didn't," Humphrey said, and it was one of the few truthful things he would say to the crowd because, among other things, APO and Julian's Book had taught him the art of lying while weaving in a few stray facts. The crowd had begun to murmur, and Humphrey held up his hand. "Here is what happened. A few hours ago, I came back to make peace with my brother. I wanted to settle down in west Caxton, at the manor left to me by my father. Over the years, when I was away, I had thought about what I had done, and I had come back to ask my brother's pardon. For Owen, as you know, was an honorable man, and I was certain he would forgive me."

"Liar," Sir John yelled.

Humphrey's voice rose. "Are you suggesting that my brother wasn't an honorable man?"

"Of course not!" came the thundering reply, but there was a note of defensiveness in Sir John's voice.

"It seems to me you are," Humphrey said accusingly. "That's what I hear. And my brother was indeed an honorable man, was he not?"

"Aye! Aye!" many in the crowd agreed, glancing at Sir John.

"Yes, my brother was an honorable man. And merciful, too. Sir John, didn't he pardon you for your crimes?" Humphrey asked, and the big man, with the crowd watching, stirred uneasily. "When you stole a Book of Everything, disobeyed Owen's orders, and attacked the barracks in Greendale, where you killed men from families all over Caxton, didn't my brother pardon you?"

Sir John's face was red, and someone from the crowd said, "My cousin was killed in that fight."

"Aye," another voice said. "So was my uncle."

"And my brother." This last was from one of Humphrey's men, but the crowd didn't realize this, and none of them knew that the man had six sisters but no brother.

There was a murmur that came from the crowd, and some of them glared angrily at Sir John, who looked guilty and took a step back.

"But that's not all, is it Sir John?" Here Humphrey pointed his finger accusingly at the big man. "You killed Feste, a man everybody loved."

From Julian's Book, Humphrey had learned all this, and he had also learned that not many people knew how Feste had died. There was a collective gasp from the crowd, and Sir John's face went from red to white. Grief-stricken, he remained silent.

"For shame!" one of Humphrey's men yelled. "To kill the man who juggled, sang, and entertained us."

"For shame!" others in the crowd yelled, and in that instant, Humphrey sensed that the mood had changed from celebratory to belligerent.

"Lock him up!" someone called.

Then it became a chant. "Lock him up! Lock him up!"

Holding up his hand, Humphrey pressed his advantage as the crowd quieted down. "Now, I bet you all thought that in his own way, Sir John was an honorable man. True, he's always been somewhat of an ass." Here the crowd snickered. Sir John's exploits were well known. "But despite his flaws, we never doubted Sir John's loyalty. And there was a time when I respected him. But look at what he did."

"He disobeyed the duke and killed Feste," one of Humphrey's men called out.

"What a rotter!" another of Humphrey's men added.

The word "rotter" swept through the crowd in an ugly wave along with "Lock him up!"

Rhys, Harry, Molly, and Jem looked at each other, and Rhys said, "We've got to get out of here." Molly nodded, but as the four tried to edge back, they found they were hemmed in by Humphrey's men, who all had knives drawn.

"I knew then that it was over," Rhys would say later.

But Humphrey was not finished. "Men can change. They can so easily go from being honorable to dishonorable." He shook his head sadly. "Look what happened to Sir John. And the same thing happened to my brother. I'm sure he never showed it, but over the years, Owen's anger at me grew and grew. When his Book told him I was here, he used it to travel from Camburgh to Caxton, where I was waiting for him in the keep. As soon as I saw him, I bowed to him, asking for forgiveness, and he struck out at me." Humphrey winced, patting an imaginary wound on his shoulder. "He stabbed me in the shoulder as I knelt before him. I really do think he was going for my throat, but he missed."

The crowd listened in shocked, sad silence. Humphrey knew this did not seem like anything that their beloved duke would have done, but then again, he also knew they had never imagined that Sir John had killed Feste. They had been told Feste had died in Greendale, but other than that, the details had been sparse, and those who knew more had said nothing. Most of the people in the crowd were bleary-eyed from all they had had to drink, and Humphrey was confident that their thinking was not as clear as it might have been.

"Luckily, I had a couple of men with me," Humphrey said. "In their rush to protect me, Owen was killed and unfortunately, so was Duchess Celia, accidentally, when she tried to intervene." The crowd gasped. "It pains me to give you this news." Humphrey bowed his head for a moment and brushed away a tear that wasn't entirely false. "I didn't come back for that. But what could we do? We were attacked, and we defended ourselves."

"Rightly so," someone called out.

"Didn't have a choice," called another.

"Self-defense!" called yet another.

"Liar!" Sir John had finally found his voice. "Owen would never do that."

"Were you there?" Humphrey asked. "Did you see what happened?"

"No, but I knew Owen," Sir John replied firmly, and for a moment, the crowd was caught between the two men.

"And I thought I knew you," Humphrey retorted. "I never dreamed you would kill Feste, your best friend, and when I first heard it, I could hardly believe it. But it's true, isn't it?"

"Yes, it's true." Sir John's voice had become small again, but by the way he stood there, looking down at the ground, it was clear that Sir John had admitted that he had killed Feste.

"Take him away," one of Humphrey's men yelled.

"Aye!" someone replied, and then more and more people yelled, "Aye, take him away."

"And his friends, too. We don't want them helping him to escape, the way they did last time."

"Aye, Aye, take them all away. Lock them up!"

Humphrey nodded, and his men grabbed Sir John, Harry, Molly, Rhys, and Jem, who all went without a word.

As the prisoners were being led away, one of Humphrey's men proclaimed, "Long live Duke Humphrey!"

The crowd took up the chant. "Long live Duke Humphrey."

With the bonfire still burning, Humphrey closed his eyes as he listened to the citizens of Caxton cry out, "Long live Duke Humphrey!" And although Humphrey knew he would miss many things about Earth—the technology, the conveniences— it felt good to be back where he belonged, in Caxton, as its duke. This time things would be different, Humphrey decided, as he basked in the glow of the bonfire and the crowd's cheers.

It wouldn't be until the next day, when all the mess had been cleared up and the bodies of Duke Owen and Duchess Celia had been spirited to the tombs below the keep, that Humphrey remembered Julian's Book had told him Owen had two children, a girl and a boy. And both seemed to be gone from the city.

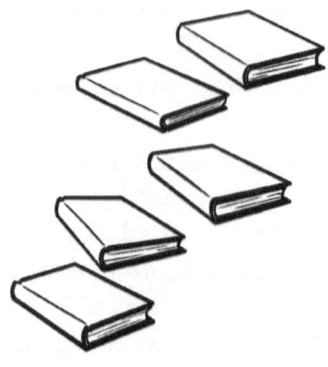

19: To Mortmain

In Julian's parlor, Maya sat quietly, shocked about what Cinnial would be able to do with the green Book and Ariel. Find his way to the Great Library? Maya had never considered this, had never wondered why Cinnial had waited for so long before planning his conquest of the Great Library. But it all made sense now. The way was blocked to him, and only a Book of Everything could show him the path. Cinnial was being lured to the Great Library, and Ariel and the green Book were the bait. In despair, Maya thought, "Sydda never mentioned that part of the plan. And neither did Ariel."

Maya was in a chair by the fireplace, and both her feet and her hands were bound, but not tightly. If Maya had worked at it, she could have slipped from the handkerchiefs—both clean, Julian had assured her—he had used to tie her up.

Hurrying from his bedroom to his parlor, Julian grabbed books and papers and set them on a table not far from his bookcases.

"What in the world do you want to bring back from this miserable planet?" the Book asked impatiently. "Mortmain has everything you could need or want."

"No, it doesn't," Julian insisted, as he tucked some books, given to him by his students, into a large rucksack on the table. Opening one, he stared longingly at the inscription and read aloud, *"To One of the Best Teachers We Have Ever Had.* And look! There are the names of all the students that were in this class."

"You have gotten soft," the Book said witheringly.

"Maybe," Julian replied. "But some of my books are coming with me."

Maya could tell from Julian's stubborn expression that he was not going to give in.

Apparently, the Book realized it, too. "All right, then! Hurry up!"

But Julian did not hurry as he went through his many books and papers, trying to decide what to leave and what to take.

"You can always come back," the Book snapped.

"I can't come back," Julian said in a low voice. "You know I can't. I can fetch Chet and bring him to Earth, but I can't stay here again."

"And why not?" the Book asked, its voice shrill.

"Because it won't be the same with Duke Owen gone. Who knows what will happen to the university and to its library?" Here Julian's voice caught a little. "And to the students. No, I'll never be able to stay here again."

Maya listened carefully. It was clear to her that despite all the plotting and maneuvering, things were not going according to the Book's plan.

"This is all Maya's fault," the Book practically shrieked. "And that old hag who helped her."

"Maya?" Julian asked, stopping with a book in hand. "How is this her fault? Yes, she stabbed me, but Evangeline was the one who gave me the mint."

"And where do you think Evangeline got that mint? It had to be Maya. There are no mints like that on this planet. The old woman is pretty good," the Book admitted. "But not that good. She never could have come up with something to wipe your memory for so long. No, that mint had to come from somewhere else."

Julian stared bemusedly at Maya. "Did you give Evangeline that mint?"

Maya nodded. "I did."

"But where did you get it?"

There seemed no point in lying. "From Mortimer," Maya replied. "At the Great Library."

"I remember Mortimer. He used to lecture me about my temper. 'Julian, you need to learn to control it,' Mortimer would say. 'Or your temper will control you.' The old man was right," Julian ended sadly.

"Enough!" the Book commanded. "Continue with your packing."

Julian stared at the Book, which was open on the table in front of the bookshelves. "You know," he said in a firm voice, "I think you need to rest while I finish packing. As soon as I'm done, I'll open you, and we'll return to Mortmain."

"No!" the Book cried. "Don't shut me!"

Ignoring the Book, Julian closed it with a snap, and there was a welcome silence. "There, isn't that better?" Julian asked.

"Yeah," Maya answered. "How can you stand it? My Books were never like that."

Julian's reply was crisp. "A different person made those Books. I created my Book, and I gave it too much of what was wrong with me. The examiners at the Great Library caught it. So did Sydda. I needed more time before I could make a Book of Everything." Julian shook his head. "But then again, maybe there never would have been enough time."

"I'm sorry," Maya said, seeing Julian's pain and regret.

He gave her a sharp look, and for a moment, Maya saw a flash of the old Julian, but then he shrugged. "It's in the past. It's on the time line. It can't be changed."

"Are you sure?" Maya asked softly.

With a slight frown, Julian regarded her. "I'm pretty sure."

"What about going forward? Not everything is fixed, you know."

Julian opened his mouth, closed it, and then replied, "I have to go back to Cinnial."

"Why?" Maya asked.

Julian sat down in the chair across from her. "I don't know why I should tell you. After all, you're just a kid."

"I'm not a kid," Maya retorted. "I'm fifteen. Almost sixteen."

"A kid," Julian repeated, peering at her. "But you're more than that, aren't you? You've had your eyes peeled. How? Where?"

"By the Toad Queen. On this planet."

"Now you can really see."

"Yes," Maya replied, shaking her head. "Sometimes too much."

"But not everything, of course."

"No one can see everything," Maya responded, thinking of the Toad Queen.

"But you see a lot." Julian rubbed his face, and he looked so tired that again, Maya felt sorry for him. "Oh, why not tell you? Once you're with Cinnial, none of this will matter."

Maya thought, "Maybe it won't, but maybe it will." However, afraid that she would appear too eager to learn about Julian and Cinnial, Maya didn't say anything.

"We met at the Great Library," Julian said with a sigh. "We were both apprentices. Right away, there was a bond between us. It was as though we had been waiting all our lives to be friends with each other. I suppose that doesn't make a lot of sense to you."

Maya shrugged. "It's never happened to me, but that doesn't mean I don't understand."

"It's almost as though we completed each other. When we had been friends for a while, we even finished each other's sentences."

"Was he your boyfriend?" Maya asked in a hesitant voice, not sure if she was getting too personal.

Julian shook his head. "No, it wasn't like that. It was more like finding a long-lost brother, or even a twin. Cinnial is dark, and I am blond. He is deliberate, secretive, controlled, and I am impulsive, thin-skinned, quick to get angry, quick to strike out. It was as though we were half of a broken coin, and when we came together, we were whole."

"That's why he didn't kill you when you messed up on Copernia and killed Alani's family?"

Remembering, Julian shuddered. "I wasn't supposed to kill any of them. Instead, I was supposed to convince Henrem, Alani's father, to accept one of Cinnial's Books and come to our side. Henrem was on the edge about this, but in the end, he refused. He said things that got to me, so first I stabbed him, then the whole family, except Alani, who was away at school. Instead of opening things up for Cinnial and Chaos, the killings solidified the opposition, who, under the guidance of Copernia's Book of Everything, took control. So Cinnial sent me here, indefinitely, to Ilyria, with only my Book to guide me and no other support."

"How long have you been here?" Maya asked.

"A long time," Julian replied. "I was sure Cinnial had forgotten me, but my Book assured me that he hadn't, that I just wasn't ready to go back to Mortmain."

"Are you ready now?"

Julian laughed shortly and without humor. "No. Something happened that none of us planned on. You came, and my memory was taken away."

"You don't have to go back," Maya said urgently, almost forgetting that part of the Great Library's plan was for her to go to Mortmain, to Cinnial, and that Julian was her way of getting there. But right now she wasn't thinking about herself. Instead, her concern was for Ariel and the green Book, which were already inside the rucksack. Then Maya thought about the Great Library. Swallowing, Maya wondered why the plan was to allow Cinnial to find the path to the Great Library.

Julian looked at his Book. "Cinnial and my Book would never forgive me. I would be completely alone."

Maya was beginning to understand. "I have one more question."

"It had better be your last," Julian said, his voice a combination of stern and sad. "We can only put this off for so long."

Maya shuddered as she thought about facing Cinnial. "I know. But what about your Book? Why are you two so close? Is it because you've been together for such a long time?"

Julian nodded. "That's right. At the Great Library, once an apprentice makes a Book, it doesn't stay with him or her. It goes in a special room. No attachment is formed between the maker and the Book. But my Book has been with me since the beginning, for a lot of years. We've formed a bond that's just as tight as the one I have with Cinnial. With my memory gone, I didn't miss my Book. But on Earth, with Humphrey, it must have been hard for my Book."

"You had six happy years without your Book, didn't you?"

"I did. But now I remember, and I can't just pretend that the bond isn't there."

Julian glanced at his Book, and Maya sensed affection mingled with impatience. Then he stood up. "All right. Enough questions. I need to finish packing."

Maya was quiet as Julian chose the books he wanted to take back to Mortmain. She thought of all that Julian had told her, and Maya had the feeling that she had gained valuable information.

When Julian was finished packing, he slid the straps of his rucksack over his shoulders, went over to Maya, and untied her. Then picking up his Book, Julian opened it.

"Are you finally ready?" the Book asked in a sulky voice.

"As ready as I'll ever be," Julian said.

"Pull yourself together!" the Book retorted. "He'll know something is wrong if you don't snap to."

"He'll realize something is wrong, whatever I do. You know that. And it can't be helped." Julian shrugged. "Whatever happens, happens. I've done my part." He put his hand on Maya's shoulder. "Now take us to Mortmain, to Cinnial."

Maya blinked and then blinked again. They were in an office with windows, one huge metal desk with a massive computer screen, and one big, black chair that looked as though it had been designed for someone who played a lot of computer games. Other than that, the room was bare. There were no pictures on the wall, no plants on the window ledge, no clutter on the desk.

Behind the desk sat a man who was so darkly handsome that at first Maya wondered if Julian's Book had made a mistake and had brought them to the wrong person. Then the man looked up, and Maya felt as though she were being held in place by his intense blue eyes. She blocked his gaze the best she could, but Maya could feel him probing, probing. How much did he see? But suddenly the probing stopped as Cinnial considered Julian.

He nodded slightly, and there was even a hint of a smile. "Julian."

Julian nodded back. "Cinnial."

There was silence as the two men gazed at each other, and Maya could feel the strong bond between them, even though they had been apart for so many years. Julian had not been exaggerating when he had stated it was as though they were each half of a broken coin, waiting to come together.

Finally, Cinnial asked, "You've brought me what I want?"

Julian patted the rucksack. "Two of them. In here."

"And the girl?"

"Her name is Maya. She might be useful."

"Useful?" Cinnial briefly regarded Maya but then quickly turned his attention to Julian, as though he couldn't bear to look away from the blond man for very long.

"Maya is quite resourceful," Julian replied. "Don't let her size fool you."

"She is very small." Cinnial frowned at Maya. "Do you have anything to say to me?" His stare was more intense than ever, but holding her head high, Maya didn't look away. "Choose your words carefully," Cinnial warned.

Somehow, despite his good looks, Cinnial reminded Maya of every tyrant she had ever seen on *Dr. Who,* and there wasn't an ounce of humor to leaven this man who took himself far too seriously and probably always had. Even though Maya was so nervous that her hands were sweating, and she had to tuck them in the folds of her dress so they wouldn't distract her, she perversely wanted to pierce Cinnial's inflated self-regard. Maya remembered the fourth Doctor's flippant question when he had been captured by a tyrant with a shrill voice and a monomaniacal desire to control the universe.

"Could I have a cup of tea?" Maya asked.

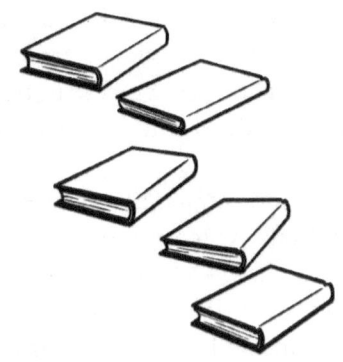

20: Stolen and Retrieved

Whistling, Jeff Perry drove down the road to Hartland, to the library where the blue Book of Everything was being held. Because of the device Jeff was carrying in his pocket, the Book didn't know he was coming for it, and Jeff grinned as he thought about how he would take both David and the Book by surprise.

"And everyone at APO," Jeff said to himself. "Especially my handler." Jeff stopped smiling as he thought about Lillian Rourke, her bright red lips and her disdainful face. Jeff always got the feeling that Lillian had thought APO had made a big mistake when they had given him a device. "But I'll show her." Jeff gripped the wheel. "Then she'll see why they chose me."

However, a part of him realized that he was taking a big risk by going to Hartland without telling Lillian or anyone else at APO what he was doing or indeed where the Book was. There would be no backup, no one to help him if something went wrong. On the other hand, Jeff reasoned, if no one knew, then he wouldn't get in trouble if he failed his mission. No one would be the wiser, and that would be a very good thing.

"But how can I fail?" Jeff thought, grinning at his reflection in the rearview mirror. He had a device that would shield him from the Book's notice, he had a gun, and he had an intense determination, something that had been with him since he was young.

Jeff remembered how exasperated his mother, never a patient woman, would get when he had decided he wanted something—a flashy car, his brother's girlfriend, a new job. "You just don't give up, do you?" she often asked with irritation and a small sliver of admiration.

"I got it from you, Mom," Jeff said aloud in the car, almost feeling sorry for his dull, hapless father, who had seemed to just fade away until one day he died of a heart attack while eating his cornflakes.

In Hartland, Jeff passed many decrepit houses, gray, shabby, and worn, with front yards filled with trash. Jeff wondered how David could work in a town that looked so poor and hopeless. Shaking his head, Jeff thought, "That man has no ambition. He's content to just stay in this stupid little town and work for low wages."

The Hartland Library, a tidy white house with an addition, was closed today, as Jeff knew it would be after checking the hours. However, from his conversation at the Asian Cafe with Charlotte, Jeff had learned that David always came to the library when it was closed so that he could catalog books and get other work done.

Sure enough, there was David's car, a poky white Toyota Corolla, at least ten years old, in the parking lot. The street was quiet, and hardly any cars drove by, but Jeff didn't want to take any chances of his car being spotted at the Hartland Library. Circling around, he parked his own new shiny red Mazda Miata a street away, in front of a lovely yellow Victorian, so well cared for that Jeff had to allow that not every house in Hartland was falling apart.

The library's door was locked, and Jeff knocked. He was smiling his most pleasant smile when David opened the door, but one look at David's grim face told Jeff that things might not go as smoothly as he had hoped.

"Oh, it's you," David said. "What do you want?"

Jeff thought, "Who were you expecting?" Still smiling, Jeff said aloud, "Just stopped by to take a look at your library. I've never been here. May I come in?"

"No," David replied. "I think you'd better go away."

Jeff was wearing a summer suit jacket that covered a holster, and he removed the gun. "You might want to reconsider."

David looked at the gun. "Are you really going to shoot me?"

Jeff was no longer smiling. "That's up to you."

"Is it?"

"Yeah. Shooting people isn't really my thing. But I will shoot you if you don't let me in."

David moved aside. "You're such an asshole."

Jeff stared at David. "Give me the Book. I know it's here."

"How did you find out? Charlotte told you, didn't she?"

Jeff shook his head. "Never mind. Give me the Book, and I won't hurt you."

David's face was red. "You won't hurt me? As if that matters! Instead, you'll be hurting the country, the world, maybe even the universe."

Jeff pointed the gun at David. "Give me the Book. I'm not going to ask again."

"No." David lunged, nearly knocking the gun out of Jeff's hand. With a surprised grunt, Jeff stumbled back, and when he did, he accidentally pulled the trigger. The gun had a silencer, so there was little noise, only David's startled yell as he fell to the floor.

"Why didn't you just give me the Book?" Jeff muttered, sliding the gun back into the holster. He went to David's desk, where the Book of Everything, blue and lovely, sat on top of a pile of papers amid other clutter. Jeff shook his head. "Messy." The Book was so large and heavy that Jeff could barely lift it, but finding a big bag by the desk, Jeff managed to slide the Book into it. He left the library without looking at David, who was still lying on the floor.

Knowing the bag would rip, Jeff carried the Book in his arms, and the weight of the Book made him hunch over as he walked back to his car. The streets were still quiet, and the only person Jeff passed was a beautiful, dark-haired woman wearing a sapphire blue sundress. Despite what had happened, despite what he carried, Jeff smiled at her. He never could resist a pretty woman. She smiled back, holding Jeff's gaze a moment or two longer than most women would have as she considered him. Then she hurried down the street.

"I should have known something was up," Jeff would say later, but his mind had been on David and the Book, which was so heavy that Jeff was sorry he had parked a street away from the library. Hobbling slowly, he finally reached his car. Jeff set the bag on the ground with a thump, reached for his keys, and unlocked the door to his car. Jeff turned to pick up the Book, and there was the beautiful, dark-haired woman, standing right behind him.

Jeff jumped. "Can I help you?"

"You most certainly can." The woman jabbed a needle into his neck. "I'll take that Book."

Jeff felt his legs go slack, and the woman, surprisingly strong, propped him up as she frisked his pockets and found the device and then the gun in its holster.

"What is this?" she asked, taking the device and putting it into her pocketbook. She left the gun in his pocket.

"Mine," Jeff said weakly. "And the Book is, too."

"Not anymore." She helped Jeff into the car, where he collapsed onto the seat. Putting the key in the ignition, she rolled down the window. "You're going to have a nice nap," she said, shutting the door. "And when you wake up, you'll have plenty of time to think about what you're going to tell the police."

"I didn't mean to shoot David," Jeff mumbled.

But the woman heard him. "And yet you did. I'm sure the local papers will love a story about how one librarian shot another. Well, I'd better be off. Sleep tight." Bending over, she gripped the bag by the handles and easily lifted it. The last thing Jeff saw before he lost consciousness was the woman walking away from the car, and her step was as jaunty as if she were carrying a summer dress in the bag rather than the ancient Book of Everything.

Diana Wagner, the beautiful, dark-haired woman, passed Earth's Book of Everything to President Murphy. They were in the library of the house in Bar Harbor, and outside the room came the sound of voices. Diana had traveled by helicopter to and from Hartland and had made such good time that the party still hadn't ended when she came back. Drew shook his head as he thought of all that had ensued in only a few hours. "Isn't that just like Maya?" Drew thought. "Wherever she goes, something unexpected always happens."

"There it is, Mr. President," Diana said, staring at the Book, which was now a normal-sized book. The device was hidden in a bag in her room, far from the library.

"Thank you. Will David live?" Drew asked.

"Yes," Diana replied. "He was hit in the shoulder and was conscious enough to tell me about Jeff Perry. I called an ambulance before going after the Book." She hesitated and then said, "Sir, I know it isn't my place to advise you, but you are the president of the United States. You have a duty to your country."

Drew sat stiff and straight. "I know that. You don't have to tell me."

"I'm sorry, sir, but if anything should happen to you..." Diana didn't finish the sentence.

"I have a very able vice president," Drew said firmly.

"Mr. President! The whole country will be in turmoil if you go and then don't come back."

He rubbed his face. "I know I will be going into a dangerous situation. But my daughter is there, and she is only twelve. I can't leave her on her own."

Sighing, Diana nodded. "Will you tell your wife?"

"No," Drew said, the look on his face softening as he thought about Denise. "With any luck, she won't know I've left, and Viola and I will be back before anyone notices we're gone. I don't want Denise to worry."

Diana leaned forward. "Take me with you. I can help. I can protect you and your daughter. You shouldn't go by yourself."

"If you go, it will change your life."

"My life has already changed now that I know about the Book of Everything, the League of Librarians, and APO. Please, Mr. President, don't go by yourself."

Drew considered her. Despite her beauty, Diana could fight better than most people he knew—certainly better than he could—and Drew had heard how she had taken down men twice her size. With Diana, his odds of rescuing Viola would be greatly improved. On the other hand, if this was an in and out kind of job—go to Caxton, retrieve Viola, and immediately come back—then what did he need Diana for? He'd just have to make another trip to go back and get her. Drew knew that only two people could travel with the Book of Everything at one time.

Drew said, "I'll consult the Book." And even though it had been many, many years since he had used the Book, he remembered what to do. Drew went to the entry labeled "Further Instructions."

The instructions couldn't have been any clearer. "Take Diana. Nothing is ever as simple as you hope it will be."

Drew looked up from the Book. "All right, then. The Book advises me to take you."

Diana nodded curtly. "I'll go get changed and be right back down. And the device?"

"Leave it where it is. We'll deal with it when we get back."

A short while later, Diana had changed from her dress into jeans and a shirt, and she returned to the library where Drew was waiting. Not only was she wearing a holster, but she also carried a jacket with many zippered pockets, and Drew knew that in those pockets there would be various weapons and tools to help them in Caxton. Drew wished that they didn't have to go in modern clothes, but there was no help for it. Diana would never be able to carry the things she needed wearing a dress, and it seemed simpler to have them both wear clothes from their own time.

"You'll probably feel sick," Drew said, remembering how he had felt the first time he had traveled with the Book of Everything, when he and Maya had gone to the Forest of Arden.

"For that matter, I probably will, too. It's been a long time. But it will pass soon." He placed his hand on Diana's arm.

"I'll be all right, sir," Diana replied. "Don't worry about me."

Drew just smiled as he opened the Book of Everything. "I know you can hear me, even though I can't hear you. Take us to wherever my daughter is in Caxton."

Then Drew and Diana disappeared, and the room was empty.

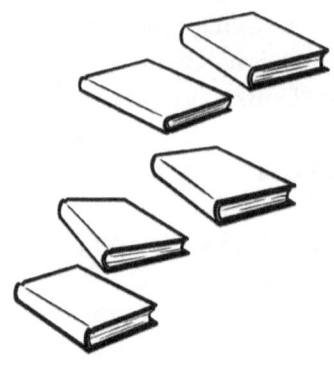

21: Going North

Simon drove the wagon north on the road going out of Caxton. They were in the countryside, and the city was miles behind them. Above them, the night glittered with stars, and a nearly full moon cast a soft glow over everything, on the rolling hills, on the road, and on the farmhouses set back in the fields. Owls hooted in the dark, and the River Caxton, a dark strip in the moonlight, flowed not far from the road.

Even though she had been given something to help with the pain, Evangeline moaned every time they went over a small bump. She was lying not far from Mémère Celine, who was sitting with her back against the wagon's seat, and Rosalind and Sebastian, both asleep, were nestled on either side of her.

Viola glanced back at the little group huddled in the wagon. Turning, she put her hand on Simon's arm. "We need to stop somewhere for Evangeline."

"Aye," Simon replied. "But I'd like to get over the River Caxton. In fact, I'd like to get to the next town. I know a baker who will help us."

"Evangeline will be all right," Mémère Celine said softly from the back. "And the children are sleeping."

"Are you all right?" asked Viola, looking over her shoulder at Mémère.

"I'm fine," came the brisk answer. "Considering that I'm on a different planet, I'm running from God knows who, and I don't have a way to get home."

Nodding, Viola turned to Simon. "What do you think happened to Duchess Celia?" she asked.

"Nothing good," he answered shortly. "Or Maya wouldn't have told us to get out of Caxton with Rosalind and Sebastian."

Viola got a sudden vision of blood and two bodies on the floor, and she felt a little dizzy. "Dead," she said softly. "And Duke Owen, too."

"That means Humphrey's back in charge," Simon replied.

"What about Maya?" Mémère Celine asked.

Viola thought, "For an old woman, she sure has sharp hearing." Aloud, she said, "I think Maya's gone."

"But not dead?" There was a slight rise in Mémère's voice.

"Not dead," Viola answered, and she could feel Mémère staring at her. Somehow, Viola couldn't bring herself to lie to Maya's grandmother. "Maya's not on this planet anymore. She's gone to Cinnial's planet."

"Where the really bad guy lives? The one with the evil books?"

"Yes," Viola answered sadly.

"Why would Maya do that?" Here Mémère's voice caught. "She's just a kid. Isn't there anyone else who could have gone?"

"I don't think so," Viola replied. "Maya is special."

"What do you mean?"

"She sees things that the rest of us can't," Viola answered. "I can see things, too, but not the way she does."

"Oh, mon Dieu," Mémère said. "She's been that way from the time she was small."

Simon turned just a little. "Maya's seen and done things that you can hardly imagine. But every time she's in a scrape, she does all right. I know. I was with her when she helped Duke Owen defeat his brother Humphrey. Maya's small, but she's tough. And she's smart."

"But she's only fifteen," Mémère put in.

However, Viola could tell from the tone of Mémère's voice that Simon had made her feel a little better, which is why Viola didn't mention that, in all likelihood, Maya was in the worst scrape she had ever been in. A dark cloud moved across the moon, and Viola shivered, even though the night was warm. She thought of Cinnial, his Books, and Chaos.

"And how old are you?" Mémère asked Viola. "Fourteen? Fifteen?"

"I'm twelve," Viola answered reluctantly, knowing what Mémère's reaction would be.

"Twelve? That's even worse than fifteen. I thought you were older. Does your father know you're here?"

"I don't think so."

"I can just picture how the president of the United States would react if he knew his daughter was here and was running for her life."

Viola could picture it, too. Most of the time her father was gentle and funny and patient. At night, in the White House, after dinner, he always played cards with her, and whenever she had problems at school, Viola went to him as often as she did to her mother, who was sometimes less sympathetic than Viola thought she should be. But whenever Viola did anything wrong, and her mother was gone, her father would give her that stern look, and then would come the lecture where he laid out the bad thing she had done, the consequences, and what she should do next time. By the time her father was done, Viola, feeling ashamed, would creep to her room and sulk for an hour or so. With her mother, it was different. Instead, there would be the shake of a finger, some sharp words, and then it would be over, with both of them continuing with whatever they had been doing.

"I bet your father wouldn't be too happy with you," Mémère said.

"No, he wouldn't be happy at all," Viola admitted, thinking that Mémère talked just as much as Maya did.

Simon spoke, "Viola didn't come here on purpose. And neither did Maya. Ariel brought them here by mistake."

"Ariel?" Mémère asked.

"Maya's Apprentice Book," Viola answered. "It took us here after we stole Humphrey's Book, and he was trying to get his Book back. Ariel brought you here, too."

"Is that why Maya wanted to go to the president's party? To steal Humphrey's Book?"

Viola shook her head. "No, she wanted to warn Dad about Humphrey. My father didn't realize who Humphrey was. When Dad was in Albion, he never saw him," Viola said, remembering what Maya had told her one night before they had fallen asleep in the bedroom in Rose Cottage. "I think Maya just decided to steal Humphrey's Book when she was at the party."

"Doesn't that sound like Maya," Mémère muttered. "She's always been impulsive. I don't know where she gets it from."

Simon laughed, and Viola joined him. Neither of them had any doubt where Maya had gotten her fiery, impulsive nature. After all, not many grandmothers, wearing pink sandals and a pink top, traveled across the universe at a moment's notice.

"I know, I know," Mémère replied. "She gets that from me. But, oh, I'm worried about her."

"Me, too," Viola said. "I hope Maya's all right."

"Maya will be fine," came a weak voice. It was Evangeline. "You'll see. Cinnial will be sorry that he ever laid eyes on her."

"Rest," Mémère said sternly, but Viola could tell she was pleased. "You didn't lose a lot of blood. But, still."

"I am resting. Here I am, flat on my back in this wagon. I'm no use at all. At least I can put in my own two cents."

"Well, you've done that," Mémère said. "Now go back to sleep."

Evangeline muttered a little but didn't say anymore, and Viola heard a little snore come from the old woman.

Viola turned a little toward Mémère. "I'm glad you're here."

"Belle jeune fille." Mémère's voice was warm. "I really don't know where I am, but I'll help as much as I can. We'll get through this together."

Viola thought, "I really don't know where I am, either." Viola was both thrilled and scared at the same time. This was the most exciting adventure she had ever been on, and she had the feeling that it would get even more exciting as time went by.

On they rode, clattering onto the bridge past the Bridge House, and Viola remembered Hildy's cozy little kitchen and her warm homemade bread. She stared wistfully at it, wishing they could stop for the night and stay in the snug house.

Simon must have sensed what Viola was thinking because he said, "We've got to keep going. We have to get as far away as possible."

"I know," Viola replied.

After they crossed the bridge, they drove past orchards, more fields, and then into the dark woods, where the trees blocked the light of the moon, and shadows crept over the wagon and the horses as they moved steadily north. Bats flew overhead, owls called to each other, and the wagon kept going until the sky began to lighten gradually and then more and more as the shadows receded from the road, moving deep into the woods. Drowsing, Viola leaned against Simon's shoulder, and the sound of birdsong woke her with a start. Embarrassed, Viola pulled away from Simon, but he smiled down at her, and Viola could tell he didn't mind that she had leaned against him as she slept. Viola could also tell that he was drooping with fatigue, and the horses looked tired, too.

"We've got to stop," Viola said. "For you and the horses."

"Not until we get to Oakton," Simon said. "It's not far away, and I know a baker there. His name is Guy. He'll help us, and so will his friend Eben. They helped your father and me when we were hiding from Humphrey's men, and I know we can trust Guy and Eben."

Viola shook her head, trying to imagine her father, at seventeen, in this world with Simon. It gave her a funny feeling to think that there was a hidden side to him that even she hadn't been able to see.

As the sun edged just over the horizon, Mémère woke up, and so did Sebastian, Rosalind, and Evangeline. A smooth head and a little curly head poked over the seat between Viola and Simon.

"Where are we?" Rosalind asked.

"I'm hungry," Sebastian put in, rubbing his eyes.

"We're just outside Oakton," Simon answered. "And soon we'll be visiting with a friend who makes delicious bread. I wager it will be ready when we get there."

"Will there be milk, too?" Sebastian asked.

"Aye," Simon replied. "And butter for the bread."

"Yay!" the children called out, jumping up and down.

"I wish I felt as energetic as they do." With a wince, Evangeline slowly sat up.

"You and me, too," Mémère said. "But we had our turn, didn't we?"

"That we did," Evangeline replied. "But it was so long ago I can hardly remember it."

The two women laughed as Rosalind and Sebastian jiggled between them. Mémère had her hand on Sebastian's back, and Evangeline put hers on Rosalind's back. Both children were held securely.

Guy, slim and dark haired, was up and pulling bread out of his oven, just as Simon had predicted. Simon drove the wagon to the back of the bakery, where flour was delivered, and hearing the clatter of the wheels, Guy came outside. His gaze swept across Simon, Viola, Mémère, Evangeline, and the children. Guy stared longest at Rosalind and Sebastian, at their fine clothes, and small though they were, the way the children stood with confidence in the wagon.

Shaking his head, Guy smiled just a little. "Trouble always seems to follow you, doesn't it?"

But Simon didn't smile back. "Aye."

Guy nodded, and his smile faded. "Come inside. There is warm bread, water for tea, and a jug of milk."

Viola and Simon clambered from the wagon. Simon opened the back, and he and Viola helped the children and Mémère get down. "Oh, I'm stiff," Mémère said, gripping Viola's hand.

Even though Evangeline protested, Simon lifted her from the wagon, carried the tiny woman inside the bakery, and brought her to the backroom, which was like a little parlor with a table, enough chairs for everyone, and a small fireplace with a kettle of boiling water. Gently, Simon settled her in a chair, and Evangeline grimaced, putting a hand to her shoulder.

Guy had followed them into the room, carrying a board with two round loaves of bread, which he set on the table. He pointed to shelves on the wall. "Everything you need is there. Crockery, butter, tea, knives, and there's a jug of milk on the floor. Most days, my wife and children join me, but later in the morning." Guy stared at Mémère's pink shirt, white pants, and sandals, but he didn't say anything.

Viola thought, "She needs different clothes." But Viola didn't say anything either. First, they would have their breakfast and then worry about Mémère's clothes.

Rosalind stepped forward. "Thank you very much." She nudged Sebastian, who was eyeing the bread. Smiling, he turned to face Guy, and there was a dimple in one of Sebastian's cheeks. "Thank you."

"You're most welcome," Guy said, leaning down toward them. "And who might you be?"

"I'm Rosalind, and this is my brother Sebastian."

Guy stood quickly, and his face was serious. "Caxton's Rosalind and Sebastian?"

"Aye," Simon replied. "We'll talk later."

"Lord help us," Guy muttered, leaving the room. "I have to finish baking the rest of my bread. Simon, when you're done, come in and tell me what's going on."

Mémère and Viola helped Rosalind and Sebastian into their chairs, and soon the table was set with plates, butter, knives, big mugs of tea for the adults, and smaller mugs of milk for the children. The room was quiet as bread was eaten and drinks were sipped.

"What good eaters you are," Mémère said as the children finished one piece of bread and asked for another.

Looking around the table, Viola could almost pretend that all was as peaceful here as it had been the day she and Simon had gone to the Bridge House, before Duke Owen and Duchess

Celia had been murdered, before Evangeline had been stabbed, before Maya had gone to Mortmain, before they had had to flee from Caxton. But Viola knew Guy was right. Trouble was following, and Viola was certain that trouble would travel much faster than the wagon had.

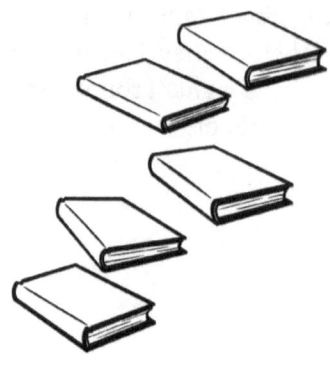

22. Hide and Seek

At first, Simon didn't want to leave Oakton without Evangeline. "You're not staying behind," he said, his fair face flushing until his cheeks were bright red. "You're coming with us."

"No, I am not," Evangeline said firmly. "You can't stay on the road, and I can't go in the woods with you. It will be hard enough with two small children. You don't need an old woman who is hurt slowing you down even more."

Guy had finished baking his bread and was with them. "We should be leaving soon. It's just past sunrise, and not many people are up and about. Not yet. But soon they will be."

He would have said something else, but his five children, used to getting up early to help in the bakery and make bread deliveries, burst into the parlor. Stopping short, they stared at the strangers who were sitting at the table.

The smallest boy, with bright copper hair, asked, "Who are they?"

"Friends," their father answered.

"I've never seen them before." The little boy stared at Rosalind and Sebastian.

"Hush, Ian," said his eldest sister. "Don't be rude."

"I'm not being rude, Becca," Ian protested. "I've just never seen them before."

Becca glanced at her father, at his tense face. "Let's go back to the house so Papa's friends can finish their breakfast."

Becca took Ian's hand, but the little boy turned to Rosalind. "Do you play stickball?"

Rosalind shook her head. "No, but I'd like to."

"Maybe you can come back someday and play with us."

Rosalind smiled. "That would be fun."

"Let's go," Becca said, pulling the reluctant Ian from the room.

"But the bread's all gone. They're done eating," Ian stated.

"Never mind that," said the eldest brother, whose hair was as dark as his father's. "They don't need you here being a pest."

"I'm not a pest, Liam," came Ian's shrill voice as he left the bakery, and the other children laughed as they followed him. "I'm not," Ian insisted.

Smiling, Guy rolled his eyes. "He is a pest."

"But much loved," Evangeline murmured.

"Aye," Guy answered, and his smile broadened.

Evangeline nodded. "Where were we?" She glanced at Simon's stubborn face. "Oh, yes. I remember. My mind is made up. I'm staying behind."

"She can stay at the farmhouse with Eben." Guy's voice was firm. "Eben has a big house with lots of rooms, and it's outside town. She can stay hidden until she heals."

"I don't like it." Simon frowned, but Viola could tell he was going to give in. Because Evangeline was right. There was no way she could go into the woods with them, on the back trail that led from Oakton's forest to Greendale and the Forest of Arden. In fact, Viola wondered how Rosalind and Sebastian would be able to travel for days in the woods, and she was also doubtful about Mémère. Viola thought, "She looks pretty old."

"We need to go now," Guy put it. "We can continue this conversation at Eben's. And the horses need tending, too."

Simon sighed. "Aye, it's time to go."

As Guy lifted the children into the wagon, he said, "Let's play hide and seek." Simon helped Evangeline and Mémère into the back, and he and Viola climbed in, too. Guy covered them all with blankets.

"Now be quiet," Guy said, patting the children's little heads before pulling the blankets over their faces. "We don't want anyone to find you."

"We'll be quiet," Rosalind promised. "Won't we, Sebastian?"

"Yes," the little boy answered. "We play hide and seek all the time, and nobody ever finds me unless I want them to. But we've never hid from a whole village."

"Now's your chance," Guy said, climbing onto the driver's seat. "Let's go."

It was only a mile to Eben's farmhouse, but it was the longest mile that Viola had ever ridden. There was just barely room for all of them, and her back was wedged against the wagon's side. Mémère's back was against Viola's face, and Sebastian was snuggled up against Mémère, who stroked the little boy's cheek with her free hand.

"Oh, you're a sweet little bonhomme," Mémère whispered.

"S-h-h-h," Sebastian whispered back. "We're hiding."

Smiling, Mémère nodded, continuing to stroke his cheek.

Hot and stuffy under the stiff blankets, crowded against Mémère, Viola was more afraid than she had been since leaving Caxton. Somehow, last night's journey had seemed dreamlike, and she had been able to sense that no one from Caxton had missed the children yet. But this morning was different. Viola knew without a doubt that the children's absence had been noticed, and even though she was only twelve, Viola had read enough to know what happened to children like Rosalind and Sebastian when their parents were murdered by a power-hungry relative. "Humphrey will send someone after them," Viola thought, shivering.

"Morning!" Viola heard Guy call to someone passing by. She stiffened, straining to hear what was being said. Mémère nodded reassuringly at Sebastian, and Simon, who was between the little boy and his sister, did the same at Rosalind. The children nodded back but didn't say anything.

"Morning!" a voice called back. "Is that a new wagon you have?"

"Nay," Guy answered. "It's Eben's. I borrowed it, and now I'm returning it."

"Never seen it before. Never seen those horses, either."

Closing her eyes, crossing her fingers, Viola waited tensely.

"Eben just got the wagon and the horses the other day," came Guy's easy reply. "He's trying to decide if he needs a bigger wagon to deliver milk. He'd be able to haul more milk and make deliveries to some of the hamlets around Oakton. With a growing family, he could use the extra money. But even if Eben doesn't expand his milk route, the wagon will come in handy for hauling bigger things around his farm."

"Aye, that it will," the man replied, and Viola could tell he wasn't in the least suspicious about what was in the wagon. The sides and the back were so high that it was impossible to see into the wagon's bed when standing on the road.

"Why would he be suspicious?" Guy would ask later. "I'm a baker, not a smuggler. Everyone in town knows that."

Viola didn't breathe normally until goodbyes had been said and the wagon was moving again. Finally, Guy said, "You can take the blankets off, but stay down until I get to the barn."

With sighs of relief, Viola, Mémère, Simon, and Evangeline rolled back the blankets. Sebastian's face was sweaty, and the curls were stuck tight to his little head. Still, he smiled, and there was that dimple. "That was fun," he said. "Nobody found us."

"Oh, you were such a good boy," Mémère replied, and Sebastian smiled even more. "And Rosalind, what a good girl you were."

"When can we get up?" Rosalind asked.

"Pretty soon. We're almost there."

Eben and some of his children were in the barn milking when Guy drove the wagon around to the open door in the back. Guy said, "Simon, you come with me. The rest of you stay here, but you can sit up."

They all sat up, and Viola heard low voices, but she couldn't make out what was being said. It didn't matter. Viola knew that Guy and Simon were explaining the situation to Eben and his children.

"Can so many people keep a secret?" Mémère asked.

"I hope so," Viola answered.

"Me, too," Evangeline said. The healer looked weary, but her face was not flushed, and it was clear she didn't have a fever.

In a little while, Guy, Simon, and Eben came back to the wagon. Simon put the back down, and Eben, a large man with blond hair, peered in. "Well, there they are." He turned to Guy and Simon. "Reminds me of old times." Eben's face was calm, but Viola could tell he was worried.

Guy ran a hand through his dark hair. "Aye, Humphrey's back in charge."

"Just like the bad old days," Evangeline said. "But we'll get through it. I know we will."

"Who is Humphrey?" Rosalind asked in her crisp voice.

"He is a man who always wants what he doesn't have," Evangeline answered. "But never mind about him. I bet this barn has a hayloft, and there might even be some kittens."

"Kittens?!" Rosalind and Sebastian called out together.

Everyone smiled, and Eben said, "Aye, kittens. Let's get you out of this wagon so you can go see them. There are two batches up there, and those kittens are some frisky."

Soon, Rosalind, Sebastian, and Eben's two youngest children were running, laughing, and chasing kittens in the hayloft. They made so much noise that it sounded as though there were a troop of children rather than just four. But Viola knew that it didn't matter how much noise they made in Eben's barn.

"It's good for them to play," said Mémère, smiling.

They were standing in a circle in the barn as they discussed what the next plans would be. To Viola's astonishment and pleasure, she had been allowed, without question, to join the circle. Viola had been half-expecting to be told to go into the loft with the children, but instead, Eben and Guy had made room for her as if she belonged, along with Simon, with the adults. Evangeline, seeing Viola's beaming face, winked at her. Viola winked back.

"You can take the horses," Eben said to Simon, Viola, and Mémère. "I don't want anyone finding out they are from Duke Owen's stables. The wagon's just a wagon. I'll store it here, but I won't use it for going into town."

"Dudley Greenwald saw me with the wagon this morning. I told him it was yours, and I don't think he thought anything about it," Guy said.

Eben shrugged. "Can't be helped. But out of sight, out of mind. I hope. And if he asks about the horses, I will tell him I sold them."

Guy nodded. "The horses will be a help traveling to the Forest of Arden. Sebastian and Rosalind can ride when they get tired. The horses can also carry supplies." He looked at Mémère. "Can you ride?"

"No," she answered. "But if a three-year-old and a five-year-old can stay on a horse, then so can I."

Guy grinned but then studied the pink top, the white slacks, and the pink sandals. "Your clothes."

"I know," Mémère said. "I stick out here like a sore thumb."

"My wife is about your size," Eben replied, regarding her.

"Can she spare the clothes?" Mémère asked.

Eben nodded. "She can. She will."

Evangeline patted the pouch she had brought with her from Caxton. "Don't you worry about that. I always keep some coins in my pouch. Eben's wife will get material for new clothes."

Eben smiled. "Thank you."

Evangeline waved her hand. "Oh, pish! The important thing is to make sure those children are safe."

Everyone nodded, and Guy said, "There's a trail through the woods from here to Greendale and the Forest of Arden. It should be fairly easy to follow. But if you get lost, go east toward the rising sun. If you travel at night, follow the North Star."

"Aye," Simon said. "I should be able to find Greendale."

"The woods can be tricky," Eben warned.

"I know," Simon replied. "But I know the woods, too. I've been in Caxton for six years, but I haven't forgotten."

"I'll take you to the hideout," Guy continued. "With Duke Owen, there was no need for a hideout, but we kept it for a hunting lodge, so it's still in good shape. There are even some supplies there. I'll show you where the path starts and go with you for a while. Wish I could go with you all the way to the Forest of Arden. I could leave my wife and children in charge, but it would look suspicious if I suddenly left for a few days this time of year, when we don't normally stay at the hunting lodge. We do that in the fall. But I'll be sure to come back with a few rabbits so nobody will wonder where I've been all day. We get rabbits year round, and Eben lets me hunt on his land anytime I want."

"I'll manage just fine," Simon replied.

"Viola and I will be there to help," Mémère said stoutly.

Viola nodded as she thought about going into the woods with Simon, Mémère, and the children to the Forest of Arden. Maya had told Viola all about the Forest of Arden and the lodge, where she and her father had stayed with Duke Owen. On their last night at Rose Cottage, Maya had told her about the giant Toad Queen who had peeled Maya's eyes. Viola shuddered a little, thinking of the pain and thinking about how really seeing had changed Maya's life.

"I hope it's worth it," Viola thought, shivering as she imagined the dark and the chaos that Maya must be facing.

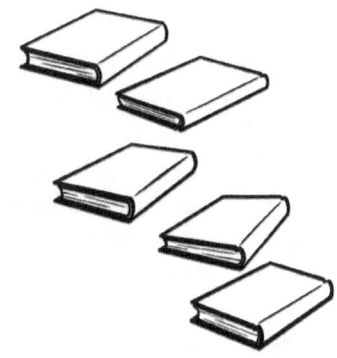

23: In Pursuit

Chet watched Humphrey as he paced back and forth in what had been Duke Owen's office but was now his. As he paced, Humphrey grew angrier and angrier, and Chet thought, "This one needs to learn how to control his temper. In fact, he should have learned a long time ago." But he said nothing.

"Why wasn't I told sooner?" Humphrey asked. "Didn't you know that Owen had two children?"

"There was a lot going on last night," Chet replied. "None of us were thinking about the children."

"And what about their nanny? We can't find her either. Where is she?"

"With the children?" Chet suggested. The tracker was wrong about this and would learn later that the nanny had been with a young man in town the night before, and that as soon as she had heard about Duke Owen's and Duchess Celia's death, she had left Caxton.

Taking a deep breath, Humphrey unclenched his fists, and Chet could see that he was calming down. "Maybe. But when did they leave? And where did they go?"

"Somebody must have warned the nanny," Chet said.

"Like who?"

"Maya. We caught her outside this office, snooping on us. Before she started spying on us, Maya must have warned the nanny."

"That means..." Humphrey stopped.

"Right. At least to some degree, Maya knew what was going on. The children and their nanny must have left before you took over. Otherwise, one of your men would have seen them last night in the crowd."

With a thump, Humphrey sat down behind the desk, and Chet could see that all the anger was gone from him. "That Maya!" Humphrey said. "She's quite the one, isn't she?"

For the first time there was a flush on his face, and Chet retorted, "She's a menace, that's what she is. To everyone's plans, including Cinnial's." He thought about Maya's blonde curls and where he had seen her before, but Chet didn't mention this to Humphrey.

Humphrey sat up straight. "Right now, there's nothing we can do to warn anyone. We don't have a Book. We'll just have to hope that Maya, formidable though she might be, will be no match for Cinnial. After all, she's just a kid."

Chet nodded. He was uneasy, but he knew that Humphrey was right. There was nothing they could do to warn Julian or Cinnial, and it was just a waste of energy worrying about it. Long ago, Chet had learned that there was no point in brooding about things that were out of his control.

"I wonder if Maya warned anyone else," Chet said.

"Like who?"

"The first time I saw her, she was with a red-haired boy and a young girl with dark hair."

Humphrey shook his head. "I don't know who the boy is, but I'm guessing the girl is Viola Murphy, President Drew Murphy's daughter."

Chet looked startled. "Drew Murphy? He was a senator when I left."

"While you were gone, he became President Drew Murphy. And that dark-haired girl you saw must be his daughter. She's here with Maya. Julian confirmed it when he came to get me on Earth. President Murphy knows this, too. He was with me when Julian used his Book to bring me back to Caxton."

Chet thought, "There's a longer story here." But aloud he said, "We need to find out who the red-haired boy is. He might know something useful."

A little while later, they had the answer. From one of Humphrey's men, Chet and Humphrey learned that the boy was Simon Forster, who took care of the horses in the castle's stable, and that he lived with Sir John at Rose Cottage.

"Simon Forster, of course," Humphrey said. "Julian's Book told me about Simon and how he helped President Murphy when he was in Albion. The boy came from Greendale but stayed in Caxton when Owen took over. I wonder if Simon is at Rose Cottage now."

"Tell me where Rose Cottage is, and I'll find out," Chet replied.

Twenty minutes later, Chet knocked on the green door at Rose Cottage. All around the door and twined around the windows in front, roses bloomed in a jumble of colors—white, yellow, and red. Their sweet smell made Chet feel sick to his stomach. He hated all flowers, but roses were the worst, flowers of love for sentimental fools. Bees buzzed around the blossoms, and although Chet stood impassively, waiting for someone to answer the door, his skin crawled a little as he listened to the bees. Chet wasn't afraid of them, but they made him nervous. All that pollinating, all that honey, all that life. It was too much for him.

An older woman answered the door, and her face looked tired and worn. "What do you want?" she asked. "My master's not here."

"I know where your master is," Chet answered shortly. "Are you the housekeeper?"

Her voice was just as curt as Chet's. "Aye, I'm Mrs. Hall."

"Is Simon here?"

Mrs. Hall stared directly at Chet. "He's gone."

"Do you know where he is?"

"No."

"Was Viola, a dark-haired girl, staying here, too, along with Maya, a girl with blonde curly hair?"

"Aye, but they're both gone, too."

The woman began to close the door, but Chet stopped it with his foot. "Did Viola go with Simon last night? And when did they leave?" He grabbed her arm and squeezed hard. "Tell me what you know, or you'll be sorry. Duke Humphrey sent me here."

The woman flinched but didn't look away. "Duke Humphrey," she said, as though there were something unpleasant in her mouth. "Why does he want to know?"

Chet squeezed harder. "That is none of your business."

"I don't know much," the woman said, gasping a little. "All I know is that late last night, Simon stopped by with a wagon. I had come home early from the bonfire and went to bed. But I'm a light sleeper, and I woke up when he came in. I got up to see what was going on, and he left with two women." Mrs. Hall shook her head. "One of them was wearing trousers, and Simon was carrying the other one. She seemed to be hurt."

"Trousers?" Chet thought. He squeezed harder still. "I could break your arm, and nobody except for you would care. Do you know who Simon was carrying?"

"Evangeline," Mrs. Hall gasped. "But I don't know who the other one was. And, yes, Viola was in the wagon. But Maya wasn't."

Chet squeezed even harder. "Anyone else?"

"Two children!" Mrs. Hall cried out, no longer looking at Chet.

Nodding, Chet dropped her arm, which was bruised but not broken. Without saying a word, he turned to leave, pausing to smash a bee that had landed on the front stoop. As he ground the bee with his foot, he heard Mrs. Hall mutter, "You won't catch them."

Swiveling around, Chet smiled at her, patted his knife, and left.

Twenty minutes later he was back at the keep, in Humphrey's office. "There was no mention of the nanny. But the housekeeper told me that two kids were with Viola and Simon. Evangeline was with them, too. There was another woman wearing trousers. Probably not the nanny, but let's not worry about either of them right now. Let me go after the kids. They're the ones you're looking for. I'm sure of it."

"But you don't know Caxton." Humphrey was drinking a mug of ale. "Do you want a mug?"

"I don't drink," Chet said stiffly, standing by Humphrey's desk.

"You're a weird one," Humphrey remarked casually, and Chet couldn't argue with this. "But we get on well together. Really, better than Julian and I did."

Chet thought, "He geared you up. I calm you down."

Humphrey asked, "Why do you want to go after the children?"

"I'm a tracker. That's what I do. If you give me a map, I'll be all right."

"Can you ride?"

"I grew up on a farm," Chet answered. "I can ride."

"Which way would they have gone?" Humphrey mused. "In or out of Caxton?"

Chet asked, "Is there a place in the duchy where they could go where they would be safe?"

Humphrey's face was grim. "Oh, yes. And because he's from Greendale, Simon would know all about the Forest of Arden."

"What about it?" Chet asked.

"It's not like other forests," Humphrey answered. "Its trees are knowing, cunning. Only people they like are allowed into the forest."

"I have no idea what you're talking about," Chet said. "What can trees do?"

"I don't really understand it either," Humphrey admitted. "All I know is that when I was duke and Owen was hiding in the forest, me and my men could never find him, no matter how hard we looked. We'd go in, wander around for about an hour, and then be right back where we started, at the edge of the forest."

"That's creepy," Chet said, twitching a little. Even as a child, he had never liked living in the country. As soon as he was old enough, Chet had left, making his way to New York City, and he never went to Central Park unless it was absolutely necessary.

Humphrey leaned forward. "If Simon brings Rosalind and Sebastian to the forest, we'll never be able to find them."

"Then I'll have to get them before they reach the Forest of Arden." Chet smiled as he pictured the chase. "It shouldn't be too hard to catch up with a group that has two kids and an old woman who's hurt."

"Do you want to take anyone with you?"

"No," Chet answered. "I travel better by myself. What do you want me to do when I find the kids?"

Humphrey was silent for a moment, and Chet could tell he was struggling with this decision. Finally, he said, "Take care of them."

Chet nodded. "All right."

A half an hour later, Chet was on a large gray gelding, and he rode into town, which was still quiet from all that had happened the night before. Few people were out and about, and this suited Chet just fine. He found wagon tracks in front of Rose Cottage and followed them on the road that led out of town and went north. Chet came to a place where the dusty road split in three, and he studied each road carefully. "Lucky it didn't rain last night," Chet thought. "And lucky not many people are out."

The wagon's tracks were clear, going on the road to the far left, and Chet followed the road that went through open fields, bright under the morning's sun. The River Caxton flowed nearby, and Chet saw a bird of prey swoop down into the river. Catching a fish, the bird gave a shrill cry and flew up with the fish twitching in its talons. Smiling, Chet urged his horse into a trot.

As the day wore on, people, with eyes bloodshot from drinking too much ale, came out to work in the fields, and wagons filled with hay rolled past Chet. But it didn't matter. Chet had carefully studied the map, and he knew the wagon was heading toward Oakton, where it must have stopped. Chet reasoned that the children and the old woman would need to rest, as would the horses. From time to time, he puzzled about the woman in the trousers, but Chet couldn't figure out who she might be, and he gave up thinking about her. He would find out soon enough. As for the nanny, she had obviously deserted the children. "Out of the picture," Chet thought.

Chet stopped once to let the horse nibble on grass and drink water from a trough by a small roadside tavern while he ate a hard roll and some sausage. As Chet sat on the ground not far from the horse, he again thought wistfully about a cold Diet Dr. Pepper and Vienna Sausages, so little, so moist, so easy to chew. "Not like this tough thing," Chet thought, as he took another bite of the sausage.

Then Chet was back on the gray horse, and by late afternoon, they were in Oakton. By this time, many wagons had gone up and down the main street, and Chet dismounted, studying the tracks. After tying the horse to a hitching post outside Oakton's general store, Chet walked up the street, studying the dusty road as it left town, but there were too many tracks for him to tell if a set belonged to the wagon he was following. Were Simon, Viola, and the children here in town? Or had they moved on, heading toward Greendale, which was two days away? Chet came to a place where a small lane split from the main street, to curve behind the shops on the left.

"For deliveries," Chet thought. There were several sets of tracks, and Chet decided to follow them.

Outside the baker's shop, some children—three boys and two girls—were playing a game that looked something like stickball. "Damned waste of time," Chet thought. "They should be working." The children's clothes, dusty with flour, indicated that they had been working, but Chet disapproved of games of any kind. Nevertheless, Chet made his face as pleasant as he could, and while he didn't exactly smile, his normally grim expression was smoothed into a neutral look.

"You need more players for your teams," Chet said.

The children stopped playing to consider him. The eldest child, a slim boy with hair so dark it was almost black, said,

"Aye, the others are all working right now, but pretty soon we'll be meeting on the green for a proper game. We're just practicing before we get together."

The youngest child, a boy with bright copper hair, put in, "There were two children here this morning, but they left."

A girl who was obviously the eldest sister nudged the small boy's arm, and the rest of his siblings frowned at him. Ignoring them, the child continued in a rush, "The boy was too little, even smaller than me. But the girl could have played."

"Shut up, Ian," the eldest brother said, and Chet caught a note of warning in his voice.

"Make me, Liam." Ian stuck out his tongue at his brother. As Liam moved toward Ian, the little boy stuck out his tongue again and then darted into the bakery. Liam didn't follow him.

Chet nodded at the four remaining children, and as he left there was something like a smile on the tracker's face. Two small children had been at the bakery in the morning. However, they were no longer there.

"Could have been village children," Chet thought. "But if they had been, why did Liam want Ian to shut up?" Chet's tracking instincts were seldom wrong, and they told him that the two children, a girl and a boy, were Rosalind and Sebastian.

"Where did they go?" Chet asked himself as he made his way to where his horse was tethered. "Back on the road toward Greendale?"

That was the most logical choice. After all, there were two small children and an old lady who was injured. Why would they leave the road? "Because Simon knows that Duke Humphrey will send someone after them. He doesn't know it's me, but he knows that Rosalind and Sebastian are in danger. They might ditch the old lady and take to the woods." From Humphrey, Chet had learned that before coming to Caxton, Simon had been good in the woods and knew how to hunt and fish. Julian's Book had told Humphrey many things about Simon, and fortunately, Humphrey had remembered them.

"The Book knew it might be important," Chet thought.

Riding out of town, Chet glanced at the village green to his right, and this was no doubt where the children played a "proper game," as Liam had put it. Chet went up a hill, and there, on the left, was a long driveway leading to a large white farmhouse with an attached shed and barn. Chet stopped to consider the farmhouse, the broad sweep of field behind the house, and the dark green forest on the far edge of the field. In the field leading to the woods Chet could see a path, and on that path was a man walking toward the farmhouse. As the man got closer, Chet could see that he had hair so dark it was almost black and that he was slight and quick.

"Just like Liam," Chet thought, considering the path. Smiling grimly, the tracker nodded and rode his horse to the other side of the road, behind some bushes, where he wouldn't be seen but could keep watch. Tonight, the moon would be bright enough for Chet to follow the path, but the night would be dark enough to provide cover for him and the horse.

"Tonight," Chet thought, dismounting the horse and settling down to wait. "Tonight."

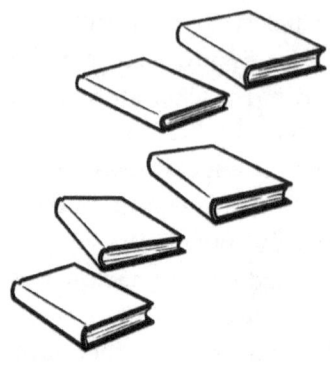

24: Into Deeper Woods

While Simon slept for a few hours at the hunting lodge, Guy, Sebastian, Rosalind, Mémère, and Viola went to a nearby stream. While the children and Viola splashed joyously in the water, Guy went upstream and did some fishing, using one of the poles from the hunting lodge. Mémère sat in the cool green of the woods on the bank. Nearby, in a small fenced-in pasture, the horses grazed, their tails swishing.

From time to time, Viola stopped splashing to glance at Mémère, who didn't look like Mémère anymore. Gone were the pink sandals, the pink top, and the white pants. Instead, Mémère wore a modest brown dress, a white cap, and sensible black boots with laces.

"I feel like I just stepped out of a book about the olden days," Mémère had said after changing into the clothes.

"I know," Viola had replied, smoothing the skirt of her yellow dress. "I felt the same way, at first. Now it seems normal."

Mémère had shaken her head. "I don't know if this will ever seem normal, but at least I don't stick out so much now."

Mémère had insisted on tucking her shirt, slacks, and sandals into one of the packs that went on the horses. "I'll want the clothes when I go back," she had said. "And those sandals are brand new."

While the children played and Mémère rested, Guy caught six fish. After cleaning them, he sat beside Mémère on the bank. Viola joined them, but Rosalind and Sebastian stayed in the water to flip over small rocks and look for crayfish.

Guy was the first to speak. "You're both from Andy's world?"

Mémère nodded. "You mean Drew Murphy, I suppose. Yes, we are."

"And I'm Andy's daughter," Viola said softly.

Guy frowned. "It doesn't seem possible that Andy would have a daughter as old as you are. The last time I saw Andy, he couldn't have been more than seventeen, and that was about six years ago."

Mémère stared thoughtfully at him. "You know about Books of Everything?"

"A little," Guy answered.

Mémère laughed. "Me, too."

Viola ran a hand over some soft moss that grew next to where she sat. "The Books can travel through time and space. What was six years for you was about thirty years for my father."

"Plenty of time to have a daughter who's twelve," Mémère said.

"I don't understand how books can travel through time and space. But here you two are." Guy squinted at Rosalind and Sebastian, who had just found a crayfish and were squealing with excitement. "And here we are. With Humphrey in charge again."

"We can't let him get Rosalind and Sebastian," Viola said, and there was a firm, resolved expression on her face.

Mémère patted Viola's shoulder. "You look just like your father."

Guy said, "That she does. I remember how determined he was the first time he came to my bakery. He and Simon had been in the woods for quite a few days, and let me tell you, they were more than a little dirty."

"Why did they come to you?" Viola asked.

"They were hungry. They wanted bread. Simon knows how to hunt and fish. He kept them fed. But there's nothing like bread."

"Especially good bread like yours," Mémère replied.

Guy smiled. "My father was a baker, and his father before him. And I think that Liam, my oldest son, will be a baker, too. He's got a feel for the dough." Hesitating, he looked at Mémère. "Are you sure you want to go on to the Forest of Arden? You could come back with me and stay with Evangeline at Eben's place."

Mémère answered firmly, "I'll miss Evangeline, but I belong with Simon, Viola, and the children. I'm old, but I'm in pretty good shape. And I can help. I know I can."

Viola nodded. "She belongs with us. If someone gets hurt, Mémère will know what to do, just like Evangeline."

Guy nodded back. "All right. I wanted to be sure. The woods can be pretty tough. And if you've never ridden before, you might not feel so good by the end of the day."

"I'll be fine," Mémère said. "My first aid kit will be coming with me. I have some ointment in there I can use if I need to."

Guy stood. "We'd better get back to the lodge and fry these fish so that you can be on your way. It's midsummer, and it will be light out for quite a while. You should be able to put in some miles before the sun sets. Maybe even get to Beaver Pond."

Mémère and Viola shepherded a reluctant Rosalind and Sebastian from the stream, dried them with a blanket they had brought, and followed Guy back to the lodge. Soon, the fish were frying in pans over a small fire in the big hearth, and bread was cut up in large slices to go with the crispy fish. Simon, who had been sleeping in one of the beds in the huge loft overhead, came down to join them.

"Those fish smell good," Simon said, sitting at a big round table with Viola and the children.

Mémère, who was helping Guy fry the fish, replied, "Nothing better than fish rolled in a little cornmeal and fried in fat. My husband, Roland, goes fishing with his friends. I've cooked fish like this many times."

Viola thought, "Mémère sure knows how to do a lot of things. I don't think Mom or Dad would know how to cook fish like that."

After a lively lunch where Sebastian, with Rosalind's help, explained the ins and outs of hunting for crayfish, they were back in the woods on a trail that was faint but visible.

"This is probably the best it's going to be," Guy warned. "Eben and me and friends from the village use this trail quite a bit. It will take you all the way to Beaver Pond. The trail will pick up across the pond. It will be fainter, but there are slashes on the trees to mark the trail. I've heard that it goes all the way to Greendale, but I've never followed the trail that far. If you do get lost, follow the rising sun." He gave Simon a compass. "And go north. You'll eventually get to Greendale and the Forest of Arden."

Guy traveled with them for about an hour. Rosalind and Sebastian had walked for a while, but they had soon gotten tired and were on one of the horses, a dark brown mare named Treacle.

Mémère, however, had walked along with Simon, Viola, and Guy. "I'll only ride if I really need to," she had said, and so far, Mémère had had no problem keeping pace on foot.

Finally, Guy stopped. "I've got to be heading back." He looked up at Sebastian and Rosalind, who both smiled down at him. "I wish I could come all the way with you to Greendale. You could use the help."

"Aye," Simon said. "But it's best you get back. We don't want anybody to be suspicious."

Guy shook his head. "By now, the word must be out in Oakton about what happened last night in Caxton. I'm sure pigeons have been sent to all the towns."

"No doubt," Simon replied.

"We'll be fine," Mémère added firmly.

"You'll be in our thoughts." Guy looked as though he would have liked to have said more, but instead, he grabbed Simon's hand and shook it hard. Hesitating just a little, Guy patted Mémère's shoulder and then Viola's. Finally, he tweaked

Rosalind's and Sebastian's feet. "You two behave. You do what you're told."

"I will," Rosalind said. "And I'll be sure that Sebastian minds his manners. Sometimes he forgets."

"Do not!" Sebastian protested, squirming around to glare at Rosalind.

"Do, too!" Rosalind retorted.

"None of that now," Mémère said in a stern voice. "You were good in the wagon. Now be good on the horse."

"Maybe Sebastian would like to ride on his own horse," Viola suggested, sensing that there would be pinches, pulled hair, and tears if the two stayed together much longer.

"Good idea," Simon said, helping down the little boy, who looked eager to get away from his bossy sister.

Laughing, Guy left with a wave of the hand. Sebastian now rode on Raisin, a blue roan, and for a while nobody said anything, not even the children. Viola knew they all missed Guy.

"Guy reminds me of my brother when he was young," Mémère finally said. "Always knew what to do, no matter the situation."

"You seem pretty handy, too," Simon stated.

"I had to learn." Mémère laughed. "I come from a small city, the same one that Viola's father came from."

Simon grinned. "Andy didn't know much about the woods."

"But he knows a lot of other things," Viola replied loyally.

"Of course he does," Mémère put in quickly. "It's no small thing to be president of the United States."

"I meant no disrespect," Simon said. "I helped Andy, but he helped me, too. Without him..." Simon didn't finish the sentence.

Viola got a flash of the lost, angry boy that Simon had been and how her father had shown Simon how to be brave. In a daze from the vision, Viola nodded at Simon to let him know that she understood. Viola had realized for a while that her ability to see things was stronger here than it was on Earth. It was almost as if there was a current in Caxton that was missing on Earth, and because of that current, Viola's perceptions were sharper than they ever had been. Viola knew it was a help to be able to sense things the way she did, but it seemed like a burden, too. "It must be hard for Maya," Viola thought. "Her vision is even stronger than mine is."

But Viola didn't mention this to Mémère or Simon. Instead, she asked Mémère, "Where did you learn to do so many things?"

"When my daughter Lily was three, we moved to a large farmhouse in East Vassalboro, about ten miles from where Roland and I grew up. Roland wanted a big, big garden. He just had an urge to grow things. I don't know where he got that from, growing up in the center of Waterville. But he had it, and with a big garden comes lots and lots of food. I had to learn how to can vegetables and make jelly and all sorts of things."

"And fry fish," Viola added.

Mémère laughed. "And fry fish. As long as Roland cleaned them, which he did." Mémère stopped talking, and she looked serious as well as a little sad.

"We'll get back to Earth," Viola said. "I know we will." She might have added, "It might take a while." But she didn't. Viola wanted to make Mémère feel better, not make her worry.

Mémère replied quickly, "Of course we will." She glanced at the two horses with their young riders. "In the meantime, we have a mission."

Rosalind, who had been following the exchange, asked, "What mission?"

"To take you to a special forest," Mémère answered.

"One where your father used to live," Simon added.

"Won't that be fun?" Viola asked.

Rosalind nodded. "But I miss Mama and Papa. And Nanny. Will they be coming, too?"

Mémère patted Rosalind's leg. "No, just us, petite bonne femme."

"When will we go back home?" Rosalind asked.

Mémère shook her head. "I don't know."

Mémère's voice was so calm, so matter-of-fact, that the little girl accepted the answer without a fuss. Rosalind's small back was straight as she rode Treacle, and she held the reins as though she knew how to ride.

"Have you given her riding lessons?" Viola asked.

"Aye," Simon answered. "I was starting to teach Sebastian, too. On ponies, of course. I didn't know it would come in handy."

"No," Mémère said, "I don't suppose you did. How could any of us have pictured this?"

For the rest of the afternoon, the progress was slow. They had to stop many times for the children, who sometimes wanted to walk and sometimes wanted to ride. The path became narrow, and they had to walk in single file, with Simon leading Treacle and Rosalind, if she was riding, and Viola leading Raisin and Sebastian, when he wasn't scampering beside them. Mémère brought up the rear, and Viola frequently glanced back, to see how the older woman was doing. In her black boots, Mémère marched gamely on, but Viola could tell by the droop of her mouth and shoulders that Mémère was getting tired.

"How long do you think it will be until we get to Beaver Pond?" Viola asked.

"Not long," Simon replied. "Guy said it wasn't too far away."

"Good," Mémère said. "My feet are killing me in these boots. When we stop, out come my sandals."

Viola thought, "Tomorrow you're riding. Either Treacle or Raisin can hold you and one of the kids."

When the woods were full of shadows, but it was still light enough to see, when a little bird with a lilting voice began to sing, they reached Beaver Pond, cut in two by a large beaver dam. Beaver Pond was small enough to see across but large enough to be able to swim in. Off to one side of the path, there was even a little area for camping, and it had a small stone fire pit, just the right size for frying fish or cooking a rabbit.

Simon said, "I'm going to set snares and go fishing on the other side of the dam where the stream runs in." Sebastian glanced at Rosalind, Mémère, and Viola and then stared wistfully at Simon. "Do you want to come with me, Sebastian?" The little boy nodded vigorously. "You'll have to be quiet when we fish and do just what I say."

"He's a big boy," Mémère said. "He'll be fine. Won't you, Sebastian?"

Nodding, Sebastian went and stood by Simon as he took what he needed from the packs, which had been tucked to one side of the campsite. The horses were nearby, grazing in a clearing made by the beavers.

"Will the horses be all right?" Mémère asked. "Will they run off?"

"They'll stay nearby," Simon replied.

"How do you know this?"

Simon smiled. "Because I know horses, and horses know me. When it gets dark, they'll be with us. You wait."

Simon was right. When night came, Raisin and Treacle moved from the meadow and stood at the rim of the campsite. The mosquitoes were out in full force, but Mémère had insect repellent in her first aid kit, and she told everyone to rub some on their face, neck, arms, and hands. Then, they were able to settle comfortably by the fire while the fish sizzled in a skillet. Nobody complained about having fish for two meals in a row. After walking for most of the afternoon, everyone was hungry, and they ate gratefully.

"Oh, you're good, Simon," Mémère said. "I wish you could meet my husband. He'd love to go fishing with you."

Smiling, Simon ducked his head. "It's been a while. I wasn't sure if I'd remember."

"It's not something you forget," Mémère said, stretching out her legs. By the glow of the campfire, Viola could see the pink sandals.

Beside them, having finished eating, Rosalind and Sebastian rubbed their eyes and yawned, and Mémère regarded them. "Time for these two to get some sleep."

The children didn't protest, and out came the blankets because even though the night was warm, it was damp, and it felt good to be wrapped in a blanket. Mémère tucked the blankets around their small bodies and kissed them on their cheeks. Soon, Rosalind and Sebastian were asleep, and Mémère settled next to Simon and Viola by the fire.

"Is anyone after us, do you think?" Simon asked softly, when he was sure the children were asleep.

Closing her eyes, Viola sent her senses out into the forest. She saw a fox hunting for a rabbit, bats flying in the night, and owls gliding through the trees. But Viola didn't sense any humans other than the five of them. Later, Viola would learn what Maya had discovered, that Chet had a way of masking himself, of closing himself off. But that night, by the fire, Viola didn't know this.

"Just animals out there," Viola replied. "No people."

She heard both Mémère and Simon sigh with relief.

"So far, so good," Mémère said.

"We still have two days to go," Simon replied.

"Would anyone think to look for us here, in the middle of this forest by Beaver Pond?" Mémère asked.

Simon rubbed his forehead. "I don't think so. But Humphrey knows about the Forest of Arden and how it protects some people and keeps others out. It wouldn't surprise me if he guesses the children are being taken there."

"That's some forest," Mémère said, and Viola could tell that after all that had happened, Mémère wasn't fazed by the idea of a forest that allowed some people in and kept others out.

"Aye," Simon said. "I lived on the edge of the Forest of Arden with my mother. And even though I can't see things the way Maya and Viola can, I could feel its presence. Always. And I had the feeling that the forest would let me hunt and fish on the edge, but that it didn't want me to go in too far."

Mémère asked, "What if the Forest of Arden doesn't let us in?"

"It will," Simon answered. "The Forest of Arden protected Duke Owen. It will protect his children."

Mémère scratched a mosquito bite on her foot. "Wouldn't Humphrey think we'd go by the road?"

"It all depends on who he sends," Viola said softly. Although she couldn't sense Chet's presence, Viola knew about the tracker. Maya had told her all about Chet, whom she had called the Man Who Didn't Smile, and how he had been able to track people and Books of Everything.

"He's one of the best," Maya had said simply.

"One of the best," Viola said to herself, hoping that Chet wasn't after them. But she said nothing about the tracker and instead watched the fire and listened to loons call from the far edge of the pond.

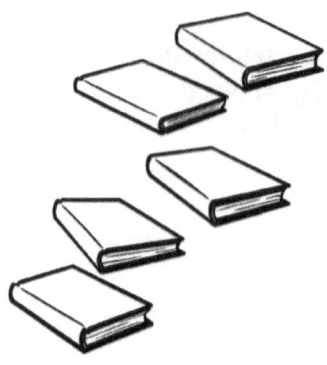

25. Chet Goes into the Woods

Chet had underestimated how dark the woods would be, even though the moon was full, and how slow his progress would be on the narrow path. He didn't dare urge the horse to go any faster on a path that was full of roots and stones. As it was, the horse tripped from time to time, and once Chet was nearly thrown. He gave the horse a hard thump on the neck, but the horse kept tripping anyway, and Chet realized that it was too dark for the horse to see well enough to make its way.

"I hate the woods," Chet said to himself, grimacing. "All these stupid trees hemming me in. If I were in charge, I would cut them all down so that I could see for miles around, in the moonlight as well as the sunlight." Chet smiled a little as he thought about the mighty crack the big trees would make as they fell with a crash.

He was just about to stop for the night—there really was no point in going on like this—when Chet came into a clearing and by the glow of moonlight, saw a lodge. It was completely dark, and the tracker could sense that there was no one there. By the lodge, there was a small lean-to, and Chet tethered the horse inside.

"I'll sleep here beside the horse," Chet thought. "And look around in the morning."

The mosquitoes were so bad that Chet had to cover himself with a blanket from his pack, and he spent a restless night listening to insects whine as they hovered around him and the horse. When he finally fell asleep, Chet dreamed about the small farm, with its gray house and even grayer barn, where he had grown up. He saw his mother, with her red hands that were chapped from so much scrubbing. He saw his father, with his long face and his down-turned mouth. Then there were his three brothers and two sisters, all doing chores in the barn. There was no laughing. No teasing and no talking. Just a grim sense of getting things done. On the barn's wall, by the door, hung a long black strap. Chet had felt that strap many times. All his sisters and brothers had.

"It kept us in line," Chet said to himself in his dream. "He taught us to behave."

Over and over, in a dreary loop, Chet fed chickens, collected eggs, worked in the garden, and mucked stalls. His brothers and sisters worked alongside him, and no one said a word.

Fortunately for the tracker, the night was short, and when dawn came early in the morning, Chet was more than ready to start the day. He felt weary, as though he really had been working on the farm for endless weeks. Shuddering just a little, Chet stepped outside the lean-to and saw a small fenced-in pasture. Chet led the horse to the pasture so the horse could graze while he looked around. The fence was in good repair, and it confirmed Chet's suspicions—this was no abandoned cabin. It was used regularly.

"Was it used yesterday?" Chet asked himself, and as he left the pasture, he saw fresh manure. "Horses were here not long ago. Let's see what's in the cabin."

The door was unlocked, and Chet walked into the cabin. He squinted in the dim light, at the large room with several tables and many chairs, at the big stone fireplace, at the loft overhead. Chet sniffed, catching the scent of fish, and going to the fireplace, he noted the pile of ashes. There was no doubt about it. Someone had been here recently and had fried fish. But who? Was it just the dark-haired man Chet had seen the day before? The fresh manure in the small pasture told another story. Horses had been here recently, but the man had been on foot.

Still, Chet wanted to be sure that he was tracking the right people. Chet went outside and spotted a narrow path. He followed it to a stream and found out what he needed to know. There was a jumble of footprints in the soft dirt by the stream, three sets of varying sizes, but all belonging to adults. Then Chet spotted the indents of little bare feet. There were two sets, one smaller than the other, and Chet was certain that these prints belonged to children, one older than the other.

"They were here yesterday," Chet said, and he actually smiled. Chet knew that even though Simon and his party had had a head start, one man could travel faster than a group of people with two small children. With any luck, he would overtake them by midafternoon, but he would hide in the woods, leaving the horse tethered to a tree some distance away. Chet would wait until night to strike, when he could take down Simon and Viola first and whoever else was traveling with them. He was fast, and it wouldn't be hard. Then the children would be easy to deal with.

Whistling a little tune, Chet washed in the stream, filled his waterskin upstream, and ate some dry bread for his breakfast. Within an hour, he was back on the trail. Intense and alert, Chet leaned forward in expectation. Soon, soon.

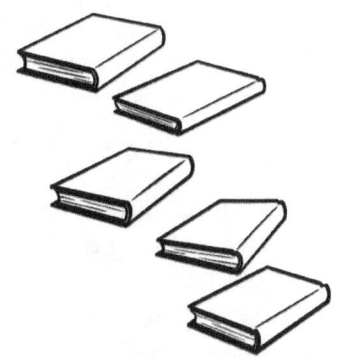

26: Unexpected Visitors

T he next morning, as Viola watched Mémère move stiffly around the campsite, she asked, "Why don't you ride with Rosalind for a while?"

"All right," Mémère agreed reluctantly, glancing at Treacle. Her black boots were back on, but the laces were tied loosely.

"She's a sweet mare," Simon said, patting Treacle's side. "That's why she's named Treacle. You've nothing to be afraid of."

"I'm not afraid," Mémère replied stoutly, but she continued to stare reluctantly at Treacle, who gave a soft nicker.

"No, Mémère, ride with me!" Sebastian sat on Raisin's back. "It will be fun."

Rosalind, who was on Treacle, frowned at her brother. "Viola said Mémère should ride with me, not you, Sebastian."

Sebastian's face went into a pucker, and it looked as though the little boy was going to cry.

"No bickering now," Mémère said. "First I'll ride with Rosalind and then Sebastian."

"And I'll lead you," Simon said to Sebastian. "How will that be?"

Sebastian sighed, but the pucker went away, and only a few tears slid down his cheeks. Viola could see that the little boy was as attached to Simon as he was to Mémère. "All right," Sebastian said. "But remember, Mémère, you promised to ride with me."

"I won't forget," Mémère said as Simon helped her mount Treacle. "And I take it Raisin is as sweet as Treacle?"

Simon grinned at Mémère. "Aye, that's why I chose her. They have the same mother."

"Good thing we have Simon with us," Viola thought, not knowing that her father had thought the same thing when the two had been in the woods together, heading to Caxton to take back Earth's Book of Everything from Julian.

Simon found the trail on the other side of the pond, and Guy was right—the path was even fainter than the one they had been on the day before. But there were marks to point the way, and the little party followed the path deeper and deeper into the woods.

"I don't know how long we'll have those marks," Simon said, looking at the compass that Guy had given him. "But we're going in the right direction, and we'll follow the marks for as long as they are there."

The day fell into the same pattern as the day before. Sometimes the children rode; sometimes they didn't. When the sun was high in the sky, they stopped for a lunch of bread and cheese. At one point, when they were on the trail, three deer came crashing out of the woods, crossed the path, and disappeared into the trees on the other side.

"Something's chasing them." Simon's hand went to the knife he was wearing.

"Yes." Viola sensed a sleek presence, a big cat. "But it's stopped chasing the deer and is going the other way."

"That's good," Simon said with a sigh.

"What are Treacle and Raisin going to eat?" Viola asked.

"Let's hope this trail leads to another beaver pond with a meadow," Simon replied.

"Could we be so lucky?" Mémère asked.

"Aye, it's possible," Simon answered. "The trail goes this way for a reason, and I'm thinking it's for both horses and people."

Simon was right. By midafternoon, they came to another pond, bigger than the previous one, with a dam. A large meadow spread beside the pond, and it wasn't long before the grateful horses were eating the rich, green grass that grew there. Later, Viola would learn that this trail went from pond to pond so that traders and trappers could travel through the woods with their horses. But for now the three were just thankful that the path had led to a place that had fresh water, plenty of grass for Treacle and Raisin, and a place to camp.

"It's good to be off those horses," Mémère said as she helped Viola gather wood for the fire. They had found another campsite on the edge of the meadow near the pond. "But Simon is right. They are sweet horses. Another few days of riding, and I might actually get used to them."

Rosalind and Sebastian were beside them, gathering small twigs for kindling for the fire.

"Oh, they're good kids." Mémère smiled as she watched them. "They know how to pitch in and help. And you, too."

Viola smiled back at Mémère. "When we moved to the White House, Mom said that I still had to make my bed, put my clothes away, and keep my room picked up. She's always telling me that I need to learn how to do things for myself."

"That's one smart mother you have," Mémère said.

Viola stopped. "I miss her. And Dad, too."

Mémère stopped as well. "I know what you mean. I miss my home, my husband, my daughter, and especially my granddaughter. If anything happens to Maya..."

Viola shivered, thinking yet again about what Maya had to face.

Mémère shook her head. "But we have a job to do, and we're going to get those children to the Forest of Arden."

"Right," Viola said, moving a little closer to Mémère.

"Right," Rosalind and Sebastian echoed, dropping their bundles to chase a toad that had crossed their path.

"Don't hurt that toad," Mémère called.

"We won't," they called back.

By the time night came, they were clustered around the fire. Simon had been able to snare two birds, and they had them for their supper.

"Makes a nice change," Mémère said. "Although truthfully, I'm so hungry by the end of the day that I could eat almost anything."

Simon smiled. "Aye, being in the woods works up an appetite."

Viola sat scrunched up, resting her face against her knees. "I don't ever remember being in the woods for so long. But Mom and Dad have told stories about how they used to go camping before I was born, before Dad became president."

"Those were good times," a voice said, and they all jumped. Springing to his feet, Simon pulled his knife from its sheath.

Two people, a man and a woman, were standing just outside the ring of firelight. Viola leaped up and ran to them. "Dad! Diana!" She gave her father a fierce hug, and he held her tightly in his arms.

"Andy?" Simon said, staring at the older man who stood before him.

Mémère scrambled to her feet. "President Murphy?"

Sitting by the fire, Rosalind stared coolly at the new arrivals. Sebastian, nearly asleep, stuck his thumb in his mouth.

"What should I call you?" Simon asked.

"You can call me Andy," Drew replied. "That's how you knew me when I was here." He looked at the campfire. "Just like old times, Simon."

"Aye," Simon answered. "But this time we're heading toward Greendale, not Caxton."

"I know." Drew held up the blue Book of Everything. "I read about what happened." Looking at the children, he didn't go any further.

"President Murphy, will you join us by the fire?" Mémère asked.

Drew nodded, and he, Viola, and Diana settled by the fire with Mémère and Simon. "You're Celine Turcotte?" Drew asked Mémère. "Maya's grandmother?"

"Oui," Mémère said. "But here it seems that I'm everybody's mémère, and you can call me that, too, if you want to."

Drew smiled. "All right." He introduced Diana as his assistant, and for a while nobody said anything. The fire crackled, and a gentle wind moved through the tops of the pines.

"Dad, what are you doing here?" Viola finally asked.

"I thought it would be obvious. I've come to take you home."

Viola frowned. "Home? I can't leave now. We have to take Rosalind and Sebastian to the Forest of Arden."

"But, Viola, you don't belong here," Drew said.

"Why doesn't Viola belong here?" Rosalind asked.

Mémère stood, brushing crumbs and dirt from her brown dress. Again, she was wearing her pink sandals. "Rosalind, it's time for you to go to sleep. I know you're tired. And look at your brother. He's nearly asleep."

"I'm not tired," Rosalind protested, but her eyelids fluttered as she said this.

"Oh, yes, you are," Mémère said firmly. "Let me get your blankets, and you can lay down right beside us."

Soon the children were tucked in their blankets, and Sebastian immediately fell asleep. Rosalind struggled to stay awake, but it wasn't long before she was asleep, too.

"There," Mémère said as she stroked Rosalind's cheek, and the little girl didn't move. "Now, we can talk."

Drew chuckled. "I can see who Maya takes after."

Mémère smiled. "She's a lot like me, but she's like her father, too."

Drew said, "I met Giles at a party. We were both at NYU at the same time."

"You knew, of course, that he would be Maya's father?" Mémère asked.

"I did." Drew looked from the sleeping children to Mémère, Viola, and Simon. "Duke Owen and Duchess Celia..." He stopped, staring at his daughter.

Viola nodded sadly, and so did Mémère and Simon. Even though the children were asleep, Viola could tell that nobody wanted to say too much, just in case.

Drew frowned. "Humphrey."

Diana's lips curled. "Jay Sheldon."

Simon said, "No matter what his name is..."

"He's a rotter," Viola finished.

"He certainly is," Drew said. "I wish I had known sooner. Maya came to Bar Harbor to warn me." He stared at Viola. "And then she got you involved."

"But we didn't come here on purpose," Viola answered. "Ariel, her Apprentice Book, took us to Caxton when Humphrey broke into my room to get his Book back."

"That's when I hit him on the head," Diana put in. "And both girls were gone."

Viola leaned against her father. "Dad, we have to help Simon with the kids. We can't just leave them."

Looking around the campfire, Drew nodded. "I know. I've got Earth's Book of Everything, but it can only transport two at a time. One by one, I could take you all to the Forest of Arden, where it's safe. Then from there, you, me, Diana, and Mémère could return to Earth. It would be slow, but we might be able to slide both the children in with one adult. They are little, and that's what happened when Alani came to Caxton with Elspeth and Maya. The two children combined are probably smaller than Alani."

"What about the horses?" Simon asked.

Drew replied, "As I see it, you have two choices. Either leave the horses on their own, or stay behind and make your way with them to the Forest of Arden."

"Is there anyone left at the lodge in the Forest of Arden?" Simon asked.

By the light of the fire, Drew consulted the Book and flipped the pages to the Forest of Arden entry. Then looking up, he said, "A small group stayed there. Duke Owen wanted the lodge to be ready. Just in case. The children wouldn't be alone."

As Simon thought about his choices, the group was quiet. The fire hissed and crackled in the fire pit, and Viola stared into the flames, trying to picture what it would be like to return home and never see Simon, the children, and Caxton again.

From behind came the loud snap of a broken branch, and Diana turned quickly, looking into the dark forest. "There's something out there."

"An animal?" Mémère asked.

Closing her eyes, Viola felt something hard and determined in the woods not far from the campfire. She pushed and pushed, and opened her eyes. "No, a person. I think it's Chet. And he's watching us." Viola pointed to a spot behind her father and Diana. "He's there," she whispered. "Not far."

In one quick motion, Diana jumped up and ran to where Viola had pointed. Everyone stood, squinting into the forest. They heard a series of yells and swearing.

"What should we do?" Simon asked. "Stay with the children? Or help Diana?"

Drew gave the Book to Viola. "Take the children to the Forest of Arden. Now."

Viola shook her head. "And leave all of you? No!"

"Do it." Mémère put her hand on Viola's arm. "Remember what our mission is."

"To get the children to safety," Viola said slowly. "But Mémère!"

Drew's voice was firm. "Viola, no arguing. Diana's good. But we don't want to take any chances with the children. You can bring them to safety. When you get to the lodge and are settled, go to Further Instructions. The Book will guide you."

Trembling a little, Viola took the Book from her father and went to Rosalind and Sebastian. The commotion had woken the children, and they were sitting up, blinking in confusion.

"What's the matter?" Rosalind asked Viola.

"I'll tell you later," Viola answered, her voice low and urgent. "Now get up and hold on to my arm. You, too, Sebastian. We're going to go quickly to the Forest of Arden."

Nodding, Rosalind and Sebastian stood. One small hand gripped Viola's arm, and an even smaller hand gripped her other arm. Viola opened the Book of Everything. "Take us to the lodge in the Forest of Arden."

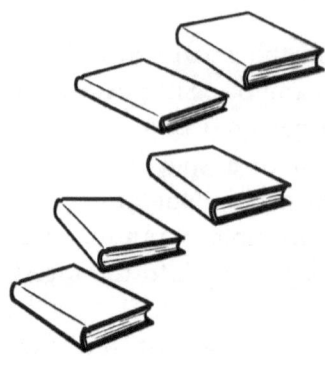

27: Fight in the Forest

Behind a large tree on the edge of the meadow but not far from the campfire, Chet watched as the little group settled by the fire and cooked their supper. There was a happy chatter as they ate, and when Sebastian sang a song about a purple turtle, everyone clapped when he was done. Then Rosalind sang a song about puppies and kittens, and again, there was clapping when she finished.

"Children should be quiet," Chet thought, thinking of the silent meals in his own home with his parents and his brothers and sisters. His father had been the only one allowed to talk, and he had never said much.

The older woman with the brown dress and pink sandals sang a song in French, and Chet asked himself, "Could this be Maya's grandmother?" Or mémère, as he knew Franco-Americans called them.

Viola sang "You've Got a Friend," an old tune Chet had heard on Earth many times when he was a young man. Chet rolled his eyes. He had hated that song then, and he hated it now. Even Simon sang a song about a young man who would never leave the girl he loved.

"It just keeps getting worse and worse," Chet thought, reflecting on how he would rather hear a song about a purple turtle than ones about friends or love.

"Will they never stop?" Chet wondered as they went through another round of songs. But even though Chet grumbled to himself, he waited patiently. He knew eventually they would stop singing, and just when it seemed as though they might be ready to settle down for the night, two figures joined them out of nowhere. Chet blinked and blinked again. Who were these people, and where had they come from? Chet crept sideways and forward until he was behind another large tree that was even nearer to the campsite. Initially, this tree had seemed a little too close, but Chet was intent on seeing the faces of the two new arrivals. Chet didn't recognize the woman, but there was enough light from the fire and the moonlight to identify the man, who was holding a book.

"President Murphy?" Chet thought in astonishment. "And Earth's Book of Everything? Of course it is. How else would he get here?" Chet stood very still, thinking about the Book he had pursued for so long, how he had nearly had it on the train from New York to Boston, all those years ago. But Mary Parsons had given it to Maya, and Chet had tracked her and the Book to East Vassalboro, Maine. He had been so sure he would finally get the Book of Everything. However, in the end, Chet had been outsmarted by a teenage girl, and thinking about it made him tremble in shame and anger. But now the Book was here in Caxton, and suddenly Rosalind and Sebastian didn't matter anymore. He had to get Earth's Book of Everything.

Chet inched around the tree to get yet a better look, trying to decide whether he should attack President Murphy, grab the Book, and run, when he stepped on a fallen branch that broke with a loud snap. The woman who had come with President Murphy sprang to her feet and raced toward the tree he was hiding behind. In an instant, Chet assessed her and knew that he had met his match. Pulling his knife from its sheath, he leaped at her as she came to the tree.

They both yelled as they rolled to the ground, and Chet slashed with the knife. But the woman was fast, slamming a knee into Chet's stomach. Winded, he fell back, and the woman stumbled to her feet. Chet watched as she withdrew a gun from its holster.

"Oh, no you don't," Chet thought, throwing his knife at the woman. It hit her in the shoulder, and she cried out in pain, dropping the gun.

Getting his breath back, Chet reached for the gun, which had fallen nearby. At the same time, the woman lunged for the gun, but she was too late—Chet had it. Just wanting to stop her, Chet aimed the gun at her leg and pulled the trigger. The woman screamed even louder and collapsed.

"I'll deal with you later," Chet muttered, racing into the clearing, toward the fire. He had to get the Book.

Three people were standing and waiting for him—the older woman with the brown dress and pink sandals, Simon, and President Murphy. The children, Viola, and the Book were gone.

Chet's face grew hot. "Where is it?" he shouted, pointing the gun at Drew's head.

Drew smiled just a little. "The Book of Everything is gone. And no matter what you do to us, you won't get it or the children and my daughter. They are all safe and beyond your reach."

Chet felt frozen, and for a few moments he just blinked at them. The Book had escaped. Again. This time with a girl even younger than Maya. And Rosalind and Sebastian had gone with her. Chet knew where they had gone—to the Forest of Arden. He had lost them all. Chet snarled, deciding that he would kill everyone here and then think about what he should do next. Chet raised the gun, pointing it at Drew.

"Run, Mémère and Simon!" Drew yelled, leaping aside, and the bullet hit him in the shoulder rather than in the head, where Chet had aimed. Drew fell to the ground.

Instead of running, Simon rushed Chet, and the tracker raised the gun, aiming it at Simon's head. But Chet never had a chance to pull the trigger. From behind, something came crashing down hard on his own head. Chet fell, but before he lost consciousness, he caught a glimpse of pink sandals.

"There!" Mémère said, holding a log meant for the fire. "Take that, you stinker."

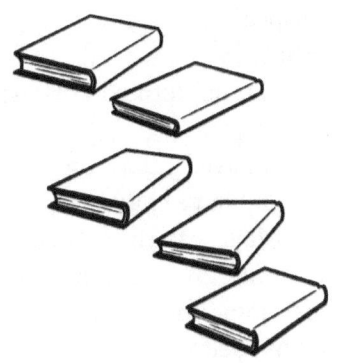

28: No Tea

Cinnial glowered at Maya, but Maya did not look away from him. She saw how displeased he was with her flippant request for tea, and Maya knew with a deep certainty that she would be punished for her lack of respect. Maya got a flash of the various devices that would be used on her, and she thought, somewhat desperately, "Why couldn't I just play along? At least for a little while." Then she remembered something her mother had said once when there had been trouble between Maya and one of her teachers. Lily had looked at her and sighed. "Maya, you always have to fight things head on."

"Mom, you are so right," Maya thought sadly, but she continued to stare defiantly at Cinnial.

Cinnial turned to Julian, who had a flicker of a smile on his face. "Do you think this is funny? Was it your idea of a joke to bring her here? Payback for being exiled so long in Caxton?"

Julian stopped smiling. "No, I didn't bring her here so that you could torment each other, even though I should have known that would happen. At least initially. As I said before, I brought Maya here because I thought she might be useful." Maya violently shook her head. "Maya," Julian said firmly, "be still and let me speak. Then, you can get yourself in as much trouble as you want."

Cinnial looked curiously at Julian. "You've changed a lot, haven't you?"

"I have," Julian answered. "But I remain loyal to you, even though I have changed."

Maya caught a flicker of pleasure from Cinnial. She understood how much he needed praise and deference, how they were something Cinnial actually craved, and how he surrounded himself with those who gave these things to him.

"Go on," Cinnial said, but his lips curled as he glanced at Maya. "Tell me again why this girl is so important."

Julian was silent for a few moments. "I could go on and on about all Maya has done, deeds that have been hidden from you because of her Books of Everything. Here's just a sample of what she has accomplished. She stabbed me with my own knife, took back the Book of Everything I stole from her, and helped Duke Owen regain Caxton. Plus, she was responsible for me losing my memory." Julian slid the rucksack from his shoulders, removed both Books, and put them on Julian's desk. "Finally, consider this blue Book. It belongs to Maya, but you will note that it is an Apprentice Book. That can only mean one thing."

Cinnial regarded the blue Book, and Maya could tell that he was shocked by the implications—Maya had been to the Great Library and had been allowed to leave with an Apprentice Book.

"The Book's name is Ariel," Maya said, even though she knew she should be quiet.

Cinnial glared at Maya, and the look on his face was so fierce that Maya wondered if she was going to survive the next five minutes. Julian held up his hand. "Before you strike, really look at her."

"I have. But she's only a young girl."

"Look again. Look more closely."

Julian turned the force of his gaze on Maya, and she cried out, feeling that she had no place to hide. Despite her best efforts to turn him away, Cinnial bored deeper and deeper into her mind until she felt nearly flayed, but even so, she didn't reveal everything. With a sob, Maya fell to her knees in front of the desk.

"Yes," Cinnial said thoughtfully. "She's had her eyes peeled, and even though she's young, her ability to see is strong."

"It's the strongest I've ever seen in one so young," Julian replied. "Stronger than mine, that's for sure. Stronger than..." Looking at Cinnial's cold face, Julian stopped. "Stronger than almost everyone's. If you could turn her and train her, then she would be a useful asset."

Maya staggered to her feet. "I'll never come to your side. Never!"

Here Cinnial actually smiled. He leaned forward a little. "You know, Maya, there are two main flaws that hold people back. One is not having enough confidence. People who are not confident are weak and ineffectual and easily swayed. They always doubt themselves. You can't really count on such people. They are only good for minor things, like cleaning the floors or tedious office jobs, and they always have to work under someone. But that's not your problem, is it?"

Maya shook her head. Not having enough confidence had never been her problem.

Cinnial continued, "I didn't think so. Instead, your problem is that you have too much confidence, and that gets you in trouble. You make rash decisions."

Swallowing, Maya didn't say anything. She was afraid she would betray Sydda and the Great Library. But she didn't look away from Cinnial's intense stare.

"Sir," said a voice Maya hadn't heard before, and with a start she realized it came from the computer. "Sorry to interrupt. But you said you wanted this message of yours to go out to the public as soon as possible. Here are some graphics to go with it."

Frowning, Cinnial stared at the huge computer screen on his desk. He nodded. "That looks good. Send it."

"Yes, sir," the computer said in a chipper but calm voice.

Cinnial looked up at Maya. "Where was I?"

"You were telling Maya that she was overconfident," Julian said.

"That's right." In his chair, he swiveled a little from side to side as he considered her. "You suffer from overconfidence, don't you?"

"Maybe," Maya answered in a small, choked voice.

"I know your type," he said dispassionately. "You're all the same, no matter which planet you come from. The cherished child of the family. Probably the only child. From the time you are very small, everyone tells you how bright you are, how much potential you have. They tell you this over and over until it becomes part of who you are. You grow up thinking that you are the best, that you can't fail."

Maya thought, "I'm not *that* confident." But this time, she wisely remained silent and let Cinnial talk. An impression of him was starting to form in her mind.

Cinnial leaned forward, and Maya felt trapped by his intense gaze. His voice became low. "But one day you will find out that you can fail, and when that day comes, well, let's just say it won't be a good one." Beside him, Julian shifted uneasily. "If you aren't strong enough, then that failure will crush you. If you are strong enough, then you will recover and achieve things that nobody thought possible. Are you strong enough, Maya?"

A little breathless, Maya just stared at Cinnial's face, darkly radiant and beautiful. Smiling at her, Cinnial continued, "We will find out, won't we? It won't be pleasant for you. Far from it. But we'll discover what you're made of. We'll see if you survive."

Shuddering, Maya glanced at Julian and saw his look of sorrow as he listened to Cinnial. Maya thought, "He really does feel bad for me."

Cinnial brought his hands together. "Enough of this. I have far bigger things to attend to than to worry about one young girl who can see and who has potential. I'm going to turn you over to someone who is more than capable of finding out if you're made of the right stuff." Cinnial was wearing an earbud, and he pressed it, saying, "Bigly, come to my office. I have a job for you."

Julian shook his head. "Bigly's still here."

"Of course he's still here." Cinnial's voice was sharp. "Bigly's served me well. He does exactly what I tell him to do. He doesn't go off the rails."

"The way I did," Julian said quietly.

"The way you did," Cinnial replied, just as quietly, and the two men stared at each other.

It wasn't long before the door opened, and a short, squat man with a huge, wedge-shaped head came into Cinnial's office. His sparse hair was light brown, and the thin strands looked as though they had been glued in place. Pockmarks dotted his large face, and his small eyes were a pale blue. Maya had never seen such a homely man, and later she would learn that he was, in fact, a troll, one of thousands who worked for Cinnial.

"So ugly," Maya thought, but now she was not looking at his face. Instead, Maya was going deeper, seeing Bigly's vicious nature, his idolatry of Cinnial, and his intense jealousy of Julian. Maya realized with a shock that it had been Bigly's idea to send Julian to Caxton. With Julian gone, Bigly could bask in Cinnial's attention.

With a fierce snap, Bigly cut off her probing, and he did it with such efficiency that Maya knew he was someone to be reckoned with.

Standing beside her, Bigly clicked his little heels together and said in a surprisingly deep voice, "Sir."

Cinnial nodded regally. "Bigly. As you can see, Julian is back."

"So he is." Bigly glared spitefully at Julian.

"Always so charming," Julian murmured, giving Bigly a pitying look that indicated he knew the troll would never be first in Cinnial's affection. That spot would always belong to Julian, no matter how loyal or helpful Bigly was. Maya could tell that Bigly knew this, too.

Bigly stiffened. "I hope you've learned your lesson after all those years in Caxton. You were gone a long time."

Julian smiled. "Bigly, I've learned more lessons than you could ever imagine, but the lessons I've learned are quite different from the ones you intended. And surprise! I even lived to tell the tale. You didn't expect that, did you?"

"My only intentions are to serve sir," Bigly retorted.

"Right," Julian replied, giving Bigly another pitying look. "Before I lost my memory, I had a lot of time to think about things when I was in Caxton."

"I hope you reflected on how you could be more like me and learn how to better serve sir." Bigly clicked his heels again.

Maya thought, "Why is Cinnial letting them talk to each other this way?" But then she noted Cinnial's smug, pleased expression and saw that Cinnial actually enjoyed pitting Bigly against Julian.

Julian shook his head, and there was a flash of anger, of the old Julian before he had lost his memory. He glared at Bigly. "I thought about Cinnial. I thought about him a lot. But I thought about you, too, Bigly, and what a hateful little maggot you are. Before I lost my memory, I vowed that I would come back and squeeze your nearly nonexistent neck until you were dead." Julian was breathing hard, and his face was flushed. Closing his eyes, he took a deep breath, and then opened them. "Watch out," Julian said, with his dangerous glitter. "I might have changed a lot, but I still have a little chip of anger that will never go away."

Cinnial said firmly, "All right. That's enough. Bigly, I called you here because I have an important job for you."

Bigly leaned forward eagerly. "Yes, sir?"

"You are to take this girl, Maya, to the Office."

Bigly blinked, opened his mouth, and then shut it again. He finally asked, "To the Office, sir?"

"To the Office," Cinnial replied. "I want you to find out how strong Maya is and whether she will ever come to our side. She's been to the Great Library. She knows Sydda."

Bigly nodded miserably. "Yes, sir."

"Bigly, Julian thought Maya was important enough to bring her to Mortmain. I can trust you. You'll be able to see what she's made of."

"But, sir," Bigly asked slyly, "wouldn't this be a better job for Julian? After all, he's the one that brought her here."

"No." Cinnial's tone of voice suggested that the discussion was over. "You're the one for the job. After a while, you'll realize it, too. Now, go, and bring her to the Office."

Again came the clicking of heels. "Yes, sir." Bigly grabbed Maya's arm and squeezed hard. "Come with me."

Grinning, Julian waved. "Goodbye, Bigly. And good luck. With Maya, you will have met your match."

Bigly didn't say anything. Instead, he pulled Maya by the arm and marched her out the door.

Maya heard Cinnial say, "Now, let's see what we can find out from those Books." Maya could tell that she was no longer a concern of Cinnial's, that all his attention was focused on the Books and finding the path to the Great Library. As Maya left with Bigly, out of the corner of her eye, she saw Cinnial reach for the green Book.

"Oh, Ariel, you'll be next," Maya thought sadly, and to her surprise, even though Ariel was still closed, Maya heard a faint response. "Maya, I'll hold out as long as I can."

Keeping her face neutral as Bigly marched her along, Maya asked silently, "How come you can talk to me when you're not open?"

Ariel replied, "Because you're connected to everything in a way that most people are not. Remember that, Maya. You don't need me as much as you think you do. After all, you came to the Great Library with the help of one acorn."

"And Time," Maya thought.

"Yes, and Time, which is all around you."

"Even here?"

"Even in Mortmain and even on this planet—Tufrak. Time is everywhere. Chaos might be able to suppress Time, but never eliminate it."

Maya almost stopped walking, and she murmured, "All around me, even here on Tufrak."

Bigly jerked her arm. "What are you doing? Keep walking!"

"I was thinking," Maya said defiantly. "And there's nothing you can do about that."

This time Bigly stopped, and he slapped her hard across the face. "You don't want to be with me, and I don't want to be with you. But sir has given me an order. I will carry it out. In fact, I'm looking forward to wiping that impudent look off your face."

Maya put her hand to her stinging cheek, but she said, "You're not going to break me. So why don't you save yourself some trouble and crawl back into whatever hole you came from."

Bigly slapped her again and again until her eyes watered. Then he stopped abruptly, muttering, "Enough of this. I need my devices, and then you'll see what happens."

In mincing steps but with a firm grip on her arm, Bigly pulled Maya down a long gleaming hall. And in a daze from being slapped so many times, she stumbled behind him. They came to an elevator, and Bigly pushed a button. Immediately, the door opened, and he shoved her inside. Bigly pressed the lobby button, and the elevator shot downward. Nearly falling, Maya grabbed frantically for the railing and managed to stay upright.

Bigly glared at her. "First we get rid of that ridiculous dress. Ilyria is such a stupid, backward planet."

Maya didn't say anything, but she thought, "Ilyria is a beautiful place, even though it doesn't have much technology. Cinnial will never get it. Never!"

The look on her face must have betrayed her thoughts because Bigly slapped her again. "Did you think I was joking? You had better start taking me seriously."

Maya thought, "Oh, I do. Believe me, I do." And she bit her lip to keep herself from crying.

"That's better," Bigly said. "Much better."

The elevator stopped at the lobby, and it looked much the way a lobby would in any building in a big city on Earth. There was a large central desk with a man and a woman sitting behind it. They were both slender and fair, and they wore dark, crisp uniforms and small pointed hats. They stared curiously at Maya then nodded respectfully at Bigly.

Bigly nodded back. "Ferd, Ina."

"We didn't see that one come in," Ferd said, his deep voice anxious.

"She didn't come the usual way," Bigly replied. "You didn't miss anything."

Again, in mincing steps, Bigly herded her down the gleaming hall, and Maya heard Ina say, "Of course we didn't miss anything. Why would you even suggest that we did?"

Ferd muttered something, but his voice was so low that Maya didn't hear what he said. She felt the fear that was inside both of them, and she understood that it was always there and always would be with Cinnial in charge. As if to reinforce that Cinnial was constantly watching, there were giant pictures of him lining the walls of the lobby. Some were simply headshots of Cinnial while others showed him addressing crowds. Then there were the ones of him posing by dead animals he had killed with the sleekest gun Maya had ever seen. Looking at the dead animals, Maya shuddered.

Bigly and Maya came to huge glass doors, and a doorman, wearing the same kind of uniform that Ferd and Ina wore, opened one of the doors. With Maya in tow, Bigly trotted outside onto the street.

In amazement, Maya looked around, swallowing. As far as Maya could see, on both sides of the street, were tall gray buildings with no distinguishing features. They rose high into the air, and the buildings gleamed as though they had been taken care of with ruthless efficiency. On the streets, there were no trees, no flowers in boxes, no awnings to break the grayness, but on some of the buildings there were huge screens, and Cinnial's face flashed out from all of them. Maya looked way up, catching a glimpse of a blue sky, a sunny day, but it hardly seemed to matter—the buildings blocked most of the natural light, sending slanting gray shadows onto the street and sidewalk. Even the few men and women on the street wore gray suits, and they were dressed so similarly that it looked as though Cinnial had imposed a dress code.

Later, Maya would learn that was exactly what he had done. No bright colors were allowed. Only sober gray and black.

Directly across the street was a building so tall that Maya had to tip her head back to take in its size. Lines of windows went up the building, and it was as though there were hundreds of dark eyes balefully watching the street.

Maya thought, "That's the Office. I know it is."

Small gray cars, big enough for only two people or trolls, zipped by, and Bigly took her to the edge of the sidewalk. A troll in a uniform with a badge was waiting, and he wore a huge whistle around his short neck. Nodding respectfully at Bigly, the troll blew into the whistle. A mighty blast went up and down the street, and Maya staggered back a little, surprised that such a loud sound could come from such a small device. As the cars screeched to a halt, the troll held up his hand. Gripping Maya's arm, Bigly was about to cross the road, when a high-pitched voice stopped him. "Mr. Bigly, Mr. Bigly!"

Turning, Bigly stopped, and Maya turned, too. A slim troll with a head even larger than Bigly's hurried toward them as fast as she could, but her progress was slow, and Maya noted her tiny feet and skinny legs. With a slight smile, Maya saw that Bigly's and the officer's feet were also tiny, and she suddenly realized that because their heads were so big and their feet were so small, the trolls couldn't move very fast. That was why Bigly took such mincing steps. She should have realized this sooner, but she had been preoccupied with Cinnial and Mortmain.

Frowning, Bigly stopped. "What is it, Tonim?"

Even though Tonim wasn't moving very fast, the troll was out of breath, and she gasped, "Someone's hacked into the system. Look at the screens."

They all looked up. Instead of Cinnial, there was a picture of a man and a woman, each wearing a bright blue mask, and the skin on their necks and hands was blue as well. The woman held a sign that read *Resist Lies,* and the man held a sign that read *Facts Do Matter.*

"No!" Bigly exclaimed as he stared at the screens, and in his shock, he dropped Maya's arm.

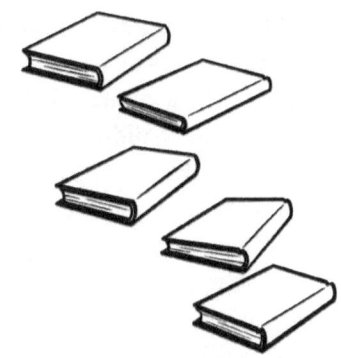

29. Kissed by Chance

Maya didn't hesitate. She bolted down the street, away from Bigly, the officer, and Tonim. Behind her, the officer's whistle blared, and Bigly yelled, but Maya didn't look back or slow down. Running as fast as she could, she turned down a narrow alleyway that connected two streets and then another alley. Fortunately for Maya, most people and trolls were at work, and the sidewalks were nearly empty. The few who were out just stared at Maya as she sped by in her red dress.

Streets, alleys, streets, alleys. Maya didn't stop until she came to a street with a delivery truck with the back open. There was no one around, except for a slight woman with brown hair and blue eyes, and Maya had the strangest feeling that she had seen this woman before. Looking at Maya, the woman nodded at the truck. Maya's intuition told her to trust this woman, and Maya sprinted up the ramp. The truck was empty, except for some blankets in the back corner, and she hurried to the pile, burying herself in the blankets.

Maya heard the door slam shut, and then a few minutes later, the sound of the engine. The truck moved slowly, alternating between stopping and turning, and Maya's heart beat hard and fast as the truck wound through the streets of Mortmain.

Maya wondered, would there be a roadblock? Would all cars and trucks leaving the city be searched? Hiding in the blankets, Maya waited, but the truck kept going. After an hour or so, the truck didn't stop as much. When it began to pick up speed, Maya knew the truck had left the city. She poked her face out and lay nestled among the scratchy blankets. The truck was dark, Maya was warm—but not too warm—and the motion of the truck made her feel drowsy. Maya tried to keep her eyes open, but it was no use. As the truck drove on, Maya fell asleep.

Maya woke up with a start. The truck had stopped, and Maya had no idea how much time had passed. Hearing the back door open, Maya burrowed beneath the blankets and waited. But nobody came in, and she cautiously peeked out. No one stood by the open door. Maya listened for voices, but all she heard was the loud humming of some sort of machinery. Hugging the wall, starting and stopping, Maya crept cautiously toward the door and looked out. There was a large gray building of some kind with a long concrete ramp leading to the truck's metal ramp. There were no people or trolls to be seen, and again Maya didn't hesitate. She hurried out of the truck and found herself in a parking lot with a row of trucks parked by ramps leading to a factory's warehouse. Scuttling around the front of the trucks, Maya didn't stop until she came to the end of the line and a concrete wall.

"Now what?" Maya muttered, crouching beside the last truck. As relieved as she was to be away from Bigly, the Office, and Mortmain, Maya was beginning to wonder if she had done the right thing. After all, hadn't she come to Mortmain on purpose, to discover something that would help the Great Library? However, when her chance to escape had come, Maya hadn't given it a second thought, and off she had sprinted. "What a coward I am," she said scornfully to herself.

Sagging against one of the truck's big tires, Maya slid down until she sat on the ground.

"Don't be discouraged," a clear voice said. "Escaping was one of the choices you could have made, and it's not a bad one. In fact, I'm beginning to think it might be a very good one."

Startled, Maya looked up to see the slight woman with brown hair and blue eyes she had seen in Mortmain. The woman wore a gray shirt and pants, just like everyone else in Mortmain, but there was something different about her, a shining quality missing from the other people she had seen. And somehow, Maya was not afraid of her.

"Who are you?" Maya asked.

The woman smiled. "I'm Chance. I think you've seen me before you came to Mortmain, haven't you?"

"Yeah," Maya replied. "At President Murphy's party."

Chance nodded. "That's right. I was there. I've been with you, off and on, since you left New York City to go to Maine. Of course, I can't be with you all the time. Others need me, too. But Time wants me to pay special attention to you, so here I am."

"Will you stay with me while I'm here?" Maya asked hopefully, standing up.

"Oh, no. As I said, others need me, too. Besides, I can't stay here very long, or Chaos will discover me. And if Nemesis is sent, it won't be good for you. So listen carefully to what I have to say. I only have a few minutes."

"Okay," Maya answered a little breathlessly.

Chance handed her a rucksack. "Here are some clothes so that you'll fit in. That red dress really makes you stand out. You're about five hours from Mortmain, in a factory town called Roford. Here, trolls and people work side by side to produce things for Mortmain and the country. To the west, toward the setting sun, lies Black Mountain, and that's where you should head. A resistance is hiding there. Find them. You'll be able to help each other."

"What about Bigly? Will he use a Book to find me?"

"Bigly doesn't have a Book. He doesn't have to. He has a network of spies, both online and actual, and this country, Caldor, is in the tight grip of the trolls who work for Bigly. They are everywhere. They might not be able to run fast, but they have other qualities. So be very careful. But Maya, not all trolls are bad, despite how they look. Let your intuition guide you as to which ones you should trust."

"But will Bigly tell Cinnial and have Cinnial use his Book to find me?"

Chance shook her head. "Bigly won't tell Cinnial." Shuddering a little, Chance winced. "Cinnial has his own plans, and Bigly won't want to bother him. Also, Bigly won't want to admit that one kid from Earth got away from him. Right now, you're safe from Cinnial's notice. Like Chet and Humphrey, he's underestimated you. But now I've really got to go."

Maya nodded, even though she had more questions she wanted to ask Chance. "All right."

"Goodbye." Chance kissed Maya on the forehead, and Maya caught a scent of spring flowers and freshly cut grass. "Sorry I can't stay longer, but I don't want Nemesis to know I've been here, and so far, so good."

Then Chance was gone, leaving Maya standing with the pack.

Hiding between the last truck and the wall, Maya glanced around. The yard was still empty, and Maya saw that the sun was setting in a hazy sky. For the first time, Maya noticed that the air around her smelled acrid, and her eyes stung a little from whatever made the odor. Blinking, she dug into the pack and found a gray shirt, gray pants, a black cap, and black shoes that were made out of cloth. Maya changed quickly, folding the red dress stained with blood and dirt and tucking it into the pack. Because the dress came from Caxton, a place Maya had come to love, she couldn't bear to part with it. Besides, if she left it behind and someone found it, the dress would most certainly arouse suspicions. Maya was sure that nobody in Roford had a dress like that, vibrant and hand stitched with lace.

In the pack were a map, a compass, a thermos of water, a small purse with some coins, and a dozen wrapped energy bars. For the first time since arriving on Tufrak, Maya realized she was hungry and desperately thirsty. Grabbing the thermos and opening it, Maya gulped down some water and then quickly ate two of the bars. She could have eaten a third but decided she'd better ration them. "Who knows what else I'll get to eat here?" Maya thought. "Or how long it will take me to find the group on Black Mountain?"

Slipping on her pack, Maya began to walk along the wall to look for a way out. It wasn't long before she came to a large gate, closed but not locked, that went across the entrance to the yard.

Opening the gate and slipping through, Maya found herself in the huge, empty courtyard of a factory that loomed so large she couldn't see anything beyond it except for rows and rows of smokestacks. In the corner was a tall tower, and to one side of the tower, a long wall with rows of doors. As Maya stood and stared, a piercing shriek came from the tower, and startled, she jumped back, hitting the gate with her pack. The doors opened, and workers started coming out of the factory. Soon the court-yard was filled with people and trolls, talking quietly as they headed for the front gate. The people moved quickly, and Maya noted that although many had the same color skin as she had, others were deep blue, like the two she had seen on the screens in Mortmain. The trolls, with their small feet, followed behind. But troll or human, they were all wearing the same sort of clothes as Maya had on—gray shirt and trousers, black hat and shoes.

Maya decided to slip in among them and head for the front gate, which was wide and open. Turning once, Maya glanced back and saw a troll standing on a balcony that jutted out above the main entrance. Maya felt her piercing gaze as she surveyed the crowd, and Maya was glad she was small enough to be hidden among the crowd.

Nobody paid any attention at all to Maya, and she went out the front gates with everyone else, away from the factory, away from the sharp attention of the troll. "Is she looking for me?" Maya wondered. "Has Bigly spread the word about me?" She felt it was likely, and suddenly Maya was grateful that she had dyed her hair blonde. The blue people had dark hair, the trolls had sparse, brown hair, but the people with Maya's skin color had blond hair. There were plenty of children walking with the adults—some of them were even shorter than Maya—and she fit right in with them. Many of the workers wore the same kind of pack that Maya had on her back. There was nothing about Maya to set her apart from any of the others.

Outside the gate, for as far as Maya could see, there were streets with rows and rows of concrete apartment buildings, five stories tall and all with small balconies. On the ends of some of the buildings there were big screens, similar to the ones Maya had seen in Mortmain, and Cinnial's face flickered on all of them. He was giving a speech about how even though their country, Caldor, had been oppressed by decadent elites, their country's time of glory was coming. Cinnial then called all men and women who were brave and ambitious to join him and his troops in Mortmain so that they could be part of this triumph. When the message ended, the screen showed a still of Cinnial with the words, "All patriots work hard for the glory of Caldor."

Most of the people and trolls gave the screens an anxious glance before moving on, but a few stopped to gaze at the screen, and Maya could see they had been moved by Cinnial's message. Some of them, she knew, would quit their factory jobs to go to Mortmain to be part of Cinnial's forces.

Thinking about Cinnial and his plan to take over the Great Library, Maya shuffled along with the people. "What am I supposed to do?" Maya thought desperately. "Because Chance is right. I am just one kid from Earth." The despair and panic she felt almost overwhelmed her, and walking even slower, Maya wondered how she would be able to go on. But then she felt something warm and bright on her forehead, where Chance had kissed her, and the warm feeling spread through her, calming her down, giving her confidence. Maya sighed with relief, knowing that for now, at least, a bit of Chance would be with her, to guide her and to give her help when she needed it most. Gripping the straps of her rucksack and holding her head high, Maya walked down the street, away from the factory.

The houses by the factory were in good repair, but the farther west Maya walked, the shabbier they became. However, children, clean and well fed, played in the streets, and older people, chatting and watching the children, sat in lawn chairs on the sidewalks. There were few cars, and Maya passed shops where people were stopping on their way home. Through the windows and open doors of the shops, Maya could see racks of brown bread. Underneath the acrid odor that permeated everything—Maya now realized that the stench was coming from the smokestacks—came the aroma of cabbage, potato, and onion soup from the open windows of many of the apartments. It was a homely, honest smell, and even though Maya had had two energy bars, her stomach rumbled, and she wistfully pictured herself eating a steaming bowl of soup with a thick slice of brown bread spread with butter. She considered stopping into one of the shops for a loaf of the brown bread, but Maya was afraid that she would give herself away by not knowing how much the coins in the purse were worth.

So onward Maya walked, until she came to a river, dark and dirty, that ran on the edge of town. There were boats and loading docks along the river, and when Maya looked west, in the distance she could see a dark, towering mountain. "There it is," Maya thought. "That's where I need to go." But Black Mountain seemed so far away. How would she get there?

In the large parking lot around the docks, trolls in electric carts zipped from boat to boat. Blue-skinned men, silent and grim, unloaded cargo from the boats to trucks waiting to drive inland. Maya made her way to the end of the loading area, where the boats and docks got smaller and smaller, and there were no trolls in carts and no blue-skinned people unloading cargo. At the very end was the smallest dock of all with a sturdy boat that was large enough to carry some cargo in sheds on its deck yet not too big to navigate smaller waterways.

A young troll sat on the dock, and as Maya considered him, the spot tingled where Chance had kissed her. "Okay, okay," Maya said to herself, and she made her way to the young troll, who was fishing.

As Maya stepped onto the dock, the young troll looked up and warily regarded her.

"Hello," Maya said a little shyly. The only troll she had spoken to had been Bigly, and the exchange had not been a good one.

The young troll nodded in a neutral but not unfriendly way.

There was a bucket beside him, but Maya wasn't near enough to see into it. "Catch anything?"

"Not yet," he answered in a gravelly voice. "Not much to catch in this dirty river, but I like to try."

"Is it all right if I sit on your dock?" Maya asked, standing some distance away.

The troll shrugged. "I guess."

"Thanks," Maya said as she settled beside him, close enough to be able to talk but far enough away to give him some space.

Removing her pack, she set it on the dock. "I'm Maya."

"I'm Jeam."

"Is that your boat?"

"In a way. It belongs to my grandpa, Captain Creb. You're not from around here, are you?"

She shook her head. "No, I'm from away. How could you tell?"

With a grave expression, Jeam regarded Maya. "You don't talk the way we do."

Maya smiled. Earth's Book of Everything had connected her to the common language of the universe, but it couldn't give her each place's accent and intonations. Slipping off her pack, Maya reached in and pulled out two energy bars. "Want one?" she asked.

Nodding, Jeam took one of the bars. "Thanks."

"You're welcome."

For a while, Maya and Jeam didn't say anything as they ate their bars and sat side by side on the dock. Dirty water, littered with plastic, paper, and some kind of oily sludge, swirled beneath them.

"Too bad the river's so dirty," Maya said.

"Grandpa Creb can remember the Ashwillot when it wasn't dirty like this. He said big fish used to come upriver in the spring, and it was a real sight to watch them jump."

"Dirty rivers can be cleaned," Maya said, thinking of the Kennebec River that ran through central Maine, not far from where her grandparents lived. She had heard Mémère speak of this many times and how the Clean Water Act had saved the river.

"How?" Jeam asked.

"The government can make rules that don't allow the factories to dump waste into the river."

Jeam snorted. "That's not likely to happen anytime soon." Then he looked fearfully at Maya. "Of course, Caldor and Mortmain matter more than the Ashwillot." But Maya could tell he didn't mean what he had said.

"Don't worry," Maya said in a low voice. "I know how bad it is here. I escaped from Mortmain. And I need help getting to Black Mountain."

Jeam stared at her. Even though his small troll face, wrinkled in a frown, was just as homely as Bigly's, there was something underneath that came through and made Jeam shine with beauty. Maya realized it was a basic decency that neither Cinnial nor Chaos could destroy, and she suddenly felt very humble. Maya thought with a shiver, "What would I be like if I grew up here?" She hoped she'd be like Jeam, but Maya had to admit that she really wasn't sure. If she had been born in Caldor, would she be drawn to Cinnial and Chaos? In the United States, where Time, so far, had mostly kept Chaos at bay, the choice had seemed easy, at least for her and for her parents. However, Maya knew that this wasn't true for everybody in the United States. On the Internet, Maya had read some hateful comments—sometimes from kids in her own school—that were as far from decency as it was possible to get.

Finally, Jeam nodded at her, and Maya could tell that he had made up his mind to trust her. "Maybe Grandpa Creb would let you ride on *The Resilience*. We follow the Ashwillot to the ocean, and from there we follow the coast until we come to the Nokom River, which goes by Black Mountain. He could drop you off at one of the towns on the Nokom. Let me go ask."

Setting his pole on the dock, Jeam scurried as fast as his little feet allowed toward the boat. He clambered up the ramp, disappeared, and was gone for a while. Maya wondered about Grandpa Creb. Would his grandson be able to convince him that it was safe to allow Maya on the boat, that she wouldn't betray them? Even though she had only been in Caldor for a short while, Maya realized that trusting the wrong human could be a matter of life and death.

Then Jeam scuttled back down the ramp and beckoned to her. Slipping into her pack and picking up the pole and the bucket, Maya headed toward the boat. As she drew closer, Maya could see *The Resilience* painted in white letters on the side of the blue hull. Taking a deep breath as she prepared herself to meet Captain Creb, Maya walked up the ramp.

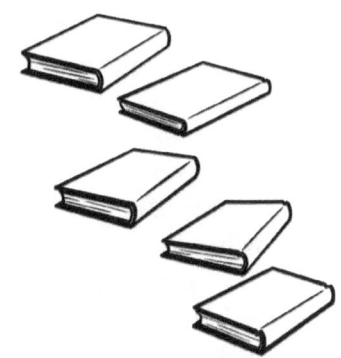

30: On Board *The Resilience*

Captain Creb was waiting for her on the deck. Taller than Jeam, Captain Creb wore a hat with a visor, much like a ship's captain on Earth would wear. His sparse hair had turned white, and his face was wrinkled and brown from spending so much time in the sun. Although he leaned against a cane, Maya got the impression that this troll knew how to keep his balance, even when the seas were rough.

"So," he said, studying her intently as she walked up the ramp and came closer, "Jeam tells me you want to find a town near Black Mountain."

"I do." Maya looked around. "But it might be dangerous for you."

"Would it, now? How much trouble can a small thing like you be in?"

"A lot," Maya said in a low voice.

"A runaway?"

"Kind of." Maya wondered how much she should tell Captain Creb. On the one hand, he deserved to know just how bad it would be for him and Jeam if they were caught with Maya. On the other hand, she really wanted to go to Black Mountain, and this seemed like her best way to get there. Maya was afraid that if Captain Creb knew about her involvement with Cinnial and Bigly, then he wouldn't want to take her on his boat.

Captain Creb held up his hand. "Never mind. I don't want to know. Welcome aboard."

"You'll take me?"

"I will. Jeam said I should, and he's hardly ever wrong."

Maya regarded Jeam, who stared solemnly back. This time, she looked even deeper into Jeam, past his basic decency, which blazed so brightly. Of course. Jeam could see, just the way she could, and it was nearly as strong with him as it was with her. But because he was a troll, Maya hadn't noticed it before. Again, Maya felt humbled as she realized that seeing wasn't limited to humans, that sentient beings across the universe could see, just the way she could.

Maya bowed her head, first to Jeam and then to Captain Creb. It was a spontaneous motion, and Maya could tell the captain was pleased.

The captain nudged Jeam. "See! Didn't I tell you they weren't all bad."

Jeam rolled his eyes. "Grandpa, I know."

The captain winked. "Just remember you heard it from me first."

Jeam rolled his eyes again, but his lips quirked into a reluctant grin.

"We'll be leaving tomorrow," the captain said. "Jeam, you'd better take her below deck so that no one knows she's aboard *The Resilience*."

"Thank you, Captain Creb." Maya followed Jeam down some stairs to a small room, a combined parlor and kitchen that had everything the two trolls needed to be comfortable. There was a stove, a tiny refrigerator, and cupboards that latched securely. There was a small table with padded benches that wrapped around it. Across from the table, there was even room for two comfortable chairs, small and bolted to the floor.

Jeam pointed to a door nearby. "That's the bathroom." He then pointed to two doors at the end of the room. The doors were open, and Maya could see neatly made beds, small stands with attached lamps, and shelves with books held securely in place with strips of wood.

Jeam saw her look at the rooms. "That's where Grandpa and I sleep. You can have my room," Jeam offered shyly. "And I'll sleep out here."

"No," Maya said firmly. "I'm not kicking you out of your room." She glanced at the padded benches. "I'm small enough to sleep here."

"You're sure?" Jeam asked.

"I'm sure."

Jeam opened a compartment under one of the benches. He moved some things around and made a space big enough for her rucksack. "You can put that here."

"Okay," Maya said, but before tucking the rucksack under the bench, she dug into it, taking out the purse. Opening it, Maya dumped the coins on the table, and Jeam nodded appreciatively. "Because I'm from away, I don't know much about the money here. Could you help me?"

"Sure," Jeam replied, and they sat side by side on one of the benches. Jeam picked up a large coin, and Maya could see that it had a profile of Cinnial's head etched into it. "This is worth the most. You'd only use it for something that costs a lot. Otherwise, you'd get more change back than would fit in your purse. And people might wonder why someone like you would have so much money."

"I knew it." Maya thought of that brown bread and of her reluctance to use the money to pay for a loaf.

There were three of those coins, and Maya pushed two of them toward Jeam. "Would anyone be suspicious if your grandpa had these coins?"

Jeam shook his head. "No, Grandpa often makes this much money after selling nuts and herbs he gets from Black Mountain. But only if the season is good, and we haven't had much rain this year."

"Take them, then."

Jeam hesitated. "Are you sure? That's a lot of money."

"I'm sure. I'll save one for when I get to Black Mountain. I might need it there."

Jeam took the two coins. "I don't know what Grandpa will say."

But the captain didn't refuse when Jeam gave him the coins. "These will come in handy," Captain Creb said candidly. "*The Resilience* needs some repairs, and to tell you the truth, I was wondering how I was going to afford them. I've heard that the drought has hurt the harvest of nuts and herbs from Black Mountain. Our take might not be so good this year. But we will soon see because that's where we're headed."

Maya nodded. "Good. Glad it will help."

Then it was time for a supper of meat and cabbage soup and brown bread. The soup was delicious, just as Maya had imagined it would be when she walked through Roford, and it had a flavor she couldn't recognize, something that gave the broth a rich, nutty taste.

"So good," Maya said with a sigh as she ate her soup.

The captain smiled. "Glad you like it. I splashed a little hua oil in it."

Maya shook her head. "I don't know what that is."

The captain studied her seriously. "You really are from away, aren't you?"

"I am," Maya replied. "Very, very far."

"Hua oil comes from the hua tree, pines so dark green that they look almost black. They grow all over the mountain, which is why we call it Black Mountain."

"I love Black Mountain," Jeam said dreamily as he stirred his soup with his spoon. "I wish we could live there."

The captain smiled sadly. "I know you do. But you're stuck with me on this boat."

Jeam shook his head. "Not stuck."

Maya looked from the captain to Jeam.

The captain cleared his throat. "Nedra, Jeam's mother, was from Black Mountain. She and her family had land and grew hua pines and harvested the nuts. But then she met my son, Ralden, and they made their home in Roford, where they worked in one of the factories."

"But there was a fire," Jeam said in a whisper. "And they were both killed."

The captain's eyes were bright. "So now Jeam lives with me."

"I'm sorry," Maya said softly, and both trolls nodded. "What about Nedra's family?"

"Eventually, they sold their land and came to live in Roford so that they could work in the factories," the captain answered. "The money's a little better, and the work is more regular. After his parents died, Jeam went to live with his Aunt Trahet, Nedra's sister."

"But I like being with my grandpa," Jeam put in, smiling at the older troll, who ruffled Jeam's wispy hair. "I get to be on *The Resilience*, and I get to go to Black Mountain sometimes."

"Do you go to school?" Maya asked.

"No," Jeam replied. "I'm ten, and I don't have to go anymore if I don't want to."

Maya thought about the children she had seen at the factory, and she now understood that they no longer went to school and instead were working alongside their parents. Something made her think about Chet and how he had worked hard as a child. She remembered his scornful question: "You've never had to work for anything, have you?"

Maya realized Chet was right. Her parents had enough money so that Maya could go to theater camp and do pretty much anything else she wanted. But now Maya's easy days were over, and she was working harder than she had ever imagined she would.

After they had finished with the soup and bread, Captain Creb set out a plate of cookies filled with golden nuts. He made some tea and set steaming mugs in front of Jeam and Maya. She ate one cookie, which was crunchy, nutty, and not too sweet. Seeing there were plenty of cookies on the plate, Maya took another.

The captain smiled. "So you like hua nuts, too?"

"I do," she answered. "They remind me of nuts we have back home."

Captain Creb sniffed. "Those that live in Mortmain think hua nuts are common, and they prefer nuts that are shipped from other parts of Caldor."

"But it's good, in a way, isn't it Grandpa?" Jeam asked, reaching for another cookie.

Captain Creb scratched his head. "Aye, Mortmain leaves Black Mountain alone. The mountain doesn't have anything Mortmain wants. Just hua nuts and other herbs. But in Roford and in other cities along the Ashwillot, the nuts and the herbs sell just fine. Some of us can even make a living from it. It's a good kind of life, considering all that's happened."

Maya nodded wistfully, picturing herself living on the boat with Captain Creb and Jeam. There wasn't enough room for her, but she imagined it anyway—being on the water, away from the cares of the Books of Everything and the Great Library.

The captain stared curiously at Maya. "You're carrying a heavy load, aren't you?"

"Yeah," Maya answered, leaning against the back of one the benches.

"That's why we have to help her," Jeam said softly but firmly. "Even though she looks the way she does, Maya's on our side."

Captain Creb stared sternly at Jeam, and he would have said something if Maya hadn't started laughing. For the first time, Maya realized that she appeared just as homely to the trolls as they did to her. On Earth, Maya knew that most people thought she was pretty, but not here, not with the trolls, and somehow this struck her as funny as well as illuminating.

"I suppose where you come from, you're quite the little fetching one," the captain said shrewdly, but he was smiling. Jeam, nervously glancing from his grandfather to Maya, smiled, too.

Maya just nodded. She was laughing too hard to answer.

When she finally stopped, Captain Creb said gruffly, "Everybody thinks their own kind looks good."

"Of course they do." Maya wiped her eyes. "I just never thought about it before."

"It's good to think about it. Your kind doesn't hold back when it comes to letting us know how ugly they think we are." There was a bitter note in Captain Creb's voice, and nobody was smiling anymore.

"I'm sorry." Maya's voice was low. "It's not right."

"No, it isn't," the captain replied. "But we trolls are just as bad. However, since we're not in charge, it's worse for us."

"I understand," Maya said softly, vowing never again to judge creatures or beings solely by their looks.

Maya offered to help the captain and Jeam with the clean-up, but Captain Creb waved her aside. "In this small kitchen, you'd just be in the way. Jeam and I have a system."

"Okay," Maya said, settling back on the bench. Closing her eyes, Maya felt the gentle motion of the boat, and she must have dozed because she jumped when she felt a hand on her arm.

It was Jeam. "Maya, wake up," he whispered. "Some of Grandpa's friends are on deck. Grandpa's up there, holding them off, but sooner or later they're going to want to come down for a drink. And not all of Grandpa's friends like humans."

"Where can I hide?" Maya whispered.

"In my room, under my bed. I'll move some things. But hurry."

Maya quickly followed Jeam to his neat, little room. Under his bed was a compartment, much like the ones under the benches in the kitchen. But this compartment was deeper and taller. Jeam closed his bedroom door and just in time. Maya heard voices as the trolls came down the stairs.

Quickly, Jeam opened the door of the compartment, grabbed some of his clothes, and stuffed them in a small chest wedged between his bed and the wall. There was just enough room for Maya to crawl into the compartment, and Jeam shut the door.

"I'll stay here with you," Jeam said in a low voice as he settled against the door of the compartment. "Grandpa's friends are loud. Most of them can't hear very well, and they have to shout to make themselves heard. And they always tell the same stories over and over."

Jeam wasn't kidding. The noise from the other room was so loud that it sounded to Maya as if there were a hundred trolls crammed into that small parlor rather than just five, as the captain would tell her later. Inside the compartment under

Jeam's bed, it was dark and stuffy, but Maya could feel Jeam's comforting presence just on the other side of the door, and she wasn't afraid.

Several times, the door to Jeam's room opened as one of Captain Creb's friends looked in on him. The comments all followed the same course.

"You're quite the one for reading, young troll, aren't you?"

"Why don't you come out and join us?"

"Always got your nose stuck in a book, don't you?"

Jeam gave the same patient answer every time. "No, thanks. I like to read."

"Suit yourself, young troll."

Then the bedroom door would slam shut.

Held by *The Resilience*, rocked by the Ashwillot River, guarded by Jeam, Maya again fell asleep. Going to Mortmain, the encounter with Cinnial, escaping from Bigly, and wondering what she should do next had completely worn Maya out, and despite the noise that the trolls were making, she slept soundly.

When Maya woke up, the boat was quiet, and the door to the compartment was open. Except for the small glow of a night light, the room was dark. Above her, Maya could hear Jeam's deep breathing as he slept. A blanket covered her, and a pillow had been slipped under her head. Snuggling into the blanket and pillow, Maya went back to sleep.

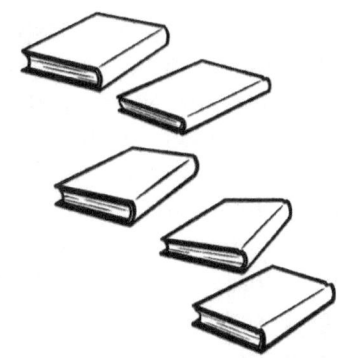

31: At the Lodge

Viola and the children landed with a thump in a parlor lit by the soft glow of lamps. There were two chairs by the fireplace, and in one sat a small, plump, bald man. In the other chair sat a tall woman with a white cap and gray curls. They both sprang to their feet. Rosalind and Sebastian cried out and then threw up on the floor behind the chairs. Viola was more prepared, and although her stomach felt queasy, she grabbed the back of one of the chairs to steady herself, and the sick feeling went away.

"Merciful heavens!" the plump man exclaimed.

The woman stared at the two children and Viola. "Who are you, and how did you get here?"

"I'm Viola Murphy." She let go of the chair and held up the blue Book. "Do you know about Books of Everything?"

"Aye," they answered together, staring thoughtfully at the Book. "That we do."

Viola nodded. "That's how we got here."

"And the children?" the woman asked.

"Rosalind and Sebastian," Viola answered.

The woman blinked anxiously. "Duke Owen's Rosalind and Sebastian?"

Viola crouched by the children, who were crying, and placed her hands on their shoulders. "Yes."

"Merciful heavens," the man said again, but his voice was brisk. "Let's get this mess cleaned up."

"And get some tea for the children to settle their stomachs," the woman added.

Within twenty minutes, the mess was cleaned, and three more chairs were pulled by the fireplace, which had a small fire and a kettle of simmering water. Although it was summer, the room was not hot. As Viola would discover, the stone lodge always remained cool, even on the warmest days.

Rosalind and Sebastian had stopped crying and were drinking their tea. There was a plate of sugar cookies on a table between the children, and they nibbled on cookies, too. Viola drank tea but didn't eat any cookies. She was too shaken by all that had happened, and her hand trembled a little as she reached for her cup. The Book of Everything lay in her lap, a solid, soothing weight on her legs.

The man's eyes, as dark as a bird's, took it all in, and beside him, the woman nodded. But he said mildly, "My name is Elwyn Brooks, and this is my wife, Sophie. I'm the lodge's steward, and Sophie is the housekeeper."

"We take care of things for Duke Owen," Sophie added, in a voice deep and gruff.

Viola stared curiously at this odd couple. It wouldn't take her long to learn that Elwyn was sterner than he looked, and Sophie was softer than her severe features and sharp voice indicated. Together, they were a team, and they ran the lodge and the surrounding tenants in a way that was firm but fair and orderly.

Having finished their tea and eaten some cookies, Rosalind and Sebastian began to sag in their chairs.

"Put Rosalind and Sebastian in our bed." Sophie looked at the children. "Tonight we'll sleep in the room next door. Tomorrow, we'll get a room ready for them."

"I'll sleep with the children tonight," Viola said. "If there's enough room."

"Oh, surely," Elwyn said cheerfully. "They're small, and you're not too big. You'll be cozy, but you'll manage."

In another twenty minutes, Rosalind and Sebastian were tucked in a bed in a room just off the parlor. Gazing down at the children's smooth faces, Viola brushed the hair away from their foreheads and kissed them on their cheeks, just the way her parents had kissed her when she was small. Viola thought of how she was too big now for goodnight kisses and was old enough to be giving them to Rosalind and Sebastian. Shivering, Viola was suddenly aware of the passage of Time.

Closing the door to the bedroom, Viola joined Elwyn and Sophie by the fire, and they were on their second cups of tea. "More tea?" Sophie asked.

"Yes, please," Viola answered, glancing at Earth's Book of Everything, which was on the table by the plate of sugar cookies.

"You had better tell us what happened," Elwyn said with a sigh. "But I don't suppose it's anything good."

"Otherwise, you wouldn't be here with Rosalind and Sebastian," Sophie added.

"It's nothing good," Viola agreed sadly, and she began by asking Elwyn and Sophie if they remembered a boy named Andy.

"We remember him, all right," Elwyn said, glancing at his wife, who nodded neutrally.

Viola noted the exchange but continued with her story. She went on to explain that she was Andy's daughter, and how he was a leader in her country. Viola then related all that had happened since she had left Earth and had come to Caxton with Maya. Finally, after correcting herself several times, Viola was done, and she slumped back against her chair.

"Duke Owen and Duchess Celia dead," Elwyn said, his voice choking a little.

Sophie wiped away tears. "And Humphrey back in charge."

"He's a rotter," Viola said fiercely.

Elwyn shook his head. "Aye, always wanting something he doesn't have."

Sophie added, "And then when Humphrey gets what he wants, he ruins things."

"Why do people follow him?" Viola asked, leaning forward. "Why can't they see how he is?"

Elwyn gave her a shrewd look. "Not everyone can see the way you and Maya can. The way Feste could. It's a talent most folks don't have."

Sophie sat with her back straight against the chair. "Most people see what they want to see."

Viola nodded. "My father and mother couldn't see how Humphrey was. They wanted him to give money to my father's campaign."

"Money's the worst," Elwyn said. "That and the desire for power can really cloud a person's judgment."

"But my parents are good!" Viola exclaimed.

Sophie glanced quickly at Elwyn before turning to Viola. "It can happen to good people, too. My own sister and her husband were taken in by Humphrey. Lucky for them that Duke Owen was merciful and pardoned them when he was duke again."

"Humphrey has a way of drawing people to him," Elwyn said. "He knows where they are weak, and he knows how to attack. He also makes wild promises that people are all too eager to hear. I will admit that even though I was always loyal to Duke Owen, sometimes Humphrey's words moved me."

Sophie gave a little shudder. "I am glad we are safe in the Forest of Arden, far away from Humphrey. He can't reach us here. The forest won't let him."

Elwyn considered Viola. "And you are Andy's daughter? It doesn't seem possible."

Viola told Elwyn and Sophie the same thing she had told Guy. "For you, it wasn't that long ago, but on Earth, it was over thirty years ago. The Book of Everything can travel through time and space."

Elwyn and Sophie were both staring at her, and there was something in their looks that Viola couldn't read. As Maya had learned, Viola was discovering that some people were good at blocking themselves from those who could see. It had happened to Viola with Chet, and it was happening now with Elwyn and Sophie. However, Viola did sense that it had something to do with her father. What had happened while he was here?

But Viola was too weary to give it much thought and had started sagging in her chair.

"You need to get some sleep," Sophie said. "Will you be staying more than one night with us?"

"I'll check," Viola said, taking the Book of Everything from the table and turning to Further Instructions. Viola read aloud, "For now, stay in the Forest of Arden with the children. Your father, Simon, Mémère, and Diana are safe. Chet is their prisoner."

"Everything is all set with them, then," Elwyn said. "Tomorrow, we'll get a room ready for you, too."

Yawning, Viola nodded. She gathered the Book, stood up, and headed toward the room where Rosalind and Sebastian were sleeping. Before going into the room, she said, "Thank you for taking us in."

"That's what we're here for," Sophie answered sadly. "Duke Owen knew that something like this might happen."

"And he was right," Viola thought with a sigh, settling under the covers beside the sleeping children. She hadn't really known the duke, but young though she was, Viola had been able to tell from the bustle and energy in Caxton that Duke Owen had been a good leader. "Now he's gone, and so is his wife."

As Viola fell asleep, she wondered what would happen next, and she heard a faint song, beautiful, but without words. It seemed to be calling to her, but Viola wasn't sure if she wanted to answer the call or not. The song stopped suddenly, and Viola slept soundly until morning.

She woke up to find two little faces staring at her.

"Viola," Rosalind whispered. "Where are we?"

"We're in a lodge in the Forest of Arden," Viola whispered back.

"My father's lodge?" Rosalind asked.

"Yes."

Sebastian put his small hand on Viola's cheek. "Where are Mémère and Simon?" He, too, was whispering.

Smiling, Viola sat up. "We don't have to whisper. We're safe here. Mémère and Simon stayed behind. But they'll be joining us soon."

Rosalind pointed to the Book of Everything, on a table beside the bed. "Did that book take us here?"

Viola nodded. "It did. It's special and can do all sorts of magical things. But let's not worry about the Book right now. We'll just leave it on the table. Are you hungry? Would you like some breakfast?"

"Yes!" the children shouted together.

Sophie was waiting for them in the parlor outside the room. She was sitting in one of the chairs, and she was knitting something small—as it turned out, a stocking for Rosalind.

"Up bright and early," Sophie said, smiling at them. "Are you ready to eat?"

"Yes, please," Rosalind answered.

"I'm very hungry," Sebastian added, smiling back at Sophie.

Sophie put her knitting in a basket beside her chair. "Follow me, then."

Elwyn and Sophie's chambers were on the second floor of the lodge. Viola and the children followed Sophie down a long hall until they came to a massive stairway, which led to a great hall with long tables and benches. Without pausing, Sophie walked briskly along the edge of the hall, and Viola and the children had to hustle to keep up with her. Glancing quickly around the room, Viola noticed a long row of windows at the far side of the hall and beyond that was a shimmering green.

Sophie led them to a dining room directly off the kitchen. There was one long table with chairs, with place settings for ten. There were windows on one wall, and Viola could see a large kitchen garden outside.

"Sit down," Sophie said, pointing to three chairs, and Viola and the children sat where the housekeeper indicated. Soon a plump, young girl with light brown hair came out, setting a platter of scrambled eggs and a plate of sausages on the table. Grinning, Sebastian squirmed with anticipation, and even Rosalind bounced a little in her chair. An older man, as plump as the young woman and with the same shade of light brown hair, brought out a platter of buttered toast.

"Toast." Viola smiled, and the man nodded with an answering smile, clearly pleased that the three guests were eager for his food.

Soon, ten people were sitting around the table, and Elwyn introduced them to Viola and the children. The plump older man was Maxwell Vos—the cook—and his assistant was his daughter Emilie. Robbie Herbert, a tall teenager with hair so blond it was almost white, took care of the horses in the stable, and Annie and Gwen Littleton, slim sisters with strawberry blonde hair, were maids who helped Sophie. They all lived in cottages that surrounded the lodge, but they came together in the morning and at noon to eat their meals together. Viola could tell they were a tight group who worked hard to take care of the lodge for Duke Owen.

After the introductions, nobody said anything for a while, and Viola could feel everyone's grief. "Of course Sophie and Elwyn told them about Duke Owen and Duchess Celia," she thought sadly.

Nevertheless, platters were passed, plates were filled, and everyone ate.

Finally, Emilie, noting the children's hearty appetites, said, "You're hungry this morning."

Sebastian's mouth was full, and he was about to say something, but Rosalind gave him a warning look. Instead, he just nodded vigorously.

"We've been in the forest for two days," Rosalind answered for him.

Sebastian swallowed. "I rode a horse named Raisin."

"And I rode Treacle," Rosalind added.

"After we're done, would you like to see the horses in the lodge's stable?" Robbie asked.

"Yes, please!" Rosalind and Sebastian said together.

The children finished eating before the adults, and Rosalind asked, "May Sebastian and I go outside and play?" She looked from Viola to Sophie.

Viola turned to Sophie, who nodded and answered, "Yes, you may." She pointed out the window to the area by the kitchen garden. "But stay right out there where we can see you."

"And don't trample the herbs," Maxwell added.

"Maybe they'd like to take Luna out and play ball with her," Emilie suggested. "Beyond the beds, there's a bit of lawn."

"Who's Luna?" Rosalind asked.

"My dog," Maxwell answered. "Right now she's in her bed by the kitchen fireplace. If you play with Luna, you must promise not to pull her ears or tail."

"I promise," Rosalind said. "We'd never hurt her, would we, Sebastian?"

"No," the little boy answered simply. "We love dogs."

Maxwell smiled. "All right, then. Emilie, go get Luna."

Emilie left the table and soon returned, followed by a small white dog with pointed ears and a little tail that stood up straight. Luna's eyes and nose were black and shiny, and she walked with a jaunty spring.

"Come on, Luna," Rosalind said, taking a ball from Emilie. "Let's go!"

Soon, Rosalind and Sebastian were shrieking and laughing as Luna chased a ball at the edge of the gardens.

For a while, everyone at the table smiled as they watched the children and the dog, but then Elwyn said to Viola, "I've told everyone what happened."

Viola nodded. "I know. I could tell."

Sophie sat tall and straight. "Now we have another job besides taking care of the lodge and the gardens. We must also take care of Rosalind and Sebastian. They are Caxton's rightful heirs. We don't know how long they'll be here, but it might be a long time."

"They'll need a nanny," Emilie said.

Robbie took another piece of toast. "My sister Meg would be good. She loves children, but she hates working in the gardens. Meg would be happy to leave outside work and come to the lodge."

"Very good suggestion," Elwyn replied.

"We need to call a meeting," Sophie said, and everyone nodded. "For all who live in the cottages. That way, they can hear what happened directly from Viola. But the children can't be at the meeting, of course. They'll have to be told sometime, but not yet. They're too young."

"Do Rosalind and Sebastian nap?" Annie asked.

"They will if we keep them busy this morning," Viola answered.

Robbie grinned. "Then let's keep them busy."

All morning, Rosalind and Sebastian were directed from one activity to the other. When they were done playing with Luna, Robbie took them and Viola to the stables, where they met the horses, who were afterwards let out into an adjoining pasture where they could graze. After that, Robbie, Viola, and the children all went back to the stables, to the hayloft, where Rosalind and Sebastian spent a happy hour jumping in the hay.

Off to one side, Robbie and Viola sat on two stools and watched the children play.

"Have you always lived here?" Viola asked.

"Nay," Robbie answered. "Me, my parents, and my brothers and sisters are from Thorndike, the town one over from Greendale. But we came here when I was young, and I really don't remember what it was like outside when Humphrey was duke. But I've heard it was bad. My brothers are older, and as soon as Duke Owen took Caxton, they went back to Thorndike, to run my parents' farm."

"Have you been outside since?" Viola asked.

"Aye," Robbie said. "I go to Greendale for supplies, and sometimes I visit my brothers. But I love it here in the Forest of Arden. I wouldn't want to live outside."

After playing in the hayloft, the children were hot and dusty, and they went to the kitchen for a drink of milk and some of Emilie's sugar cookies.

When they were done, Robbie asked, "Want to see the brook?"

Rosalind nodded, and Sebastian asked Viola, "May we get wet?"

Viola replied, "Oh, why not? It's a hot day."

After splashing in the brook, and then running around in the sun to dry off, Rosalind and Sebastian were ready for a noonday meal. When they were done eating, the children didn't argue about taking a nap, and just down the hall from Elwyn and Sophie's apartment, they were shown to their new room that had two small beds covered with bright quilts. Off the children's bedchamber, there was a connecting room with a bigger bed for Viola.

Viola sat with the children until they fell asleep and then left the room to find Sophie waiting for her in the hallway.

Sophie hesitated and then said, "Everyone is below in the great hall. My advice is that you don't tell them you're from a different planet and don't mention that you're Andy's daughter. It will just confuse things. Instead, say that you are from a distant land and that you came to Caxton with Maya. Tell them that when you were in the woods, your father came to help you with his own Book of Everything. That will be enough, and everyone in the forest knows about Books of Everything."

Viola studied Sophie, and she could tell the older woman was hiding something. But all Viola said was, "Okay."

Nodding, Sophie turned, walking in her brisk way down the hallway. Frowning, Viola followed her.

About forty people sat at the various tables in the great hall, and Viola felt self-conscious as everyone watched her come down the stairs. But Viola held her head high. With her father and mother, she had met many leaders on Earth, and from her parents, Viola had learned that it was important to look calm and in control.

"All right," Sophie said when she and Viola had taken their places beside Elwyn at one of the tables. "The children are asleep. We can begin the meeting."

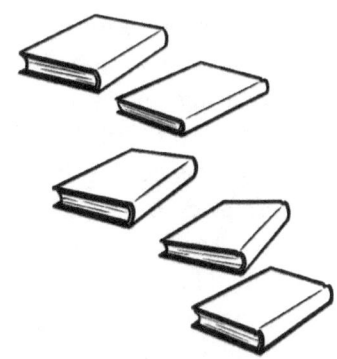

32: Viola Learns the Truth

Viola stood with her back to the long row of windows that overlooked the broad sweep of gardens, the cottages rimming the edges, and the dark green forest waiting just beyond. She told the forest's residents, adults as well as children, what had happened to Duke Owen and Duchess Celia. There were loud gasps and then silence as Viola described fleeing with Rosalind and Sebastian from Caxton, hiding in the wagon in Oakton, and the escape into Oakton's forest. There were more gasps as Viola told about how Chet had stalked them in Oakton's forest, and how, using her father's Book of Everything, Viola had escaped with Rosalind and Sebastian to the Forest of Arden.

When Viola was finished, there was more silence, and she sat down between Elwyn and Sophie. Clearing his throat, Elwyn stood. "This is a terrible shock and a terrible loss to Caxton. Unfortunately, Duke Owen knew Humphrey might return someday. This is why some of us stayed in the Forest of Arden. So there would be a refuge here should it be needed."

There were bowed heads, and many of the adults put their hands over their eyes, but everyone nodded. Elwyn continued, "Sebastian and Rosalind might have to stay here for a long time.

Who knows how long Humphrey will remain in power? Sometime soon, Viola will be returning to her own land, and we will need a nanny for the children. Meg, Robbie said you might be willing to be the children's nanny."

Meg was sitting by her parents, Robbie, and her other brothers and sisters, and in a group, their blond hair glowed brightly. "Aye!" she answered quickly.

"You'll have to come live at the lodge," Elwyn said.

"That's all right," came another quick answer, and despite the seriousness of the situation, everyone laughed.

"There you go, Meg," said Robbie. "No more working in the garden for you."

Meg didn't say anything. She just smiled in reply.

A middle-aged man stood. He had dark hair and a lean face. "Are we just going to let Humphrey get away with this?" he asked urgently. "Aren't we going to fight back?"

The adults in the room stirred uneasily, and Elwyn was silent for a few minutes before he spoke, "Gil, we are all here to take care of the lodge, to grow food, and to be as self-sufficient as we can. True, we get supplies from Greendale, but we don't know how long it will be safe to do that. I'm sure many of you remember how dangerous it was outside when Humphrey was duke."

People nodded, and some of them muttered, "I remember."

"However," Elwyn continued, "if any of you want to leave, then there is nothing to stop you. All of you are here because you want to be. You are free men and women. The choice is yours. But Sophie and I are staying here to take care of the lodge and to help Rosalind and Sebastian."

"Thank you, Elwyn," Gil said, sitting down. "I'll let you know what I decide." Most people shook their heads, but a few looked thoughtful as they considered what Gil had said.

Viola looked around the room. "How many will stay, and how many will leave?" she thought. Even though she had been in the Forest of Arden for only a short time and really hadn't had a chance to wander around, Viola could sense peace and order, a welcome relief after fleeing from Caxton with the two children. Then she thought about how her father, when he was seventeen, had been here with Maya. "Something happened with Dad, but what?" Viola wondered, and she was determined to talk to Sophie about it after the meeting.

However, Sophie had other ideas. When Viola approached her, the housekeeper said, "Annie, Gwen, and I have a full afternoon of cleaning. We have a weekly schedule, and I like to stick to it. Maybe Robbie will show you around beyond the stable and the stream."

Robbie, who was nearby, said, "Oh, aye."

"What about the children?" Viola asked.

"I'll have Meg stay here, and I will introduce her to the children when they wake up. She needs to spend time with them. It will be good for them to be used to her before you go."

"After you're done cleaning, I want to talk to you about my father," Viola said so softly that only Sophie could hear.

"I was afraid of that," Sophie replied just as softly. "Come to my parlor for afternoon tea. We'll talk then."

Thinking about her father and worried about what she might discover, Viola followed Robbie. They went out the front door, away from the gardens, on a well-traveled path that led directly into the woods. At first, absorbed with thoughts about her father, Viola hardly noticed the forest or the trees. But gradually, her busy mind stopped scrambling, and Viola became aware of a still, green presence that felt very old, and she began looking at the giant trees around her. Some of them were so tall that Viola had to tip her head back to see their leafy tops. Although birds sang and squirrels chittered, there was an underlying serenity so profound that it filled Viola with the same sense of awe she had felt when she had visited cathedrals in France with her parents. Stopping and closing her eyes, Viola put her hands on one of the trees—an oak—and she felt a slow, deep thrumming. Opening her eyes, Viola put her hand on another oak, and there was that same thrumming.

"The song of the trees," Robbie said, his face bright with joy.

"There are other songs," Viola replied, remembering the one she had heard last night.

"Aye," Robbie said. "And they all come together in the Forest of Arden."

Viola looked at the forest that stretched in every direction. "No wonder you don't want to leave." She thought about her hectic life on Earth, how she could never go anywhere by herself, how her schedule depended on what her parents were doing, how there was always a tension hanging over their lives because her father was the president of the United States. Before coming to Caxton, Viola hadn't realized how tired she was of it all—she had only been nine years old when her father had been elected—and she said sadly, "I don't want to leave, either. I love this forest."

"Couldn't you stay here?" Robbie asked. "And help Meg take care of Rosalind and Sebastian?"

"No, my father would never let me."

"Are you sure?"

"I'm sure."

"Then let me show you something to remember," Robbie said. "I came upon it by accident. But you have to promise not to tell anyone. I don't think anybody else from the outside has seen what I want to show you. Not even Maya."

"I won't tell anyone," Viola answered. "I promise."

"We'll have to walk for a good hour before we get there."

"I don't mind."

Robbie nodded, and deep into the forest they went, following a path so faint that Viola didn't know how Robbie could even find it. All around, she felt buoyed by the forest, which filled all her senses until she walked in a sort of swoon, forgetting about herself, her father, and their problems. Above her was blue sky, and the sun filtered through the deep green leaves, leaving patches of gold wherever it landed. There was a smell so fresh that Viola knew she could never get enough of it, and she breathed slowly and gratefully.

Viola followed Robbie, and what took over an hour seemed like minutes, until finally they came to a shimmering lake. Looking at her, Robbie put a finger to his lips and crept slowly toward the lake, moving to the left. Viola followed him as quietly as she could, and it wasn't long before she heard the sound of running water. Robbie stopped, motioning for her to come stand behind a tree so large that there was room for both of them to hide. Viola joined him, and Robbie whispered into her ear, "Peek slowly around the edge and look at what's swimming in the stream."

Viola did as she was told and nearly cried out in wonder when she saw winged creatures, no bigger than dragonflies, but with bodies that looked human. They were splashing in and out of the small, glittering stream, and if she listened closely, Viola could hear their high-pitched squeals of laughter. Some of the creatures had blue bodies and wings, others were red, and still others were black and gold. They flew and dipped so fast that it made Viola a little dizzy just watching them.

"What are they?" she whispered.

"We call them sprites," Robbie whispered back. "This time of day, they always come to the stream to drink and bathe."

Robbie and Viola watched until the sprites were done bathing, and they flew away in a sudden rush, banking together in perfect precision as they avoided trees and branches. Viola listened as the high-pitched laughter grew fainter and fainter until there was only the sound of water.

Robbie said, "We can go to the stream now."

The stream sparkled with glittering flecks left behind by the sprites, and Viola could sense a pulsing energy coming from the water. On the banks, the tall ferns seemed to shimmer. A fox with golden eyes came to the stream and paused to look at Viola and Robbie. Robbie nodded at the fox, and the creature nodded back. After taking a quick sip, the fox turned and, with a flick of a tail, disappeared into the forest.

Robbie and Viola sat by the stream, and bending down, she gazed into the water.

"Don't drink from it," Robbie warned. "Who knows how it will change you? That fox is no longer quite a fox anymore, and we think those sprites were once dragonflies."

"I won't," Viola answered, even though she was tempted to dip her hands in the water and take a sip. "How did the dragonflies become sprites?"

"I'm not sure, but I think it has something to do with the Old Oak that lives on the other side of the lake. It's ancient, and it has special acorns. The Forest of Arden gets its energy from the tree and the acorns. The closer you get to the tree, the stronger the energy, and it changes creatures who live next to it in all sorts of unexpected ways."

"Like the Toad Queen," Viola said.

"You know about the Toad Queen?"

"Maya told me."

"Aye, she had her eyes peeled by the Toad Queen. A brave lass. I'm not sure I would have the courage. But then again, I've never been called."

"Do you know Maya?" Viola asked.

"Not really. I saw Maya when she was here six years ago, with a boy named Andy, but I didn't get a chance to talk to her or to him."

"Andy," Viola said softly.

"Do you know him, too?" Robbie asked.

"I do."

"How well?"

"Very well," Viola answered, even though she was beginning to think she didn't know her father at all.

Robbie stared closely at her. "You look like him. Are you related?"

"Yes," Viola answered reluctantly, digging at the ground with one of her hands. Then shaking the dirt from her hand, she looked up at Robbie. "Tell me what happened with Andy. Something did. I can feel it when Elwyn and Sophie mention his name."

Robbie turned away, staring at the stream, and his usually bright face was serious. "I don't think I should. Especially if you're related to him. Besides, I was young when it happened, and I just heard bits and bobs from my older brothers. So it might not even be the whole truth."

"Tell me," Viola urged.

Turning, Robbie considered Viola, and she put her hand on his arm. "Please, whatever he did, it's worse not knowing."

Robbie sighed. "First tell me how you're related, then I'll tell you. Are you his sister?" Viola shook her head. "His cousin?"

"No."

"Then what?"

Viola's voice was flat. "I'm his daughter."

"His daughter?" Robbie looked so startled that Viola could tell that he didn't really believe her. "How can that be?"

Yet again, Viola explained how the Book of Everything could travel through time as well as space, that Andy was now a middle-aged man, old enough to be her father.

There was a panicked expression on Robbie's face, as though Viola had trapped him. "If he's your father, then I don't think I should tell you."

Like her father, Viola was slow to get angry, but when she did, it vibrated through her whole body, making her feel cold rather than hot, and she said in a crisp, precise way, "Robbie Herbert, you are a coward. You said you would tell me about Andy if I told you how I was related to him. Now, you're going back on your word." Jumping to her feet, she held her head high. "I'm going back to the lodge, and I don't need your help. Just leave me alone."

Standing, Robbie flushed. "I'm not a coward."

Whirling away from him, Viola marched through the forest, away from the stream.

"Wait!" he called.

But Viola ignored him, striding among the trees and the golden sunlight, and she had the strongest feeling that she was going in the right direction, that the trees were showing her how to get back to the lodge.

In an instant, Robbie was by her side, and he grabbed her arm. "Stop!"

Viola pulled away from him. "Don't you touch me. Just go away. The trees are showing me how to get back to the lodge."

Robbie grinned. "Look where you are."

Viola blinked. Somehow, she was back where she had started, by the stream.

Taking a deep breath, Viola burst into tears, surprising herself just as much as she surprised Robbie. Viola prided herself on her ability to stay cool in almost any situation. Her friends commented on it. Her parents praised her for this trait. But with everything that had happened in such a short time, it was all too much, and covering her face with both hands, Viola sank to the ground and sobbed louder than she had in a long time.

Crouching beside her, Robbie patted her shoulder. "All right, all right. I'll tell you. Please stop crying."

It took Viola a while, but gradually she stopped. Her head felt terrible, and her nose was stuffy. Robbie handed her a handkerchief. Nodding gratefully, Viola took it and blew her nose. Tucking the handkerchief in the pocket of her dress, Viola looked at Robbie, and she waited with both dread and anticipation.

"First, it wasn't all Andy's fault," Robbie began, staring intently at Viola. "Sir John egged him on. Sir John was tired of hiding in the Forest of Arden with Duke Owen. He thought it was time to attack Humphrey, who was planning to burn down the Forest of Arden."

"No!" Viola gasped.

Nodding grimly, Robbie looked away from Viola, and he gazed at the stream. "I remember when Duke Owen told us what Humphrey had planned. The duke had called a meeting, a lot like the one we had today. Right away, Sir John wanted to leave the forest and attack Humphrey. But Duke Owen wanted to take time to train the men. Most of us here are farmers and tradesmen. What did we know about fighting?"

"If you had attacked Humphrey directly, then you probably would have been smashed flat."

Smiling, Robbie looked at Viola. "Aye, that's just what my little brother Davy told Duke Owen. And Maya agreed. Even though she was young, she helped Duke Owen with strategy. Duke Owen and his men would hide in the woods and take Humphrey's men by surprise. And it worked. My older brothers were with Duke Owen, and what happened is almost the stuff of legend. Humphrey's men were unprepared, and we hardly lost any of our own men."

"But what about my father?" Viola asked. "What was his part in all of this?"

"You've heard about Feste, and how he took Maya under his wing?"

"Yes," Viola answered. "Maya told me a little about Feste."

"Well, Sir John took Andy under his wing, just like Feste did with Maya. Except that Sir John is..." Robbie paused. "He's unpredictable. His moods change just like the weather. On top of that, he's stubborn. When Sir John gets a notion in his head, nobody can stop him, and as I told you, he wanted to attack Humphrey. Immediately."

Viola had a bad feeling about what was going to come next. "What did my father do?"

"He stole Maya's Book of Everything and gave it to Sir John. After that they left the lodge, went to Greendale, and attacked the garrison there. They won, but then Julian stole Maya's Book of Everything, and Sir John, well, he killed Feste." Robbie's voice was low. "Not on purpose, but as my mother said, dead is dead, no matter if it's an accident."

Viola sat very still. During their late night talks at Rose Cottage, Maya hadn't told her any of this. Viola finally said, "It doesn't seem possible that my father would steal the Book of Everything from Maya."

Robbie shrugged. "He was young. And Sir John can be persistent."

"But my father was older then than I am now! Why didn't he see how Sir John was?"

"Viola," Robbie said gently, "not everyone can see the way you and Maya can. I know I can't."

Viola shook her head. "Elwyn said the same thing to me."

"Aye," Robbie replied. "'Tis true. Must be a bit of a burden, though."

Looking away, Viola blinked rapidly, afraid that she was going to start crying again. "Yes, it is," she answered in a tight, choked voice. "Sometimes I wish I didn't have it."

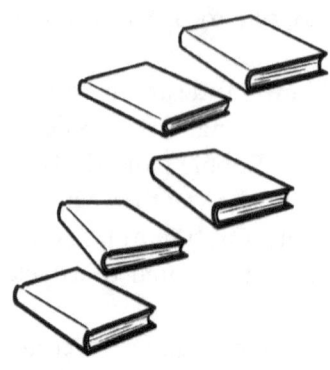

33: Viola to the Rescue

L ater that afternoon, Sophie filled in the gaps of what
Robbie had told Viola about her father. They were
sitting in Sophie's parlor, and there was tea. Meg and the children were outside, and Elwyn was in the garden, discussing
crops with the head gardener. The window was open, and warm
air flowed inside, but in Sophie's parlor, it was cool and quiet.
The room was at the front of the lodge, away from the gardens
and the bustle of the cottages.

Sophie said, "Aye, it's true that Andy stole the Book of
Everything and gave it to Sir John. Then the two hotfooted it to
Greendale and convinced the villagers to attack the garrison. In
the process, Julian stole the Book of Everything and returned to
Caxton. Sir John did indeed kill Feste, and what a loss that was
to all of us." Sophie sighed. "There isn't a day that goes by when I
don't think of Feste. Both Elwyn and I miss him very much."

"But it was an accident, wasn't it?" Viola asked anxiously,
thinking of the large, generous man who had let her and Maya
stay at Rose Cottage.

"It was." Sophie finished her tea and picked up her knitting
from the basket by her chair. She was making good progress on

Rosalind's little stocking. "When Duke Owen regained his title and retook Caxton, he sent us a long letter explaining all that had happened when Andy and Sir John left the Forest of Arden. Feste and Maya went to Greendale to bring Sir John and Andy back to the forest. There were hard words, and Sir John lost his temper. He punched Feste square in the face. Sir John's a big man, and Feste was slight. It was too much for poor Feste."

"How could Sir John have done that?" Viola asked in a low voice.

"He was angry," Sophie answered simply. "And when people get angry, they sometimes do bad things."

"Then what happened?"

"Duke Owen banished Sir John and Harry from Caxton, and he placed your father under house arrest at Duchess Celia's. She lived in Greendale then and wasn't married to Duke Owen. But your father escaped and met the very same Simon who helped you flee with the children from Caxton. Simon and your father reunited with Sir John and Harry, who, as it turned out, didn't leave Caxton as they were instructed. Instead, Sir John and Harry joined with other men who were plotting to overthrow Duke Humphrey."

Viola sat quietly, thinking about how even though she and Maya had talked late into the night at Rose Cottage, there was a lot that Maya hadn't told her. And Simon? He had never mentioned any of this to Viola. So much had been kept from her. "What did Maya do?" Viola asked after a while.

"After Feste died, Maya went to get help at a place called the Great Library."

Viola said, "Maya did tell me about the Great Library. It's where Books of Everything come from."

Sophie nodded. "Aye, Maya came back with an Apprentice Book, and two women, Elspeth and Alani. They joined with Andy, Simon, Sir John, and men from the surrounding villages to help take back Caxton for Duke Owen. Without their help, who knows what would have happened?"

"Did it make up for what my father and Sir John had done?" Viola asked grimly.

Sophie stopped knitting. "I can't answer that. But I do know that not much blood was spilled when Duke Owen retook Caxton. We've had six very good years. Elwyn and I don't travel far from the Forest of Arden, but we do go to Greendale from time to time, and we can see how prosperous and orderly the town has become. Duke Owen must have thought it was enough because he pardoned Sir John, Harry, and your father."

"Right," Viola replied. "That's why Sir John and Harry were living in Caxton, in Rose Cottage. Where do you think they are now that Humphrey's back in Caxton?" Somehow, with all that had happened, this was the first time Viola had wondered about Sir John.

Sophie sighed. "I expect Sir John is in jail. And Harry, too."

"What will Humphrey do to them?"

"I think you know the answer to that," Sophie said, resuming her knitting.

Yes, Viola did know what Humphrey would do to Sir John and Harry. Despite what the big man had done, Viola was filled with sorrow when she thought about how he would be executed.

"Does Sir John deserve to die?" Viola asked. "He killed Feste."

Sophie stopped knitting again. "Duke Owen didn't think so. He banished Sir John instead of having him killed on the spot. And no one loved Feste more than Duke Owen did."

"What do you think?"

Sophie shrugged. "I'm glad it wasn't my decision to make. But one thing I know. Duke Owen ruled with both his heart and his head. He chose mercy whenever he could. Yet he was strong. And wise, even. There aren't many leaders like Duke Owen." Sophie put a hand to her eyes, and Viola could see that she was crying.

"My father's like that, too." Viola's voice was little more than a whisper. "He's pardoned a lot of people. Do you think Dad learned that from Duke Owen?"

"Aye," Sophie said, sniffing. "It wouldn't surprise me."

Viola thought of the Book of Everything on the table in her bedchamber. "I could save Sir John," she said suddenly. "And Harry, too. If the Book of Everything would let me."

"I suppose you could. With all the talk about Duke Owen, Duchess Celia, and the children, I haven't been able to think of much else."

"Me, neither. Where would I take Sir John and Harry?"

"Why don't you consult the Book?" Sophie smiled just a little. "I just pray it isn't here."

Sophie's prayers were answered. When Viola consulted the Book of Everything and went to Further Instructions, the Book said, "Bring Sir John and Harry to Eben's hunting lodge in Oakton Forest. Rhys, Molly, and Jem are imprisoned, too. Bring them to the hunting lodge as well."

"That's a lot of rescuing," Viola said to herself, wondering how her stomach would feel after so much traveling. Nevertheless, she was ready to do it.

Sir John, Rhys, Harry, Molly, and Jem sat despondently in the small jail in Caxton. They had been tried and found guilty, and the next day they were to be hanged by the neck until dead. There were two cells, side by side, with Sir John, Rhys, Harry, and Jem in one cell, and Molly in a cell by herself. Nobody spoke, not even Sir John. They just sat on the floor, and each person was absorbed with his or her own thoughts. Both cells had one small barred window at the top, and no matter how bright the day, only a dim light filtered into the jail.

But there was plenty of light to see the young girl who suddenly popped into the cell with Sir John, Rhys, Harry, and Jem. The girl was holding a book, and she staggered back a little, clutching her stomach with her free hand.

Jumping, the men peered at her. "Viola?" Sir John asked, his voice raspy.

Rhys stared at the girl. "Is that a Book of Everything?"

"Yes," Viola whispered. The Book had told her that the guard in the next room was napping, and the sheriff was conferring with Humphrey at the keep. But Viola wasn't taking any chances. "I've come to rescue you and bring you to Eben's hunting lodge in Oakton."

For a moment, with their mouths slightly open, the men just stared at Viola. Then Jem went to the side of the cell, where the two adjoined, and in a whisper told his mother what was happening. Viola heard a choked sob coming from Molly. Shivering, Viola thought about what it must be like to be sentenced to death and then rescued at the last minute.

"Who wants to go first?" Viola asked, still whispering. "I have to take you one by one."

"Let Jem go first," Rhys replied softly. "He's the youngest."

Before Jem could protest, Viola put her hand on his arm and in a low voice said, "Take us to Eben's hunting lodge in Oakton Forest."

One by one, Viola took the men to the lodge. Sitting around a table as they waited for their stomachs to settle down, they nonetheless looked around in wonder at the lodge.

"Never thought I'd come here again," Sir John said.

"Me, neither," Rhys replied, swallowing.

"Traveling with that Book is like a kick in the gut." Jem rested his head on his arms on the table.

Viola's face was pale, but she was getting used to traveling with the Book, and she actually didn't feel that bad. Viola said, "Now for Molly."

Back to the jail Viola went, to fetch Molly, and just in time. In the next room, the guard was waking up. Viola could hear him yawning and stretching.

After Molly had recovered from traveling with the Book, everyone looked expectantly at Viola. They were all sitting at one of the tables.

"Tell us how you escaped," Rhys said. "And did you take Rosalind and Sebastian with you?"

"Yes," Viola answered. "Simon and I took them away the night of the bonfire. Maya told us to go. She knew something bad was going to happen to Duke Owen and Duchess Celia."

"Thank God for Maya," Molly said.

"Aye, but it's too bad she couldn't have saved Duke Owen and the duchess." Rhys scowled. "They are dead, and Humphrey is duke again."

"I don't think Maya could have saved them," Viola said wearily, remembering the conversation between Evangeline and Maya in Duke Owen's parlor. She regarded the blue Book on the table. "I think the Books have their own plans." Shivering, Viola had a sudden flash of illumination. "And above the Books are Time and Chaos."

The room was quiet as everyone thought about what Viola had said. "Where are Rosalind and Sebastian now?" Rhys finally asked.

Viola told them all that happened, and when she was done, Sir John wiped his eyes. "Safe in the Forest of Arden," he said. "Thank heavens!"

"You and Maya are quite the pair." Molly patted the girl's arm.

Viola shook her head. "Maya's so much better than I am. So much braver."

"Maya's unique," Rhys said. "But don't downplay all that you have accomplished. Those children would be dead right now if it weren't for you and Simon."

"And my father," Viola said suddenly. After listening to Robbie and Sophie, Viola had only been able to think about the bad things her father had done, and she hadn't really considered what would have happened to them all if her father hadn't arrived just when he did with Earth's Book of Everything.

"Aye," Harry agreed. "Chet might have killed you all. And we would have been hanged on the morrow."

Sir John's face was red. "That Chet. If ever I get my hands on that man, he'll wish he had never come to the Duchy of Caxton."

Rhys smiled just a little. "Not that he had much choice. Maya brought him here."

"But Chet didn't have to go after those children," Molly said grimly. "He had a choice in that."

"Aye," Rhys replied. "But Chet chose his path long ago, and now he's so set on it that it's all he can do."

"Plus he's a rotter," Viola said. "Just like Humphrey."

"That he is," Harry agreed, and everyone nodded.

"Can a rotter ever change?" Viola asked.

"Not likely," Molly said, then glancing at Sir John and Harry, she added quickly, "Course, sometimes people make big mistakes. They're sorry afterwards and try to make up for what they've done. That's different from being a rotter, who only thinks about himself."

Sir John and Harry were looking down at the table, and Viola realized that no matter how sorry they were, what they had done would be something that would be with them for the rest of their lives. Viola thought, "I wonder if it's the same for my father?"

But Viola kept these thoughts to herself. Instead, she said, "I should get back to the Forest of Arden. Will you be all right here?"

"Oh, aye," Rhys answered. "Sir John, Harry, and I have spent quite a lot of time at the lodge. And now, at least, we have one of the best cooks in Caxton to keep us going."

Molly smiled sadly, but she didn't say anything, and Jem patted her arm.

Viola stood. "Well, if I don't see you again, good luck. I don't know how much longer I'm going to stay in the Forest of Arden."

After everyone thanked her, again and again, for rescuing them, Viola had the Book of Everything take her back to the lodge in the Forest of Arden.

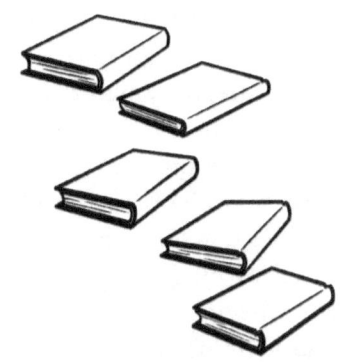

34: Viola Is Called

Back at the lodge in the Forest of Arden, everything was quiet. It was that glimmering time between late after-noon and dusk. Meg, Rosalind, and Sebastian were still outside. In the kitchen, Max and Emilie were cooking the evening meal. Robbie was tending the horses, and Annie and Gwen, finished with their day's work, had joined their parents in one of the little cottages edging the garden. Elwyn and Sophie were in the office directly off the great hall, and they were going over the lodge's accounts, planning a trip the next day to Greendale to stock up on supplies.

The Book of Everything brought Viola directly to the office, and she landed with a soft thump in front of the large desk Sophie and Elwyn were sitting behind.

They both jumped. "Viola!" Elwyn exclaimed. "Merciful heavens, you have a way of startling us."

Viola smiled. She was beginning to feel like a pro when traveling with the Book of Everything, and her stomach wasn't at all upset. "Sorry!" she replied.

"Oh, that's all right," Sophie said. "Pull up a chair and tell us what happened."

There were extra chairs lining the room, and Viola brought one over, setting it in front of the desk. Sitting down and taking a deep breath, Viola told them all that had happened, how she had been able to rescue Sir John, Rhys, Harry, Molly, and Jem.

Sophie smiled. "That's going to give Humphrey a little surprise, when he finds out that they've all escaped, and there are no clues to tell him how they did it."

Frowning, Elwyn set down his pencil. "Surprise probably won't begin to describe Humphrey's reaction. No doubt he'll send men into every town to search for Sir John, Harry, Rhys, Molly, and Jem. And Greendale will have a target on it because of the Forest of Arden."

"Good thing we're going into town tomorrow," Sophie said. "How long do you think we have before Humphrey sends men to Greendale?"

The Book of Everything was in Viola's lap. "Do you want me to check and see how long you have?"

"Why, yes," Elwyn said. "By all means. Very handy to have a book like that."

Turning the pages, which seemed to go on and on, Viola stopped when she came to Humphrey's entry. "Humphrey is furious that his prisoners have escaped," she read aloud. "And he's beginning to wonder what has happened to Chet. Humphrey plans to send bands of men to each town, to track down Chet, the children, and the prisoners. He will send more later as he rebuilds his forces. Humphrey's men will reach Greendale in four days."

"Four days will give us enough time," Sophie said.

"After that you won't be able to leave the Forest of Arden?" Viola asked anxiously.

"Not with our carts and not in any numbers," Elwyn replied. "We'll be able to sneak into town from time to time to get supplies we can carry in packs on our back. And folks from town will bring things to us. But they can't be conspicuous about what they're doing. If any of them should be caught before they get into the Forest of Arden..." Elwyn's voice trailed off.

"It wouldn't be good," Viola finished.

"They'd be killed," Sophie said flatly. "So we have to be careful."

Elwyn agreed. "Careful is right. Not only do we have to watch out for Humphrey's men, but there's always a chance that someone in town will be turned."

"What do you mean?" For some reason, Viola was nervous about what the answer would be.

Elwyn shook his head. "There's been talk that when Sir John attacked the garrison in Greendale, someone had warned the troops, and they were ready. In the end, it didn't matter. Sir John and the men in Greendale took back the town. But we have to be vigilant."

"Did you ever find out who it was?" Viola asked.

"No," Elwyn answered.

Sophie looked at Elwyn. "That might just be a rumor."

"I don't think it was just a rumor," Elwyn said in his soft voice, but there was also a firmness to it that indicated his certainty. "I've heard that a lieutenant of Humphrey's knew who betrayed the town. He was going to tell Duke Owen and barter for his freedom. Duke Owen was staying in Greendale Manor, and the lieutenant was to be brought to him. But the lieutenant died before he could tell the duke, and no one ever found out who it was. I suppose the lieutenant didn't tell anyone else because that was his trump card, and he wanted to make it pay."

Viola swallowed. "I wonder who it was."

Elwyn shrugged. "That secret apparently died with the lieutenant. Funny thing, though."

"What?" Viola asked.

"I've heard that the lieutenant's wounds weren't that bad."

"Do you think someone killed him to keep him quiet?" Viola asked.

Elwyn shrugged again. "It wouldn't surprise me."

"Elwyn Brooks," Sophie said sharply. "This is all speculation and gossip. You don't know any of this for a fact. The lieutenant probably just caught a fever and died. It happens all the time."

Elwyn nodded. "We'll say no more on the subject." But he gave Viola a look that suggested he was right, and Sophie was not.

Viola left Elwyn and Sophie so that they could continue making their list of items they wanted to stockpile. She carried the Book up the stairs, to her bedchamber. Suddenly, the Book seemed heavy to her, and Viola knew that it wasn't because the Book had gained volume, the way it could if it wanted to. Instead, it was because of her low spirits and her dread of what she might find inside the Book. Viola realized this wasn't exactly fair. It wasn't the Book's fault that she had found out what her father and Sir John had done. The Book hadn't mentioned anything about it when Viola had turned to Further Instructions. Instead, Viola knew it was her ability to sense things, sharper than ever now that she was in Caxton, that had led to that discovery. Nevertheless, Viola felt uneasy. What would she discover next?

"Maybe I don't really want to know," Viola said to herself, putting the Book on the table beside her bed. "Maybe it's better not to know, especially when there isn't anything I can do about it."

For a while, sitting on the bed, Viola stared at the Book, serene in its blueness, and she brooded about knowing and not knowing.

During dinner in the little dining room off the great hall, Viola was quiet as everyone talked and ate. Viola noted how much Rosalind and Sebastian liked Meg. They were sitting on either side of her, and Meg smiled calmly as she responded patiently to their many questions.

Viola thought, "They'll be fine without me when I return to Earth. That's good. They've lost a lot, even though they don't know it yet. It's great that they like Meg and their new home here in the forest."

In a way, Viola wished she could stay right here with them and never have to go back to her old life or face her father. What would she say to him? Viola felt that their relationship would not be the same now that she knew what her father had done.

Robbie wasn't at the table, and Viola missed his bright presence. Instead, he was at his parents' cottage, where he ate his evening meal most nights.

After the meal, she went outside with Meg and the children so that there could be one last game with Luna before it was bedtime. While Luna and the children ran after the ball, Meg glanced quizzically at Viola.

"You seem sad tonight." Meg was nearly as tall as her brother, and she had the same bright aspect.

"I am a little," Viola answered with a sigh.

"Are you sorry to be leaving the children?" Meg settled on a bench at the edge of the kitchen gardens, and Viola sat beside her.

"Yes." Viola looked around at the golden shadows and the deep green that came with dusk. "I'd like to stay in the Forest of Arden with them."

"I wouldn't like to leave either," Meg said. "But the Forest of Arden is not for everyone. My older brothers couldn't wait to get back outside and run the family farm. Too quiet here for them. No tavern where they can drink and lark about with their friends."

"It is quiet here," Viola said. "But I like it. I've traveled a lot with my parents. It's not as much fun as you think it would be."

Meg nodded. "Some of us are homebodies. And as my mother says, for us, home is best."

"I don't even know where my home is anymore," Viola said sadly. For three years, they had lived at the White House. If her father didn't get reelected, Viola wasn't sure where they would live. Her parents hadn't discussed it with her, although she knew they would eventually. But wherever she and her parents lived, they would still be guarded by the Secret Service. Once again, her life would be closed in.

"I wish I could stay here," Viola repeated.

"Why can't you?" Meg asked, just as Robbie had.

"My father would never let me."

Meg frowned. "Most parents like to keep their children nearby. But aren't you nearly old enough to be striking out on your own?"

Viola shook her head. "Not really. Twelve is pretty young where I come from. And in my land, my father's a leader. Just like Duke Owen. Actually, higher than Duke Owen. More like your king."

Gasping a little, Meg said, "I'm surprised, but I'm not. This afternoon, you came down that staircase just like you were royalty."

Viola smiled a little, but she said seriously, "If I suddenly just went away, there would be so much trouble. And my mother, well, she would make a big stink." Viola grimaced. "When Mom gets on a roll, she can go on for a long time."

Meg laughed. "Aye, I know what you mean. My mother's like that, too. My father's a forester, and I think he's glad to be able to spend so much time in the woods." She put her arm around Viola. "Well, however long you stay, you are welcome. You saved Rosalind and Sebastian, and somehow, you fit right in here."

Viola felt it, too. But she didn't say anything and instead leaned her head against Meg's shoulder.

Later that night, after the children had been tucked in their beds, and Viola was in hers, she took the Book of Everything from the table beside her bed. By flickering candlelight, she opened the Book and skimmed through its seemingly endless pages. She read her father's entry and learned that he was recovering from being shot and that Mémère was taking good care of him.

"How are we going to explain that when we get back to Earth?" Viola asked softly. Diana, too, was recovering, but her injury was more serious. Again, Viola wondered how this would be explained.

With trembling hands, she turned to Maya's entry, and there was a picture of Maya's determined face. Viola gasped a little as she read the simple entry: *Maya must be in Mortmain as we can no longer find her.* "Oh, Maya," Viola whispered. "Good luck."

Hesitating just a little, Viola turned to Simon's entry, but there was nothing about his time in Greendale. Instead, the entry explained how he was helping Mémère by hunting for food and guarding Chet. It ended with the admonition that Chet, though a captive and tied up, was still dangerous, and that Simon and Mémère should be careful.

Viola wasn't sure whether to be relieved that she hadn't learned anything about Simon's time in Greendale or be worried about what Chet might do to her father, Simon, Mémère, and Diana.

Finally, and slowly, Viola turned to her own entry. A picture, taken with her mother and father when they were in Rome, just a few months ago, was by her entry, which read:

Eventually, you must return to Earth with your father. But you know that. However, your father needs to heal first, so you will have some time in the Forest of Arden. Tonight you will be called, and you will have a decision to make. The decision is yours and yours alone. Do not worry about what others have chosen.

Viola sat very still. She knew exactly what the Book meant. Hadn't she heard the song calling her? Shivering, Viola closed the Book and set it back on the table beside the bed. She blew out the candle and settled into bed. It took her a long time to fall asleep, but finally she did, only to be woken up a few hours later by the song without words. This time it was louder, stronger, and it seemed to tug at her. Viola slipped quietly out of bed, took off the nightdress Sophie had given her, and put on her dress and shoes. She crept past the sleeping children, slid into the hall, and closed the door softly. Down the stairs and across the great hall Viola went, and it felt as if she were gliding rather than walking. All around her was the song, guiding her gently but insistently through the large doors at the end of the great hall.

Surrounded by the song, Viola sped past the gardens and into the woods. The night, illuminated by soft moonlight, was nevertheless dark, mysterious, and a little dangerous. Viola heard odd noises that she couldn't quite identify. One, a cross between a yip and a cat's meow, was so close that it made her jump. But the song enveloped Viola and brushed away whatever was making the strange cry. Viola heard the sound recede farther and farther away from her until she couldn't hear it anymore.

As the song swept her through the forest, Viola felt co-cooned and safe from all the creatures that prowled and hunted. However, Viola trembled a little as she thought about what she was going to face.

After what could have been ten minutes or two hours, Viola was brought to a clearing where there were hundreds and hundreds of small toads. They were all singing, singing for her. On the other end of the clearing, next to a massive oak tree, sat the Toad Queen, and her song was the loudest and strongest. The Toad Queen glimmered in the moonlight, and Viola caught a flash of the red jewel in her head.

Viola took a tentative step into the clearing, and the song stopped. Viola stumbled, and little toads leaped away from her. But Viola didn't fall, and standing still, she gazed in wonder at the massive Toad Queen. Viola curtsied, as she had been taught to do when meeting royalty.

"Welcome, Viola," the Toad Queen said. "Our song has brought you here, but you must come the rest of the way freely, by your own choice."

Nodding, Viola stepped carefully among the small toads, who made a path for her as she approached the Toad Queen. It seemed to Viola that she would never get to the Toad Queen, but eventually she did, unable to look away from the regal creature in front of her.

"You know who I am?" The Toad Queen asked.

Viola licked dry lips. "Yes, Maya told me about you."

"And you know what choice you must make?"

"I do," Viola heard herself say faintly, as though she were speaking down a long tunnel. But she continued in a clear if soft voice, "I have to decide whether or not to have my eyes peeled."

"That is right. And what is your decision?"

Viola didn't say anything. Instead, she stood silently in front of the Toad Queen and the Old Oak. Around them the forest was quiet and still, as though it, too, were waiting for her answer.

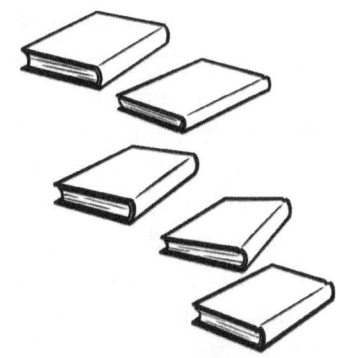

35: To Black Mountain

Maya stayed with the captain and Jeam for three days as *The Resilience* made its way down the Ashwillot, along the coast, and then up the Nokom River to Clamic, the port where the captain stopped to get hua nuts and herbs. From Clamic, Maya would be able to find a trail that went up Black Mountain, and Jeam had drawn a little map for her that outlined the route.

Maya had to stay below deck. There were too many boats going along the coast for her to be up with the captain, which is where Maya wanted to be. She wanted to feel the sun on her face, smell the salt air, and watch the various seabirds. She wanted to see the stars in the night sky, which Maya knew would be different than the ones she was used to seeing on Earth.

But Maya sensed it was much too dangerous for her to be on deck, where other trolls would be able to spot a short human girl with blonde curls who looked suspiciously like the one Bigly was hunting for. Maya had no doubt whatsoever that word about her had spread through the troll grapevine from Mortmain to Roford to all the boats cruising along the coast. Whenever a boat passed *The Resilience,* and Maya heard the gruff hail from another troll captain, she could almost feel sharp eyes peering into the boat. If she was in the parlor, then Maya would hide under the table and stay there until Jeam would tell her that it was all right to come out. Maya knew that the room's windows were too high and too small for anyone to easily see her, but she wasn't taking any chances.

As it turned out, Maya was right to be cautious.

"Trolls have better vision than humans do," Jeam said the first time she hid. "They probably can't see you through those little windows, but it's better if you're under the table. Just in case."

Through it all, Jeam mostly stayed with her, only going on deck from time to time so that none of the other troll captains would be suspicious and wonder why Jeam wasn't out with his grandfather. In the cozy parlor, Maya and Jeam sometimes played a game that was very much like checkers. Sometimes Jeam read to her from a book called *The Adventures of Tempus Troll*, who sailed the ten seas of Tufrak and got into one scrape after another but always managed to prevail in the end. Sometimes Jeam and Maya just talked, telling each other things they never would have told anyone else. Because despite their age difference, despite the fact that Jeam was a troll, and Maya was a human, they instinctively knew they could trust each other. In a very short time, they had become good friends.

Jeam confided to Maya that he was afraid his grandfather would die before Jeam was old enough to take care of himself. Then, he would have to go back and live with his Aunt Trahet.

"Was she mean to you?" Maya asked anxiously. She had noticed how Captain Creb coughed loudly in the morning when he got up, and she thought that Jeam was right to be worried.

Jeam shook his head. "No, but she doesn't care for me as much as the captain does. Aunt Trahet just took me in because my mother was her sister. But Grandpa likes having me here. He wants me to be with him."

Maya understood. "I hope the captain lives for many more years." Then she got a flash of Jeam, a little older but not yet a grown troll, at *The Resilience*'s helm. "You don't have to be an adult to be captain of this ship. You know more than you think you do."

Jeam nodded. Although Maya had confirmed his fears about the captain's health and death, she could tell that she had also reassured him. Jeam would stay with *The Resilience,* even when the captain was gone.

Then Maya told Jeam a little about Ariel and the Books of Everything, the Great Library, and Cinnial.

"Cinnial's a bad man," Jeam said almost in a whisper, as though someone might be listening.

"Yeah, he is," Maya agreed. "I'm supposed to do something to help save the Great Library, but I don't know what. And I don't even have Ariel to help me."

In his gentle way, Jeam looked deep inside Maya, and she didn't block him. Blinking, he pulled back. "You know more than you think you do, too."

Maya sighed. "That's what Ariel told me just before I escaped from Mortmain. But I don't understand what that means."

"How did Ariel help you?"

"Ariel gave me advice. But the best thing was that Ariel could move me through time and space and take me anywhere in the universe."

Jeam whistled softly. "Wow."

"Right? How cool is that? But Ariel is in Mortmain, and now I have to travel just like anyone else."

"Maybe not," Jeam said.

"What do you mean?" Maya asked. Ariel had hinted at something similar just before she had left Mortmain. Maya didn't understand it then, and she didn't understand it now.

"You might be able to travel like that on your own."

"What did you see?"

Jeam frowned. "I didn't really see anything. It's just a feeling I got. That you could go wherever you wanted."

"But I don't know how. It seems impossible."

"Maybe you have to really want to."

"Maybe, but for now I'm on *The Resilience,* with you and Captain Creb."

"Wish you could stay longer," Jeam said wistfully.

"Me, too." She had made a permanent bed under Jeam's bunk, so now there really was room for her on the ship. But Maya knew it wasn't safe for the captain and Jeam to have her on board *The Resilience*. Maya shuddered as she pictured what would happen to those two if another troll discovered her hiding below deck. And besides, her mission wasn't to sail the ten seas with the captain and Jeam. It was to go to Black Mountain and somehow find the resistance that was hiding there.

"But how can there be a resistance in Caldor?" Maya wondered aloud. "Why hasn't Cinnial discovered it?"

Jeam shrugged. "I don't know about a resistance, but I do know that high in Black Mountain there is a group who lives there and saves seeds. Some say that Black Mountain has strange powers when you get high up and that the mountain lets the seed savers stay there. But most humans and trolls keep to the edges down below where the hua trees grow thickest. Hardly anybody ever goes to the top. Too many avalanches, both in summer and winter. And you never know when one is going to happen. Even I like to stay on the edges of the mountain where there are lots of trees and no avalanches."

"Do you think the seed savers belong to the resistance?"

Jeam shrugged again. "I've never heard of a resistance, only the seed savers. But you'll find out."

"I'll find out."

Late on the night of the third day, with *The Resilience* docked at Clamic's small port, Maya reluctantly said goodbye to Captain Creb and Jeam. In her pack, there was now one of the captain's jackets, which fit Maya pretty well, a flashlight, the map, a compass, some sandwiches and cookies, and a thermos of tea.

They all stood awkwardly in the parlor that had come to seem like home to Maya. Finally, Captain Creb said, "Well."

Blinking rapidly, Maya nodded.

"We'll miss you," Jeam said in his soft, gravelly voice.

Nodding again, Maya impulsively hugged Captain Creb. She could tell he was startled, and Maya knew that he had never hugged a human before. But the captain tentatively hugged her back and even gently patted her on the shoulder, the way her mother or grandmother might have done. Then Maya turned to Jeam, and he hugged her as tightly as she hugged him.

"Good luck," he whispered softly.

"Thank you," she whispered back.

Pulling away, Maya sniffed and cleared her throat. "Thank you so much for taking me in. I'll remember you two always."

Captain Creb cleared his throat, too. "It was nothing. It's what any decent troll would have done."

Maya's voice caught. "You've taught me a lot."

The captain smiled but then said seriously, "But remember that not all trolls are decent."

"Just like humans," Maya replied.

"Just like humans."

Crying a little, Maya quickly left *The Resilience*, not looking back, even though she knew Jeam had come on deck and was watching her as she left the docks. The city streets were mostly empty and quiet. It was late enough that even the bars had shut down for the night, and all Maya saw were a few stray animals that looked a lot like cats as they prowled, hunting for animals that looked a lot like rats and mice. Maya heard several loud squeaks as the hunters caught their prey, and she felt the passing of little lives. Shuddering, Maya strode on, only stopping to check the map and the compass, to make sure she was going in the right direction.

By dawn, Maya was out of the small city and into the Forest of Black Mountain. Gazing around at the dark trees and listening to the wind move in a whisper through the branches, Maya understood why Jeam loved this place. Although the Forest of Black Mountain felt wilder and sharper, there was something about it that reminded Maya of the Forest of Arden. However, Maya could sense that its power didn't come from an ancient oak. Instead, it came from something elemental deep in the mountain itself.

When Maya was far enough away from the city to feel safe, she left the trail to sit by a tree. She had a breakfast of tea and a sandwich, made from a hua-nut spread that was a lot like peanut butter. Leaning her head against the tree she was sitting by, Maya listened to the sounds of the forest—the birds singing and small creatures rustling in the underbrush. In the distance, she could hear the sounds of Clamic as humans and trolls woke up and went to work.

"It's the same no matter where you are," Maya thought as she pictured the morning bustle. Occasionally, she could even hear the tooting of a loud horn, and it made her feel homesick for New York City.

Underneath the whisper of the forest and the noise of the city was a deep thrumming sound, and Maya knew it was the voice of Black Mountain. There would be no more need for the map and compass. All she needed to do was follow the sound. "But how will I find the resistance or the seed savers or whatever they are?" Maya thought as she stood up, brushed herself off, and packed her rucksack.

As it turned out, the resistance found Maya. By midafternoon, Maya was high enough up the mountain so that she could no longer hear city noises. The trees were smaller and had started to thin out. Maya stopped to rest and take a few sips of tea and a bite of sandwich. When Maya looked up, a woman with blue skin was standing in front of her. Maya jumped, sloshing her tea.

"Are you Maya?" the woman asked.

Putting down the cup, Maya scrambled to her feet. "Yes."

The woman nodded. "I thought so. My name is Arless. Will you come with me?" Arless looked to be as old as Maya's mother, and there was a worn, tired look on the woman's face. Yet there was also a sharpness that kept Maya from seeing too much. The woman's dark hair was cut in a bob, and she wore gray clothes similar to Maya's.

"Are you with the resistance?" Maya asked, knowing the answer even as she asked the question.

"Yes," Arless answered. "For the past few days, we've been waiting for you. Today we spotted you on our screens, and here I am to take you to our headquarters."

"All right," Maya said. "I'll come with you. But how did you know who I was?"

"You'll see," Arless answered curtly. "It is my mission to take you to headquarters, not to fill you in."

Maya bit her lip but didn't say anything as she put the thermos and half-eaten sandwich back in her pack. Then she followed Arless farther up the mountain. Looking at the woman's stiff back, Maya wished she were back on *The Resilience* with Captain Creb and Jeam, and she shook her head in amazement as she realized she would rather be with those two trolls than with Arless. Maya sensed the woman didn't really want to be bringing her to the resistance's headquarters.

"There are a million places I'd rather be," Maya thought impatiently as she hurried to keep up with Arless. "But here I am. She could at least be nice."

Stopping, Arless snorted. "I am being nice. You should see me when I'm not."

Nearly running into Arless, Maya felt her face flush with anger. "I don't care how much you can see. You shouldn't do that," Maya retorted. "It's not polite. You're old enough to know better, and I won't let you do it again. I'll be ready next time."

Arless snorted again, but her lips twitched as she tried not to smile. "Come on, we're almost there, and then you'll find out what you need to know."

"What I need to know," Maya thought. "That's all I'm ever told." But she didn't say anymore as she followed Arless.

The sound of Black Mountain, so strong when Maya had been alone, receded until it was just a deep undertone, and Maya understood that the mountain had been guiding her up, where she would be found. Arless and Maya came to a section of the mountain that looked just like any other, but stopping, Arless removed a device from her pocket and pressed a button. A piece of the mountain slid open, revealing a lighted room. Maya gaped.

"Come on," Arless repeated impatiently. "Let's go."

Into the mountain they went. Once inside, Arless pointed the device at the open door, and it slid shut. There was an elevator on the opposite wall, and Arless pushed a button. Nothing happened for a long time.

"That's the slowest elevator," Arless grumbled. "It takes forever. Sometimes I think I'll die of old age before the door opens."

Now it was Maya's turn to try not to smile. Maya had finally met someone who was even more impatient than she was.

"What?" Arless asked. Maya just shook her head.

Eventually, the elevator door opened, and they stepped inside. "Going down?" a man's gentle voice asked. Maya realized it was the elevator that was speaking.

"Of course we're going down," Arless snapped. "Where else would we be going? You're up as far as you can go."

"No need to be grouchy," came the elevator's unperturbed voice. "Just asking. And this must be Maya."

"Yes," Arless answered. "This is Maya." She glanced sideways at Maya, looked as though she wanted to say something, and then shook her head.

"Maya is smaller than I thought she would be," the elevator said.

"Cormec, what do you know about young girls?" Arless asked. "There are no children here."

Maya stood straight and held her head high. "I'm older than I look."

"My apologies, Maya," Cormec said. "I've just heard so much about you. How you escaped from Mortmain, were kissed by Chance, and traveled with two trolls. I thought you'd be older somehow."

"Where did you hear all this?" Maya asked curiously.

"Why from..."

But Arless cut the elevator off. "Never mind where you heard it. Maya will be debriefed downstairs. Zip it, Cormec."

Cormec actually sighed. "As you wish. Just making conversation."

"Well, don't. It's not appreciated."

"Not by you, but Maya might think otherwise."

"Cormec," Arless said, and there was a note of warning in her voice.

"All right, all right. I'll be quiet."

For the rest of the way down, Cormec didn't say anything until they stopped at the bottom.

"There you go," Cormec said. "Thank you for riding with me."

Striding out of the elevator, Arless muttered, "Oh, for God's sake."

Maya, however, lingered for a few moments. "Thank you, Cormec. Is she always like that?"

"Always," Cormec replied. "But I don't let her get me down, and you shouldn't either."

"I won't," Maya said, and then an image of Bigly came to her. "I've met worse."

"Oh, dear," Cormec said sympathetically.

"Maya!" Arless called. "Come on!"

"Coming!" Maya called back. "Thanks again."

Maya joined Arless. "Cormec was only being friendly. Can you imagine what it must be like for him, going up and down like that all the time?"

"That's what he was made for," Arless said, but her voice wasn't as sharp. "It's his job."

"Still," Maya replied.

"I hate chitchat," Arless said. "It clutters my mind."

Maya nodded. "Just like my mother."

"Your mother?"

"Yeah, you're even about the same age. Except she doesn't mind if other people talk, even though she doesn't say much." Maya's voice ended with a catch as she thought about her quiet, gentle mother. Would she ever see her again?

For a moment, Arless had an expression that looked sympathetic. But Arless didn't say anything. She just shook her head as they hustled down a long corridor with rooms on either side. All the doors had windows, and Maya peeked into the rooms as they hurried by. Most of the rooms were offices, with blue-skinned people sitting at a desk and staring at a screen. Half-way down the hall, there was another corridor that went to the right, but Arless and Maya kept going straight. They passed a large dining area where a few people were gathered around a table. Maya could smell roasted hua nuts, and she sighed wistfully as she thought of the cookies she had eaten with Jeam and Captain Creb.

"Later," Arless said. "First you need to be debriefed."

At the end of the corridor was a double set of doors. Opening the doors, Arless strode into a large room filled with big screens on the walls. There were six desks clustered in the middle of the room, and people were staring either at the big screens or the smaller ones at their desks. There was the soft sound of conversation that stopped as soon as everyone noticed Arless and Maya. But as Maya passed the desks, she could hear her name being whispered.

Arless didn't say anything to any of the people. She just walked across the room until she came to another door. Stopping, Arless knocked. "Come in," a woman's voice said.

Arless and Maya went into the room, a large office with a desk, some chairs, and bookshelves filled with books. On the top shelf, on a stand, was something that made Maya gasp. It was an open Book of Everything, and Maya was as drawn to it as she had been to Earth's Book and Ariel.

"Here?" Maya asked, for once nearly speechless. "How?"

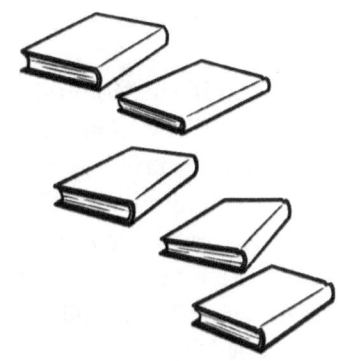

36: A Visit Cut Short

B ehind the desk sat a woman, blue-skinned like Arless. Although she smiled, Maya got a sense of seriousness, of extreme caution and reserve.

"Maya, welcome." The woman motioned to two chairs in front of the desk. "Please sit down. You, too, Arless."

Arless nodded slightly as she sat down. "Yes, ma'am."

Putting her pack by the chair, Maya sat down as well, but she kept glancing at the Book of Everything on the shelf to her right.

"Blindon, I told you Maya would be surprised when she saw me," the Book said in a soft but firm voice.

The woman at the desk nodded. Her dark hair was longer than Arless's and pulled back into a bun. Even though Blindon was dressed in the same gray clothes as everyone else, there was an elegance in the way she wore them. Blindon asked, "And why wouldn't Maya be surprised? A Book of Everything so close to Mortmain. And by the way, I'm Blindon Ava, and you, of course, are Maya Hammond."

Maya nodded absently, still looking at the Book. "What are you doing in Caldor, so close to Mortmain?"

"I was here long before Cinnial came to Caldor," the Book said.

"In Black Mountain?" Maya asked.

"In Black Mountain."

Blindon rubbed her forehead. "Caldor has been a mess for the past hundred years. In fact, the whole planet has. The seas began to rise. Coastal cities flooded and then had to move farther inland. Blue people fought against white people, and everyone fought against the trolls." Blindon shook her head. "Too many were killed. Then came the water and food shortages to much of the planet, especially here. War broke out everywhere. My grandfather was prime minister of Caldor then, and he made a decision that we hope will save this planet."

"What decision?" Maya asked.

"Hide me in Black Mountain," the Book answered. "Trolls had lived here for centuries, so the tunnels were already dug. But the trolls left after they mined all the precious metals, and it had been empty for quite a while."

Maya looked around. "But how did your grandfather fix the place like this without anyone knowing what he was doing?"

"He pretended he was building this complex for something else," Blindon said. "To save seeds. In fact, he did send people here to save seeds, and we still do. The Book of Everything chose people who could be trusted, and it has continued to do so over the years."

Maya frowned. "But some people must have known about the Book of Everything. Isn't that why your grandfather hid it? Because bad people were after it?"

"That's right. Things were terrible here, and my grandfather could see, much the way you can. He knew things were going to get even worse." Blindon sighed. "So my grandfather did something that made people think the Book had been destroyed."

"What did he do?" Maya asked, not sure if she wanted to hear the answer.

Blindon shuddered a little. "Burned down the library where the Book was being held. All the books were burnt to a crumble, and everyone thought the Book had perished in the fire. Nobody guessed that my grandfather had hidden the Book in Black Mountain, with the seed savers, who live very quietly. They only come and go to get seeds and to get supplies. The seed savers are hardly noticed."

"And Black Mountain has helped us," said the Book. "Its avalanches discourage most everyone from coming up this far. A lot of humans and trolls even think that a spirit lives in the mountain, and they respect but fear it. In a way, they are not wrong. But nobody cares if a small group of people wants to live in the mountain and save seeds. Cinnial certainly doesn't care." The Book paused. "He has his eyes on bigger things."

Blindon continued, "So when the last Great World War broke out, about fifteen years ago, only a few of us knew the Book of Everything was here. During the war, my parents sent a small group, including me, to stay with the Book. Turned out to be one of the smartest decisions my parents ever made. My mother was prime minister then, and she and my father were killed in the war, along with most of the other people in top posts. That's when Cinnial came to power." Swallowing, Blindon stopped.

Arless finished the story. "When Cinnial took over, we were safely in Black Mountain, but because of our Book, he doesn't know about us. He doesn't even know there is a Book of Everything on this planet. That's why he chose to come to Tufrak. As far as Cinnial knows, it has technology but no Book of Everything. Like everyone else, he thinks that the Book was destroyed in a fire over a hundred years ago and that no new Book was sent to this planet."

"It is not hard to hide from Cinnial and his Books," the Book of Everything said a little smugly.

Maya muttered, "Sydda never mentioned you."

The Book's voice was firm. "Maya, by now you know that you must find some things out for yourself."

Maya stared at the Book. "This is a big thing."

"It is." The Book hesitated. "I suggested telling you, but the Great Library's Book thought otherwise. The Book, along with Time, wanted to leave some things to Chance, and this was one of them."

Blindon looked at Maya's forehead. "And Chance found you, didn't she?"

Nodding, Maya touched the spot on her forehead. "Can you see it?"

"Just the faintest glimmer," Blindon replied. "But if I weren't looking for it, I wouldn't know that Chance had kissed you. But now, Maya, it's time for you to tell us what you know. Something that might help us."

Maya shook her head. "I don't know what that could be."

Arless said, "Chance sent you here for a reason."

Maya shrugged. "Maybe, but she didn't give me any details."

"Tell us what happened since you came to Mortmain and Caldor," Blindon suggested. "Maybe we can glean something that you missed."

So Maya told them about coming to Mortmain with Julian, Ariel, and Caxton's green Book of Everything and how Cinnial now had both Books. Then she described how she had escaped from Bigly when the screens on the buildings flashed images of two people holding signs.

Blindon stared at Arless. "I had not approved this. It was still in discussion." Arless actually looked sheepish but didn't say anything. "You went behind my back. What if Cinnial finds out where the message came from?"

"He won't," Arless answered shortly. "We have two of the best hackers on the planet who know how to hide their work. They are better than any of Cinnial's trolls."

Blindon's mouth was a grim line. "We'll deal with this later. Go on, Maya."

Maya described how she saw Chance, hid in a truck that took her to Roford, saw Chance again, and found Jeam and Captain Creb, who took her away from Roford, up the Nokom River, to the small port city of Clamic.

"And here I am," Maya finished.

"No one recognized you? No one followed you?" Blindon asked anxiously.

But it was Arless who answered. "We've been keeping even closer track than usual of who's on the mountain. Nobody followed her."

"Thank goodness for that," Blindon said. "If anyone should ever discover there's a Book of Everything here, then it's over for this planet."

Frowning, Maya regarded Blindon and saw how great her fear was. Maya really couldn't hold it against Blindon for being so afraid. "After all," Maya thought, "Didn't I run away from Bigly the first chance I got?" Still, there was something about Blindon's fear that bothered Maya.

The Book of Everything said, "I would like to speak to Maya. Alone, please."

"Alone?" asked Blindon.

"Alone."

Blindon left reluctantly, and Arless, with a speculative expression, followed her.

When the door to the office closed, the Book said, "You see how it is, don't you?"

Maya thought about Blindon's fear and suddenly understood how that fear kept everyone paralyzed at Black Mountain. "Yeah. Blindon is so afraid that she doesn't dare do anything."

The Book's voice was weary. "I have spoken to her over and over again. I've encouraged her to be bolder, that the time for action is coming. But I just can't convince her. She won't budge from Black Mountain. She'll send a few people out on scouting trips and to get seeds, but that's it. She won't make contact with other people and trolls who would help her."

Maya said in a low voice, "In a way, I don't blame her. Mortmain is a scary place. And Cinnial..." Maya stopped, unable to continue.

"I know all about Cinnial," the Book said shortly. "He is a formidable opponent who has Chaos on his side."

"That's for sure."

"Nevertheless, he will be leaving Mortmain soon,"

"To go to the Great Library," Maya whispered, her heart beating fast.

"Yes," the Book said, and there was a deep sadness in its voice.

"Do Blindon and Arless know this?"

"No, I haven't told them yet. They just know that Cinnial is planning something big. They don't know how big, and they don't realize that Cinnial can find the path to the Great Library with the two Books that Julian gave him."

Maya shivered. "I hope you Books know what you're doing."

"Me, too," the Book replied.

"And what am I supposed to do?"

"Things are in flux right now, and I really don't want to give you too much advice," the Book answered. "But I have the feeling you will know what to do when the time comes."

Maya shivered again, but she was curious about something, and she had to ask, "What color are you?"

"Come see," the Book replied, and she caught a note of amusement in its voice.

Maya rose from her chair and went over to the Book of Everything. Carefully, she flipped back to the cover and saw the glossy sheen of black.

"A black Book of Everything in Black Mountain," Maya said.

"Appropriate, isn't it?"

"Yeah," Maya answered. "Was it planned?"

"Not really. It just worked out that way."

"What color is Cinnial's Book?"

The Book sighed. "You people are so concerned about color."

"I know, but what color is it?"

"Red," the Black Book answered. "Cinnial's Book is red."

There was a knock on the door. "Yes?" the Book asked.

The door opened a crack. "Are you and Maya done in there?" Arless asked. "It's time for dinner."

"We're done," the Book said. "Blindon's off by herself brooding?"

"You got it." The door opened wider, and Arless poked her head into the room. "Come on, Maya. The rest of us are waiting for you. And some of us have been traipsing around the mountain. We're hungry."

"Okay." Standing and grabbing her pack, Maya moved toward the door.

"Good luck, Maya," the Book said.

"Thanks," Maya replied. "And good luck to you, too."

Arless led Maya to the dining area they had passed, stark and clean, with several stainless steel tables and matching chairs. There were fifteen people, all with blue skin, seated around the various tables, and Blindon came into the room right after Maya and Arless had taken a seat. She sat with them and three others— two women and a man. Blindon was still brooding, and her mood filled the room. Nobody said anything, and the silence was so uncomfortable that Maya thought longingly back to her meals with Jeam and Captain Creb, to the lively conversations and stories, to the general happiness of the two trolls.

Finally, Arless said, "Oh, snap out of it, ma'am. It had to be done. You kept dithering."

"You went behind my back."

At the next table, a man and a woman looked down at their laps. By the door to the kitchen, the cook and her assistant, in white aprons, stood still with steaming platters of food.

"And then the Book wants to talk to Maya alone, like I'm the one who can't be trusted." With an angry twitch, Blindon rose, but Maya put a hand on her arm.

"Don't be mad. The Books work on their own. They tell us what they want us to know, and believe me, there's a lot they leave out."

Blindon swallowed. "How old are you?"

"I'm nearly sixteen."

"Young."

Maya said wearily, "Sometimes I don't feel very young. I've been to a lot of different places, and I've seen a lot of things."

"I used to go to different places," Blindon said slowly. "But for the past fifteen years, I've been here."

Maya thought, "Where it's safe." But she didn't say anything.

Blindon saw the cook and her assistant by the door. Sitting down, she motioned with her hand. "Bring in the food. Let's eat."

Platters of noodles with a cheese sauce were set on the table. There were rolls sprinkled with hua nuts and a spicy herb salad.

"How do you get supplies?" Maya asked after taking a bite of the pasta.

"On the other side of the mountain we have a landing pad," Blindon said. "Most things are flown in, and because the landing pad is on the other side of the mountain, it's hidden from the city of Clamic. The less the people see, the better."

Nodding, Maya was about to take another bite of the creamy sauce and noodles, when an image came to her of Ariel on a table under a bright light. The Book was in a device much like the ones Maya had seen at the Great Library. But instead of giving information, these devices were sucking information out of Ariel. Maya could feel the intense suffering and pain of the Apprentice Book, who was still holding on, not giving Cinnial the information he wanted. But for how much longer?

"Ariel!" Maya cried. Her fork fell with a clatter onto the plate.

"Where?" Arless asked suspiciously, looking around the room.

"Do you mean your Apprentice Book, the one that's in Mortmain with Cinnial?" Blindon asked.

"Yes," Maya replied breathlessly, suddenly knowing what she had to do. She couldn't just leave Ariel in Mortmain to be tortured and destroyed by Cinnial's team. Maya shook her head ruefully. She should have realized that she'd feel this way, that she could never abandon Ariel. Yet again, Maya chided herself for bolting away from Bigly.

Maya scrambled from her chair. "Ariel needs me. I have to go back. Now."

The room was no longer quiet as everyone began talking at once.

"Maya, no!" Blindon said, looking alarmed. "Cinnial might find out about us. You can't go back."

"I have to," Maya replied fiercely. "I never should have left in the first place. I was only thinking about myself."

Blindon stood, and there was a closed, stubborn expression on her face. "I won't let you leave."

But Maya didn't back down. "How are you going to stop me? Are you going to lock me in a room?"

The two faced each other, and Blindon glared at Maya. "If I have to. But Cormec won't take you topside. I won't allow it."

Arless also stood. "No, you're wrong. Cormec likes Maya. He'll take her up if she wants to go."

The room became quiet as Blindon and Arless stared at each other.

Then Blindon asked, "You want my job, don't you?"

Arless gave Blindon a withering look. "I don't want your job. I don't want to sit behind a damned desk and do paperwork from morning until night. I just want you to do the right thing, to be ready to act when the time comes."

Blindon's voice was almost a whisper. "But if we lose our Book of Everything..."

"It would be a terrible thing," Arless replied. "But finally we'll have a chance to do something other than hide in this mountain. Cinnial has those two Books of Everything for a reason. He's going to do something with them. He's not going to hang around in Mortmain."

As Maya shrugged into the rucksack, which had been tucked under her chair, she made a decision to tell them about Cinnial's plan. She didn't know if the black Book of Everything would approve, but she didn't care. Maya agreed with Arless— the time for action had come. Maya said, "Cinnial wants to take over the Great Library. But Time hid the pathway from him, and Cinnial thinks he'll find the way from the Books of Everything that Julian brought him. His team is pulling information out of Ariel and the green Book."

For a few seconds, there was silence, and Blindon stood so still that it looked as though she were stuck in place. Then again everyone started talking at once.

"Blindon, did you know?"

"What's going to happen if Cinnial takes over the Great Library?"

"Arless is right. We can't just hide here while the universe goes to pieces."

People rose, clustering around Blindon, and Maya quietly slipped from the room. Running down the hallway, she saw that Cormec's doors were opened, waiting for her. Maya was nearly at the elevator when a voice called, "Maya, wait!"

Maya didn't look back to see who it was. A little breathless, she sprang into the elevator and said, "Cormec, take me up."

"Let's wait for Arless," Cormec said in his unflappable voice. "She's a bit of a grump, but her heart's in the right place, and I think she might be of service to you."

Turning, Maya saw Arless sprinting toward her. The woman jumped into the elevator and said, "Take us up."

"As you wish," Cormec replied.

"Why are you here?" Maya asked Arless.

"Because Cormec is right. I can help you. How did you plan to get back to Roford from Clamic? Swim?"

Shaking her head, Maya reluctantly grinned. "I hadn't thought about that."

"Well, maybe you should start thinking," Arless snapped. "I don't understand how you got this far, the way you just go off without planning."

Maya continued to grin. "And yet I did." She could see that even though Arless was gruff, she also had a fierce courage and a desire to help her country, her planet, take a better course. And deep inside Arless, there was even a glimmer of a sense of humor.

Arless's lips twitched, but she didn't smile. "I know some people who have a boat. For a price, they'll take you back to Roford."

"I have money," Maya said. "One of those coins with Cinnial's head on it."

Arless whistled. "That should do it. I'll take you to Clamic, to the people who have the boat. After that, you're on your own to Roford and Mortmain. I have to come back to Black Mountain." Arless shook her head. "Look, Maya, Blindon is not wrong to be worried about what you'll say when you go back to Mortmain. You'll be caught. You'll be tortured. Eventually, you'll tell them what they want to know."

"I don't think so," Maya replied. "The Books wanted me to go to Mortmain. Something is going to happen, but I'm not sure what." Then, shuddering, Maya thought about Bigly and the Office. "But you never know. Talk to your Book of Everything. It will know whether you should stay here or leave."

Arless looked grim. "I'm sure that's where Blindon is right now, but God knows if she'll follow the Book's advice if it suggests it's time to leave."

They were quiet as the elevator reached the top. When the doors opened, Cormec said, "Here we are. Goodbye and good luck, Maya. I doubt we'll meet again."

Maya stepped out of the elevator. "No, probably not. Goodbye and thanks for taking me up."

"My pleasure," Cormec answered. "Also my job. And, Arless, you be careful. There's a lot going on out there. Things are starting to move."

Leaving the elevator, Arless grunted but didn't reply.

"Cormec, how do you know so much?" Maya asked.

"I talk to the Book, of course," Cormec said as the doors closed. "Not only humans can communicate with Books of Everything."

Maya smiled. "No, I suppose not."

But there was no reply as Cormec headed back down.

Arless said, "You've certainly stirred things up, even though you haven't been here very long."

"Yeah," Maya said, shaking her head. "That seems to happen wherever I go."

"You're a real pain, aren't you?"

"That's what my father says," Maya replied.

"Well, he's right." But Arless was finally grinning.

Maya grinned back, and the two headed outside onto Black Mountain.

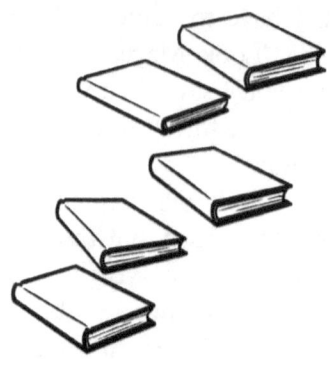

37: Evacuation

At the long table, Sydda sat in the boardroom in the Great Library. Except for Astrid, all the others had left to begin preparations for evacuation. Astrid sat beside him, and she had that stubborn expression she got whenever Sydda wanted her to do something she didn't want to do. It didn't happen often—mostly they were in agreement about the way things should be run at the Great Library—but when Astrid had that look on her face, it took all of Sydda's powers of persuasion to convince Astrid to go along with what he was suggesting.

Sydda stared steadily at Astrid, letting her emotions run their course. After a while she said, "No." Her mouth trembled just a little. "I'm not leaving you alone. I'm staying, too."

"To what end?" Sydda asked.

"To be with you," Astrid answered softly. "You must know that I couldn't leave."

Sydda nodded. He did know. For over a century, Astrid had been his companion, his friend, his wife. He remembered how beautiful Astrid had been when she had first come to the Great Library—her blonde hair, her deep blue eyes, her pale complexion, quite a contrast to his own dark skin. And to Sydda, Astrid was still beautiful, even though her face was creased with wrinkles now. As they looked at each other, Astrid blinked, trying not to cry.

Sydda reached across the table and put his dark hand over her pale hand. "There, Astrid. We all have to go sometime. Even here, at the Great Library, where we live longer than we normally would on our own planets."

Tears slid down her face. "I know. But all alone like this?"

"It is best, Astrid," Sydda said gently. "The staff needs you. The Great Library needs you. In fact, the universe needs you."

Sighing, Astrid wiped the tears from her cheeks. "Yes, I am needed. But what am I going to do without you?"

"You will manage. You know you will. And if things go our way, then you'll have quite a job on your hands when you come back."

"And if things don't go our way?" Astrid asked.

"Then you will have an even bigger job."

"To protect the Great Library's Book of Everything and to help the other Books."

"That's right."

Astrid frowned. "But why can't someone else take the Great Library's Book? There are plenty of able people here."

"Astrid, nobody can handle a crisis the way you can. There have been many over the years, and you always find a way to navigate through them. It will mean a lot to me to know that the Great Library's Book of Everything will be in your capable hands."

Astrid nodded, but there was still a stubborn look on her face. "It doesn't seem right that we are leaving this fight to others, especially to one so young."

"Maya is young," Sydda agreed with a sigh.

Astrid leaned forward. "Maya might get sidetracked, as teenagers often do. We should stay here and defend our library."

"There's a part of me that feels the way you do. But I believe the Great Library's Book of Everything is correct in predicting that Cinnial will be expecting us to fight. He'll be coming with a lot of firepower. But if we play our cards too early, Cinnial will flee back to Mortmain. And now that Cinnial knows how to get here, he would be a constant threat. An empty library will throw him off-guard. When the real fight comes, he will be unprepared. You know this is true."

"But how will Maya know what to do?" Astrid asked.

"Trust me," Sydda said, smiling just a little. "If Maya gets this far, she will know what to do."

"And if she doesn't?"

"Then it will be up to you to groom someone else," Sydda said. "There are many other candidates, some of them as talented as Maya. But so far, she has come the furthest and has the best chance."

Nodding, Astrid put her free hand on top of Sydda's hand. "All right, Sydda. I'll do as you ask. But it won't be easy."

"None of this is easy," Sydda replied. "But sometimes we have to put aside what we want."

Astrid sniffed. "I know."

"Of course you do," Sydda said, and although he was outwardly calm, inwardly he trembled as he thought about facing Cinnial alone. He looked out the window, at the terrace, at the gardens, at the small but wide forest that started where the gardens ended.

"Astrid," he said, "let's take a cart and go see the Ancient One."

Astrid blinked at Sydda. "Do we have time?"

"I believe we do," Sydda replied. "Maya has left Black Mountain and has just reached Roford by boat. So far, the Books, bless them, are holding their own against Cinnial's team. Despite being blocked by Cinnial, we will know when one of our own falls. Even he can't hide that. And when a Book falls, it will be time to evacuate."

"Which Book do you think will fall first?" Astrid asked in a choked voice.

"I think it will be the green Book. It's my guess that Cinnial will focus more on that Book rather than on an Apprentice Book. He'll underestimate Ariel, just the way he's underestimated Maya."

Astrid squeezed Sydda's hand. "And us. Cinnial thinks we'll fall like sparrows. But we'll show him. Yes, let's go to the Ancient One for the last time."

A little while later, Astrid and Sydda were in a small electric cart. Astrid was driving, and Sydda sat in contentment beside her. They passed the gardens, clear of vines and other plants. The air was cool but crisp rather than cold, and the leaves in the forest blazed with an intensity that moved Sydda. It almost seemed as though they were bidding him farewell. Sydda shook his head, knowing this was a fanciful thought.

Into the forest they went, on the broad path that led to the Ancient One. They passed by a rushing stream, full from the autumn rains. Above them, birds called, and the cart was so quiet that Sydda could hear them clearly. Many birds had left for a warmer climate, but there was always a handful that stayed year round, the "true blues," as Sydda called them, and he especially loved the birds hardy enough to survive the cold of winter.

They rode under the blazing canopy, which seemed to light up the entire forest. "So very lovely," Sydda thought.

It wasn't long until they came to the Ancient One, an oak which had been at the heart of this planet, indeed the heart of the universe, for as long as anyone could remember. The tree's limbs were so thick and gnarled and expansive that it didn't seem possible the Oak could stay upright without any cables to secure the branches. And yet it did. The Oak shimmered with an inward glow, and on the ground all around the tree were golden acorns, waiting to be gathered and sent to various planets in the universe along with Books of Everything. Sydda wondered, would they be sent this year? Would Cinnial destroy the Oak and the acorns? Shuddering, Sydda thought it was likely, and he was about to tell Astrid to gather some acorns, just in case. However, Astrid had already slipped from the cart and was putting acorns into a small cloth bag she had brought.

Sighing, Sydda closed his eyes. Astrid always knew what to do, which was why he was sending her out with all the others. But how he would miss her, at the end of all things. Sydda found he was actually weeping, but he didn't try to stop the tears. Instead, Sydda sat very still in the cart, and as he wept, picturing what Cinnial would do, he felt a presence. It was the Oak, serene and shining, giving him comfort in this time of danger and grief, reassuring Sydda that with the acorns Astrid was gathering, along with all the other trees already planted on the various planets, the Oak would continue. Cinnial could no more destroy this vital force than he could destroy Time, and it was only arrogance and the desire for revenge, stoked by Chaos, that allowed Cinnial to think that he could.

"But Cinnial can make things bad for a long, long time," Sydda thought, his eyes still closed.

Something like a chuckle arose from the Ancient Oak, as though it found Cinnial's machinations amusing in a small kind of way. "I wish I had your confidence," Sydda whispered sadly, and he felt the tree's energy wrap itself around him, holding him close, stilling his fears. Sydda stopped crying and opened his eyes. Astrid was in the cart, and Sydda could barely look at her grief-stricken but peaceful face. Nodding, she put her hand on his arm, and Sydda knew that the Ancient Oak had communicated with her as well.

"It's good we came here," Astrid said softly. "And not only for the acorns."

Sydda nodded. "For us, too. We needed it."

Later that afternoon, the green Book fell. Sitting at his desk in his office, Sydda felt it like a blow, and beside him, the Great Library's Book of Everything actually cried out. For a few minutes, Sydda sat still, gathering himself for what would happen next. Then slowly, Sydda rose, went to a panel on the wall, and pushed a button. Throughout the Great Library, to the very top where the retirees lived, came a loud, incessant chime, calling everyone to assemble in the great hall.

Gently, Sydda gathered the Great Library's Book of Everything in his arms. "Time for you to leave, old friend."

"I am sorry it has come to this," the Book replied.

"So am I. So are we all. But here we are. Astrid will take good care of you."

Closing the Book, Sydda took one last look at his tidy office and left, shutting the door gently. People were dashing madly around him. Alani whizzed by with a red Apprentice Book tucked under her arm. Sydda knew she was looking for

Alexander, the head librarian of the main floor stacks. They had recently been married, and they would be leaving together, traveling to a planet Sydda had suggested.

As Sydda made his way to the great hall, he went over what he was going to say. He had rehearsed this farewell speech many times, but now his throat was thick with anxiety and his mind nearly a blank as he entered the great hall. The room was almost full, and yet more people, all clutching Apprentice Books and large packs and suitcases, came into the great hall. After placing the Great Library's Book by an empty seat at the head table, Sydda went to the dais by the long windows overlooking the gardens. He waited until people stopped trickling into the room, the bell ceased chiming, and Astrid came in, sitting at the empty seat by the Great Library's Book.

Surveying the people he loved, Sydda took several deep breaths and began. "The day that we have dreaded is finally here. Ilyria's green Book held out valiantly but finally fell, revealing the pathway to the Great Library. I have no doubt that Cinnial is well prepared for this day and is gathering his forces as I speak. Time will do what it can to slow Cinnial and his forces down, but now that the pathway has been revealed, Time has little choice but to let things take their course. Thus it has been, and thus it will always be, with Time and Chaos wrestling with each other to gain ground. Sometimes Time wins, sometimes Chaos wins, but the struggle continues."

Heads nodded, and Sydda could hear the sounds of sniffing and crying and the blowing of noses.

"You are right to be filled with sorrow," Sydda continued. "An epoch is ending, and we don't know what will happen next. We hope that Time will prevail, but Cinnial, allied with Chaos, is strong now. However, Time, like Chaos, can never be vanquished, only subdued. And here is where it comes down to you and the Apprentice Books you hold. Go out across the universe to the planets you have chosen. Do what you can to oppose Chaos and assist those who are working with Time. Chance will help you as much as possible, but watch out for Nemesis."

Sydda looked at various upturned faces. Some were wet with tears, some were stern and sad, all were resolved.

Sydda said, "It has been a great pleasure and a joy to have been your director, to have served the Great Library and Time. This is a place like no other. Now go forth, all of you, and do what you can to suppress Chaos and tip the scales back in Time's favor. I will remain here, until the end, but the Great Library's Book is going with Astrid. To which planet, I don't know. That way, Cinnial won't be able to get that information from me. But I have been told temporary headquarters have already been set up, and a small data team will be with Astrid. They will keep things going, but it won't be anything like what we have here at the Great Library. Much of the time, you will be on your own and will have to rely on your own intuition. But I have every confidence that you will all do your best for the planets you go to, for the Great Library, and for Time. Goodbye and good luck to you all."

At first there was silence and then clapping and cheering, interspersed with shouted farewells. Alani and Alexander were among the first to leave. But the rest of the librarians and staff vanished so rapidly that within ten minutes, the room was silent, and for the first time since it was built, the Great Library was nearly empty.

Along with Sydda, four people remained—Astrid, holding the Great Library's Book of Everything, as well as Mortimer, Ebeneezer, and Ichabod.

Sydda nodded at the three old men, who all held Apprentice Books but didn't look as though they would be leaving anytime soon. Going to Astrid, Sydda put his hands on her shoulders and kissed her on the lips.

"Goodbye, Astrid," he said and stopped, unable to say more.

There were tears in Astrid's eyes. "Goodbye, Sydda." Then she and the Book were gone.

Clearing his throat, Mortimer said in his soft voice, "That was hard, seeing her go."

"Of course it was hard," Ebeneezer snapped. "This whole damned thing has been hard."

Ichabod put in, "If any of us had known what Cinnial would become, we would never have let him put his big toe in the Great Library."

"Gentlemen," Sydda asked sternly, "why are you still here?"

"Because this is where we belong," Ebeneezer said defiantly. "We've been here just as long as you have."

Sydda frowned. "Your staying here serves no purpose."

"We are not jumping ship." Mortimer's voice was as stern as Sydda's. "We are staying until the end."

"Come on, Sydda," Ichabod said. "Don't be such an old stick. You know you want us here."

Sydda continued to frown as he regarded the three men. Ichabod and Ebeneezer glared back at him, and Mortimer's gaze was steady but cool. Gradually, Sydda's frown went away. His lips quirked into a grin, and he shook his head. "All right, all right. You are three stubborn old fools."

"There's a fourth one here, too," Ebeneezer replied, and Sydda actually laughed out loud.

"Do you think there is time for tea?" Mortimer asked, smiling.

"Gentlemen, there is always time for tea" Sydda replied.

And when Cinnial, Julian, and the forces stormed the Great Library, they found the four old men drinking tea as they sat clustered around the head table in the great hall.

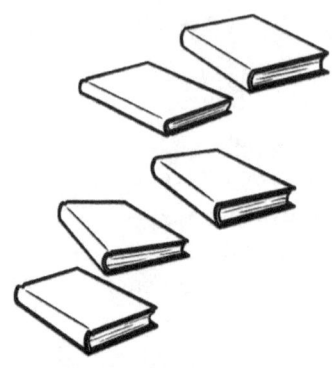

38: Library Lost

Cinnial's jaw was clenched as he regarded the old men drinking tea, but Julian bit his lip to keep from laughing. Before losing his memory, Julian would have been just as enraged as Cinnial and probably would have rushed forward to slit the old men's throats. Cinnial, of course, would have called him back, wanting to get whatever information he could before killing them. But losing and regaining his memory had given Julian some much-needed distance from his hot impulses, and he admired the old men's audacity. Clearly they knew Cinnial was coming—the Great Library seemed empty of all the staff except for the four sitting at the table— and yet here they were, calmly drinking tea. They couldn't have chosen a surer way of goading Cinnial, of pricking his pride.

Cinnial was surrounded by ten men and women, all dressed in black combat armor, all carrying sleek silver pistols in one hand and a Book in the other. Cinnial, his jaw still clenched, pointed his gun at the old men, and the team cautiously made their way to the head table.

Sydda stared evenly at Cinnial. "Oh, for heaven's sake. Lower your weapons. We are unarmed and are no threat to you."

"That remains to be seen," Cinnial replied in a tight voice.

Looking around the room, Julian listened to the emptiness that had settled over the Great Library, very different from the bustling place he remembered. All he could hear was the stomping of feet as Cinnial's forces searched the Great Library. Julian said, "I think he's telling the truth."

Cinnial's gun was aimed at Sydda's head. "There could be an ambush, a force hiding in some other part of the Great Library. This is a big place."

"Don't be such a fool," Ichabod snapped. "Can't you sense that we're the only ones here?"

Cinnial's guards gasped at Ichabod's disrespect, and Julian thought, "Ichabod will be the first to go."

But Cinnial wasn't quite ready to begin shooting, and he turned to his guards. "Go by the doorways and stand watch while I talk to these four."

"Would you like some tea?" Ebeneezer asked as the guards tucked their Books in their back pockets and left to take their posts by the room's doorways. "Taking over the Great Library must be thirsty work."

"He really hasn't had to do that much," Mortimer observed.

"Oh, but the excitement of conquest," came Ebeneezer's quick reply. "It can really dry a person's throat."

Cinnial slammed his gun down on the table, and the four old men jumped. Smiling just a little, Cinnial surveyed them. "Not quite as confident as you seem."

Sydda spoke quietly and with dignity, "Of course we're not. We know you are going to kill us when you are ready."

Cinnial frowned. "Then why isn't there anyone here to protect you?"

Mortimer answered with the same dignity, "We are librarians. It is not our job to fight and kill. It is our job to make books and to make sure people get them. And all kinds of people, not just a certain few."

Ichabod shook his head. "Once, you were a librarian, too, Cinnial."

Cinnial leaned forward. "And it's your fault that I'm no longer a librarian. I had more talent than anyone here, yet you rejected my Book." He stared down at his red Book, and his hand shook a little.

"Put me down on the table," the red Book said, and Cinnial followed its instructions.

Julian put his own black Book beside the red Book, and he sat down next to Mortimer. The two men nodded at each other.

"You've changed," Mortimer said, staring at Julian.

"I have," Julian admitted. "But I'm still with Cinnial."

Mortimer sighed. "You two always brought out the worst in each other."

Cinnial was still standing, and he glared at Mortimer. "I thought Ichabod would be the first to go, but now I'm reconsidering."

"Enough of this," Sydda said firmly. "Cinnial, what is it you want to know before killing us?"

Cinnial's voice was soft. "You are no longer in charge. Remember that. I am." Picking up his gun, he aimed it at Mortimer and pulled the trigger. There was a high-pitched whistle as a bullet flew toward Mortimer and struck him in the forehead. Mortimer didn't even have time to cry out. The force of the bullet threw him from his chair and onto the floor.

Swallowing, Julian looked away, and Sydda, Ichabod, and Ebeneezer were very quiet.

"Now that I have your attention," Cinnial said, "I do have a few questions before I kill the rest of you. Where is everyone?"

"They've scattered across the universe," Ichabod said, subdued but still defiant. "You'll never be able to track them all down. Not if you live for a thousand years, which you won't."

Nodding, Cinnial raised his gun and shot Ichabod. He, too, fell to the floor.

"How did you know I was coming?" Cinnial asked.

Ebeneezer took a deep breath. "The signs were everywhere. You might be able to block yourselves from us, but not your dirty deeds. We knew this day was coming, and when the green Book went down, we were ready."

Shaking his head, Cinnial shot Ebeneezer. "All right, Sydda, you're the last one. Do you have anything to say before I kill you?"

"I'm not sure that I do," Sydda said calmly, even though he looked grief-stricken.

"Tell me where the Great Library's Book has gone," Cinnial demanded, pointing his gun at Sydda.

"I don't know," Sydda replied. "That information was kept from me. On purpose. That way you wouldn't be able to get it out of me."

"Why kill him?" Julian asked quickly, trying to sound disinterested. "Why not make him our prisoner so that he can see all that we do here at the Great Library? And Bigly could use his devices on him. Sydda must know something that will help us."

The red Book spoke, "If Sydda were just a normal person, then that would be a good idea. But Julian, do you really think any prison cell would hold Sydda?"

Julian opened his mouth and then closed it. Sydda was alone, defenseless. He didn't have a Book of Everything to help him. He didn't even have an Apprentice Book. How could Sydda escape?

The red Book laughed, a low unpleasant sound. "Julian, Sydda doesn't need a Book of Everything to travel. He's been at the Great Library so long that he's connected to it all, just the way we Books are. He could leave anytime he wanted. You could leave right now, couldn't you, Sydda?"

Sydda nodded. "I could. But I would never willingly leave the Great Library. My place is here."

Cinnial muttered, "What a fool you are. Just like your friends. And now they are dead."

"We all die," Sydda said. "And we four stayed loyal to this place we love, right to the end. Will you be able to say that when your time comes, Cinnial? Have you ever been loyal to anything except your own monstrous ego?"

Grimacing, Cinnial pointed his gun at Sydda, but the red Book said, "Don't kill him just yet. I have a few things to say first." Cinnial, his face clenched with fury, reluctantly lowered his gun. The red Book continued, "Now, Sydda, tell me, if Cinnial's ego is so monstrous, then why did you let him come to the Great Library to begin with?"

Sydda smiled sadly. "I suppose it was because of our own egos. We thought we could guide Cinnial, to help him learn to think of others, not only of himself. But we were wrong."

"We?" the red Book asked slyly.

Sydda cleared his throat. "Me. I was wrong. My vote was the deciding one that let him come here. There were four in favor and four against." With a look that was almost soft, Sydda turned to Cinnial. "You had such ability. You still do. But after you made your Apprentice Book, I saw how wrong I was. I had hoped you'd get over the disappointment and stay here to help run the Great Library, maybe eventually become the director. But again I was wrong. Ichabod, Mortimer, and Ebeneezer suggested sending you home, but I wanted you to stay here, where I could keep an eye on you."

"But you underestimated Cinnial, didn't you?" the red Book asked, with a note of triumph in its voice.

"I did," Sydda answered. "Nobody can see everything, and the higher up you go, the more you have a tendency to underestimate those below you."

Later, Julian would remember Sydda's words. But right then, in the Great Library, with three dead men on the floor and Sydda soon to follow, Julian's focus was only on the present, not on the future.

"So in a way," the red Book said softly, "it was your own arrogance that created Cinnial. You thought you could change him. You underestimated his strength. You underestimated Chaos."

Sydda swallowed. "Yes." He stood, staring with love and affection at Cinnial. "Please forgive me. I forgive you."

"Now!" the red Book commanded. "Kill him now!"

However, Cinnial stood perfectly still. His gun was in his hand, and it was pointed at Sydda. But he didn't shoot.

Julian thought, "Will he let Sydda live?" And for a brief moment, Julian felt hopeful.

"Kill him!" the red Book shrieked. "Don't let Sydda get to you. Remember how he rejected you, of all people. He doesn't deserve to live."

Nodding and with a tremor so slight only Julian could see it, Cinnial pulled the trigger and shot Sydda. Like the others, Sydda was killed instantly, and he fell to the floor.

"There!" the red Book cried triumphantly. "It is done. Sydda is finally gone, and the Great Library is ours."

"Ours," Cinnial said faintly, but there was no look of triumph on his face. Instead, he looked hollowed out, and Julian wondered if Cinnial was going to faint.

"Sit down," Julian said to his friend. "Get your bearings." Cinnial sat across from Julian, and Julian called to the guards by the kitchen door. "Go find us something to drink. Something strong. Now!"

Two guards, a man and a woman, rushed into the kitchen and returned with a bottle with clear liquid and two glasses. "Good!" Julian said. "Now go, all of you. Two of you stand guard in the foyer by the door to this room. The rest of you help secure the Great Library. Not that you'll have much to do, but the Great Library should be searched from top to bottom. Just in case."

As soon as the room was empty, Julian snapped both Books shut. The last thing Julian wanted was needling comments from either Book. He poured the clear liquid into the two glasses and gave one of them to Cinnial. "Drink," he said. Taking a drink, Cinnial grimaced and coughed a little. Julian took a drink, and he, too, grimaced as the liquid burned down his throat. When he could speak again, Julian said, "Take another drink."

Cinnial took another drink and another and another. When Cinnial's glass was empty, Julian refilled it, but Cinnial only drank half. The color had come back to his cheeks, and Julian saw that the hard look of arrogance had returned to Cinnial's eyes.

But when Cinnial spoke, his voice was soft. "It's done."

Julian nodded. "And what's done is done."

Cinnial studied Julian. "You didn't want me to kill Sydda."

"No, he was our teacher. And so were the others."

Cinnial's face was hard. "But they rejected our Books."

"Yes, they did."

"They got what they deserved."

"They need to be buried," Julian said quickly, not wanting to agree with Cinnial but not wanting to disagree with him, either. "And the floor needs to be cleaned."

"I'll allow them to be buried in the Great Library's cemetery."

"Very magnanimous of you," Julian said, and he received a sharp look from Cinnial, who was alert for any signs of sarcasm, but there were none. Julian was very much aware of all the things Cinnial could have chosen to do with the bodies, and burying them in the cemetery was not the first thing that had come to Julian's mind.

"And let the bells ring their deaths," Cinnial said. "So that all the people on the mainland know that the Great Library is no longer run by Sydda."

Within a day, Sydda, Mortimer, Ichabod, and Ebeneezer were buried in the cemetery, and the floor of the great hall was scrubbed clean. Within two days, the mainland received notice that Cinnial was now in charge, and the Great Library was no longer open to the public. And within three days, the Ancient One had been chopped down and burned with the remaining acorns. Its smoke, sweet and sad, billowed over the Great Library and drifted to the mainland, to Watertown, the small city across the bay from the Great Library. The smoke carried glittering particles of bark and acorns. The glitter fell on the roofs of the houses. It fell on orchards and onto the apples not yet harvested, and it fell into streams and lakes, making its way into drinking water. Soon everyone in Watertown had either eaten or drunk some of the fine gold dust from the Ancient One and its acorns.

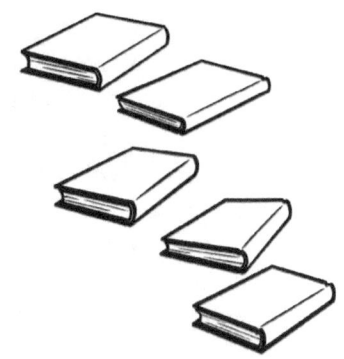

39: Maya, Let's Go for a Walk

Maya sat huddled in a corner in her small cell, which was so dark that it didn't make any difference whether her eyes were opened or closed. She rested her throbbing head on her knees and wept softly. In Roford, after getting off the boat during the night, she had been spotted by a group of trolls and had been captured, both her legs and hands shackled so that she couldn't escape. Maya really hadn't envisioned how she would return to Mortmain, but she had always assumed that she would slip in as easily as she had slipped out. But no. Before the trolls, someone else had spotted her—Nemesis—and there had been a glitter of triumph in her eyes as she had considered Maya, who stopped briefly to stare at the familiar blonde woman. Maya had hurried on, but not long afterwards the trolls had found her.

And here she was, in a dark so oppressive that Maya wasn't sure how long she had been in the cell. The dark squeezed and pushed down on her, and if Maya hadn't been so worn out, she would have panicked, flinging herself against the walls. Instead, all Maya could do was sit in the corner and cry. Her one consolation was that Ariel was still alive. She could feel the Apprentice Book's presence, weak but holding on. Maya also knew that the green Book was gone. She could sense nothing at all from Ilyria's Book.

Maya tried not to think about Bigly and the devices he had used on her, but she couldn't help replaying the scenes in her memory—a silver cap, which felt so tight that it seemed as though it were actually boring into her head. But there was no blood as the cap squeezed and squeezed, trying to get information from Maya. When that didn't work, Bigly, muttering to himself, produced a large silver ring and slipped it onto Maya's head.

"I hope this doesn't kill you," he said, peering at Maya's drawn face. "I know sir wants you alive."

"You're wasting your time," Maya said, licking dry lips. "I'm just a kid from Earth. I don't know a thing."

Bigly snorted. "You might be just a kid, but Julian thinks you're worth the bother, and sir always listens to Julian." Bigly's voice ended on a bitter note, and there was an ugly expression on his face.

"Julian has changed," Maya said, hoping to buy some time, but for what she didn't know. Sooner or later, Bigly would activate the silver ring that rested lightly on her head. "Julian's not as hard as he was. He lost his memory for six years, and he lived a different life in Caxton. He taught classes. He had students who really liked him." A startling thought came to Maya. "Julian was happy."

"Happy?" Bigly spat the word out. "Julian wasn't sent there to be happy. He was sent there to learn from the error of his ways. Julian made a big mess of things. Yes, he did. Sir should have executed him, but when it comes to Julian, sir has a blind spot."

"Cinnial loves Julian," Maya whispered, marveling at how a man with such a huge ego could love anyone else. But it was true. Julian had spoken of it before they left Caxton, and in Cinnial's office, Maya had been able to feel the tight bond between the two men.

"Love!" Bigly said, indignantly. "How could anyone love that blond fool who always goes off half-cocked and kills before he thinks." Bigly trembled a little, and there was a look of such misery on his face that Maya actually felt sorry for him. Bigly knew he would never even come close to competing with Julian for Cinnial's affection.

Bigly noted Maya's look of pity, and with a clenched jaw, he pushed a button on the side of the silver ring. With a deep chirp, it disappeared, sliding into Maya's head, boring into her thoughts and memories. The pain was so intense that Maya couldn't even scream, and if her will hadn't been as strong, then the ring would have wormed its way completely in, finding out all that she knew about the Great Library and about the Book of Everything in Black Mountain. But Maya held on to her memories. She threw up and nearly passed out, but she didn't give in.

"All right, missy," Bigly said at last. "Enough for today. But I'll be here tomorrow and tomorrow and tomorrow. Eventually, I'll get what I need."

Then two trolls had dragged Maya back to her cell and had shoved her in a corner, where she had collapsed.

"Tomorrow and tomorrow and tomorrow," Maya thought bleakly, knowing Bigly was right. She could only hold out for so long.

"What am I going to do?" Maya thought. "There's no one here to help me. I am all alone."

Maya cried until she fell into a deep, exhausted sleep, and as she slept, she dreamed. Instead of being in a dark cell, she was with her mother in New York City in their brick house, bright with art and color. Instead of being fifteen, Maya was five, and she sat in the living room, playing with her toy ponies. She had lined them up on the coffee table and was in the process of braiding their manes. Even though red was her favorite color, her favorite pony was blue, and Maya had named her Misty. Maya had slipped silver beads in with the braids, and she was admiring how pretty Misty looked.

Maya's mother came into the room. Smiling at the array of ponies on the table, Lily said, "Maya, let's go for a walk."

Maya jumped up. "Okay. Can I bring Misty? See how pretty she looks."

"Yes," Lily answered, "you may bring Misty. And she does look pretty. I really like that silver against the blue mane."

Now it was Maya's turn to smile. Even at five, she knew how much her mother noticed colors. But Maya had something else on her mind. She was nearly six—her birthday was in a few days—and Mémère had sent her fifty dollars to buy more ponies to add to her growing collection. With that much money, she might even be able to buy a little castle for them to live in.

"Can we go to the toy store?" Maya asked. "Mémère sent me birthday money."

"Yes, we can go to the toy store," her mother replied. "But, Maya, I think you should let me carry the money."

Frowning, Maya shook her head. "No, I want to carry it in the pocketbook Mémère sent me with the money." It was shiny and red and had gold handles. Maya had never seen such a beautiful pocketbook.

"What if you lose it?"

"I won't. I'll be careful. I promise! Please, Mom, please."

"All right. But hold onto it."

"I will. I will."

Out they went into the street by their house. The day was so warm and sunny that it was dazzling. A part of Maya knew she was, in fact, in a dark cell in the basement of the Office. But another part of her went eagerly with her mother. In one hand, Maya gripped her pocketbook, and in the other, she held Misty.

"Maya, look at the shadows that the sun on the gate makes," her mother said.

But Maya wasn't concerned about the shadows. Instead, she was thinking about Misty and how something bad and dark was after her. "Go, Misty, go!" Maya said, making Misty gallop along the gate.

There were trees lining the street, and Lily stopped under one. "Look up, Maya. See how the sun filters through the green."

Maya looked up and said in a high voice, pretending to be Misty, "Oh, sacred tree, help me escape from the dark."

Smiling, Lily shook her head. "You're just like your father. With you two, it's words and stories. But maybe you can learn to see, just a little." There was a wistful note in Lily's voice that younger Maya had not understood but older Maya did.

"With me and Dad, Mom feels left out," Maya thought, and then she was back in the dark, dark cell. All alone.

"No," Maya whispered fiercely. "I don't want to be here. I want to be with my mother. In the sunny streets. I want to see the gate's shadows and the way the sun shines through the leaves."

The two images shimmered before Maya, and her longing for them was so intense that she could feel herself beginning to slip away from the dark, which stubbornly held her in place.

Again, Maya heard her mother's voice. "Maya, let's go for a walk."

All those walks where Lily had tried to show Maya the world of light and shadow, colors and patterns. However, Maya hadn't really paid attention. Instead, she had played and imagined.

But now Maya was paying attention to it all, to Spot, the black and white dog that had his own balcony and barked in a friendly way whenever Maya and her mother walked by.

"Hello, Spot!" Maya would call joyfully, and Spot would bark again.

There was the little corner store that sold papers and milk and candy. Once in a while, but not too often, Lily bought a candy bar for Maya. On that day, just before her birthday, when Maya had carried her new pocketbook and Misty, Lily let Maya have some candy, and Maya picked Peanut M & M's.

Maya focused on the yellow packet holding the M & M's. On Spot. On the tree. On the gate. On the shadows. They all came together in a vivid intensity so dazzling that Maya just stared in wonder.

"Maya, let's go for a walk."

"Yes," both Mayas replied, "let's go for a walk."

And suddenly, in that dark cell, the way was clear to Maya. She saw a shimmering line connecting to her younger self and to Lily and the sun-dappled street. The line beckoned. All Maya had to do was let go and follow the line.

"Mom, I'm coming," Maya cried. "Wait for me!"

Smiling, Lily waited.

Maya let go, following the line. She felt herself hurtle through space along the line, and she felt Time's presence wrap itself around her, guiding her to that day when Lily had taken Maya for a walk.

With a gasp, Maya stumbled onto the street. But her mother and her younger self didn't stop, didn't notice her.

On they went, for their walk.

About Laurie Graves

I like to say I was born in County Tolkien, but really I was born in County Kennebec in Waterville, Maine.

I write essays and fiction from my home in the Maine hinterlands. For many years I was editor and co-publisher of the magazine *Wolf Moon Journal*. My essay, "On Being Franco-American" has been read on the radio and used in a French studies class at the University of Maine at Orono. My work has also been published in the anthology *Heliotrope: French Heritage Women Create* and in magazines and journals. *Maya and the Book of Everything* was my first novel. The story of Maya, Viola, and the Books of Everything continues in the third novel in the Great Library series, available in the fall of 2020.

You can find out about my rural day-to-day life at my blog Notes from the Hinterland (hinterlands.me). It features posts about writing, books, nature, food, and people. I also post lots pictures of flowers and the Maine countryside.

To get information about my upcoming books see Hinterlands Press (hinterlandspress.com).